MARRY ME

Reviewers Love Melissa Brayden

"Melissa Brayden has become one of the most popular novelists of the genre, writing hit after hit of funny, relatable, and very sexy stories for women who love women."—*Afterellen.com*

To the Moon and Back

"*To the Moon and Back* is all about Brayden's love of theatre, onstage and backstage, and she does a delightful job of sharing that love... Brayden set the scene so well I knew what was coming, not because it's unimaginative but because she made it obvious it was the only way things could go. She leads the reader exactly where she wants to take them, with brilliant writing as usual. Also, not everyone can make office supplies sound sexy."—*Jude in the Stars*

"Melissa Brayden does what she does best, she delivers amazing characters, witty banter, all while being fun and relatable."—*Romantic Reader Blog*

Back to September

"You can't go wrong with a Melissa Brayden romance. Seriously, you can't. Buy all of her books. Brayden sure has a way of creating an emotional type of compatibility between her leads, making you root for them against all odds. Great settings, cute interactions, and realistic dialogue."—*Bookvark*

What a Tangled Web

"[T]he happiest ending to the most amazing trilogy. Melissa Brayden pulled all of the elements together, wrapped them up in a bow, and presented the reader with Happily Ever After to the max!"—*Kitty Kat's Book Review Blog*

Beautiful Dreamer

"I love this book. I want to kiss it on its face...I'm going to stick *Beautiful Dreamer* on my to-reread-when-everything-sucks pile, because it's sure to make me happy again and again."—*Smart Bitches Trashy Books*

"*Beautiful Dreamer* is a sweet and sexy romance, with the bonus of interesting secondary characters and a cute small-town setting."
—*Amanda Chapman, Librarian (Davisville Free Library, RI)*

Two to Tangle

"As usual, Brayden delivers with great dialogue, likeable characters, and emotional turmoil."—*Bookvark.com*

"Melissa Brayden does it again with a sweet and sexy romance that leaves you feeling content and full of happiness. As always, the book is full of smiles, fabulous dialogue, and characters you wish were your best friends."—*The Romantic Reader*

"I loved it. I wasn't sure Brayden could beat Joey and Becca and their story, but when I started to see reviews mentioning that this was even better, I had high hopes and Brayden definitely lived up to them." —*LGBTQreader.com*

Entangled

"*Entangled* is a simmering slow burn romance, but I also fully believe it would be appealing for lovers of women's fiction. The friendships between Joey, Maddie, and Gabriella are well developed and engaging as well as incredibly entertaining...All that topped off with a deeply fulfilling happily ever after that gives all the happy sighs long after you flip the final page."—*Lily Michaels: Sassy Characters, Sizzling Romance, Sweet Endings*

"Ms. Brayden has a definite winner with this first book of the new series, and I can't wait to read the next one. If you love a great enemies-to-lovers, feel-good romance, then this is the book for you."—*Rainbow Reflections*

Love Like This

"Brayden upped her game. The characters are remarkably distinct from one another. The secondary characters are rich and wonderfully integrated into the story. The dialogue is crisp and witty."—*Frivolous Reviews*

Sparks Like Ours

"Brayden sets up a flirtatious tit-for-tat that's honest, relatable, and passionate. The women's fears are real, but the loving support from the supporting cast helps them find their way to a happy future. This enjoyable romance is sure to interest readers in the other stories from Seven Shores."—*Publishers Weekly*

"*Sparks Like Ours* is made up of myriad bits of truth that make for a cozy, lovely summer read."—*Queerly Reads*

Hearts Like Hers

"*Hearts Like Hers* has all the ingredients that readers can expect from Ms. Brayden: witty dialogue, heartfelt relationships, hot chemistry and passionate romance."—*Lez Review Books*

"Once again Melissa Brayden stands at the top. She unequivocally is the queen of romance."—*Front Porch Romance*

"*Hearts Like Hers* has a breezy style that makes it a perfect beach read. The romance is paced well, the sex is super hot, and the conflict made perfect sense and honored Autumn and Kate's journeys." —*The Lesbian Review*

Eyes Like Those

"Brayden's story of blossoming love behind the Hollywood scenes provides the right amount of warmth, camaraderie, and drama." —*RT Book Reviews*

"Brayden's writing is just getting better and better. The story is well done, full of well-honed wit and humour, and the characters are complex and interesting."—*Lesbian Reading Room*

"Melissa Brayden knocks it out of the park once again with this fantastic and beautifully written novel."—*Les Reveur*

Strawberry Summer

"This small-town second-chance romance is full of tenderness and heart. The 10 Best Romance Books of 2017."—*Vulture*

"*Strawberry Summer* is a tribute to first love and soulmates and growing into the person you're meant to be. I feel like I say this each time I read a new Melissa Brayden offering, but I loved this book so much that I cannot wait to see what she delivers next."—*Smart Bitches, Trashy Books*

First Position

"Brayden aptly develops the growing relationship between Ana and Natalie, making the emotional payoff that much sweeter. This ably plotted, moving offering will earn its place deep in readers' hearts." —*Publishers Weekly*

By the Author

Waiting in the Wings

Heart Block

How Sweet It Is

First Position

Strawberry Summer

Beautiful Dreamer

Back to September

To the Moon and Back

Marry Me

Soho Loft Romances:

Kiss the Girl

Just Three Words

Ready or Not

Seven Shores Romances:

Eyes Like Those

Hearts Like Hers

Sparks Like Ours

Love Like This

Tangle Valley Romances:

Entangled

Two to Tangle

What a Tangled Web

Visit us at www.boldstrokesbooks.com

MARRY ME

by
Melissa Brayden

2021

Credits
Editor: Ruth Sternglantz
Production Design: Stacia Seaman
Cover Design by Jeanine Henning

Acknowledgments

Call me a romantic, but I've always believed that meeting the right person can transform anyone into the best version of themselves, from caterpillar to butterfly, and wanted to explore that concept in *Marry Me*. I also very much enjoyed delving into a character like Allison Hale, who thinks she knows themself until...she finds out she doesn't. The journey commences!

Gratitude to Bold Strokes, Radclyffe, and Sandy Lowe for being the best possible publishing partners I could ask for. To my editor, Ruth Sternglantz, for keeping me grounded when I need it, and cheering me on just as often. To Jeanine Henning for another striking cover I keep staring at. To Stacia, Toni, Carsen, and the rest of the behind-the-scenes folks who work hard to make these books come to life. To Alan for the brainstorming sessions and laughs and love along the route to publication. My gorgeous kids for making everything worthwhile. To my pack of book friends, Georgia, Nikki, Rey, Paula, Carsen, Kris, Fiona for simply existing and making my life that much better. Lastly, to you. The person reading this book and walking down this path with me and the characters on the page. From the bottom of my heart, thank you.

For those regular folks who are anything but.

PROLOGUE

Wake up. You're dreaming. But she wasn't.

It was the kind of moment that didn't feel real, when reality suspended itself. Ally felt like she was looking in on her own life from a safe distance. She stared up at the colorful fireworks exploding in the sky all for her, the cascading hues and the loud bangs overwhelming her senses. Her family and friends applauded, stealing glances at her to reassure themselves of her joy, and to absorb all they could secondhand. She knew this moment meant just as much to them as it did to her. Brent, at her side, clasped her hand tightly and, every once in a while, gave it a little squeeze.

They were engaged.

He'd asked her to marry him just five minutes ago, and yet she still didn't feel any different. Still just Allison Hale, fourth-grade teacher, but maybe with a little more behind her. She was going to be a Carmichael, for God's sake. That would take some getting used to. As a girl from humble beginnings, marrying into one of the richest families in Dallas hadn't really been an option on her radar. She was just…her.

They'd discussed marriage after dating for close to a year, but for some strange reason she never actually imagined it would be her reality. Why was that? Yet following a candlelit dinner at the rooftop restaurant in Dalliance, one of Dallas's upscale hotels, Brent had suggested they take a stroll around the deck and take in the view. Hand in hand, they'd walked along the railing, all the twinkling lights of the city glistening back at them. Brent had given her hand a tug, bringing them to a pause just as Allison was explaining that their dessert had been clearly sent from God because of the quality of the whipped cream. Ally quirked her head because Brent seemed distracted, like he had something on his mind more important than whipped cream, and honestly, what could be more important than that? His dark eyes met hers, and she stared up at his six-four frame that often made her feel smaller than she was.

"I think we're meant to be, Ally."

"You do, huh? I think the whipped cream was meant to be part of our lives as well," she said with a lighthearted grin, oblivious at the time. But he wasn't smiling back. Weird. He had perfected the thoughtful smolder, and it was on display now. God, look at him. How did someone like him end up interested in her? She was pretty enough, but no huge head turner, especially compared to the women who ran in Brent's circles. She was self-aware enough to get that.

He ignored the whipped cream reference and pressed on. Almost as if he had a script. "We fit together, and you're everything I'm looking for in a partner, someone to share my life with. You're beautiful, kind, and you put up with my idiot ideas, at least long enough to explain to me that buying a six-pack of huskies is maybe not the best plan for the long term."

"Maybe just start with one," she said gently.

"See? That's exactly it. You level me out. You're what I need, and I love you so much." He was beaming, on some sort of high.

"I love you, too," Allison said. "Wait, what's going on?" To her left, she became aware of someone snapping a photograph of them. That was odd. She raised an eyebrow. Another click of the shutter. "Why is he doing that?" she asked Brent, slightly concerned by the photo stalker.

Brent grinned at her, proud and unwavering. His confident gaze then swept the terrace, and out of thin air, her parents approached, clutching each other. What in the world? Then came her older sister, Betsy, looking gorgeous with her blond hair, the same shade as Allison's own, swept up, walking alongside her husband, Dell. On the other side of them stood Brent's parents and his younger brother, Jeff. Okay, so this was not a coincidence. This was an actual event, and now her hands were numb and her mind was on fast-forward, trying to catch up. Understanding dawned just as Brent sank to one knee and pulled a velvet box from the pocket of his blazer. Oh God. Shove the whipped cream to the side. This was happening. And it was happening in front of everyone, thirty-two stories in the air.

"Yes," she said, without even giving it any thought, and here they stood, staring up at the fireworks as a happy group, only she was watching from somewhere nearby, unable to fully absorb the turning of the wheels already in motion. But there was nothing to be afraid of. This was Brent and her. They got along great. He was tons of fun, better looking than she ever would have hoped for in a husband, relaxed, easy to get along with, and richer than God. And somehow, Brent saw something in her that appealed to him. As of this moment, her life was figured out and all right there in front of her. Laid out with certainty. That counted for a ton, and she should be flying high. Instead, she watched the gleeful scene from a measured distance. That was strange, right? She swallowed the question and tried to focus.

Ally exchanged a smile with her sister and beamed up at the fireworks that were commissioned for the occasion of her very own engagement. Surreal. She tried not to think about what would have happened if she'd said no. This whole setup must have cost a ton, and everyone had dressed up and driven over, given up their whole evening.

She tried to anchor herself in the moment and shut down her racing brain. She took in the familiar scent of Brent's cologne and forced herself to absorb every detail, as it would surely be one of her fondest memories when she looked back over her life, years from now.

"Are you happy?" Brent asked quietly.

"Yes," she said automatically. "Are you?"

"I'm the luckiest guy alive. Are you kidding? And everything went like clockwork." He chuckled quietly. "I love it when that happens. All for you. Well, *us*."

They were an *us* now, always and forever. Whoa. The world was a crazy place.

When the fireworks reached their crescendo, an amazing spectacle of a colorful finale, a server appeared with a large bucket with two sweating bottles of champagne and glasses. They all gathered together on the terrace for a bubbly toast given by Brent's father, Dalton Carmichael. "I toast to my eldest son, his future wife, and the joining of two families. Today is a special day." Allison watched as her parents practically vibrated with joy, their smiles bigger than she'd ever seen them. Her mother had clearly had her hair done into a fancy updo and wore a new dress that looked more expensive than anything she'd ever seen her in. Seeing her glow more than warmed her heart. A union with the Carmichaels was good for her family in more ways than one, and now it was all happening. She beamed back at them, pleased to have been the one to make them proud, a spot usually reserved for her older sister. But tonight was *hers*. Her father had his arm tightly around her mother as if he was the luckiest guy on Earth.

They sipped and stared and sipped some more. "Now what?" she asked the group, who answered with laughter.

Brent raised a victorious eyebrow and lifted his glass. "Now is the fun part. We get to plan a wedding."

CHAPTER ONE

From the boardroom on the fourteenth floor of the Wilton Office Suites, Megan Kinkaid studied her bulleted notes, her dark hair pulled into what she called her smooth-serious-business ponytail. "Where are we on the Adams wedding?" she asked her team. "Someone update me."

Kelsey, her right hand at work and closest friend, jumped on the question. "Bride is pivoting from the interlocking hearts ice sculpture. She's worried it's gaudy and cliché."

"She wouldn't be wrong," Miranda, another employee, murmured from her spot next to Kelsey. She was never one to hold back her snark.

Kelsey continued, "I've tried to direct her to something classic, timeless, or even memorable. But what she wants, she gets."

"Can't argue with that," Megan said. "Good. Any fires I should know about?"

"Not today. She's surprisingly calm." Kelsey checked her watch. "Give her time."

Megan smiled. "Perfection. You seem to have things under control."

Her team of five was made up of smart, patient multitaskers with a mixture of personalities, on purpose. Megan appreciated their individual talents and recognized that they each served a fantastic purpose at Soiree, the wedding and event planning company she'd started twelve years earlier. Back then, it was just Megan working alone from her studio apartment, handling one wedding a weekend for very little, wearing her customary navy dresses and suits to the events, and meeting clients at cafés and coffee shops to consult. Since then, she'd grown the business exponentially, building on one referral after the next. She'd ascended the ranks of the in-demand event planners until she sat at the top of the heap as Dallas's most sought after, and notably most expensive, event coordinating company. They still wore their signature navy to each and every event, but nowadays, Soiree worked for top echelon clients, tackling corporate events, weddings, anniversaries, and even the occasional political gala, provided the candidate was on the correct side of the fight. Megan Kinkaid knew her business and the value she brought to her clients and had no problem charging for it. The fruits of her labor were on display in their high-end suite of offices located in the heart of downtown. Gourmet coffee, fresh pastries, and colorful floral arrangements were delivered daily from preferred vendors. Only the finest furnishings and finishes accented the suite so that it felt both sleek and comfortable for the staff and their clients. Megan aimed to impress from the moment a client walked in the door.

"About the sculpture, have your client look through Glacial Art's portfolio. That guy might be more what she's looking for," Cade, her one male staffer, said to Kelsey from behind his laptop. "His stuff is a bit more stylized and less in-your-face about love and forever. If she's going for regal and subtle, he might be the one."

"Great rec," Kelsey said, pointing at him with her pencil and jotting the note. "I'll also pull his stuff for our next meeting, so we can all familiarize ourselves."

"I love it. What else?" Megan asked from her seat at the head of the table.

"Mason wedding is this weekend," Lourdes noted. She was a go-getter and the newest hire, having just completed her first year with the company. Young, just out of business school, but already a contender. "We're ahead of schedule. I just need to confirm minor details with our vendors, and Elaine, the bride, was hoping you would be calling the ceremony personally. I told her I'd find out your schedule."

Megan smiled. "You can tell Elaine that I will most certainly be there, calling the show from my headset. In fact, I'll join you for the meeting, so she knows I'm in the loop." Megan understood that people booked with Soiree because of her personal reputation, and though she wasn't project leader on every event, she tried to be as present as possible. "This afternoon, yes?"

"You got it. And it would definitely put her at ease. She's starting the week-of unravel." Megan knew it well. It landed approximately five days before the big day and left a bride second-guessing every decision she'd made until she was relegated to a crying mess in the corner of her designer bedroom, clutching a bag of chips like a lifeline to Jesus.

"Then it's our job to take that stress right off her," Megan said calmly. She was always calm. A gift. She then picked up the lifestyle section of the *Dallas Morning News* and held it up. "Next order of business." Five heads swiveled. "I'm not sure which of you saw, but there's an engagement announcement for Brent Carmichael in this morning's write-ups."

"Get out," Cade said. "Someone wrapped him up? How did we miss this? And how many Dallas women are sobbing on their drives to work this morning? We need to start a count."

"I'd heard he was seeing someone, but I didn't know we were close to marriage," Megan said and dropped the paper onto the table. "Yet here we are. Lucky us."

Eyebrows rose and her team exchanged glances, well aware that the Carmichaels' oldest son's wedding would be the society event of the year. Megan pressed on, "While it would be great to have our name all over this one, I want everyone to play it cool. Let the Carmichaels come to Soiree if they think we can get the job done. They're going to want the best at the helm, after all. No hiccups."

"And that's us," Cade finished.

She smiled at him. "Exactly. I know Brent Carmichael, and he'll get it. We've handled the BeLeaf Foods Christmas party for years now, and they fall all over themselves in amazement at what we've managed to pull off." The Carmichaels owned a hugely popular chain of organic grocery stores in Dallas and had systematically taken in a larger share of the market each year they'd been in business. They were big players in the community and highly respected for all that they'd brought to the city. They were, quite frankly, Dallas royalty and at the top of any important guest list.

"I'm not worried. I'd say that wedding is as good as ours," Kelsey said confidently, as if she couldn't imagine any alternative.

Megan held up a hand. "The real question is how we make room for such a huge event on the schedule, especially if it's quick."

Cade nodded. "If they're looking at anything this side of a year, it's going to tax us. We're already up to our eyeballs."

Megan folded her arms and regarded her team. No. *Challenged* them. "Are we up for it?"

After a pause, five faces nodded eagerly back at her, and she knew she could count on this rock-solid group.

"Who's the bride? Do we have a name?" Demi, their office assistant, asked. Young, blond, wide-eyed, and eager to please. Megan saw her going places and hoped to groom her into a coordinator over the next year or two.

"Interestingly enough, I've never heard of her," Megan said, turning the newspaper around to face the group once again. "Allison Hale. Anyone?"

"Hmm." Kelsey squinted. "There's the Hale family from New York. The fitness empire people with all the apparel. Maybe she's one of them?"

"Anything is possible, but Ms. Hale landed herself the biggest fish in Dallas. But yes, there will be throngs of socialites crying into their pillows after they see this announcement."

Miranda grinned, gleeful. "Read 'em and weep, girls. Literally."

Cade stared at her. "You take joy in pain."

She didn't blink. "I bathe in the tears of the privileged."

"So bad," Kelsey said with a laugh. "But I think I'll follow you to hell. Life is short."

The meeting concluded, and after a long day of client consults and negotiating with vendors on the phone, Megan arrived at her favorite bar in downtown Dallas, Shakers. At last, she could be a person, breathe, and live life for herself. Something that didn't happen often enough these days. It was close to eight, and she easily found Kelsey sitting at the bar, looking like the knockout she was. After a rapid-fire day at Soiree, her best friend still wore her stilettos just to grab a drink. Megan would give her one thing—they made her legs look killer. That was for damn sure. Her dark hair was clipped to the side with a stylish barrette that matched the damn shoes, and her skin was flawless. Not fair.

"I'm afraid I don't have your shoe commitment," Megan said, sliding onto the stool next to Kelsey's. "At a certain hour of the day, the pretty ones have to come off. Mandated. I'm not even going to apologize for it."

"I'm glad. My only time to sparkle is when you don't have it in you to try." Kelsey sipped her drink delicately and batted her lashes. "My endurance is my saving grace."

"No need to gloat."

Their favorite martini spot with the calm blue lighting scheme was just beginning to pick up as they shifted into midevening, though the larger crowds arrived after ten, prime hookup hours. Megan planned to be home by then, hopefully a little more relaxed after a mango martini with an extra splash of lime. She signaled the bartender, who knew her drink. She'd earned it.

"Plus, I believe in fighting for my cause," Kelsey said and sipped her London Fog.

"And that would be?"

"Attracting the hottest woman in this bar and using these shoes to do it."

Megan surveyed the room on Kelsey's behalf. "Lots of options, K. Though it is only Tuesday. Maybe pace yourself."

"Why? I could be hit by a cab tomorrow. Gotta live while I can." She sighed. "Same old faces, though. I'm bored with Dallas. Let's move west."

Megan laughed. "And what would we do there?"

"Hollywood calls. We need our own reality show. A day in the life of two kick-ass wedding planners."

"Please. This is our town and we're not giving it up."

"Texas, man. As a Black woman, I have a love-hate. I hate its overconfidence, its audacity, but love that I've conquered this city anyway."

Megan could identify. She took after both her white father and Black mother, and the noticeably white Dallas society had not always made it easy for her on her way up the ladder. Yet she'd refused to let outdated rules hold her back. She'd clawed her way to the top, kicking in doors that had been otherwise closed, and was now damn proud of the credit associated with her name. People respected her, and that mattered.

Kelsey touched her glass to Megan's. "Cheers to us. Renegades that we are." She then folded her arms on the table and leaned in, perfectly glossed mouth pursed in anticipation.

"Yes?" Megan asked, amused.

"Speaking of bold moves, how was your thing with Selena the

other night? That was her name, right? The one who kept overarching her eyebrow when she looked at you?" Kelsey demonstrated with an exaggerated raise of her own.

Megan nearly spit out her drink. "That's too good an impression."

"I pay attention. Now answer my question."

Megan nodded and looked skyward, not exactly proud of herself. "Dinner was mediocre. The conversation was surface level." She sighed.

"So a no-go."

"I still took her home with me. I'm apparently that girl." She winced.

Kelsey shook her head, smiling and staring straight at her. "You little minx. I love it when you indulge. It's rare."

"Don't minx me. It only encourages my bad behavior." She bit her lip in thought. "The thing is that I'm too tired to be good and sort through the masses. I'm starting to think I'm a puzzle piece without a match."

"No, you're not. And with Selena, I totally get it. Bird in the hand," Kelsey said coolly. "Plus, I tend to think if you had felt something, you wouldn't have taken her home."

She frowned, not following. "What does that mean?"

"You don't do emotionally vulnerable. You never have. The day you meet a woman who does that for you, your world is going to tremble."

"Maybe it's better I stay as aloof as you, then." Megan sipped her drink, not believing a word of it. She wanted to find someone. She did.

"I'd say you're not far off."

"That's both complimentary and terrifying."

"Then it should send you screaming."

"Not funny."

"Not wrong."

Megan held up a hand. "All right, all right. So I'm not good at taking emotional risks. That doesn't mean I can't be in the future. I just need to meet the right person, the one who makes me want to take that scary leap all for them."

"I look forward to seeing it happen." She laughed behind her martini, and Megan balked.

She turned and studied the room behind them. Beyond the sleek bar with the soft blue illumination and sculpted gray barstools, a more relaxed conglomeration of couches allowed for lounging and mingling over cocktails and small bites. There was a small dance floor, but honestly no one at Shakers ever used it. This was a place for Dallas singles to gather, carouse, and pair up. But Kelsey was right. She should maybe try to allow herself to feel something without allowing the terror to creep in. Who knew what might happen? Daily, she watched as couple after couple walked through the doors of her office, declaring their intention to spend forever together. Maybe Megan simply wasn't the type, and that was totally okay. But she preferred to believe that she just wasn't ready yet. One day, she'd find her own love story. Right?

"Let yourself off the hook," Kelsey said. "You don't have to be perfect all the time. You wanted a little action, and you got it with Eyebrow Arching Selena."

Megan winced. "Action sounds so crass."

"An amorous encounter then, Jane Austen? Do you feel better?"

Megan smiled. "Yes. I can live with an occasional encounter on my résumé."

"My kinda girl. Oh, who's she?" Kelsey asked, following a tall blonde as she moved across the room. "Hello."

"That's the deputy sheriff's wife, so maybe no."

Kelsey raised a nonchalant shoulder. "Says who? She just smiled at me, and it wasn't the platonic kind."

"Lord above, please help my friend Kelsey not go to hell or jail," Megan said with a laugh. "But if she goes, maybe take me with her."

Kelsey bumped her shoulder. "This is why we're ride or die. You tell me what not to do but always let me do it anyway."

"Like I can stop you."

"True."

"But damn, it's also fun to watch. My own personal soap opera."

Kelsey scrunched her shoulders and bounced her eyebrows. "Mine better be rated R."

"Oh, trust me."

Megan limited herself to one drink and took her leave, though Kelsey stayed behind for one more and who knew what else. Probably a little flirtation with the off-limits blonde. Megan hoped it would stop there but preferred not to interfere. The less she knew, the less she'd worry. She headed home, a two-block walk to the Union Towers

Condominiums. She nodded to her doorman, Chip, who was expecting a baby soon.

"Any sign of the smaller version of Chip yet?"

He shook his head. "I keep checking my phone, ready to dash out of here."

"Dammit. I've been anxious."

"*You're* anxious?" Chip said, opening the door for her. "I sleep twenty-five minutes at a time. I'm like a wired squirrel."

"That little girl will be here before you know it."

"Good. I don't know how much more I can take."

She rode the elevator to the sixth floor and let herself in to her favorite place on Earth, her two-bedroom apartment, professionally decorated to her carefully explained taste. The mostly white kitchen was complemented by the blue, gray, and cream accents throughout her soft but sophisticated living space. Dark woods anchored the room and made it somewhere she never wanted to leave. Her bedroom was to the left, and a second bedroom that she'd turned into her own private study, complete with towering, full bookshelves, jutted off to the right.

She immediately changed into an oversized striped button-up sleep shirt and panties and slipped beneath the cool sheets, exhaling from her day. It would be a busy one tomorrow, and as she closed her eyes, she went through a mental checklist of all on her agenda the next morning, her nightly routine. Sterile? Sure, but that's how she'd found success. She put her job first, and she did it well. Nothing wrong with that. Some people drifted off dreaming of puppies, kittens, and rainbows. Megan put her ambition first. She really liked her life and had so much more to accomplish. She sighed, letting her muscles sink into the soft mattress, knowing sleep would claim her shortly.

Tomorrow was just one more step in her journey.

❖

Allison sank into the worn-in chair behind her desk twenty seconds after arriving back in her empty classroom. The hard part of her day was behind her. She'd just dropped her fourth graders at their buses and various after-school programs, or handed them off to their parents. Today had been school picture day and thereby a whirlwind of hairbrushes, insecurities, refusals to smile, and nervous energy. She needed two minutes of quiet just to reclaim herself and remember that she was a person outside of *Ms. Hale, what are we doing today? Ms. Hale, can I use the restroom? Ms. Hale, why do shoes squeak?* She loved her kids and her job, but the life of a teacher was definitely an exhausting one. Her desk was a wreck, too, like she'd been to war with a band of angry mice.

Luckily, it was the last Wednesday of the month, and that meant happy hour with Betsy. Her sister would no doubt want to talk about the wedding plans, and that was good because she could use the tips and a swift kick to jump-start her progress. Her sister absolutely lived for planning her own wedding a few years back and had learned the ins and outs. Ally was more of a go-with-the-flow kind of girl. She'd be thrilled with any kind of gathering of her family and friends as long as everyone was having a good time. But she knew expectations would be high for the Carmichael family, and that's why she needed Betsy. She was too far out of her depth.

Rather than one of their usual meetup spots, they decided to meet back at their childhood home where they could spread out a bit at the kitchen table and relax. Betsy was already mixing drinks in their parents' kitchen when Allison arrived. "Martinis. You game?"

She paused in front of the kitchen table. "Bringing out the big guns. You realize I'm not very sophisticated, right? I've had maybe two martinis in my life."

"Exactly why we're doing this. You're about to be a Carmichael, and that means acting the part. Plus, this is a big day. We're planning my little sister's wedding. I can't believe I just said that." She shook the shaker, looking like an ad. Betsy had inherited all the looks in the family. Gorgeous, thick blond hair. A pronounced dimple in her left cheek and sparkling blue eyes that everyone made such a big deal about. *Would you look at that little girl's eyes. Gorgeous!* Allison had gotten the dulled-down version of all those features but didn't mind. She liked her appearance and just smiled when people would fawn over Betsy growing up. She also wasn't someone who sought the limelight, so her sister had been the perfect choice to absorb most all of it.

"I honestly can't believe it either." Allison blinked at the counter. "I'm engaged, Bets. It's a done deal."

"Your life is about to transform," Betsy said, making the gesture of an all-encompassing rainbow probably made of glitter from the land of fashion-forward unicorns.

"Well, somewhat. The basics will stay the same."

"What? You're going to teach fourth grade and shlep for Mom and Dad at the shop in the summers after you're married to Brent? No way."

Allison frowned. "Well, yeah. Why would I not?"

"Because you're marrying into lots and lots of money and status. Ally. Come on. You're not going to have to work. Ever. There will be other expectations, though. Charities, child rearing, social projects."

"But I like my job, and Brent knows that."

Betsy laughed in the way that said she knew better and that Allison was too preciously naive to be real. "I give you a year before you quit."

Allison opened her mouth but swallowed the argument on the tip of her tongue, knowing it was enough that she'd eventually prove her sister wrong. She couldn't imagine life without her kiddos and her classroom, even as much as it kicked her ass every day. She believed she'd found her calling. Plus, she liked helping out their parents at their small health food store, being part of the family business when she could, and spending time with them.

"Voilà. One shaken martini, straight up, for the bride."

"Thank you," Ally said, accepting the martini glass, and feeling a little fancy and not minding it.

"Let's get started," Betsy said, taking a seat at the table next to Allison.

"Okay." She was nervous and excited but ready to do this.

Betsy regarded her with overly sincere eyes. "I want to start by saying that this is a journey, and each detail will take time." She covered Ally's hand. "Trust me. I've been there."

"And I do," Allison said, nodding.

"It's best to start with the big details and work down. But you'll need someone to organize it all for you. A planner, or you'll go out of your mind and crash and burn a fiery death."

"You?" Ally asked. "Can't you save me from the death of fire? That doesn't sound like something I'm interested in experiencing."

Betsy laughed. Loudly. "Me? Good God, no. I'd love to help and will certainly offer my opinion, but I'm talking about a professional. I used Hand in Hand, the wedding planners we met that day at the Bridal Fair, but do you know who I dreamed of having plan my wedding?" Ally shook her head. The details were fuzzy. "Soiree." Betsy left a large pause so the word could shimmer in the ether for a moment. "They're *the* planners in Dallas. The sought after."

"Then why didn't you use them?" Allison asked, really enjoying this martini and the way her neck muscles had gone loose. Maybe she should have cocktails after school more often. Cue the debauchery and rebellion. The thought made her laugh to herself.

"Soiree? Oh, well, they're impossible to book, Ally. I couldn't get in, and trust me, I tried. Megan Kinkaid is the empress of events, and if she takes you on, listen to me"—she adopted a feisty stare— "you're golden." Next, a light bulb seemed to click on over Betsy's head. "But you know what? You're not in my shoes. You're marrying a Carmichael, for God's sake. I have a feeling that might make a huge difference. Allison, whoa."

"What?"

"You could land *Megan Kinkaid* as your wedding planner." The look on Betsy's face was now equivalent to someone having dropped a million dollars in hard cash over her head.

Allison was skeptical. "Not if they're booked solid. Brent and I were planning on getting married in the summer, and that's less than a year away at this point. It's already autumn."

Betsy deflated. "You might want to make an exception, change your plans if it's the difference between Soiree and another option. Trust me when I say that these are the people."

"I do—I trust you," Ally said, still not entirely sold on there being only one company capable of pulling off the kind of wedding Brent's family would want. Then again, she really didn't want to blow this, her first official act as a member of their family. They did have incredibly high standards. Suddenly, the pressure seemed oppressive, and her cheeks went hot. She rolled her shoulders. "Yeah, okay. Soiree it is, then. I'll see what I can do to make it happen."

"Hidey ho!" their mother said, popping into the kitchen through the garage door, arms full of food from the shop, a grab-and-go health food store where they crafted and sold all sorts of creative and fresh foods. With her fiery red hair swept up into a now collapsing twist, she dropped her bags on the counter and beamed at her girls. "Well, just look at the two of you. Heads together at the kitchen table just like the days you did your homework in that very spot. Don't move." She took out her phone and snapped about eight photos in a row. "Darling."

"Who are these people in my house?" her father bellowed, joining them inside. His hair was mostly gray now and his stomach a little more pronounced, but he still had that same playful gleam in his eye. Such a softy. "How did they get in my house? Who are they?" he asked their mother sincerely. He placed a hand over his chest as if startled. "Oh. It's just you two."

"Hi, Daddy," Betsy said. "Good day at the store?"

Her father shrugged. "Customer traffic could have been better, but we did okay." Her parents had always been entrepreneurs. In Allison's lifetime, they'd cycled through half a dozen businesses, some more outlandish than others, but the Nutcase had been the longest lasting, having stayed open for close to a decade now. Nestled in a pretty popular strip mall, they'd established a good batch of regular morning customers, who picked up breakfast and a drip coffee to go. Her parents' crown jewel was their grab-and-take oatmeal bar, the Dash Bar, which they sold fresh in the store and packaged in boxes of six. Pop the bar in the oven, and you had fresh, warm oatmeal in bar form, perfect for eating in the car or in the midst of work. No spoon required. They baked them fresh in-store but had started moving into licensing them for retail, her father's lifelong dream. They were already in a couple of local mom-and-pop grocery stores and looking desperately to grow to the big-box chains. The Nutcase would be a thing of the past once, and if, the bars took off at the licensing level the way her parents were hoping. They were ready to put everything they had behind the product, believing in it that much.

"How's working with that new manufacturer on the Dash Bar?" Betsy asked, turning around her chair. "Able to cut your margins yet?"

"Not yet." Her mother's face brightened. "They've been a dream, though, in every other sense. So much better than the last manufacturer, who cut corners on the recipe. The bars now taste almost like we make them fresh in the shop."

"That's fantastic." Allison smiled, rooting her parents on. She actually really enjoyed the bars and ate them several times a week on her way to school. "I'm glad you got it all sorted out."

"We're in the big time now, kids," her dad said with a proud smile.

His business was everything, and he stayed up many nights, trying to figure out how to make it all come together. Her parents had always lived paycheck to paycheck and were looking to capitalize on this new wave to solve their financial woes. "The Dash Bar is on its way." He turned to Allison. "Dalton, or should I say your future father-in-law, pulled me aside the night of the engagement to set up a formal meeting. Not just talk anymore. It's serious."

"Get out," Betsy said. "You're going to be in the BeLeaf stores? That would be insane. There are a million of them in Texas alone."

Her mother smiled demurely. "Well, we don't know for sure, but Dalton seemed to think that with you kids getting married, the families should have a conversation." Her parents, sometimes to her embarrassment, had been talking up the Dash Bars to the Carmichaels since the moment they'd met. Ally had asked them to put the brakes on, and they'd been nice enough to respect her wishes. But it seemed their seed planting might have taken root. "Ally, if this deal goes through, you'll be the hero." Her mom ruffled her hair the way she used to when Ally was five.

"I didn't do anything but hit it off with Brent. The business stuff is all you guys."

"How's the wedding planning going?" her father asked, referencing the martini glasses with a grin.

Betsy lifted hers. "Well, we've accomplished two things. Number one, martinis. Number two, we've decided on a planner. Once Soiree is on board, I have a feeling all the doors will fall open, and we'll have access to all the best venues and vendors." Betsy sat back. "I'm jealous just thinking about it."

"Your life is perfect," Ally said. "Your husband is. Even your lawn looks like a commercial."

Betsy didn't hesitate. "It is perfect. But Dallas society didn't fawn over an invitation to my wedding the way they will yours. That's a pretty big coup, little sister. Even I can admit that, as competitive as I am."

Allison shrugged it off. That part didn't matter to her, but she was happy it brought joy to her family, and if it helped her parents ease their business struggles, well, that was a pleasant bonus.

"You guys want to stay for dinner? I can whip up some chicken tenders and cream gravy," her father offered, always the handy cook.

"I'm on Keto," Betsy said, standing. Her perfect figure didn't need it. "The martini was a splurge."

"Oh, I'll stay," Allison said with a smile. "Brent is working late, and I need Dad's chicken to survive this week."

"That's my girl," her mom said. "Let me change, and we can set the table together."

Allison relaxed, enjoying time at the house where everything always felt simple and easy. With Brent, as much as she adored him, there was always an element of keeping up, making sure she was up on all the latest news or gossip. It was pressure she put on herself unnecessarily, because he didn't care, but it was there all the same. Tonight, she would simply enjoy herself in her childhood home with her cute, creative parents and some comfort food.

She could tackle the wedding world tomorrow.

It wasn't going anywhere.

CHAPTER TWO

Megan stared at her laptop and blinked at the ridiculous explanation from their supply company as to why they'd been short four tables at the Gallagher wedding the weekend prior. Their driver had read the order wrong. Why had no one higher up double-checked? Sure, in the moment, she'd been able to pull a rabbit out of a hat and have a backup vendor bring over four closely matching counterparts, but it never should have been an obstacle on her client's big day to begin with.

She typed back a very curt response, thanking them for their effort but expressing her disappointment in the service they'd received. No need to be petty, though she downgraded their status from her go-to supply company to backup and would alert her staff to do the same for their own clients.

"Megan, call for you on four," Demi said through the phone's intercom.

"Who's calling?" Megan asked, really not wanting to be pulled from her email if it wasn't dire.

"Allison Hale."

"Can you take her information, or hand her off to Kelsey."

There was a pause. "Allison Hale, remember? Her fiancé is Brent Carmichael."

Megan closed her eyes, grateful for Demi's persistence and annoyed she'd overlooked the name. "Of course. Thank you, Demi. I'm on it."

She took a deep breath and clicked on to the call, sending it to her wireless headset. "Ms. Hale? This is Megan Kinkaid."

"Hi," the friendly voice said. "I'm so sorry to bother you."

"No bother at all," Megan said, using her most soothing, professional voice. "You're getting married. Congratulations! We were so thrilled to hear."

"Oh, thank you. Yes. My fiancé and I got engaged just over a week ago, and I know this is a long shot, as in incredibly lofty to even ask, but I was hoping we could discuss your availability." A small pause, almost as if she hated to play this card. "Brent Carmichael is my fiancé."

Ah, well played, Allison Hale. Use what you got. "Brent's a dear friend, and such a charmer. You've got a good one there, and I always aim to accommodate friends. When were you thinking of getting married?" The answer didn't matter. Megan was bound and determined to handle this wedding personally.

"We're thinking summer. June."

"Popular month and not far away."

Allison sighed. "I know. You're surely booked, and of course, we understand."

"I have room for a June wedding." Megan left off the part where they'd turned down dozens of brides-to-be with the same request just that week alone.

"You do? Wow. Oh, this is fabulous. I didn't anticipate you having an opening. What's next?"

"Why don't we set up an appointment for you to come in? Brent is invited as well, of course."

"I think he's giving me the reins on this one, but I'm sure he'll be available to consult throughout the process."

Megan smiled into the phone. "That's fairly standard. We don't see as many grooms. How about Monday? Are you free?"

"Anytime after three forty-five. Sorry for being so specific, but I'm a fourth-grade teacher and have to make sure each of my kiddos makes it to their bus."

An elementary school teacher? That pulled Megan's interest. She'd always imagined Brent would end up with a full-time socialite, a fashion designer, or even a model. This romance just got more and more interesting. A teacher? How pedestrian and, honestly, refreshing. Good for Brent. "Let's say four o'clock. You can be my last consult of the day."

"I'll be there, and you don't understand how great this news is."

"For us both," Megan said, smiling. She liked this woman.

And at three fifty-eight in the afternoon, Allison Hale kept her promise. Megan peered with interest through the small window of her office as Demi greeted Allison in their lobby and escorted her to their lounge area, which was essentially a sitting room made up of soft Italian leather couches with fresh flowers on either end table. Perfect for getting comfortable with clients.

"Allison Hale is here for you," Demi said, poking her head around Megan's door.

"Thank you." She gathered her notes and new client forms that she would fill out for Allison as they spoke and made her way into the lounge to find Allison examining the artwork above the couch she sat on.

"Oh, hi there." Allison smiled unabashedly. Her cheeks dusted with pink at having been caught midperusal, and her eyes shone brightly. Megan could already tell she was the cheerful type. "I hope you don't mind my admiring your Richter. I'm a fan."

"Really?" Megan smiled because not too many people could have spotted a Richter in the wild. "Gerhard Richter caught my eye on a recent getaway I took to Europe. I had to have something of his. Not an original, but I splurged on one of his limited lithographs. No regrets." She smiled at the abstract. "You can get lost in it."

"I already have."

She extended her hand. "Megan Kinkaid."

Allison stood and accepted it as if forgetting herself. "I'm sorry. I should have told you who I was before launching into an artistic confession while remaining a stranger in your office."

"It's completely okay."

"And honestly, I don't know a ton about art, just a novice, but I've collected a few favorites in my brain. And I've done it again. Still a stranger. Allison Hale." She nodded like a punctuation mark in human form. "That's my name."

"Well, Allison Hale, I don't think you have a thing to be sorry about. You have fantastic taste. Shall we sit and get to know each other?"

They did. Allison, who had blond hair that fell past her shoulders in layers and light blue eyes, pursed and unpursed her lips. She seemed out of her element, which was not a problem at all, but still surprising, giving her engagement to such a high profile person like Brent Carmichael. You'd think she'd be aware of her status and own any room she walked into.

Megan decided to just jump right in. Something about Allison made her relax and give in to her own curiosity about the unlikely pairing. Allison was quite pretty, but in a girl-next-door sense. Very much against type. This was no sex kitten. "So, I'm going to get a little nosy here, especially since Brent's an old friend. Where did the two of you meet?"

"Oh, at a retail conference in Orlando. My parents own a health food grab-and-go where they sell a lot of their own products, and I work with them part-time and in the summers when school is out. The Natural Food Retailers Association had a session on getting your product into big-box stores. Brent was on the panel, and I stayed after and talked his ear off, taking notes. He probably thought I was a lunatic."

"I doubt that," Megan said and smiled demurely.

"Well, we then ran into each other back home at the opening of that new movie theater near Fair Park, and he asked me out. I guess he likes lunatics, which might be a red flag, but I've chosen to ignore it."

Megan laughed. "I love that story. It sounds like it was meant to be."

"Yeah." Allison nodded, a far-off look in her eyes. "We have the ability to talk about anything for hours. Do you believe in fate?"

"I do." She gestured around her. "I don't think I could work in the wedding industry if I didn't. What about you?"

Allison smiled, and not the kind that was for show. When this woman smiled, she meant it. Megan was captivated. "Jury is still out on that one. I have lots of fanciful notions, but I'm not sure if I've made up my mind about the hand of fate. It's kind of nice being kept in suspense."

Megan had never thought of it that way. "Well, you keep me updated. Shall we talk about your wedding?"

"Oh God, yes. I'm going to need you for this one. I'm afraid I'm wildly unprepared and out of my depth when it comes to big events. Fourth-grade Christmas parties with construction paper garland? I'm your girl. I can arrange kids on a set of risers like nobody else. White tablecloths and place settings? I defer. Please help."

"Well, we can always talk tablecloth color down the road." Megan liked this woman even more in person. She was very open and honest and engaging as hell. What you saw was what you got. She glanced behind her. "It's late in the day, and you're my last appointment. Some champagne? Wine? To celebrate the occasion."

"Do you have any white?" Allison asked with a devious grin. "I'm a fruit chaser."

"You've come to the right place."

Allison laughed, full and melodic. "Happy hour it is."

Demi brought them two glasses of chardonnay, and they went through a brief question and answer session, so Megan could best gauge some of Allison's likes and dislikes. What she learned was that Allison wasn't so sure of her own taste.

"What do *you* think looks best? Lots of flowers or the minimalistic approach?" Allison asked.

"I don't think it matters what I think," Megan said gently. "But if you're asking about a family like the Carmichaels—"

"I am. Bingo. Now you're talking. That's exactly what I'm asking."

"The high society families tend to like to…display a little bit more. That doesn't mean excessive amounts of floral decor, but they'll want a good showing of the elegant variety."

"Expensive flowers for all the world to see. That's what you're trying to say in a very polite and professional way." Allison took a sip of her wine. "You can just say it. They need to show off."

"Exactly that," Megan answered with a laugh. The wine had loosened her up, and she found herself really enjoying her afternoon. Not always the case in her line of work. Most of her clients came in with a strong idea of exactly what they wanted and planned on Megan simply going out there and getting it for them. Allison Hale was a breath of fresh air.

"Are you married?" Allison asked. Then she covered her mouth. "That's a really nosy question. You should shoo me out of this office right now. I'm out of control." She pointed to her glass in blame.

"I'm not, and I don't mind you asking."

"I just wondered what it would be like to plan your wedding when you have so much knowledge at your fingertips." She gestured to lookbooks spread out around them. "Infinite experience to draw from."

Megan smiled. "I have ideas of what I would want at my wedding, sure." She turned the stem of her glass, melting into the daydream. "But I think it would depend on who I was marrying and what they were like. I would want it to suit us, you know? Not just me."

A long pause. "I really like that answer," Allison said. "I have a feeling you'd choose a guy with a lot of style."

"A woman," Megan corrected as she gathered the books they'd sorted through. She'd already made notes of some of the photos Allison had gravitated to.

"Oh, fantastic."

"Is it?" Megan asked with a smile.

"I think so. Even better if she's into the planning. Brent is pretty much agreeable to whatever I decide as long as *it's lit*. His exact words."

"Forever a frat boy. He means well, though, and luckily has a kind heart."

Allison laughed. "Both are true."

"And a jawline like a superhero."

"Again, I can't argue." She paused. "So, what do we do now?"

Megan took out her appointment book. "We schedule a follow-up. I've got your basics down and have some idea of some options to pull together for next time, so we can work on narrowing our focus. Your homework assignment is to take a look at my website and some of the photographs of weddings we've done in the past. Make note of any detail that stands out to you. Flag things that you like and things that you don't."

"I can do that," Allison said. "Honestly, seeing all of the images helps me navigate through my very cluttered brain, and you keeping track of everything for me is just, wow."

"All part of my job."

Allison gestured to the larger office beyond the lounge. "I notice you have lots of people working here. This is a major operation." She made a gesture as if her brain was exploding.

"There are six of us on staff and a variety of part-time helpers for weekend events."

Allison stood, gathering her things. "Do you meet with everyone personally? That must be exhausting."

"Actually, I don't. I have a handful of clients who are mine, and I help oversee my staff as they handle their own events and clients. We're all project managers here."

"Oh." Allison's mouth fell open. "Well, then I'm honored. Thank you so much for taking the time to see me." She held up a finger. "But I'm guessing this is more of a Carmichael thing."

Megan smiled. "Well, the Carmichaels are a big client. We handle so many of their corporate events that I wanted to handle your wedding personally. It's my honor and pleasure."

"I won't argue. I won't balk. I'll take all the help I can get, and I can already tell the rumors are true. You're amazing. A wedding genius sent from above to save me from what I simply do not know."

"Well, thank you for saying so, but wait until I force you to start making the hard decisions."

Allison grimaced. "I get nervous just thinking about it. I have Tums in the car."

Megan placed a hand on her shoulder. "I will hold your hand and not let you fail at this. Got it?"

"Got it," Allison said quietly. "And now I will leave, so you can go home and concentrate on your own life." She looked around. "What's it like to work in a place as sophisticated as this? I'm passing out tissues and redirecting kids away from jokes about bodily functions."

"Honestly, it's a dream job, but I bet yours is equally fulfilling if not more."

Allison scrunched her shoulders. "It's true. I love it. Immature jokes and all. While I envy you, I know I've found my calling."

"Doesn't that feel amazing?"

If Allison could light up any more, she did in that moment. "Like the coziest of gloves. The kind that have become overly fuzzy from so much wear, but you're planning never to get rid of them because they are *the* gloves."

"I've never considered the wonder of overly fuzzy gloves."

"Well, you must," Allison said in earnest. "They're a gift to us all, and I demand you seek some out. Though it takes time to accomplish. The fuzz generation."

"I'll never take them for granted again."

With a wave, Allison was off, and Megan was left with a smile on her face.

"I guess the Carmichael meeting went well. You're grinning," Kelsey said.

"It went fine, it's just…she's fun. Different." She shook her head, trying to pinpoint it. "Easygoing, I guess, is the best way to describe her. Extra talkative, but I got the feeling it was because she was nervous. A nice person. Go, Brent."

Kelsey exhaled. "Thank God. We have enough high maintenance women to keep happy and a few demanding men."

"Do you have many extra fuzzy gloves?"

Kelsey paused, squinted, and quirked her head. "I don't have any."

"Total shame," Megan said and headed back to her office to do a little more work.

❖

"What do you mean you booked Soiree? Just like that?" Betsy shrieked like a fourteen-year-old girl at a BTS concert. Allison reflexively covered her ears. At her sister's invitation, she'd joined Betsy for her nightly speed walk through her neighborhood. Apparently, now that Allison was a bride-to-be, her sister thought she should up her fitness game. With a shrug, she'd tossed on her old tennis shoes and made the drive to Betsy's posh neighborhood with all the sculpted shrubbery and stop signs with actual landscaping around them.

Allison tried to mimic her sister's fast-paced arm movements that made her look more than a little silly. She went with it anyway, hustling like a suburban she boss. "I dropped the name Carmichael, and the magical doors opened. I've already had my first consultation."

Betsy let out another scream. Those should really come with warnings, or else she needed earmuffs for these encounters. "I can't decide if I'm thrilled or jealous. I think it's both, but I'm leaning in to thrilled. What was it like? Who did you meet with?" Her arms still shuffled a mile a minute like a wind-up toy.

"Megan Kinkaid."

"You did not." At the mention of Megan's name, Betsy upped her arm hustle, so Allison followed suit.

"I did so. She took the meeting herself. She was both beautiful and smart. And oh my God, you should see her gorgeous skin."

"I've seen photos. It's a treasure."

Allison thought back on the moment Megan had entered the room. Her dark hair had been down and her brown eyes large and luminous. She'd wore a tan business suit and matching heels that made her look like what her father would deem a million bucks. "She also comes with this calming presence that just takes over the room. She had my nerves in check in under a minute."

"This is why she's on the map. Did you settle on a date?"

"She suggested the first week of June, and I'm great with that."

"That's a killer date, and she knows it. Damn, she's good."

"I had no idea there were killer dates."

"Well, there are. And you snagged one, you lucky thing."

"How long do we have to do this?" Allison asked, already feeling a little winded. "People are likely laughing at us, you know."

"Are not. Suck it up. Another mile."

Allison gasped. "Fabulous. You're trying to kill me because I'm a June bride. This is a cruel way to go. Death by maniacal arm movement."

"You're going to thank me one day."

"No, I never will."

They fell into quiet huffing, and Allison reflected on her meeting with Megan and how happy she was that someone now had the reins and would help her through this monstrous task. Not only that, but she'd really liked Megan Kinkaid. She was confident and warm at the same time, the kind of person who made an impression on you and stood out in a group.

"Mom says that the BeLeaf meeting went well." The statement pulled Allison immediately from her thoughts. That's right! She'd been so caught up with Soiree, she'd forgotten that the meeting had been today.

"Really? That's fantastic. Tell me more."

"I think the deal is a go."

"They're interested in putting the Dash Bar on the shelves? Brent hinted that his father was serious about the Dash and told the buyers as much, but I was still holding my breath, you know?"

"We all were." Betsy looked over at her. "Don't tell Mom and Dad, but I was really worried. They need this, Ally. So very badly."

"I know. Things have been tight."

"It's worse than that. I'm not sure you realize this, but they've invested far too much money in the Dash Bar."

"Really? Then I'm so glad this is happening. They just think it's the next big thing, and you know what?" Hope filled her heart. "Maybe it will be. Maybe the stars have finally aligned. God, I hope so. They work so hard, Bets."

"Dad barely sleeps he's so worried."

Ally nodded. "Mom has been stress gardening."

"God, I hope this goes through." Betsy paused them for a car to cross the intersection. "If it doesn't, I don't know what's going to happen. They can always move in with me, I suppose."

Allison turned to her sister as they resumed their walk. "Well, we can't think like that, because it sounds like it's all moving in the right direction. I'll check with Brent tonight. We're having a late dinner after his conference call with the board. The new BeLeaf is opening in Oak Lawn, and deadlines are tight."

"He's been pulling late hours?"

"Sure, but that's not new."

"That might have to change once you two start a family, which I recommend you get to immediately."

Allison laughed. "No, no, no. Let's not get ahead of ourselves."

Betsy tossed her a glance over her double-timing shoulders. "I'm quite serious. A man like Brent is going to want children and likely soon."

A man like Brent? The thing was, Allison knew Brent and Betsy didn't. At least not that well. Her sister was more worldly than she was, but sometimes her proclamations came without merit. Brent was a Carmichael, sure, but he wasn't a *Carmichael*. He would never demand anything of Allison that they hadn't thoroughly discussed and agreed upon.

"I'll keep that in mind," she told Betsy, not really one to make waves. Ally preferred to keep things comfortable, and sometimes that meant agreeing with her sister for the sake of peace.

They finished their walk, and after a quick shower, Allison made the drive to Brent's house in Highland Park. Correction, her future home. It was honestly too big for two people, but gorgeous nonetheless, a custom remodel spanning two and a half stories over a sprawling five thousand square feet. The circular driveway made for a regal arrival, and the soaring ceiling of the entryway into the living room was only the first wow factor. A person could easily get lost there, Allison often reminded Brent, who would laugh at how cute she was. Coming from the complete opposite of her humble upbringing, Brent had always had money at his fingertips and very much took it for granted. She didn't blame him for what he hadn't experienced, but sometimes she worried that he couldn't relate to a large part of the world.

"There you are," he said, when she made her way into the great big living space. He wore dark jeans and a forest green sweater. Even after a long day, he looked bright, focused, and ready for more. "I ordered Mr. Eggroll. Is that cool?" He leaned down for a quick kiss. "The usual."

"I will forever be in your debt. Betsy made me do one of those speed walks, and I feel like I should be rewarded."

"What? Like the women in the mall in the jogging suits?"

She followed him to the gray and white kitchen. "But with extra added intensity. Her shoulders move like Mighty Mouse, Brent. I'm not built that way. I was lucky to survive."

"Betsy doesn't mess around. Reminds me of the hard-core girls from Penn. Crab rangoon?"

She snagged one as he plated the rest of the food. "She was floored that Megan Kinkaid is personally planning our wedding. I still am, too, if I'm being honest."

"Oh, I gave her a call today. Just to say hello. Courtesy, you know."

"She mentioned you were friends."

"We ran in the same social circles for a while, back when I was a gentleman about town." He adjusted his imaginary tie.

"Oh, you mean the wild and crazy days."

He kissed her lips with a smack. "Until I met the woman who tamed me for life."

They both knew that wasn't the case. Brent did everything on a timeline, and when the alarm clock in his head went off, he knew, probably because his father once told him, that he needed to settle down and look toward the next phase of his life. And here she was. "I can't take credit for that. You have a plan for everything. What did you two talk about?" She slid into the sleek leather bench seat that surrounded the large square kitchen table, big enough for eight.

He took a swig of his beer. "We shot the breeze for a bit, and I let her know how much you enjoyed meeting with her. Gave her our budget and some special liquor requests. We'll need the good stuff for my guys."

"And I wouldn't have a clue what that would be, so I'm glad you stepped in." A pause. "So…what's she like? Outside of work." She couldn't help but wonder after having been so struck by the woman.

"Megan? Smart and always the responsible one in any group. Killer dancer and hot as hell when she's doing it. Likes the ladies, though."

"So she said." Ally chewed her food. "I wonder what it's like to be so put together? I'm envious."

"Of Megan? Please. I much prefer my everyday girl." He squeezed her hand and went back to his food. Brent liked that she wasn't overly glamorous or complicated, and she had no problem owning it. Not everyone could be special.

"Speaking of meetings, I heard the one with my parents went well," she said, moving them out of it.

He nodded vigorously. "If all goes according to plan, we'll set them up with some of our manufacturers, and that should ease their costs." He cracked his knuckles, and Ally flinched. Not her favorite. "And we'll look at getting the Dash Bar on BeLeaf shelves a few months down the road."

"Brent Carmichael. That's the most amazing news I've heard in a long time."

"Yeah? Well, if you're happy, I'm happy. It's not a bad little bar either. Your parents have something there. We'd want it on our shelves regardless of the familial connection."

She felt herself light up. "I think it's fantastic, too. And their customers at the shop can't get enough. It's why they wanted to license it in the first place. They saw something unique."

"They were spot-on, and we'll do right by them. They're family now." He smiled, and she did, too.

That night, they watched a movie. A later installment of *Fast and Furious* that Brent picked out for them. It held her interest for a short time until it just didn't anymore. She wasn't a huge fan of action movies and fell asleep next to him. She found herself eating dinner at a lovely little outdoor spot with lots of friendly people. Delicious-looking cocktails went by on a tray, and Allison considered ordering one because they looked refreshing and it was warm out.

"You should do it," a voice said. She turned to her dinner companion, and Megan Kinkaid gestured to the tray. "I hear they're amazing. In fact, let me order you one. I insist." She did. The drink arrived in seconds. Citrusy and delicious. They spent the next stretch of time just talking beneath the setting sun. The next thing she knew they were walking along the beach and Megan took her hand, laced their fingers, and smiled over at her. Allison had never felt more at peace or quite so happy in her entire life. She reached over and touched Megan's bottom lip with her free hand and watched how she reacted, as if struck by the gesture, moved by it. Her heart squeezed pleasantly.

"Babe, we're at the credits." The voice didn't match Megan's even though her lips moved to the words. "Movie's over, Sleeping Beauty. Good guy won." And then she watched as Megan, beautiful as ever, slowly faded away.

Allison's eyes fluttered open, and it took her a minute to understand where she was. Towering ceiling. Large television. Right. Brent's. The egg rolls. The racing. The beach and Megan Kinkaid had been a dream. That's all. A really realistic dream she wasn't sure she wanted to end.

"You should stay over tonight," Brent said, giving her chin a shake. "You're exhausted."

She nodded and allowed him to pull her onto her feet. "Good idea." She'd not moved in with him because her place was much closer to school, and well, she also liked it a lot. They'd agreed that she'd begin the move as they got closer to the wedding date. For now, they stole time at each other's houses, occupying drawers and closet space as needed. It wasn't how other people would have done things, but they did what worked for them. The arrangement offered them their time together but also a little bit of space. Betsy recoiled at the description, but Allison thought it was actually quite mature of them, seizing upon what worked rather than what was assumed of them.

"Okay, but don't let me oversleep. It's another twenty-five minutes on the road in the morning, and I have to account for it. Fourth graders can't be kept waiting."

"I'll shove you out the door if I have to. Scream expletives until you get the hell out of here."

"Now we're talking."

"Should we just crash?" he asked. It was a question of sex, which she could take or leave. Their connection in the bedroom was fine but had definitely wound down from their early days together.

"Yes, please."

They fell into bed in Brent's oversized king, and Ally hoped to return to that rather pleasant dream. She didn't know why, but she felt awfully at home there on that beach. It beckoned her. Would be a nice way to spend the evening. When her alarm went off at five forty-five a.m., she frowned. The grumpy alligator that had followed her around in her slumber was a far cry from the serenity of the earlier dream with a beautiful woman. Friend. "Interesting," she muttered as she showered for school, in regards to both dreams. Yet only one of them stuck with her as she moved through her day. Like a happy little getaway tucked in the recesses of her brain that she could take out whenever she wanted.

Strange, yes. But Allison also noticed that she wasn't complaining.

CHAPTER THREE

Allison Hale seemed different at their second scheduled consultation. Megan couldn't quite put her finger on what it was, but it snagged her attention right off the bat. She'd come into the suite, several minutes early again, and Cade had directed her to Megan's office. She looked less like a teacher today—her blond hair carried lazy waves, and she wore calf-high gray boots. Not only that, but her clothes were sleeker, more like a woman out for a day of shopping rather than instructing nine-year-olds. She looked, quite frankly, really attractive.

Megan relaxed into her chair and smiled up at Allison as she entered. "How were the kids today?"

"I wouldn't know. Teacher workday, and we were dismissed by noon in a happy turn of events. I got to have lunch out with my sister, and then we got our nails done." She waved her newly pink fingers at Megan, who nodded her approval.

"The color suits you."

"Thank you. I get flustered when they ask me to choose, and I just close my eyes and point. Sometimes I live with those unfortunate consequences."

"Living on the dangerous side." She gestured to the cream sofa across from her desk as a bolt of unexpected energy struck. Where had that come from? "Come on in and have a seat. I thought we'd meet in here today." She'd been exhausted from a nonstop afternoon, but somehow seeing Allison had woken her the hell up. Her friendly vibe must have been infectious.

Allison took a seat and looked around the room. "You have a nice office. I mean, really."

Megan saw the space through Allison's eyes with pride. "I wanted something that felt professional, yet comfortable."

"You've definitely achieved it. I'd sleep in here." She patted the couch. "Or there. Or even over there on the soft-looking carpet. You could rent it out."

Megan laughed out loud, caught off guard by the comment. "Thank you?"

"Definitely a compliment. As a teacher, I sometimes go too hard, so I'm always on the lookout for comfy spots to crash." She laughed. "I'm just kidding about renting it out. Sometimes my jokes aren't clear."

"No, no. I was with you." Again, incredibly endearing. And cute.

Megan opened the Hale/Carmichael file on her computer and turned the oversized monitor so it was visible to both her and Allison. "I went over some of the photos you flagged for me since we chatted last."

"I'm all over the map on style, aren't I?"

"Actually, no." Megan brought up four of the photos and placed them side by side. "In terms of hue, you like bronzes and champagnes with little pops of bright color. Very elegant, in fact. I like it."

Allison's cheeks turned red, and she sat taller. "Really? I have actual style?"

Megan narrowed her gaze because as much as she liked Allison, she sure didn't come with a ton of confidence in herself. "You do. You also sell yourself short. File that away."

More blushing. "I think that's me just knowing my lane. I'm a pretty good roller skater."

"I think it's a broader lane than that. Based on what you've shown me, I have a photographer you're going to love. Not at all cheap, but after Brent handed over the budget, I don't think we have to worry."

"Okay. I suppose that's good news." A pause while Megan pulled up the website. "I had a dream about you recently."

Megan raised an eyebrow. "Oh yeah?" She paused her file sorting and met Allison's tentative gaze.

"I don't even know why I'm bringing this up, but have you ever had one of those dreams where afterward the person in it takes on new meaning? As in, you feel like you know them when you really don't? It was like that."

Megan was intrigued. "What was the dream about?"

"We were on this beach, and we were so comfortable with each other, and relaxed. Almost like we were very close, you know?"

Megan smiled. It didn't sound half bad. "I do know. I grew up on a beach, and I could use one about now." She squinted. "How do we make that happen?"

Allison laughed. "I'm glad you don't think I'm a lunatic. The dream lingered with me a bit, and now, seeing you, it's coming back in full force." Her voice got quieter. "It's random, but really nice. Maybe we were meant to meet. Crazy?"

"Oh," Megan said, her mouth making the shape of the word. The way Allison was looking at her had pulled her up short. Like she mattered, and that Allison was happy about that. Megan held her gaze for a moment, forgetting the trajectory of the meeting altogether. In fact, she couldn't quite find the words she wanted at all. What was her name again?

"I didn't mean to derail us," Allison said finally, saving them from the silence. "Sometimes I'm a one-way segue to randomville. You can proceed with your impressive professionalism and tell me about that photographer."

Megan blinked a couple of times, grinned, and shook her head. "Right. Photos. The photos are probably more important than anything. The day will be gone in a flash, but the photos last a lifetime."

They looked through the sample shots, and Allison seemed captivated, nodding and pointing out all the minute details Megan herself had always been impressed with. "You notice the little things," Megan said.

"Sometimes big and flashy get all the attention when something amazing and less noticeable is standing right there in front of a person."

"That is such a true, and often unrecognized, statement." Somehow, Megan got the feeling that the analogy was not limited to the details in a photograph. Megan herself had even paused at Brent's choice of the schoolteacher, of all people, for his bride. But the more minutes she clocked in Allison's presence, the more she understood how thoughtful she was, how unique, and what a life force she possessed.

Allison checked her watch, probably realizing that their consultation was coming to a close. "Well, we knocked one thing off the list. Provided you can score your photographer."

"I have my ways," Megan said and tapped her temple. "Shall we schedule another meeting soon?"

"Yes, but while I have your attention, I have a favor to ask."

Megan wasn't sure where this was going, but her interest was piqued. "I'm listening."

"Career Week is approaching next week at school, and I was wondering if someone from your office might be willing to come out and speak to my class." She held up a hand. "No major speaker fee, unfortunately, but I do offer a gift certificate to the Nutcase, a fantastic healthy grab-and-go café."

"Well, how can I say no to free stuff at the Nutcase, a healthy grab-and-go café?"

Allison laughed. She had such a pretty one. Not like anyone else's. "I was hoping that would be your take."

"I'll come. Sure."

"Wait. You? You can send someone, you know. This is not a Carmichael thing, so the obligation isn't there. Honestly, event planning is just an interesting career that we've never featured before."

She grinned. "I'm coming. It sounds like a nice detour from my day-to-day."

"Oh. Well, in that case, we'd love to have you." Allison thumbed through a small notebook she pulled from her bag. "I have Tuesday, Wednesday, and Thursday afternoon available."

"Put me down for Wednesday." Megan had no idea what in the world had possessed her to say yes to speaking to a group of fourth graders, an invitation she never would have accepted normally. Refusing to analyze it any further, she smiled at Allison. "Just tell me what's expected, and I'll be there."

Allison beamed like Megan had just presented her the moon. "This is going to be fantastic."

She smiled back, wondering what in the world she'd just gotten herself into.

❖

"Who's coming today? You still haven't told us. Is it another kids' doctor?" Levi whispered as he turned in his math test. "Tired of those. They act like they're so smart."

Ally smothered a smile, because Levi had high standards. "No. Not a pediatrician, but you'll have to wait and see who is coming, though. It's a new one."

He passed her a curious gaze. "Keep talking."

"I can't—it's a secret. Now go sit down."

"Why?"

"Because you're a kid, and it's what you do."

He nodded. "Good point."

Fifteen minutes later, after the last test was submitted, in walked Megan Kinkaid wearing a belted sweater dress, heels, and what had to be a five-hundred-dollar bag. Not that Allison knew how much bags of that variety went for. Every kid in the room sat straight up. Allison waved and grinned, beckoning Megan to the front of the room.

"Everyone, I want you to meet a friend of mine, Megan Kinkaid."

"Hi," the kids said in near unison, beaming, excited to meet this new person.

"Hi there," Megan said back.

Allison continued her intro. "Have you ever seen one of those fancy weddings in the movies, or an exciting party where everything is just perfect, and wondered how all of it happened?" She doubted the answer was actually yes, but her class was clearly all-in and nodded enthusiastically. "Ms. Kinkaid, along with her staff, plans those very events. Her company is called Soiree, which means a party. The word originated from the French language."

"Do you speak French?" Augustus called out without raising his hand.

"I don't. No," Megan said with a wince.

"Oh." Augustus thought on this. "That's okay. I still think it's a good name."

"Me, too," Allison said. "It's why I've asked Soiree to plan my wedding." That did it. The class let out a collective gasp, and Megan's value in the room just went up.

Ally gestured to Megan that she now had the floor. "Ms. Kinkaid, why don't you tell us a little bit about what it's like to be an event planner?" She saw several of her students, most notably her firecracker, Haley, scribble down Megan's official title. Haley didn't like to miss a detail. She was going to take over the world.

"Thank you, Allis—Ms. Hale for having me here today." She

smiled warmly at the kids. "My name is Megan, and when I was little, I wanted to be a tightrope walker in the circus. After that, I thought maybe I'd be a zoologist. In high school, I thought of being a fashion designer. But then something happened. I learned what I was really, really good at."

"What was it?" Augustus shouted from the back. She really needed to work with him on raising his hand. She put her finger to her lips silently, a gesture for the class to listen to their speaker.

"Spotting the details it takes to get a large task completed way before everyone else. Have you ever worked on a group project?" The group of heads nodded. "Well, it's kind of like that."

Megan went on to explain, and the kids listened in awe. She had them hooked. She found a way for them to relate and built her story from there. She never spoke in complicated terms and turned on the charm, even pulling a few laughs. The kids swarmed her when it was time to say good-bye, the girls especially in amazement of her success and the fact that she got to attend an actual wedding each weekend. "Can I intern for you someday?" Haley asked. "My sister is an intern at our vet's office. I promise I have a lot to offer and will never be late."

"I believe it. Look me up when you're older," Megan said and booped her nose.

"Do you have a boyfriend?" Levi asked. "You're alluring."

Allison closed her eyes in mortification because allure had been one of their vocabulary words last week, and now it was coming back to bite her. "That's too personal of a question, Levi," Allison said.

"I don't mind," Megan said. "I don't have a boyfriend."

"Score." Levi scurried away, hanging on to his perceived victory.

Allison then stepped in to save Megan from the eager children, who would never let her out of there without intervention. As she walked Megan to the door, she leaned in. "Thank you for doing this. You were fantastic but may have unfortunately just inspired some competition fifteen years from now."

"I hadn't thought of that angle," Megan said with a sly smile. "But I'm memorizing Haley's name now."

"She's going to buy and sell all of us," Allison whispered.

Megan laughed. She was effortlessly beautiful. One of those

people. Allison had to agree with Levi. She was not only alluring, but intoxicating. Allison couldn't take her eyes off her as she presented, feeling a little drunk off the experience.

"When does school get out again?"

Allison forced herself to think. "Um, a little under an hour?"

"Want to grab a cup of coffee after? I'm not in this part of town too often."

"Really?" She was planning to work a little longer, grade those math tests, but quite frankly, they could wait. Being asked to coffee by Megan Kinkaid made her feel important. "Let's do it."

"Perfect. Do you know the coffee shop up the street? I passed it on the way here."

"Froman's. They have amazing whipped cream. Not that I sample it in large amounts or anything, except I do. By the spoonful. It's my drug of choice."

"You're the right person to ask, then. See you there when you're finished up."

Allison returned to her kids on a bit of a high. This afternoon was really going well, and the excited chatter from the kids told her they thought just as much of Megan as she did. In fact, the more time she spent with Megan, the more impressed she became. Megan had clearly been out of her element but rose to the occasion and even prepared for her talk with the kids, as busy as she was. That meant a lot and spoke of her character.

"She's pretty," Levi whispered.

"And very smart," Allison added for good measure. "Don't forget that part."

"Well, that's one of the reasons she's pretty," Levi said and grinned proudly. Wise beyond his years, that kid. One to keep an eye on.

"Shall we get back to multiplication? Let's talk about the hard problems on the test. Who had trouble with number three?"

She was met with a group groan and several exasperated bodies flinging themselves into the backs of their chairs. She had to agree with them. It was hard to return to the doldrums of real life after spending a little time with Megan Kinkaid.

❖

The quaint little coffee shop felt more like a cozy house of treats. It smelled like a chocolaty coffee heaven inside, to begin with. The space was made up of an open floor dotted with tables, flanked by little carved-out nooks for more intimate booth dining, almost woodsy in its appearance. While Megan didn't get to this part of town too often, she would remember Froman's the next time she was nearby. Unique and cozy. She'd knocked out a good chunk of her ever-arriving email by the time Allison arrived and grinned at her from across the room. Allison held eye contact as she walked in Megan's direction, and something about that connection sent a shiver straight up to Megan's shoulders and down her arms. She'd seen Allison just a short time ago, but she was already happy to see her again, now really glad she'd suggested this. The invitation had flown from her mouth on a whim. But sometimes one had to follow their instincts, and Megan's had never let her down.

"This is so sad. Where's your drink?" Allison asked when she arrived at the table and scanned it.

"I was waiting for you. It didn't feel right to inhale all the whipped cream before you had a shot at any, professed addict that you are."

Allison laughed. "You're thoughtful, too. I'm glad we met."

"Me, too," she answered sincerely. Allison must have picked up on the change in tone, and her smile dimmed to match Megan's.

"What's your poison?"

Megan thought on it. "You know what? Get me whatever you're having."

"Oh. So easy."

The drink Allison presented her with, however, was nothing like Megan would have ordered for herself, and that made it all the more fun. Allison gestured to the warm beverages on the table in curvy glasses you'd expect to see at an ice-cream shop. "Two Toffee Crunch Dreams. Basically, a latte with lots of added goodness. You're welcome and enjoy."

Megan stared at the tall glass towering with whipped cream, a drizzle of toffee sauce in an overlapping design, and what had to be toffee pieces. "I'm not sure I've ever seen coffee so decadent before. You're sure this is *coffee*, right? I'm usually a house blend with skim kind of woman and out of my depth."

"Oh no. Then it's a good thing you came to Froman's with *me* for your first time. I've saved you from utter coffee boredom. This is fun coffee. It's why we live." She pointed at the glasses. "For things like this."

Megan laughed, feeling lighter than she had in quite a while. "I'll try to keep an open mind. How do I get at this thing exactly?" She came at the drink from over the top and then from the lip of the cup, but both seemed pretty daunting.

"Tongue or spoon to start. Your choice. After that it reverts to a regular drink. Straw or not. Up to you."

Megan picked up the plastic spoon Allison had delivered along with their order and dived in, a happy kid after school. "There's something refreshing to setting aside your entire afternoon and diving into a damn dessert."

"Damn right there is," Allison said. "It's still weird to me that I'm hanging out with you in Froman's. A few weeks back you were a myth, a legend, and now you're my wedding planner, fourth-grade speaking guest, and coffee date."

"I'd like to think we're becoming friends, too," Megan said. "Aren't we?"

"Well, I can't get presumptuous. But maybe this is how it's done. Do you stay in touch with many of your clients after they're married off?"

"You make it sound like they're my children, and I've finally convinced a good man to take 'em off my hands."

Allison earned herself whipped cream on her chin when her spoon collided with her laugh. "Well, now that's always how I'm going to think of your job." She grabbed a napkin. "No, but seriously. Do you? I didn't want to assume friendship. Maybe I'm just one of the masses."

"Some of them become my friends, sure. When you work closely on a very stressful project with someone, you can't help but bond a little bit."

"Like us now?"

Megan thought on it. "Actually, no. We haven't had to make any difficult wedding decisions yet. The trauma is ahead."

"I was referencing public speaking in front of fourth graders."

Megan's eyes went wide, and she found herself confessing. "I don't often share my weaknesses as a matter of principle, but this talk today had me up late. I've spoken at women's groups, small business associations, even college entrepreneurship classes. But the idea of nine-years-olds blinking back at me was scary as hell."

"And there we go. Cue the trauma bonding," Allison said and obviously savored the whipped cream from the spoon in her mouth.

The more time Megan spent with her, the more beautiful she became, and she was already pretty. Cultivating a friendship with Allison Hale, soon to be Allison Carmichael, wasn't a bad idea. The toffee atop the latte was that she actually liked Allison. A lot. A thought hit. "I'm hosting a little girls' night out happy hour at Shakers. You should come. Let off some of that fourth-grade steam."

Allison seemed surprised by the invitation. "Oh, you don't have to do that, just because I announced our newfound bond."

"Trust me. No one ever pressured or influenced me to do anything. I'm a pretty independent woman, and I'd love for you to come out with us. Have a cocktail or, in your case, a hot fudge sundae or four."

Allison looked a little nervous, which Megan had come to understand was her built-in self-doubt. "I'm not sure I'm sophisticated enough for a cocktail. I tried one recently with my sister, and it went straight to my head. White wine?"

"I hear they're stocked with that, too."

Allison shifted her lips to the side and a small smile appeared. Megan was captivated by the transformation. "You know what? Maybe I will come out."

"I hope you do. I'll send you the Evite. No pressure."

Allison pointed with her spoon. "How's that Toffee Crunch Dream working out for you?"

She sighed. "I feel guilty as hell, but I'm also loving every moment of it."

"My favorite moments in life."

"Think you'll dream about it?"

Allison's mouth fell open. "You're making fun of my beach dream, but it was actually really nice. You need to trust me on this. We were in heaven."

Megan laughed. "I was actually just referencing the name of the latte. A pun. But I applaud your wholehearted defense of our dream life together."

"Oh," Allison said and turned tomato red. It was a sight to behold, and Megan couldn't take her eyes off the overt cuteness. In fact, her own face heated uncharacteristically, and she dropped her gaze to her drink to regain her cool-as-a-cucumber default. In the midst of it all, she was very aware of how much she was enjoying her foray into Allison's world and struck by the fact that she didn't even know Allison existed until a few weeks ago.

"Oh! I almost forgot." Allison reached into her bag and pulled out a certificate with Megan's name written in swoopy calligraphy. "A token of our fourth-grade appreciation. You'll want to frame that."

Megan laughed. "Without delay."

"And as an extra-special gift, twenty-five dollars to the Nutcase, which is actually a really nice shop. I recommend the Dash Bar if you're into oatmeal. Fresh. Just pop it in the oven, or if you buy it in the shop, they'll do it for you."

"Huh. That's an interesting concept."

"Trust me. Not your average bar. You've never tried anything like it."

Megan eyed her. "You're a little salesperson."

"On a sugar high, which makes me doubly persuasive. Plus, my parents raised me to be loyal."

Megan snatched up the certificate. "Then I have no choice but to see for myself."

Allison sat back with a gleam in her eye, and Megan grinned. "This has been fun. I mean it. It was a great way to break up my work week, and I feel like I'm breathing a little easier. Enjoying life. So thank you for having me."

"Anytime," Allison said, and Megan hoped she meant it.

CHAPTER FOUR

It was uncharacteristically cold out, and that made Allison suspect wearing a dress to Megan's cocktail gathering wasn't the most practical of ideas. But then again, sophisticated women wore dresses to these kinds of get-togethers regardless, didn't they? And heels? The fancy cocktail drinking types anyway, of which she definitely was not one. What about boots with a small heel on them? Would that count as dressy enough? Could she blend?

"What's going on in here?" Brent asked, leaning against the doorjamb with a lazy grin.

"I'm failing at being a woman about town. I'm afraid I'm not cut out."

"That's what I like best about you."

She frowned. "Not helping."

He held up a hand. "First of all, I was kidding. Second, you don't have to go at all, you know. We can stay in. I got a couple bottles of expensive wine from one of our vendors. We can watch UFC."

"Do those two things go together?" she asked with a squint, not relishing the idea of a bloody beatdown.

"If we say they do."

Allison sighed. It *was* tempting to skip out and avoid feeling like a fish out of water, but something she couldn't quite pinpoint was tugging her along, urging her to go. The Evite Megan had forwarded had included Kelsey from Soiree as one of the confirmed attendees. They'd met back at the office, so not everyone would be a stranger. She turned to Brent and took his hands. "No, I think I want to go. Push through my insecurities. It'll be good for me, right?"

He kissed her temple. "I'm sure you'll have fun once you're there. If not, you know where to find me and the fighters." He grabbed his keys and headed back to his place where he'd be more comfortable. She'd send him a text once she made it home, and they'd see each other the next day. Brent was…easy. Their life was, making it one less thing she had to worry about. She exhaled slowly. Low heeled boots it was. She chose a maroon sweater, her slim-fitting black pants, and a pendant necklace for a final top off and was out the door.

Shakers was a pretty cool bar. Not that she had a ton of downtown bar experience, but this one fell under the heading of swanky. The barstools were softly upholstered, and the colors light and airy. Definitely trying to appeal to women. Megan told her she'd find their group at a series of high-top tables at the back. Apparently, she'd reserved the entire section for their gathering. Allison took a deep breath as she approached the group of about fifteen or so. The women were talking animatedly, each holding a cocktail in a variety of glass shapes. As she approached, she was surprised, no, *relieved* to see that the women weren't all glamour goddesses, as she'd been imagining. Some looked just like her friends and neighbors, of all ages, sizes, and ethnicities. Her boots had been the right choice!

"Oh, wow. You came," Megan said, setting down her orange-colored martini and crossing the short distance to Allison. She gave her a quick hug and kiss on the cheek, smelling sweet like vanilla and cinnamon.

"Didn't want to miss the fun."

"And you haven't. White wine?" Allison nodded, and Megan disappeared, clearly in control and looking fabulous at the same time. She wore jeans, a black turtleneck, and a pair of booties that really accentuated her legs, which were…perfect. She was pulled from her thoughts by Kelsey, who *had* worn the dress and heels in spite of the cold.

"Allison, right? Awesome you made it. Is someone getting you a drink?" She searched the room for an answer.

"Megan is, yeah. It's good to see you. You look amazing."

Kelsey shrugged it off. "I'm single, so I have to turn up the volume a little bit. Find my own Carmichael."

"Well, Brent has a brother," Allison said with a laugh.

Kelsey narrowed her gaze. "What about a sister?"

Aha. Not straight. For some reason, that made her stomach tighten. "Afraid not."

"Boo."

Before she knew it, Megan had returned with her drink and escorted her through the room, introducing her to all the other women, who were warm and interested in most everything she had to say. Megan had great taste in friends.

"I'm an assistant district attorney," one woman, Cathy, said. "What do you do?"

"I teach fourth graders."

Cathy lit up and touched her glass to Allison's. "A hero among us."

"You doing okay?" Megan asked her, tugging on her elbow a short time later.

Allison grinned. "Everyone here is wonderful. That woman over there is a conservator at a museum."

She followed Allison's gaze. "I know, and amazing at it. I like smart, nice people. I collect them." She laughed, now on to her second martini. How did she manage such grace on two? "Kidding, of course. But my friends are important to me, and I try to bring us together as much as possible. Our jobs sometimes get in the way, so nights like tonight are important."

"I appreciate you including me, but then again I did introduce you to Froman's, which was a pretty big deal."

"I haven't forgotten. Speaking of new places, I have a few venues I'd like you to take a look at. Maybe we can take a little field trip next week if you can steal time."

"Field trip? You're speaking teacher language now. I'm in."

Allison stayed at Shakers much longer than she'd intended, enjoying the conversation. Only one problem. The wine was going straight to her head. The more she chatted, the more sips she absently took. She wasn't even sure how many glasses she'd gone through. Others kept refilling her, and she was not a big drinker.

"You okay?" Megan whispered as Allison searched her bag for her phone. She was in no shape to drive and would call for an Uber. She also felt a little bit giggly, her first clue that she'd had too much.

"Little tipsy," Allison said, blinking to clear her vision. "But your friend Mandy is hysterical. Did you know her dog can talk?" She giggled again just thinking about a dog saying hello because *that* was hysterical. She hoped to meet that dog one day.

"She's told me that story," Megan said and rolled her lips in.

"Oh! I should have her bring the dog to class."

"You should maybe think on that tomorrow," Megan said gently. She had the best lips. Allison couldn't stop staring at them.

"You have good lips." Oh no. Dear Justin Timberlake. Her thoughts were speaking. How did that happen?

"Oh." A pause. Allison studied them unabashedly now, and Megan seemed to notice. "Thank you."

"I promise I'm not checking you out, though. Well, your lips. Yes. But not all of you."

Megan chuckled. "Understood. Hey, why don't we sit for a little while longer and have some water before you go?" She poured Allison a full glass, which she lifted in delight. Very clear water. Moderate bubbles. Four stars. This place had the good stuff.

"You are routinely full of good ideas. Is that the right word, routinely? It sounds so weird when you say it out loud. *Routine.* Roo-teen. Teen. With a Roo. Together."

Megan smiled. "I think it's correct."

"Say it with me. So weird."

"Routine," Megan said along with Allison. "You're funny when you drink."

"Drink too much, you mean. Soused. I swear I'm not a regular souser." She waved a hand in front of her face, hoping to convince Megan that she didn't usually do this. "Total lightweight. Though I know this, the wine got away from me. People kept bringing me more. Tricky wine. Friendly people. What a combo."

"Well, I don't want to send you out into the world quite yet. Let me give Brent a call."

She imagined Brent would really enjoy this one. "Oh, he'll laugh."

Megan put her phone to her ear. "Hey, Brent. Megan Kinkaid. I have your fiancée with me and she's had a little—"

"Sauce!" Allison proudly supplied.

"To drink," Megan finished. A pause. "That's very helpful of you. I can also walk her to my place and let her crash."

"Bam," Allison supplied and sipped her water happily. "Let's do that. I wonder what it's like where you live. Gorgeous, I bet."

"He wants to talk to you," Megan said.

Allison took the phone. "Hi."

"Sounds like it turned out to be a fun night after all," Brent said. There was the chuckle she'd predicted.

"Yes. Glad I came. The women were so nice. They hand out free wine here, too."

"I have a feeling Megan picked up the tab for the event."

Allison widened her eyes and looked at Megan. "You're rich, too."

"Not really."

"Listen," Brent said, reining her back in. "I don't mind driving out there to get you."

"You have that early morning thingy. I'll Uber. Or Megan."

"Yeah, but if you need me…"

She stared at Megan, who was already right here and perfectly lovely. Flawless skin. Perfect lips. That amazing perfume. How did she manage that? Plus, her turtleneck showed little to no skin, but it certainly captured the curves of her breasts. "Nah. Megan's got it."

"I don't mind," Megan called to the phone. "Honestly."

Brent sighed. "All right then. I'll check with you in the morning and make sure you're okay. Love you, kid." He sure called her *kid* a lot. Made her feel like one when he did it.

"Love you, too. Kiddo," she tossed in. She clicked off the call and handed Megan the phone. They stared at each other for a moment.

"Looks like you're stuck with me," Megan said.

"Like glue on a construction paper Thanksgiving turkey."

Megan nodded and squinted. "Don't move. I'll settle up, and we'll hit the road."

Allison snickered, because the visual was ridiculous and funny. Smackin' that road. She watched as Megan approached the bar with her credit card in hand. Wow. When she walked, her hips swayed a little, and it made her seem soft but in charge. The combination inspired goose bumps on her arms. What must it be like to be as beautiful and confident as Megan Kinkaid, who also, to her credit, was kind. Megan would never actually smack that road.

And then she was back. "All set. How are you feeling?"

"A little less whirly." Ally stood and blinked as the world tilted. "Oh, *there's* the full whirl. This bar is a fun house."

"Here," Megan said and offered her arm. Allison looped hers

through it and followed Megan out to the street. "I live just down there. Two blocks. Not far at all."

"Oh, that's lovely. You can come back here tomorrow. Anytime you want."

"It's a perk."

They walked beneath the streetlights of downtown Dallas, and in the midst of the two-of-everything phenomenon, she still found it entirely peaceful.

"So, did you have a good time? You seemed to be laughing a lot."

Ally didn't hesitate. "The best. I don't socialize too often. Not since I've been with Brent. Mainly just have happy hour with my sister."

"I wish I had one of those. You're lucky."

"I know." They walked on. "Betsy is the reason I came to see you."

"Then I owe her."

"Nah, she can be overbearing and pretentious. But we still like her."

"We do," Megan said, laughing. "This is me. Hey there, Chip. How's the newborn?"

He shook his head. "Adorable, but there's a big problem. She doesn't sleep. Not sure how much longer we can stay up. It's like we're in a grudge match, and she's the reigning champion."

"That's what I've heard about the new ones. They tend to win."

He relaxed into a smile. "Good thing she's cute."

Allison nodded as they entered the building. "You two are friends."

"Chip's a great guy. They've been trying for kids for years, so this is a very big deal."

"Do you want them? Brent does. I do." Oh, that sounded nosy even through the wine haze.

"Kids?" Megan hesitated. "It would depend on who I'd be having them with, I think. Too hard to guess. An algebra problem without all the information."

"Good analogy, Megan." She liked her name. She liked saying it. She also liked her apartment. Very much. Light colors on dark floors. Nice accompanying touches, too. Blankets and draperies that matched. Tall ceilings. Towering shelves. "Okay. This is beautiful. Like a magazine. Are we in a magazine?" she whispered.

"Thank you, but no. I'd love to take the credit, but I splurged and hired a decorator."

Allison placed her hands on the back of the couch to steady herself. "I have a feeling I'm going to appreciate it even more when I'm entirely sober."

Megan passed her an apologetic look. "I'm so sorry the night ended with you not feeling so hot. I have clothes you can sleep in and a nice comfy bed you can crash on. Right this way."

She followed Megan into the room to the left of the living room and paused. "Halt. This looks like your room."

"It is, but I changed the sheets just this morning. All yours for the night."

"No, no. I can't steal your room." She deflated. "I may be inebriated and swaying, but I was brought up with manners."

"Me, too. And they say don't put your drunk guests on the couch. Especially the nice ones." She pointed to the other side of the apartment. "Plus, I'm going to steal a little work time in my study. Just some odds and ends that will make my morning go smoother."

Allison was too sleepy and dizzy to argue as long as she normally would have. At a loss, she gave in meekly. "Okay, if you say so."

"I more than say so. I insist."

With the alcohol gradually drifting from her system, she was able to see the evening for what it was. Embarrassment hit. "I completely ruined your party, didn't I?" She heard the crack in her voice.

So did Megan, who came to her immediately and wrapped her up in a nice hug. "Absolutely not. I thought tonight was fabulous, and I'm so glad you were there."

Allison nodded against her shoulder, inhaling the vanilla-cinnamon combo. Megan Kinkaid smelled amazing at the end of the evening, too. Her apartment was amazing, her business was, too. "Did you also get first place on field day?" Allison asked.

"Um, what?" Megan laughed at the total non sequitur. "Tomorrow you're going to have to explain all of this." Megan set out a pair of striped pajamas. "For you."

Allison's eyes were feeling heavy. She spied the clock, and it read just after eleven. Luckily, there was no school the next day, or she'd be in real trouble. "Thank you." Automatically, she pulled her sweater over her head and stepped out of her shoes. That's when she noticed Megan staring at her strangely, almost in a panic. "Are you okay? Are these the wrong pajamas?"

"No." Megan gestured behind her, averting her eyes. "You know what? I'm going to give you some privacy."

"Okay, but it's not a big..." And that's when it occurred to her that changing in front of Megan in her own bedroom might make her uncomfortable. She didn't know the rules when it came to lesbian friends because she honestly hadn't had many. She always changed in front of her female friends in school, or her sister at home, or the few times she'd gone to the gym. The intimacy of the space and the time of night maybe contributed, and now all the overanalyzation had her very aware of being half clothed in front of Megan, and her stomach did the most noticeable dip and somersault. But Megan had slipped away, and Allison was left to try to understand the past few seconds and why her body was all of a sudden very alert and sensitive. Had to be the alcohol.

As she slid beneath the cool and criminally soft sheets, she couldn't banish the moment from her brain. In fact, she replayed it several times. Megan's gaze grazing her body before dropping to the floor out of respect. Why was this even a thing she was dwelling on? Allison wasn't sure, but the room spun when she closed her eyes, so maybe she should keep them open a little while longer. She reflected on the night and the way Megan effortlessly moved through the room, speaking with her friends and making each one feel important, valued, and looked after. She was something special, and she'd come to Allison's rescue tonight when an Uber would have been just fine, if not a little scary in her condition. She exhaled slowly. People like Megan didn't come around too often.

"You okay in here?" Megan asked quietly from the doorway. The lights in the bedroom were off, but she was backlit from the hallway, wearing a T-shirt that hung past her thighs, which Allison could only glimpse. Another stomach flip-flop. Other parts of her squeezed, too, lower parts, and that was a downright shock.

"Um, all tucked in." She swallowed, finding her full voice. "And, Megan? Thank you. You didn't have to go out of your way because I screwed up my counting."

"You didn't screw up at all," Megan said simply. "And I'm happy to help." She came farther in to the room. "Not to intrude, but I brought you some water and aspirin in case you need it." She set them both on the bedside table. "Bathroom is just there." She lightly touched Allison's head. "Good night."

"Good night," Allison said.

As Megan closed the door, Ally's brain raced with the speed of a spooked horse. She didn't understand life and all of its complexities, but she knew one thing for sure. Her body was turned the hell on, and Megan Kinkaid was the reason.

❖

Megan woke the next morning, curled up on her couch with her favorite purple blanket wrapped around her. She'd always been an early riser and relished getting the day started. She had a wedding that evening, and that meant her workday would begin about two p.m. First, she'd make a little breakfast for herself and her unexpected houseguest—that was, if Ally was up for it. She was glad she'd pushed for her to crash here last night, one of the benefits of living close to the bar. Plus, drunk Allison was endearing and adorable. She flashed briefly on the image of her in her bra about to slip into Megan's nightshirt, and the perfectly round breasts that took her awareness of her friend to a new level. Sigh. Not good. She quickly moved past the image, feeling like a dirtbag. Friends didn't ogle friends. Even if they had a killer body and beautiful blue eyes to match and made you want to talk to them nonstop about anything and everything because they simply lacked an ounce of pretension. She shifted uncomfortably beneath the blanket and rolled her eyes at the gentle ache. *Oh, you stop that.*

Rebounding, she sneaked into her bedroom where Allison slept peacefully and went still at the beautiful sight of her blond hair splayed out across the pillow. *Nope. Don't.* She looked away and grabbed a quick shower in the primary bathroom, doing her best to be quiet and courteous. She then tossed on a pair of jeans and a long-sleeve white T-shirt, skipping the shoes. Allison stirred as she exited the room but had yet to wake.

It was the sizzling bacon that finally did the trick.

"Good morning. I didn't mean to outsleep you."

Megan turned at the sound of the voice to see Allison standing there in her pajamas, looking like she belonged in them. "You look better in those than I do," Megan said automatically, gesturing with the spatula.

"Do you always lie in the morning?" Allison asked. Her hair was extra tousled after having been slept on, wild in a good way.

"I would never. Breakfast, or is that a bad thing to ask today?"

Allison smiled and slid onto one of the silver-backed barstools along the oversized island. "I feel surprisingly good. What's in the water here?"

"Oh, I'll never tell." Megan slid two slices of bacon onto a plate of scrambled eggs with sliced avocado on the side. "Order up. Coffee, ma'am?" She slid the plate along with a fork in front of Ally.

"I'd love some, and you did not have to go to all this trouble. Or call me *ma'am*, but keep it up."

Megan laughed. "What trouble? It's the weekend. My chance to be home in the morning and cook. The hard part doesn't start until after lunch." She offered a wink.

"That's right. Saturday. Who's getting married today?" Ally sighed dreamily. "That's so exciting."

"Tony and Jason. We'll be outdoors, surrounded by fancy heaters."

"It's a shame there won't be snow for the photos if a wintery wedding is what they were going for."

"Well, they should have chosen a city other than Dallas."

"True. Do we like them?" She sipped the newly presented coffee.

"Tony is a peach to work with, but Jason is hard to please. They could switch today."

"Does that often happen?"

"That people get a personality transplant once their wedding day arrives? More than you'd think." Megan quickly made up a plate for herself and ate, standing across the island from Ally. The bacon hit the spot, and she closed her eyes to savor. When she opened them, she caught Allison watching with interest. She passed her a questioning look.

"Nothing. You're delicate with your food. But you enjoy it. And you don't sit."

She glanced down to see that she was in fact eating and standing. "I think that's a hallmark of often being on the go. When you sit, you lose time." Allison held out a hand and gestured to the stool next to hers. Megan smiled and came around the island to join her. "Happy?"

"Immensely." Allison sent her a smile that she felt more than she should have. Was it the domesticity of the past ten hours that was messing with her? Did their scenario somehow mimic a different kind of overnight guest? Or had Megan truly developed a minor crush on a straight woman who happened to be engaged to Brent Carmichael, of all people? She'd really gone and lost her mind this time, breaking some sort of lunacy record.

"Have you talked to Brent this morning? Let him know that I managed to keep you alive?"

Allison nodded around a bite of avocado. "Just briefly. He had an early morning work thing. A new store opening."

"The work of a Carmichael is never done."

"Don't I know it. He's tugged in a lot of different directions, but that's always been the case. He's been a vice president at BeLeaf for three years now and serves on the board of several organizations in town."

"Admirable."

"Yeah," Allison said. "And he manages it all with a positive attitude."

"Do you?"

"Actually, yes. I've always had an independent streak, so having time on my own is an ideal scenario. We work together in that sense. Our relationship is…What's the word? Unique, and we both like that about it. It serves us well."

So they spent time apart, Megan realized. It was practical, but also a little unfortunate. "I think that's very mature of both of you. Figuring out what works is how you make it last. Too many divorces out there." She winced. "I shouldn't have said that."

"Why not? It's true." She touched her chest, and Megan's gaze followed. Her own damn pajama top had a lower neckline than she'd remembered, and she immediately paid for it, swallowing. Allison wasn't done. "I'm not someone that you have to sugarcoat things around, okay? You give it to me straight. Promise? That's the kind of friendship I want us to have."

"I promise to never sugarcoat."

"Then tell me why you went weird on me just now."

Megan turned back and met her gaze. "Nope. That I won't do. But I won't lie either because that would be a form of sugarcoating." She picked up her plate and moved to the sink on the other side of the island, putting some much needed space between them, though she could feel Allison's stare on her as she moved.

"Megan."

The quiet use of her name caused her to go still and a bolt of something powerful shot through her body, followed by a shiver.

"Yeah?" she said, all confidence shot.

A long pause. "Yeah. No. Nothing." Allison picked up her plate and joined Megan at the sink, the side of their forearms touching briefly. Allison turned and looked up at her. In bare feet, Megan had about two inches. For a long moment they just stared at each other, and Megan was powerless to look away. Allison spoke, breaking the spell. "Thank you for breakfast and the bed."

Megan nodded. "Of course. You're always welcome."

"I'm just gonna..." Allison gestured in the direction of the bedroom and was off. When she emerged, she had showered and changed, carrying her bag on her shoulder.

"All set?" Megan asked, putting the last dish in the dishwasher.

"I promise to leave a favorable Yelp review."

"We appreciate you." She walked Allison to the door and opened it. Allison reached for her automatically, pulling her into her arms.

"You're a good person," she said. Megan savored the moment, trying not to think too much about the fact that she was holding Allison in her arms, but failed in that endeavor. It was all her brain latched on to.

"Be good out there," she said as she released her.

"Always. Talk to you soon." Allison offered her one last warm smile and disappeared down the hall. Megan closed the door but didn't move from where she stood, still absorbing the last day of her life and her very surprising, but no longer deniable, attraction to Allison Hale.

"Well, damn," she whispered and placed her forehead against the cool surface of the door. She lifted it up and dropped again with a thud. This was going to be a problem.

CHAPTER FIVE

"So, tell me all about it," Brent said excitedly and ran his hands up and down her shins. She had her legs propped up, sitting sideways on his couch. "You went out with some new friends, got a little drunk, and crashed at our wedding planner's place. This is one for the books. Entirely epic." He grinned like a kid because this was not the kind of thing Allison did. Ever.

"You're enjoying this way too much." She exhaled. "It certainly wasn't my proudest moment, but do you know when you're so focused on making a good impression and listening to what others are saying to you that you sip or snack absentmindedly?"

"I've heard of the practice."

"I forget. You're perfect."

"Far from it. I just don't really get nervous much these days."

Ally quirked her head and squinted. "What's it like on your planet?"

"I get it. I get it." He refocused. "So you were sipping and talking."

"And everyone was so hospitable that I didn't even notice when my glass was refilled, and it must have been. A lot."

"Fuck me. Tipsy Ally."

"So as things were winding down, and I was seeing two of everyone, I went to call for an Uber."

"You could have called me first."

"I knew you had your opening the next day, and Megan was right there to take control—and me home with her."

"She certainly knows how to stay on top, that one. She's good. I'll give her that."

"What do you mean?"

"Well, you're marrying into my family. It's big points for her if she takes care of you. She knows we'll remember it, and we will."

Ally pulled her face back. "You think she did it as some kind of business strategy to get in good with the Carmichael dynasty?"

"I know she did. Kudos to her. It was a smart move." He saw the look on Allison's face and held up a hand. "Not to say she's not a nice person. Megan's great. But she's savvy first and foremost."

"I don't think I buy that at all."

He kissed her cheek. "Because you're Ally, and you think everyone has a heart of gold. That's why I like you."

"Good thing I like you back, or I might have to wrestle you to the ground over the Megan slander."

He narrowed his gaze, amused but curious. "You really like her, don't you?"

Allison shook her head, not really knowing how to explain. "I do. A lot. And I'm not someone who goes out there and makes close friends overnight, but something is"—she shrugged—"pulling me to her."

"I guess it's meant to be." He grinned.

"No, I don't mean it like that."

"Why not? People form quick friendships all the time."

Allison relaxed a little at his description, not comfortable discussing the details of what she felt when in Megan's presence. They were new feelings and honestly a little alarming. Maybe she needed more sleep or more time with Brent. It was likely the stress from the upcoming wedding. Whatever it was, Allison planned to keep an eye on it. At the same time, she was already looking forward to the next time she'd see Megan, so it couldn't be all bad, right? "Yeah, it's a fast-forming friendship. That's a good way to categorize it. But you're wrong about her motives last night."

"Oh no, I'm not, but I don't think that takes anything away from your newfound whatever with her. In fact, marrying me only bolsters it."

So now he was insinuating that Megan was extra friendly with her because of the Carmichaels. A sinking feeling came over her because there was a small chance that was the case. "Lucky me?"

"Lucky both of us." He kissed her lips and dashed off. There was a college football game that afternoon, and he was heading to a friend's house to watch with the guys.

Alone with her thoughts, Allison melted away, letting her mind go where it chose. She closed her eyes and thought about Megan's gaze as it brushed her skin briefly the night before, the feelings it had stirred, and the way Megan'd looked in that T-shirt that clung to her thighs as she stood in the darkened doorway. Allison didn't stop herself from going where she wanted to go. She imagined lifting the shirt over Megan's head to see all that was beneath it. Her breasts. Her waist as it flared into the curve of her hips. Everything went warm, but she didn't shy away. She imagined touching Megan's breasts, lifting them to her mouth, and kissing her nipples. Her lips parted at the rush of arousal. She could almost feel Megan's smooth skin beneath her fingertips as she ran them down Megan's back to cup her ass and pull her hips close against her own. She adjusted in her chair, wet now with heated cheeks. What the hell was she supposed to do with all this? She pinched the bridge of her nose, now confident that she had a larger problem on her hands.

Her phone rang, and for a moment Allison just stared at it. Terrified, scared to death it would be Megan, yet at the same time, hoping to hear her voice. She checked the readout and relaxed. Just Betsy. *Stand down.*

"Hey there."

"Well, well, well. Word on the street is you had a wild night out."

"The street?" Allison frowned. "Where do you hang out these days, Bets?"

Betsy laughed. "When you didn't answer my text last night, I checked in with Brent this morning. He filled me in on your debauchery downtown."

"Oh, right, sorry. I had too much to drink, or I would have gotten back to you."

"It sounds like you scored a nice little invitation. Moving up that social ladder, little sister."

The social climber stigma made Allison feel uncomfortable and didn't accurately portray her interest in having a nice night out and maybe even meeting some new people. That's all it was. "It really wasn't a big deal. Drinks with some of Megan's friends and colleagues."

"It's just *Megan* now? She's taken you under her wing. Making sure you know all the proper people. Smart of her because you'll be forever grateful."

Allison frowned that she'd leapt to the same conclusion Brent had.

"I don't think it's like that. She did a presentation for my class, and the invitation to the gathering came naturally."

"Mm-hmm." She could hear the wheels turning in her sister's head. "Regardless, I'd lean in to it. She's sure to have a huge number of powerful connections."

"I'm confident she does, but what would I need those for exactly? I'm an elementary school teacher."

Her sister was quick to answer. "You never know. You're going to be a Carmichael, Ally. It's like you really don't get it. You're going to have to start thinking like one."

"I'm never going to be a socialite, Betsy. That's just not in my makeup."

There was a loud sigh. "I worry for you, Allison. I really do. I don't think you have a clue what's ahead of you."

Allison frowned. "I will be supportive of Brent and all he does. I will attend all the events I already attend with him. We'll spend the holidays with our families and go to our separate jobs every day. Hell, maybe one day we'll get a dog. Or a child. What's more to expect?"

Betsy seemed to redirect. "All I'm saying is that Megan Kinkaid could be a very helpful friend. Hold on to her."

Allison planned to do that, but not for the reasons Betsy suggested. "She's my wedding planner, so I don't think she's going anywhere." She made an excuse to get off the call because she didn't have the coping ability for the pressures that came with her sister. Alone now, she made a cup of tea and stared into its depths, letting the mug warm her hands, and knowing the Earth had shifted beneath her feet with these new realizations and not at all sure what to do about it.

❖

Megan arrived at the Great Waters Country Club twenty minutes before her scheduled meeting and tour with Allison. She preferred to arrive before her clients to get her bearings and to make sure they were on schedule to see the venue. After checking inside with her contact, Lisa, Megan walked along the gorgeous duck pond, leaning over the quaint wooden railing and watching the little guys pump their legs as they swam. She hadn't seen Allison in close to two weeks, and the anticipation had her preoccupied most of the morning, no matter how often she shoved it to the side. Just another bride. She saw throngs of them daily. If only.

She turned at the sound of a car door closing in the parking lot and caught a glimpse of blond hair headed her way. She straightened and smiled, ignoring the way her stomach danced and her skin felt extra sensitive as Allison approached. She'd be coming from school, but she didn't look the least bit tired. Instead, she was Allison, fresh-faced and seemingly full of energy.

"You got me ducks and everything?" she exclaimed as she grew closer. Her blue eyes sparkled like always.

"I heard you had a soft spot." Megan made a sweeping gesture to the dock. "Imagine the gorgeous photos here. Serene, romantic. It's possible one of these ducklings might even play along."

"Wear a tux," Allison supplied.

Megan closed one eye. "Sure. I suppose, if you were extra persuasive and tossed them some currency."

They took a moment and grinned at each other. Megan swore the air around her changed the moment Allison arrived, and she bathed in the crackle of energy now present and bouncing between them. Almost like someone had just hit the play button on her paused life. "Shall we go check out the space?"

"Yes. Any of it outdoors?" Allison asked.

"Well, they offer outdoor ceremony options, but are you trying to roast your guests? We're talking about a summer wedding in Texas. You could pull that off in early spring at the latest."

"Yeah, good point. I've always romanticized an outdoor wedding."

"I can make anything you can afford happen, but I've found the weather refuses to be bought. I've tried."

"You have a way of saying no to things with humor."

"Yeah?" Megan looked over at her. "I guess I try to soften it."

"It's a great tactic. I almost don't realize I'm being deprived because I'm grinning at you. That's a pretty color on you, by the way. Makes you glow."

Megan glanced down at the fuchsia sweater she wore, warmth springing to her cheeks. "Thank you."

"Welcome." Ally clapped once. "Lead the way. I'm bursting with excitement."

They met up with Lisa, who took them on a tour of all the club's offerings. The Carmichaels were members, of course, so they were given the VIP treatment, though they declined the champagne.

"It's gorgeous," Allison said, staring into the sprawling ballroom, currently empty but impressive still. Huge picture windows looked down over the water and golf course beyond.

"Imagine stepping out onto the dance floor with Brent about here," Megan said, moving them into an open space, "looking into his eyes as the sun sets on the party." Allison turned and her gaze found Megan's, her lips parted slightly. Was there something she wanted to say? Allison seemed struck, and for a moment the edges of the world blurred as the two of them stood on that empty dance floor looking at each other.

Lisa's voice startled her, bringing the world back to full volume. "Cake setups are generally over here, but like with everything, there's flexibility. The fountain in the atrium is always a conversation piece, so it's a lovely place to display photos or a guest book."

"I imagine that's a beautiful grouping," Ally said, but her voice was different than just a few minutes ago. Quieter. She looked back at Megan again, but then tore her gaze away. Sigh. Perhaps they needed to address whatever this was ricocheting between them. That's how Megan would handle any other snag she came upon with a client. Only this one wasn't business related, and the thought of vocalizing... her feelings left Megan terrified. And since when did anything terrify Megan Kinkaid, dammit? She'd built her business from the ground up by grinding away and doing the hard work. Surely, she could look Ally in the eye and be honest, sort this out.

"So, what did you think?" she asked after they'd said good-bye to Lisa. They stood in the opulent atrium in front of the fountain, the soft sounds of flowing water underscoring their conversation.

Allison exhaled and tilted her head from side to side, and Megan watched as she struggled with her thoughts. "I was amazed by how beautiful the room is, but I'm not sure I can see myself there, you know?"

"It's not your glove."

"Translate?" Ally frowned. "My glove?"

"Everything about your wedding should fit like a glove, a fuzzy one in your case, match your tastes and aesthetics and feel innately like you, or like you and Brent as a couple. This wasn't it. No big deal. There are dozens and dozens more."

"I've never tried to characterize our couplehood." Allison smiled thoughtfully. "Maybe I need to try, so we can capture this whole event better."

"Want to take a walk around the water and hash some of it out?" Megan also saw this as an opportunity to maybe put more cards on the table and find a way to reset them.

Allison nodded. "Pretty day. Let's do it."

Their pace was slow. It was chilly out but not cold enough to require jackets, which was nice for what was becoming winter. "Tell me about you and Brent."

"Okay." Allison nodded. "We have a lot of fun together, teasing and laughing a lot. That's a big part of us."

"Adorable," Megan said. "I think you have to laugh. It helps you through the harder times."

"I completely agree. We're also incredibly practical. As I've explained, we're not afraid of doing what works for us, which sometimes makes other people raise an eyebrow."

Megan frowned. "In what way?"

"Well, we haven't moved in together. We stay at each other's places a handful of times a week, but it's not like I count the moments until I see him again. I have my life, and he has his, and the overlap is a fantastic cherry on top."

"Right. I remember you mentioning that independence." She didn't identify with the setup but could appreciate it working for someone else.

"I've never been a starry-eyed girl when it comes to love. I don't require big gestures or box checking. I have my head on my shoulders, and so does Brent."

"Huh," Megan said. Not that Allison's description had anything wrong with it, but it wasn't often that she heard brides-to-be speak so matter-of-factly about their significant other. At the same time, going into a marriage and understanding how your relationship best operated would go a long way to keeping them happy, together. "You seem to have it figured out. Impressive."

Allison stared out at the water. "I'm not sure I would go that far. We're not perfect."

"You sound pretty ideal for one another." In a lot of ways, this was helpful for Megan to hear. Allison was happy where she was. Everything was as it should be.

"In so many ways, yes. Here's a confession for you, and I have no idea why I'm telling you this except I feel like you're my friend."

Megan reached out and squeezed her hand. "I am."

She stared out at the water. "I wonder if Brent chose me because then he will always be the one to shine."

Megan frowned. "What are you talking about? Not following."

"Well, think about it. With *me* next to him, he gets to be the shiny penny. Brent can have any woman he wants, and he chose me. Ordinary me. I'm not glamorous or exciting or rich or overly ambitious. By comparison, let's admit, he sparkles."

"No. Stop right there." Megan paused their walk to emphasize her point. Anger flared. "Uh-uh. You're in no one's shadow, and you certainly don't pale next to him. Take it from someone who can see the situation clearly. That's not the case."

"It's okay. It's a role I know well. My sister was always the dazzling one, too."

"It's not okay because it's not true." Megan turned to Ally fully and looked her straight in the eye. "I have news for you. You light up every room you walk into." Ally opened her mouth to protest, but Megan held up a finger. "No. You listen to me because I never lie. In a sea of people, you stand out as not only beautiful but *special*, and I can't stand another minute of you not understanding that. You're the shiny penny, Ally. Any person who spends five minutes with you can see that." She heard the passion in her voice and took a breath and a literal step back.

Allison blinked at her, not saying anything. The look on her face was nothing short of mystification. "Is that client talk?" The look on her face said she knew the truth.

"No. Dammit. I wish it was. It's how I feel," Megan said, all of it bubbling to the surface. "The more time I spend with you, the more I want." Why were these words falling from her lips without permission? "And that's certainly not because you're *everyday*. It's like I can't get enough."

"Do you sometimes wonder how we've become friends so fast?"

Megan rolled her lips in. "Yeah. It feels…right. Like we were meant to meet."

Allison took a step forward. "I feel that way, too. There's just something…"

"What?" Megan needed to hear the end of that sentence. Desperately.

Ally shrugged. "I don't know. I'm just thinking out loud."

"What were you going to say?" Megan asked, pressing her.

"There's just something here." She made a gesture between them. "It's been nice. And terrifying. But it's real."

Megan nodded. "I know."

Allison exhaled in relief. "Wow. Okay. So now that we've said that…"

"It's out there."

Ally nodded. "Voiced."

"And we can relax and get back to life as scheduled, right?"

They shared a laugh before the noticeable tug between them returned. Megan shifted to a soft smile. "Sometimes I think the universe has a way of knowing when two people need each other and brings them together. I don't claim to know why we've stumbled upon each other, but something tells me it's ordained."

Allison bumped her shoulder as they continued their walk. "And who would have ever predicted it? A fourth-grade teacher who looks forward to dressing like a giant crayon for the Halloween parade and Dallas's most sophisticated event planner?"

Megan closed one eye and regarded Allison. "A crayon, you say? No."

"Oh yeah. A purple one. I could set you up as orange. I have an extra."

Megan held up a hand, feeling lighter. "Nope. I'm good."

"Suit yourself."

"Want to grab a drink before we head home?"

Allison rocked back on her heels. "Okay, but only one. I can't shack up with you anymore."

"Your loss."

Okay, yes. Things were feeling a lot more manageable. The playful, casual dynamic certainly helped ease the tension. They were going to right themselves and survive this, it seemed.

Fifteen minutes later, they sat at the bar of a restaurant that neither of them had been to before, where they knew no one. In a way, it was liberating to disappear into anonymity next to Allison, who smelled wonderfully of what had to be strawberries. No. Raspberries. As they talked about other potential venues, Megan lost herself in the soft blue of those eyes, the same eyes that assumed no one ever noticed them. In actuality, she noticed everything about Ally and wondered what it would be like to show her how much she appreciated her for exactly who she was. There were no hidden agendas or wild expectations. Allison was a what-you-see-is-what-you-get kind of person in the best way possible. She had shiny hair, perfect lips, and a warm heart, but she was also out of bounds, and Megan, of all people, should know better than to wonder *what if.* But the question lingered all the same, and she cherished their easy conversation and the way Allison placed her hand on Megan's forearm when it came time to pay. She memorized the way it made her feel, and God, did she feel.

"I'll get this one." She stared down at the subtle touch, the butterflies erupting in her stomach. She clung to the warmth that began on her arm beneath Allison's fingertips and spread.

"Are we okay?" Allison asked, signing the receipt. "After our earlier discussion. I hope I didn't say anything that made things between us weird or tense. It doesn't feel that way."

She handed the leather portfolio back to the bartender and didn't hesitate to respond. "We're more than okay. I think the fact that we talked about it just goes to show how mature and open we can be with each other. Let's not lose that."

Allison nodded sincerely. "I'm in complete agreement." She gently touched the fabric of Megan's sweater. "And I stand by how great you look in this color."

Megan stared down at Ally's hand. "This isn't going to be easy, is it?"

The smile on Allison's lips dimmed. "No. It isn't. But we're going to be just fine."

"Good as new."

They stared at each other, not wanting to say good-bye. Megan held on to this little bit of time when Ally felt like hers. It was a mirage, a myth, but sometimes it was easier to lie to herself, and get lost in a fantasy.

"Shall we?" Allison asked.

Megan nodded, her heart sad. "Let's get out of here."

CHAPTER SIX

Allison would classify Lacey Turner as a friend. Kind of.
They'd taught at the same elementary school for close to six years now, and as a fifth-grade teacher, Lacey often consulted with Allison about her students, because they were Allison's former students, so it made total sense now to talk about her personal life with Lacey, who also happened to be, you know, gay. No biggie. Just two colleagues chatting. Correction, two kind-of-friends chatting. She sighed, aware of the stretch.

"Can I eat my sandwich with you?" Allison asked, popping her head around the corner of Lacey's empty classroom. The kids were at lunch, which would be followed by a recess, buying them forty-five minutes. Allison usually ate at her desk while simultaneously grading papers or completing assessments or lesson plans, but today she was willing to forgo productivity.

"Oh, um, sure," Lacey said, staring at Allison curiously, her eyes suspicious saucers, which made sense because they'd never eaten lunch together or anything even close, so why were they starting now?

"I just feel like we don't talk enough, you know?" Allison said, making herself at home on the other side of Lacey's teacher's desk.

"Right. That's not happened." Lacey pushed her phone away.

She decided to make small talk as she unwrapped her turkey sandwich. "Did you find the faculty meeting yesterday unnecessarily long?" Allison shook her head like it was the crime of the century.

Lacey nodded along emphatically. "Sometimes I think opening up the end of the meeting to questions and concerns takes a whole extra hour right when we all think we're about to be out of there."

Allison leaned in, prepared to gossip, give up her opinion on a few things to get Lacey's in return. "And I don't want to point fingers, but first grade is part of the problem."

"First grade loves drama. That's why. I hear they argue over peanut butter in the faculty lounge. Congrats on your engagement, by the way." Lacey then looked embarrassed. "I saw it in the paper. I hope that's not weird."

"Not at all, and you're sweet. Thank you." She paused as she chewed. "That's actually why I wanted to stop in today, to bend your ear."

"You wanted to talk to me about your engagement?" Lacey seemed confused and had every right. In fact, she glanced at the door, probably plotting her escape route or looking for help. "I don't know much about weddings. I'm not sure if someone is lying to you about that."

"No," Allison said calmly. "But I have been spending time with this person I met, and there's this connection that I can't seem to un-notice."

"Okay," Lacey said, drawing out the word. "Is it someone from first grade? I don't know that I would advise that."

Allison widened her eyes, clearly a miscommunication. "No. God. No one at school."

Lacey ran a hand through her short brown hair, and it sprang back into place impressively. "And this connection is a...problem?" She was searching for clarity.

Allison set her sandwich down and nodded solemnly. "I've only known her a few weeks, and already, I think about her too much for someone who's...engaged to someone else."

Lacey's lips parted and she nodded. "Her. You said her."

"Yeah."

She exhaled, and understanding seemed to hit. "I'm your lesbian fairy godmother, aren't I?"

"Well..."

She held up an excited hand. "No. Don't apologize. I'm up for this job." She rolled her shoulders as if preparing for a boxing match. "Born ready."

"I get how cliché it is of me, rushing to *you* with this little problem, but...I wasn't sure who else, and I'm not sleeping that great, as in at all, and I need a lifeline."

"Of course you do." Lacey shrugged. "Totally fine. And we don't have to call me the fairy godmother if you don't like it. Local Lesbian Consultant has a ring to it, but there's only so much insight I can offer unless I understand more." She took out a notepad and pen, poised to take it all in.

"Okay. Um, well, her name is Megan. She's my wedding planner, and I liked her right away, the moment we met."

"Your wedding planner?" Lacy shouted.

Allison threw a glance behind her and turned back, eyes wide. "Well, don't scream about it."

Lacey covered her mouth. "I'm sorry. Sorry about that. Just was not expecting it to be the wedding planner. Please go on."

"Okay, well, she's smart, successful, put together. I thought I was just in admiration of all she was."

Lacey scribbled down some notes. "And you're sure that's not it? Attraction and idolization can be confusing."

"Yes, I'm sure." She nodded for emphasis. "Sure, *sure*." She met Lacey's eyes purposefully to impart that there was not a mistake at hand.

Lacey squinted and set the pad aside. "How do you know?"

"Because I think of her in other ways."

"I'm picking up on that, but you haven't said, and if you can't even say it out loud, then I'm not sure how I can help." She held up a hand. "Again, not that I'm not willing because this is…really something."

Allison closed her eyes briefly and decided to just do it. The words would make it real, but this was for the greater good. She couldn't talk to Betsy. Definitely not Brent, and she wasn't sure she wanted to reveal trouble in paradise to the teachers on her own grade level who were so excited about the upcoming wedding. "I'm attracted to her. Plain and simple."

"You're attracted to her confidence, her exuberance for life, her success."

Allison answered with her eyes closed. Easier to blurt that way. "Yes, but I'm also attracted to her body. To being close to her. I fantasize about doing more than just being…her friend." She opened her eyes, feeling a little bit more free.

Lacy grinned and applauded. She was certainly an enthusiastic person. "And now we're getting somewhere. Has this ever happened to you before?"

"No."

"So no female crushes?"

"No, I meant this hasn't happened to me with anyone before. Male or female. She affects me in a way no one has in the past. This might be way too much information, but—"

"I think we're way past that point, but you were saying?"

"I've never been a big...luster. Is that a word? What I mean is that I've found people attractive before, enjoyed their company, and gradually grown to like spending time with them."

"Which is perfectly okay."

"Yes. I've been happy. And I enjoy sex when I have it, but I don't think about it when I'm going about my day, you know? It's a lovely perk in life, but it's never driven me...until now."

Lacey nodded sagely and set down her cup of yogurt. "Until now. Megan."

"Yeah. What do I do?"

"That's a difficult question. This guy you're engaged to, you love him?"

"Yeah, he's great. Nothing not to love."

Lacey passed her a look. "You're not even married yet. You should be head over heels for this guy, longing for his presence. Do you?"

"Do I *long* for his presence?" She took a moment to truly ask herself the question, because in the quiet of this classroom that wasn't hers, with this friend who had always been peripheral, she felt like she could be honest. The stakes were low in just answering a simple question, right? "Longing is a strong word."

"And what about Megan?"

"I think about the next time I'll see her a lot. I fixate on it and glance at the clock. Even more now that I'm aware of the fact that I do it."

"Which could easily be amplified if you found yourself in an actual romantic relationship with her."

The thought almost made her head explode. What would that even be like? Ally couldn't comprehend it and didn't allow her mind enough slack in the rope to explore the scenario. "Yeah. I would likely agree with that statement."

"So this is my early in the game semiprofessional opinion: maybe your sexuality is a little more fluid than you'd ever planned on."

"Bisexuality."

"That's not an awful thing."

"No, but lusting after someone else is when I'm months away from marriage."

"Well, yeah. Can't deny that part." She tapped her pen against her chin. "You honestly have two options. Explore whatever this is with Megan, or shut it the hell down and carry on with your life. The only drawback of option two is you'll always wonder."

"Yeah." Honestly, though, it might be the smartest route to sidestep this roadblock. She could hire another wedding planner. Make up an excuse. "I think that's what I should do. Shut it the hell down."

Lacey raised her eyebrows and nodded. "Why not? That *always* works."

"I'm supposed to get married, Lacey. Everything in my life is tied to that happening. My house is going on the market soon. My parents are going into business with his family, and my brain is already prepped for this new life. I can't just upend all of it because of a wayward crush."

"You do seem really set on the marriage happening."

Allison nodded. "I am. And thank you for helping me sort through all this. I think I know what I have to do." It wasn't going to be easy, but she had to get in front of this thing in a drastic manner before she found herself aboard a runaway train that would eventually derail her entire life as it smashed into a devastating brick wall of disaster.

"Ally?"

She turned from where she stood in the doorway, her empty lunch bag clutched at her side, motivated. "Yeah?"

Lacey's brown eyes carried kindness. "Make sure this is what *you* want. Your happiness matters just as much as everyone else's."

She heard the words but shoved them to the side. "Thank you, Lacey. Keep your fingers crossed for me. You've been a great sounding-board-fairy-godmother-consultant thing."

"Anytime. I mean it."

She didn't make it to the Soiree offices that day until close to five. A parent-teacher conference and ridiculous traffic on I-35 held her back. By the time she arrived, her heart thudded rapidly, and her palms were clammy and cold. She let herself into the office suite and was promptly greeted by Kelsey, who paused upon seeing her.

"Hey, Ally." She glanced behind her. "Did you have an appointment? I don't think that Megan realized you were—"

"No, actually. I'm here unannounced but was hoping I could steal a moment of Megan's time. Should be quick."

Kelsey frowned. "She's actually gone for the day. She has a killer weekend ahead, so she snagged a free hour."

"Oh. She's gone home?"

"Most likely home. Do you want me to call her to see if she can—"

"No, no. You've been more than helpful." She smiled, bit the inside of her cheek, and stared down at her shoes, plotting her next course of action. Her fingertips were numb, and wasn't that strange?

"Ally, you okay?" Kelsey quirked her head to the side. "You seem, I don't know, off."

"No, I'm fine. Long day." She forced a smile followed by an exaggerated exhausted look.

"I feel you on that one. Let me know if there's anything we can ever do for you. Doesn't have to be Megan, either. Any of us can help."

Kelsey was a nice person. "Thank you. I appreciate it. But I'm really good." She nodded a couple of times like a fool and gestured to the door behind her. "I'll, uh, catch up with Megan later. Thank you."

"Anytime," Kelsey said, with a curious stare, which of course was fully earned.

Allison could have gone home, left it all alone, but that would have also left her in exactly the same spot. She had to subtract herself from this situation, and in this moment she had the courage to do it. Who knew about tomorrow?

She made the short drive to Megan's building, parked on the street, and said hi to Chip, who luckily remembered her and was kind enough to let her up. Standing in front of Megan's door, she shook her hands out a few times to gear up before knocking.

Megan opened the door quicker than she'd expected, wearing jeans with a rip in the thigh, no shoes, and a slouchy red sweater that left one of her shoulders bare. Dammit. She looked more beautiful than Allison had even remembered. And if she was being truly honest, Megan didn't just look beautiful, she looked hot. Ally's mouth went dry. This just got so much harder.

"Ally. Hi," Megan said, lighting up. "I just assumed it was a package. The front desk mentioned that I had one."

"Sorry," she said, sliding her hands into the back pocket of her pants. "Not a package. Just me."

"You're even better. Come in." She stepped back and held the door open, still beaming.

"No. Don't be happy to see me. Please. I have to talk now."

"Why would I not be happy to see you?" Megan asked. Her dark hair was pulled halfway up and had come a little loose. Casual. Wonderful.

"Because what I'm about to say is not at all good. And you might hate me."

Megan frowned and leaned against her kitchen counter. Normally, Allison would have done something basic like slide onto a nearby barstool so they could chat, but today it seemed smarter to keep her distance, so she lingered close to the door.

"Tell me what's going on."

"I've decided it's best that I go with another wedding planner."

Silence. Megan stared at her for a moment, her dark eyes holding surprise, or was that hurt? Her gaze dropped to the floor before she raised it to Allison once again in question. "Is it something I said or did? I thought we'd left things in a good place."

"Yeah. Too good a place," Allison said automatically. She shifted her weight, hoping to explain better. "I think we've gotten too *close*, don't you?"

"We don't spend that much time together. A couple of extracurriculars. That's all. We can pull those back if it helps." She took a step forward. "Have I done something as your planner that you're not happy with? Has my staff?"

"No. Nothing like that. You've been perfect every step of the way. You're fantastic at your job."

"Then this is strictly about you and me."

Allison nodded.

Megan took a moment to absorb. "I'm going to say something really honest here and risk messing things up even more, but I don't like this. I don't want to say good-bye to you, and that's got nothing to do with our working relationship."

Megan's professional polish was nowhere in sight. Standing in front of her was a version of Megan that was one hundred percent the woman alone, and that made Allison's heart ache. She loved this version of Megan, wanted to spend time with her, laugh, and talk. Even right now. She wanted to pull her in and just—no. "I'm getting married, Megan. Soon. I can't. We can't."

Megan held up her hands. "I know that. I'm not trying to undo any of your plans. I would never do that. But I need to be honest." She took a moment as if to compose her thoughts. "The idea of you drifting away and then spotting you at parties across the room, a stranger, sounds like the worst kind of punishment."

"I know," Allison said. Tears sprang into her eyes, and she didn't attempt to hide them. "But what else can I do here?" she whispered.

Megan closed her eyes. It was clear she was hurting, too. "I think you're doing the right thing. I mean, I get it. Doesn't mean I have to like it." She placed a hand over her heart in the exact same place Allison felt hers aching.

"Thank you." Ally wiped a stray tear from her cheek. "For the guidance, and the friendship, and so much more."

"Anytime," Megan said and walked to her. "Come here." She opened her arms and Allison moved into them wordlessly, treasuring the feeling of being held by Megan one last time, memorizing each sensation. The cinnamon and vanilla scent, the soft skin pressed against her own, the warmth, the tension, all of it. Megan released her and took Allison's face in her hands. "You're going to have a wonderful life, Ally. Full of happiness, and laughter, and love. You hear me?"

She nodded, trying desperately to believe the words. "You are, too," she managed.

Megan nodded. "Me, too." She stepped back, and Allison immediately felt the loss of her touch, hating the knowledge that she'd never feel it again, and before she knew it, her feet were moving, carrying her right back there. She went up on her toes, took Megan's face in her hands, and leaned in, capturing her mouth. When their lips came together, every part of her went numb before bursting to life. In that moment, Allison knew she would never be the same again. Every nerve ending screamed with overwhelming sensation as if having been locked away until this very moment. Megan's mouth moved in perfect tandem with hers, and Allison couldn't get enough. This wasn't just kissing. It fell into another category entirely. And the more they kissed, the more she wanted to kiss, and God, was Megan good at it. She had her arms wrapped around Ally, her hands at the small of her back, holding her close. Her tongue slipped inside Allison's mouth, and the world faded away. Without even realizing it, she pressed Megan more firmly against the counter, molding her body more tightly to Megan's, amazed at all the things her body felt. She was lost in a haze of wonder and lust and abject pleasure.

"I'm sorry," Megan said, wrenching her mouth away. Breathing. Both of them. She pressed her forehead to Allison's. "I'm so sorry."

Allison took a moment to catch her own breath and regain her thoughts. "What are you sorry for? I'm the one who did it. Me."

"No. Not that." Megan raised her gaze. "I'm sorry for disrupting your life, for making this so difficult."

"You had no way of knowing. Neither of us did." She ran her thumb across Megan's bottom lip reverently. "Maybe I shouldn't have done that. God, now I know what it's like to kiss you. I can't unknow. How can I possibly unknow?"

"Yes, you can," Megan said, walking her to the door and nodding her encouragement. "And you will."

Allison stepped into the hall and looked back. "Good-bye, Megan."

She smiled, and Allison stole the image, burned it into her memory. "Bye, Ally."

Allison knew one thing for sure. She walked out of that apartment a different person than the one who'd walked in. She didn't call Brent. She'd get to him soon enough. Instead, she went home, made a pasta dinner she didn't eat, and stared at a television show she didn't watch, trying to figure out how she proceeded from here, how she found herself again, and would it ever be enough?

❖

As much as Megan would have preferred to delegate her appointments to other members of her team and sit in her living room alone with a bag of chips and her very raw feelings, she forced herself to put on smart-looking jeans, a navy plaid jacket, and booties and get herself to at least *inside* the office. From there, she smiled at all the right moments, held her clients' hands as they made decisions, nodded along, and even let a little of her frustration out on an innocent florist, to whom she'd then sent a bottle of expensive wine by way of apology for her tone.

"All right. What's going on?" Kelsey said, closing the door to Megan's office behind her. "The difference in you between today and yesterday is alarming. Somebody clearly made off with your favorite breakfast cereal."

"Do you ever have one of those days where you don't feel like you're really here, but you trudge along anyway? I don't think I'm really here."

"Okay, I'm tracking." Kelsey took a seat and chucked her heels onto the floor one at a time. "But why? Why are you a shell of Megan, and does it have anything to do with the Carmichael wedding? Allison Hale stopped by here yesterday, looking a lot like you do now."

Megan sighed. "We lost the Carmichael wedding. They're going with someone else. I'm letting them out of the contract."

Kelsey looked at her as if she'd just told her Dallas was outlawing toothpaste. "No way. I don't even know what to say. Why?"

Megan rolled her lips in and shook her head. Kelsey was the one person she confided in about everything. But this felt different. "I think she's looking for someone a little more removed from her world." She knew the statement was vague, but it was also innocuous, which was the point.

"Nope." Kelsey passed her a *try me* look. "You can't do this with me. I know you too damn well, and what I'm reading between the lines is that something happened between you two—a fight, or maybe you discovered she's your long-lost sister. My money is on the latter."

Megan sighed. "I wish she was my sister. It would solve a lot."

Kelsey's expression took on understanding. "Aha. So it's like that."

Megan looked around. "It's in these moments I wish I was the kind of person who kept hard liquor in my bottom drawer."

"Lucky for you I am. Be right back."

Megan, in all her misery, couldn't help but laugh sardonically.

Because of course Kelsey did. Of course. She returned with two rocks glasses, kicked the door closed behind her, and poured them each a double splash. "Swill and spill."

"I don't even know how to explain it or have the energy to try."

"Try anyway."

Megan took a swallow of the liquid and allowed it to burn a path down her throat. "She came out of nowhere. Allison. So unassuming at first. This sweet schoolteacher, trying to figure out what kind of colors she liked. But after we talked a couple more times"—she shook her head and took another swallow—"I couldn't get her out of my head. I didn't know why at first. Just someone who'd made an impression."

"I've met people like that."

"Right? It happens." She let her gaze roam to her bookcase, and her mind wandered with it. "But the more time we spent together, the more we just clicked. And that's the thing. It wasn't a ton of time, Kelsey. Little meetups for the wedding or after I visited her classroom."

"And the cocktail party. She stayed at your place that night." Kelsey paused. "You sleep with her?"

Her gaze snapped back to Kelsey. "God, no. She's engaged to Brent Carmichael."

Kelsey whistled. "You sure can pick 'em."

"The irony is not lost on me." A pause. "But we did kiss."

"Meg. Wow. No judgment. It's just not like you."

"I know." She closed her eyes to absorb the reality and instead remembered the acute reaction she'd had to Allison's lips beneath hers. "In the course of firing me and saying good-bye, it happened."

"She has similar feelings, then."

Megan nodded. "I think all of this has really affected her, and even though we vowed to keep a lid on it, she needed to extract herself from the situation entirely."

Kelsey nodded. "If she wants things to work out with Brent, it was probably wise."

Megan turned the glass in her hand. "I tell myself that, too. This is for the best, but a big part of me wishes things were different."

"How serious is this?" Kelsey took a moment. "Are you in love with her?"

"No. I don't know her well enough to say that, but I have a feeling if we'd been given that shot, I could have been."

"Still hurts like a bitch. As someone who's been in that kind of triangle, I can attest to how much it utterly sucks to be the one to bow out."

"But it's the right thing to do, so I will. Just has me here, you know?" She touched her heart and fought against the threatening tears. She was not a crier and didn't plan to start now. Hell, she couldn't remember the last time she'd cried. "Your alcohol is making me mist up."

"Yep. That's totally the bourbon. Not your own damn broken heart."

Megan raised her glass and they cheered.

"Now what?" Kelsey asked.

Megan stared at her. "I don't know. I guess I lose myself in other people falling in love from the time I get up until I go to bed. Attend their weddings, give them the most glorious days of their lives, send them off into the sunset, and try not to think about my own very empty path."

Kelsey nodded dryly. "Good plan."

CHAPTER SEVEN

And apparently the store on Windsor is killing it, out of nowhere," Brent said, completely on a high from work. "Smashing goals and records. We implemented one of those BeLeaf In Yourself loyalty programs, and people are going nuts for it. My idea, so I was nervous."

"That's awesome. I know you were worried about that store." Allison was listening, but finding it hard to engage. They sat at his kitchen table, which was now littered with the remains of their Mexican takeout. *We never cook*, she thought distantly.

"The fucking management couldn't get it together. Glad to see them on the upswing. Stronger displays, too. They're stepping up, and it makes me want to expand the loyalty program to my other stores. Just gotta convince my father."

Megan nodded along as Brent described everything that was happening at BeLeaf these days in specific detail, all the while knowing in her heart she had something bigger to talk about and waiting for her moment. She'd considered shelving the details of her and Megan kissing a few days back and moving forward with life. It didn't work. That's not who she was. She knew she had to come clean with Brent and make sure he had all the information, or it would sit on her chest like a rock. She'd never been a dishonest person and didn't intend to start now.

"The thing about the Laurel Crest store, though, is they don't have a human presence. You walk through the doors, and no one greets you. There's very little warmth. A real culture problem we can't seem to get in front of because of turnover in the store. They're cursed."

"I kissed Megan Kinkaid." Okay, that wasn't how she'd planned to break the news to him, but there was only so much grocery talk she could sit through before the information came bursting forth from her conscience.

"What do you mean? In greeting? Like the store? Is that why you said that?" He stared at her with his brow dropped.

"No." She took a moment. "I don't know how to explain it other than to say I'm attracted to her, whether I want to be or not, and when I told her she shouldn't plan our wedding anymore, I also kissed her. She kissed me back. I'm so sorry."

He looked off at the wall and then back to Allison. "This is so random. So out of the blue. I don't even know where to go with this." He stared at the kitchen table and then back at her. "You're into *women* now? Since when?" There was no anger or accusation in his voice, only the piecing together of a shocking puzzle.

"Yes, but until now I didn't know I was. This is all very new. We've spent some time together, and I slowly started to realize there were these feelings I couldn't explain, but they were there, and as I said good-bye to her, I had a moment of utter weakness and acted on them."

"Huh." He sat back in his chair.

"Brent, I'm sorry. I don't know if anything like this has ever happened to you, but if it has, maybe you could try to understand. I hope it doesn't change anything, but I also think it's something we need to talk about."

"I made out with my assistant last year."

"Wow. Okay." She paused. "We were together last year."

"I know. And I should have told you about it, but I thought it would just hurt you, and I had no interest in the woman. I see now that I should have said something."

On one hand it felt like a slap across the face, but on the other, she was relieved. She wasn't alone. "So you have been there. Developed feelings for someone."

He blew out a breath. "We were at a gathering one night. There was booze. It happened. I wouldn't say I had feelings for her. That's only been you."

"I see." Her mind scrambled to understand and figure out how she should feel, but all she could focus on was where all of this left them.

"But this is different?" His eyebrows still shaded his eyes as he pondered the implication. "You fell for her?"

"Fell for her. No." A pause. "I don't know. It was all so fast. But whatever it was, it felt…important."

"Fuck." He smacked the top of the table with his open palm. "You're going to be my wife in, what, seven months? What am I supposed to do with this? It would be one thing if it was just a fluke, but feelings?" He got up and stalked the length of the kitchen and back again. "And what about her? How does she feel?"

"I think we found ourselves in similar positions."

He nodded, anguish all over his face, and it killed her. "Great. This is wonderful." They stood in silence for several long moments, each grappling.

Finally, she looked to him. "What do we do?"

"Hell if I know." He tossed his arm in the air. A moment later, he was more composed. "I think we head to our separate corners and do some thinking."

She closed her eyes. She didn't like the sound of that but, at the same time, could concede that it was the best idea. "Yeah, okay." She stood and carried her plate to the sink but paused in front of him. "I didn't plan on any of this. I'm just as shocked as you are. I love you." She placed a hand on his chest, and he relaxed into it. "Please know that."

He nodded. "I do. Love you, too." He caught her hand and gave it a squeeze. "Maybe we can talk more tomorrow. Cooler heads. Right now, my thoughts are on top of each other, and I need a beer. No, fuck it. Something stronger."

"Okay. Let's do that." She quietly collected her things and drove home, gripping the steering wheel tighter than she ever had in her life because she needed something solid to hold on to. It felt like her entire everything she depended on had just been upended, and she was dangling in midair, gasping for breath. She didn't know how to fix any of this. All she was sure of was that she was learning things about herself and should maybe pay attention to the signs the universe was dropping at her feet. At the same time, did she have the courage?

She didn't sleep well that night, cycling through garish dreams where she searched for Megan everywhere, and no matter what she did kept running into photographs of her instead of the real thing. In another dream, Brent kept calling, but she couldn't get her phone to pick up, regardless of how hard she tried. Around four a.m., she finally gave up on sleep and sat quietly with a cup of tea, watching the rain through the window.

Brent must have slept much better because when she heard from him midmorning, he had energy in his voice and suggested they meet for brunch at Harley's Diner, between their homes.

"Here's the thing," he said as he swirled his coffee in the dark brown mug. Those things must have been standard issues for diners. They all had them. "You need to figure this thing out, and the only way for that to happen is for you to take a little time for yourself."

She stared at the strawberry pancakes she'd yet to touch. "And do what exactly? What if I don't want time to myself?"

"Whatever you need to do. Explore your feelings for women, for Megan Kinkaid, and when you're ready, you'll come back."

He was so sure, so confident. The night apart had certainly restored his sense of direction. Gone was the shock, hurt, and confusion she'd witnessed. In its place sat the business version of Brent, who always believed he'd come out on top. She had to admire him for that. She wished she felt a little bit of his direction.

"I don't understand. So this is you setting me free?"

"Not forever. But can you marry me and know for sure that it was the right decision given what you're feeling?"

What an awful question, but she understood its purpose. "No."

"Then do what you have to do. Like I said, I'll be here."

"I don't know what that is." She did and she didn't.

"You'll figure it out, Ally. You're a smart person." He exhaled. "And I know I got angry last night, but I'm glad you told me. We're able to work on something *now* that could have been a problem later. This is going to make us stronger than ever. I just know it."

"You should have told me about that assistant."

He shot her a rueful look. "Yeah. I see that now. Just a moment in time, though. A blip. Nothing for you to worry about."

She did, a little. What else hadn't he told her because it wasn't important? She stared down at her finger, at the diamond that she still wasn't used to. She slid it off her finger and held it out to him.

"I'll hold on to this for you," he said and slipped it into his breast pocket.

She nodded glumly. The action felt so final, whether it was or wasn't. Her throat constricted and ached as she watched him pay the check. She'd put them both in a tough spot, yet there was nothing she could do to remedy it fully. But she could do as Brent asked, and take some time and make sure this marriage was what she really wanted. It would give them both peace of mind, and that made it worthwhile.

"I'm still here, you know, if you need anything or want to talk," Allison told him as they walked to the parking lot. It was one of those sunny yet cold days in winter that usually got her excited to go out and do something cold-weather related. Winters were short in Texas, and she liked to take advantage.

"Same goes for you. My door is always open." He offered her a nod, gestured behind him to his Bimmer, and headed out. She just stood there in the parking lot long after Brent had driven away, trying to understand the path in front of her, and this new ground beneath her feet. There were papers to grade and probably people she should update about the engagement, but that could all wait. Instead, she slid into a pair of fuzzy gloves, added a scarf, and drove to the crowded shopping mall, where she could take a walk, disappear into the masses, and gather her courage. She was going to need it.

❖

"Amy on standby." A pause. "Send Amy. Thank you," Megan said quietly into her headset from the back of the church as she watched the second bridesmaid begin her procession, as instructed by Cade, who had the door. "Sienna on standby. That's a go for Sienna."

"*Copy*," Cade said in her ear just moments before Sienna emerged, perfectly spaced from Amy. She loved working weddings with Cade. Their communication was seamless, and the women adored his good looks and warmth. He'd been handed more than a few bridesmaids' phone numbers in his time with Soiree, but she knew she could depend on him to behave with professionalism at all times.

Megan proceeded to call the rest of the wedding before joining the formal photo session after, as Cade went ahead to the Dallas Museum of Art to be sure all was on track for the guests' arrival at the reception. Staying true to the promise she made herself, Megan remained focused on the many details she had to manage and kept her mind from wandering too much. So far, so good.

"Thank you, Megan," Kristine—the bride—said, just before

hopping in the rented Rolls for her ride to the museum, the venue she'd always imagined herself getting married in. She and Matthew, the groom, had been ideal clients, bubbling over with happiness. "I'd be a disaster without you here."

"I'm not so sure about that. But you focus on enjoying yourself, and we'll handle the rest."

Kristine beamed like a person who'd just married the love of her life and now had a fantastic party ahead of her. All was as it should be.

Thirty minutes later, Megan arrived at the reception and organized Kristine, Matthew, and their wedding party for their big entrance, which played out beautifully. Now she and Cade had a few minutes to relax as the guests were served their meal. Though she'd been invited to the sit-down dinner, Megan always preferred to eat after. Comfort food on her couch late at night was part of her post-wedding ritual along with a good glass of bourbon-barrel-aged red. Helped her unwind and celebrate a job well done. Maybe tonight, she'd pick up some of those sinful nachos at a drive-through and add the extra cheese.

"Things seem under control," Cade said. The signature cocktail— the cranberry cuddle—flowed, and the band played music mellow enough for dinner. Another fabulous wedding almost in the books.

"You want to do a lap to make sure the kitchen is ready for the cake cutting?" she asked Cade. "I want to press on just as soon as our couple is finished with their meal."

"I'm on it."

She turned and found herself face-to-face with a grinning guest. "You're Megan Kinkaid, right?"

She smiled back at the beautiful woman whose dress she recognized as Dior. Something about her was familiar. Why was that? "Yes, I am. Nice to meet you."

"Betsy Hascomb. You're planning my sister's wedding, and we are just so excited about it."

"Oh, fantastic. Who is your sister?"

"Allison Hale. Though it might be the Carmichael name that jogs your memory."

She went still but held her smile. "No need to jog my memory. Allison is great." She refrained from informing Betsy that she would no longer be planning the wedding. It wasn't her place. "How is she?"

The question was out of her mouth before her brain had a chance to censor itself.

"She's fantastic and just over the moon about the engagement, as you surely know. She's right over there, actually, at table nine. You should say hello."

Megan went still, blinked, and followed Betsy's gaze across the large room where she glimpsed Allison in a simple black cocktail dress. Her heart rate escalated without permission. Her mouth went dry. Her heart literally hurt. "Oh. I didn't see her at the ceremony."

"She just arrived. Work thing. Some kind of kids' carnival. Kristine was really more my friend growing up, but Ally would run along after us, and I suppose that was enough to score her a bonus invitation."

Megan's heart rate still hadn't settled. She didn't see Brent, and as if reading her thoughts, Betsy chimed in, "Brent probably had a board meeting or something. He's got so much on his plate in his VP role at BeLeaf."

"I can only imagine."

"Well, I'll let you get back to it," Betsy said. "I know you're fabulous at what you do."

"Thank you," Megan said, her eyes still trained across the room.

As the night played on, she kept herself focused on all that needed to be done, but she also made sure to give Ally space. Megan was always aware of where she was in the room, whether she wanted to be or not. Luckily, it helped her keep her distance. They'd agreed to stay away from each other, and the last thing she wanted was to ruin Allison's evening. Though hers no longer felt so great.

Just as Kristine and Matthew began their first dance, and the romance in the room swelled, Allison appeared at her elbow. "Hi."

Megan exhaled. "Hey. I had no idea I'd be seeing you tonight, and that's the honest truth." Damn those blue eyes and how wonderful it was to see them.

"I know. I never mentioned I had a wedding to attend. But here we are." The soft tendrils of blond hair that framed her face from the updo were gorgeous, as was the dress or, rather, how Ally looked in it. "It's really good to see you."

Megan's heart clenched. "It is? Well, good to see you, too," she said conservatively and then pretended to scan the room for any sort of wedding planner alert.

"Could we maybe steal some time to talk?"

"Tonight? Probably not. I've got my hands full." What was happening?

"Right. Well, maybe coffee tomorrow? There are some things that I want to—"

"Sundays are generally my days to decompress." More scanning of the room, anything to get them out of this. It was already painful to look at Allison, and they'd never been more than friends. She couldn't imagine the ramifications if they'd gone further. It wasn't a good idea to drag this out.

"Okay. I see." Allison took a moment. "Well, then, I'll just say that Brent and I have stepped back from each other. I returned the ring. At least for now. He wants me to take time for myself, figure things out."

Megan's gaze shot to Allison's ring finger, and sure enough, it was bare. She opened her mouth to speak, not even sure what to say, but Ally beat her there.

"So now you're caught up. One of the first people I've told." She nodded resolutely. "I'll let you get back to your life. Sorry to bother."

Megan stared after her, agape.

The engagement was off? What was she supposed to do with that information because her head was already spinning. This was an opening, yes, but was it wise to take it? Getting involved with Allison, even though everything in her screamed for the chance, also came with a lot of unknowns. First of all, she'd been straight, up until recently. Or at least thought that she was. Then there were her ties to the very powerful Carmichael family, who Megan didn't want to upset. But most of all, Allison Hale had a string attached to Megan's heart, and the power of it scared her, especially after the difficult last few weeks. Was this really a leap she wanted to make, knowing that the stakes were astronomical?

The rest of her wasn't listening.

She stole glances at Allison throughout the night, watching her with new eyes. She smiled as Allison danced with her sister across the floor during one of those fast-paced medleys designed for wedding receptions, cheesy and fun. But it was the way she danced that really stole Megan's attention. Unencumbered and having the best time like a goofball. Her shoes were off, her hair had come down, and Megan swore she could hear her laugh through all the other noise in the room.

They didn't speak again that night, but after gooey nachos and a glass of burgundy, Megan sat with her feet up on her coffee table, wondering what Allison was up to. She managed to wait until the next day to reach out, sending out a singular text message.

So…that coffee offer. For Froman's?

The response took less than an hour to arrive.

No other spot.

CHAPTER EIGHT

Allison beat her to the coffee shop this time. She stood at the counter surveying the contents of the pastry case when Megan arrived and got in line behind her.

"It's eleven a.m. on a Sunday morning. I say you go for it."

Ally turned and met her gaze. Her mouth opened and then closed before, finally, she smiled. "Hi. I didn't see you come in."

"I didn't make a big commotion. Hi."

Allison gestured to the display case. "I was investigating the options. I'm thinking about something with frosting."

"Well, that cinnamon roll looks right up your alley, then."

Allison stared at it longingly. "Should I?"

"Have the cinnamon roll. In fact, we'll take two," she told the barista, who nodded and rang them up. They ordered their Toffee Crunch Dreams, and Megan handed over her credit card. "My turn."

"I don't argue with free coffee from my ex-wedding planners."

"Wow. Your policies are specific."

Ally furrowed her brow. "Gotta be prepared, you know?"

They found themselves a quiet booth with lots of sunlight and stared at each other. "I didn't expect to be sitting with you like this again," Megan said.

Allison inhaled deeply and shook her head. "Me neither. In fact, I don't even know what to say." She stared into her lap, probably corralling her thoughts. Megan waited patiently. "Except I knew I had to see you, talk to you, let you know what happened with Brent and me. It may make zero difference to you. For all I know, you were nice to me because I was a high-profile client."

"First of all, that wasn't the case. I'm always professional, but anything beyond, well, that was all me." It was crazy that she would think otherwise. "You always undervalue yourself. Do you know that?"

Allison seemed uncomfortable. "No. I just don't overvalue myself either. I have some great qualities. Did you know I can knit? I don't a whole lot, but I can. I'm good, too."

Megan laughed. "Color me impressed, but you're so much more than you seem to understand. You do sparkle, Ally. The sparkliest purple crayon in the box. You have to trust me on that one."

"Yeah, well, you've always made me feel important."

"Good."

"And—disclaimer—I didn't come here expecting anything from you. You're under no obligation to react or even care about my situation. Hell, I hired you and fired you and kissed you."

Megan smiled because as serious as Allison was trying to be, she had a dollop of whipped cream above her lip, which was so very Allison in every way.

Ally glanced behind her, curious. "Why are you enjoying this? What's going on?"

"I'm sorry." Megan gestured to her own lip. "It's just that you've got some—"

"Oh God," Allison said, racing for a napkin. "See what I mean? Sometimes I'm such a disaster. I'm over here trying to have a serious conversation and let you off the hook while looking like the Stay-Puft Marshmallow Man who forgot to shave."

Megan stared at her, falling a little bit more. "I happen to find it very effective."

The napkin went still in Allison's hand on its way back to the table. "You do? Whipped-cream face?"

"And who said I wanted off the hook?"

"Oh." Allison looked nervous, then pleased, then confused. "Why? After everything. The way I waltz in and then out and then here I sit again, just blabbing away."

"Probably because you say things like that and have the most adorable look on your face."

Allison's cheeks dusted pink, and she smiled into her drink. "Whoa. Okay." A pause. "So what now?" she asked finally.

"Can we just continue being us? No plans or goals required."

"I like that. Low pressure."

Megan sat back. "What do you have planned the rest of the day? We could grab a friendly movie."

Ally winced. "I wish I could, but I'm scheduled for a shift at the Nutcase. I pitch in on weekends to help out my folks."

"A good daughter."

"I try to be. They haven't had it so easy in the money department, and I hate to see them struggle, so I pitch in. Volunteer a little time. Plus, it's kinda fun, working the register, talking to all the healthy people."

"Got it. Allison the friendly counter girl. I like it."

Ally beamed, and the whole coffee shop lit up. She had the brightest eyes, and Megan wasn't shy about losing herself in them for once.

"That's me."

They sipped from their oversized mugs and watched the foot traffic around them. Finally, Allison turned to her. "I'm going to tell you something."

"Okay." Megan crossed her arms.

"The last time I saw you really stuck with me."

She was referencing the way they'd kissed each other into oblivion. "I can't say I'd forgotten about it, either. You shocked the hell out of me."

"It was out of character, to, uh, ambush someone in their own kitchen."

"I didn't kick you out."

Ally set down her mug. "No, you didn't. In fact..." She raised a saucy eyebrow.

"I might have leaped right in. It turns out we kiss really well together."

Allison took a steadying breath. "Mark this down as a conversation I never thought I'd have. Evaluating my make-out session with my really attractive wedding planner."

"Substitute *client*, and I'm right there with you. I think I probably broke the cardinal rule of wedding planning."

"Thou shalt not kiss the bride."

"Bingo." She felt the need to fan herself. "We should maybe stop talking about kissing now."

Allison sat a little taller. "Why is that?" She smiled.

Oh, someone was finding their confidence and it made Megan's everything stand on alert. God.

"Because it's highly distracting. I have a leisurely day to stroll through, and you have a nuthouse shift."

"Nut*case*."

"Fine. You're a nutcase."

They shared a smile. It had been a good coffee date. Short in nature, somewhat productive, and the unforeseen bonus flirting that had her head spinning. Megan drove away feeling lighter than when she'd arrived. In fact, as she moved through the grocery store and then that cute little shoe store nearby, she thought of very little else. By midafternoon, she did something impulsive, paused her errands, and followed Google Maps to the damned Nutcase.

The shop was located in an outdoor strip mall and had a cute little sign in red featuring a squirrel chowing down on an oversized nut. Inside the store, it was small, with lots of healthy choices to buy straight off the shelves, as well as a counter farther in where you could order fresh menu items. Salads, soups, a premade sandwich option, and lots of bars. Three tables lined the far wall for those who chose to eat in the store. Very quaint.

Megan was able to peruse the space unnoticed, along with two other customers, one who waited at the counter for service.

"Hi, there! Sorry to keep you waiting. What can I get you?"

Ally.

It was fun to watch her in her natural habitat as an unnoticed observer. Exuberant, welcoming, and—yes—hot as hell, even wearing a red visor with a large squirrel on the front. Megan held a package of energizing trail mix in front of her face and pretended to study the list of ingredients as Ally and the customer continued to chat.

"I don't know what kind of mood you're in, but our customers' favorite menu item is definitely the Dash Bar. Hot oatmeal in bar form. You can take them home in a box of six, or I can make one for you fresh in the oven."

The woman nodded enthusiastically. "My friend was telling me about them. That's why I stopped in. I'm a huge oatmeal fan but never have the time to sit with a bowl. I'd love to try the hot version."

"Your friend has the best taste. I'll be right back."

Ally disappeared, and Megan worked her way to the counter, picking up a few of the fresh snacks along the way. Everything looked amazing, but the price tags were a little out of this world. Thirteen dollars for a medium-sized pack of trail mix? She was beginning to see why the store might be in trouble. Allison reappeared with a brown bag she presented to the customer, her eyes landing on Megan as she handed it over. "Well, look at that. A new customer," she mused, pointing obviously. "Welcome to the Nutcase, ma'am."

"Thank you for having me," Megan said. "I'm a squirrel fan, so I stopped in."

The customer in front of her waved good-bye, leaving them face-to-face across the counter. "I've selected my purchases." She slid the trail mix and two granola bars across the counter. "I'll also take a Dash Bar. I hear they're all the rage."

"Coming soon to a BeLeaf near you." She knocked on the counter for good measure.

"Now I'll definitely need to try one."

"Hot?"

"I just heard that's the best way."

"God, yes. Wait here and prepare to have your life changed." The life-changing part was the way Ally watched her eat the bar, minutes later. She took her time, enjoying the cinnamon and spices and Allison's eyes on her mouth. Since when had a cereal bar been so sexy?

"What's the verdict?" Ally asked, removing the visor. Her hair was up in a ponytail, which showed off the column of her neck.

Megan blinked, trying to stay focused on the moment. It tasted like hot, fresh oatmeal in her hands. "This is some Willy Wonka magic."

Ally grinned. "My dad spent a lot of time perfecting that recipe. Trying it out on the customers for a couple of years until he got it just right." She gestured with her chin. "There's nothing like it out there."

"I can tell how proud you are of your parents." She popped the last bite of the Dash into her mouth and used the napkin to dab the corners.

"They're really good people."

"They'd have to be. They raised you."

Allison scanned the store, which was now empty. "Level with me. Why did you come by?"

"I have a gift certificate I wanted to spend." That wasn't the truth.

She could gloss over most anything with other people, but Allison affected her differently, made her want to shoot straight. "Okay, here's the deal."

Allison rubbed her hands together in anticipation.

"I was thinking about you and our earlier conversation. It made me want to see you." She met those blue eyes when she said the last part and held eye contact. Allison didn't pull her gaze away. Instead, she seemed thoughtful.

"I'm done here in an hour and a half. I usually grab some dinner and take it home with me. But maybe we could—"

"Grab it together. Dinner."

"Yeah."

"Why don't I cook?" Megan asked. The idea of something a little more relaxing and casual appealed to her, and the last time they'd been in her kitchen had been a difficult conversation. Maybe they could reclaim the space on happier terms.

"No, no. I don't want to put you out and make you go to work."

Megan eased a strand of her dark hair behind her ear. "I'd like to, actually. How do you feel about sweet-and-sour chicken and veggies? I'm a wiz with a wok."

"I'd kill for it right now, but I don't want to show off how excited it makes me. Oh, damn. I think I blew that with the blurt." She frowned and then smiled.

"Oh no." Megan laughed. "Gotta work on that poker face."

"I'm afraid that ship has sailed. I'm about as mysterious as a beige bath towel."

"I like the way you own it, though."

They shared a smile, and Megan lifted her bagged purchases and gestured behind her. "I better get out of here and start cooking."

"I was wondering why you hadn't *dashed* away."

"Oh, you're still marketing. Look at you."

Ally folded her arms and grinned proudly. "Always."

"See you at seven thirty? And don't bring anything. I have wine."

"Perfect."

They shared another lingering look, and Megan headed out, once again amazed at herself for completely changing trajectories. This was the second time today she'd attempted to steal more time with Allison, and she was the opposite of a needy person. Well, at least she used to be.

"Hello, new weird version of myself," she muttered as she slid behind the wheel of her black Audi S5. It felt like she was about to embark upon something important with each new step she took. The only question was would it change her life or destroy it? If only she had some sort of reassurance, then this would all feel a little less terrifying, like walking across a frozen lake, waiting for the ice to crack beneath her feet. She closed her eyes before firing up her ignition. "Just don't fall," she said as she sped out of the parking lot.

❖

Allison closed up the shop and locked the door behind her. They'd tried keeping the store open in the evening hours, but it never pulled much traffic. Mornings were really more their time of day anyway.

She turned around to face the now darkened sky with a zap of extra-excited energy paired with a side of total terror. How could both things exist in one person? She closed her eyes and offered herself a small out-loud pep talk right there on the sidewalk.

"Allison Hale of Dallas. You're going to be fine. You'll have dinner. You'll take it moment by moment and see if there's a…spark. No pressure."

She walked to her car, internally arguing with herself because of course there would still be a spark. They sparked the hell out of their coffee date and continued sparking along at the Nutcase, where she practically drooled all over Megan, who'd never looked so good as she did on a casual afternoon out shopping. Her fingertips had gone numb as she'd watched Megan slowly enjoy that Dash Bar, then remembered her mouth and the way it felt pressed to hers. The rest of her body joined her fingertips, and her cheeks got very, very hot. Sparks were not in question.

Sitting in the driver's seat, she wrestled her phone from her pocket, not even giving it much thought. Lacey picked up after only two rings.

"Allison?"

"Yep."

"From-school Allison. Hi."

"Hi, Lacey. How's your Sunday? Tons of papers to grade?" She sounded way too chipper, even for her.

"Okay, what happened?" Lacey asked. Yep, she'd seen straight through her.

"The engagement is off. Or paused. The woman I told you about, Megan, is still the most intriguing, beautiful person I've ever met, and I'm now supposed to go to her house for dinner. What the hell am I supposed to do when I'm there? I'm freaking out. I need my fairy lesbian consultant."

"I think I have the answer." A short pause. "Eat the dinner," she said with total confidence. "I think it's customary to do the thing one was invited to do. I really think I nailed this one."

Ally pinched the bridge of her nose. "I hear you, and that part I have under control. It's…the rest. What if something happens between us? Will she expect it to?"

"I've never met the woman, so it's hard to say. There's not a universal lesbian expectation of sex if that's what you're asking. People are just people. Gay or not."

Ally sighed because of course there wasn't, but she felt like she was exploring brand-new territory without a map. "Right. But any advice?"

Lacey paused. "Trust your intuition, and try to have a good time. I think with those two things in effect, you're going to be fine."

"What if I'm overcome and want to kiss her again?"

"Do you think she'll scream and run away?"

"Well, I didn't until you said that! Is she going to scream and run away?"

A pause. "I think you're putting too much pressure on yourself, and the only reason you're calling me is because this woman—"

"Megan."

"Right, *Megan* happens to be female. Can you just forget that part and just relax?"

"Relax, relax, relax," Ally repeated, moving her limbs like they were made of Jell-O. "Sure, I can try that. I'm mellow. This is not a big deal, and I'm not swimming in attraction for a hot woman, who is about to make me dinner. In her home." A pause. "What if she's barefoot?"

"I think that's allowed. No?"

"She looks so sexy when she's barefoot and relaxed."

Lacey laughed quietly. "Oh, dude. You have it bad. And you've never been attracted to women before? I don't buy it. Are you sure?"

"That's the crazy part." Allison noticed that she was gesturing wildly, alone in her car in the parking lot. Didn't matter. Times were desperate. "More on that front. I've been paying attention to myself. So, I've never really let myself notice women before, but I'm noticing them now. A lot. Like someone turned on the lights at a mostly dim party. I see them differently after Megan. They're pretty in…other ways now."

"Kissable ways. Barefoot ways."

"But none come close to Megan. Do you understand me?" She pressed her forehead to the steering wheel, begging it to give her guidance.

"You get that you're in control here, right? It's a two-way street, so if you want to have dinner and walk the hell out of there, that's completely your choice."

She sat up, latching on to that idea and coupling it with Lacey's earlier suggestion. "I'm a mellow person on a two-way street of control."

"Hell, yeah, you are. Okay, but don't walk in the door and announce that. I can see you doing that." Lacey sighed. "And I can't believe I'm saying this, but let me know how it goes, okay? I feel invested now."

"You've got it. And hey, Lacey? Thanks for being my sounding board."

"Yeah, well, I guess we've all been there before."

Another helpful tip. Ally was not the first person to have this kind of revelation, and she wouldn't be the last. "It helps to think of it that way. One of many."

"It's the truth. Hang in there. You'll figure it out."

"I will." Allison nodded, feeling her confidence return.

She vowed to buy Lacey lunch for all her sideline coaching, swung home, and changed into what she hoped was a more fashionable yet not too dressy outfit, and arrived on Megan's doorstep at precisely two minutes after seven.

Megan swung the door open moments later with a soft smile, music playing behind her in the apartment. God, she was a lot to take in, wearing jeans, the softest looking white sweater, shiny lip gloss, and—wouldn't you know it—no shoes. "Hi, you."

"I'm mellow," Ally said.

Megan raised an eyebrow. "Are you? Good to know." She reached out, grabbed Allison's hand and pulled her inside. "Glass of white already poured for you." She picked up her glass. "Join me?"

Allison didn't need any more encouragement. The wine would relax her, after all. She followed Megan into the open kitchen and sank into the sounds of upbeat jazz. The unpredictable melody of the trumpet very much underscored her unsure footing, and in a way, that was also comforting. The music understood her plight. She sipped the wine and leaned against the counter.

Megan gestured to the speaker. "I can change it if this isn't your speed. I love jazz, and it's my favorite to cook to. Chills me out." She stared at the vegetables in her oversized pan and gave them a little toss, sexy and effortless.

"No, I like it. It's nice."

"How was the rest of your shift?" She smiled at Allison, and that also made her relax. This was just Megan, after all.

"Pretty quiet. The shop pulls in most of its traffic in the morning and slowly winds down from there."

"You look really pretty. I didn't know if you'd have much time to spare after you got off. I was expecting your polo and visor."

"Ha." Allison looked down at her brown boots with the slight heel, skinny jeans, and navy and red striped top that, yes, came with a slight dip in the neckline. "I couldn't show up looking like a clerk. Who wants to cook dinner for a clerk on the clock?"

"You could show up looking like anything you wanted, and I'd still be happy to see you."

The comment hit her square in the chest and blossomed. She couldn't have inhibited the smile that hit if she'd tried. But she was super mellow, remember? And thereby, played it cool. No big deal. Just a compliment she'd think about for hours later. "So, sweet and sour. A favorite of yours?"

Megan nodded. "Yep, believe it or not, I grew up eating a lot of Chinese food."

"Somewhere in your heritage or just a preference?" Ally asked.

"My mom's a second-generation American with family originally from Jamaica. Some are still there. And my father grew up in Oklahoma, so no. Absolutely no cultural connection at all to the East that I'm aware of."

"Jamaica. Have you been?"

Megan nodded. "Lots. My father, total white guy, was in for quite a culture shock. They all get along great now."

"And your parents are still married?"

"Yes, and bickering over the television like teenagers. He likes historical documentaries and she prefers *Real Housewives*."

"And you?"

"Give me a police procedural, and I'm yours." She went back to her pan, and Allison filed that one away.

"That easy, huh?" She kicked her hip against the counter as she watched Megan work.

"Well, no. But I can't give away all the secrets. I'm jealous, though. Of your parents living so close. Mine are in Corpus Christi, so I don't see them as often as I'd like. We talk a lot, though. They just figured out FaceTime and were upside down on our last call. It's a process."

Allison laughed. "They sound great. But as for my family, it's a blessing and curse having us all in one spot, everyone involved in everyone else's life. My family means well, but…"

"They have opinions."

"Oh yes. My sister especially. So many expectations. I don't think I could jump that high if I devoted my entire day to it."

Megan paused and turned to her. "I say this with affection. Don't let anyone pressure you to be someone you're not."

Those were big words, especially given the new terrain she found herself navigating. Self-exploration was no joke. No one knew about her attraction to women other than Brent and Lacey, and for now, she wanted to keep it that way. At least until she understood it better herself. But there was no denying its existence or sustainability at this point. It wasn't a fluke. It was a part of her. Standing in Megan's kitchen confirmed it hadn't been a momentary fixation. As she watched Megan cook, she had flashes of domesticity that sent shivers through every inch of her. She imagined coming up behind Megan as she cooked, placing her hands on Megan's waist, kissing her neck. Every part of Ally went warm. No, hot.

"Where'd you go just now?" Megan asked.

She exhaled slowly, her heartbeat accelerated and distracting. "I don't know that I can say."

Megan watched her, set her fancy cooking spoon on the counter, and closed the distance between them. "Listen, I don't have answers, either. But I know this must be scary for you in a lot of ways I don't have to deal with anymore." She took Ally's hand. "I want you to know something. You don't have to be worried or on guard with me. We're just hanging out. Spending time together because we want to. That simple. Tonight doesn't have to change your life." She gestured to the pan. "Just food."

Allison nodded, already lost in a haze of Megan. She regained her smile and the ground beneath her with those reassuring words. "What if it does?" Ally whispered.

Megan's lips parted. Her big brown eyes searched Allison's. "Well, there are some things that are beyond our control, I guess." Her gaze dropped to Allison's mouth, and it seemed like the world paused, leaving just the two of them in it. She wanted nothing more than to lean in, close her eyes, and lose herself in the caress of Megan's lips, surrender to her mouth, and let her hands explore. Loud sizzling and the recognizable scent of something burning alerted her already overtaxed senses.

"Shit," Megan said, racing back to the stove. A moment later, "I hope you like a little char on your veggies."

Allison, now alone in her space, located the air. "It's the only way I eat them."

"Bless you."

Ten minutes later, they sat across from each other at Megan's dining table, devouring the best sweet-and-sour chicken. "You don't do anything halfway, do you?" she asked.

"No, I do. But I try not to make it for public consumption. If I'm inviting you to dinner, I'm only going to cook a dish I'm certain I've got a good handle on. Just smoke and mirrors. The catastrophes are for me alone." She slid a bite of green pepper into her mouth with the grace of someone on a commercial.

Ally sat back, studying her. "You're such a perfectionist. Has it always been that way?"

"My mother would say yes." Megan sipped her wine, leaving a hint of a lip print on the glass. Sexy. "But it's definitely a quality I've watched develop over time. It serves me well in a lot of ways, but it's also…"

"Exhausting."

"Yes. That's a good word for it." She grinned as she went back to her food.

"Take it from someone who embraces mediocrity—it's okay to fail once in a while. Face-planting can actually reset the bar nicely."

"Easier said than it is to accept. I'm a work in progress."

Allison reflected on their time together. Megan always knew exactly what to say, how to put the other person at ease, and she never had so much as a hair out of place. Even when Ally had stayed over, Megan was dressed and put together well before Allison woke. She had a sudden urge to break through that barrier to the true Megan underneath and get to know her on a deeper level. She craved it, in fact. On a whim, she used her fork to toss a couple pieces of sauced chicken onto the table. "Whoops."

Megan eyed her, raising an eyebrow. "Why did that look like it was on purpose?"

"Because it was. I'm sorry about that. But now that it's done, why don't you try it?"

"Throwing food off my plate?" She laughed the suggestion off and returned to her meal.

"Scared?"

Megan balked and then narrowed her eyes, sensing the challenge. "I'm definitely not scared."

"Okay, then." Allison folded her arms.

Megan shook her head and tossed a carrot onto the table.

"Whoa." Allison stared at the offending vegetable. "What is wrong with you? It's like you were brought up in a cave."

Megan gasped and tossed a forkful of rice and chicken off her plate.

"And how did that feel?"

"Gratifying as hell." She laughed. "Happy?"

"Satisfied. And I might have a tiny crush." She was proud of herself for saying the words, owning them.

"Yeah?" Megan sipped her wine, returning to elegance and grace.

"On this chicken," Allison finished, which caused Megan to throw a piece of it at her. "Bonus," she said, scooping it up off her plate and popping it in her mouth.

They finished their dinner, stealing glances at each other and enjoying the music, updating each other on the fourth grade and

Soiree's client load, including Missy, the chronic caller. She apparently phoned the office at least three times a day, earning herself a reputation.

"I guess I freed you up in that respect," Allison said, handing over her plate to Megan at the sink. "For the difficult clients."

"And tied up my brain in other ways." A pause. Megan turned off the water and dried her hands. "So, how are you?"

Allison shrugged and accepted a refill on her wine. "I'm so many things. Scared. Sad about the state of the engagement, but also relieved. There was too much in here for such a big step." She pointed at her head. "I'm excited, too."

"About what?" Megan said, lingering close.

Allison swallowed. "Getting to know you better. Provided that's what you want, too."

"Really? There's doubt?" Megan sighed. "I stalked you at your job today."

"And I loved it," she said softly. It was brief, but she could have sworn Megan's gaze swept over her cleavage. Her breasts tingled, and she took a moment with that new feeling. "You have an effect on me that I'm still not used to. A very strong physical one."

Megan's gaze dropped again, but this time purposefully, lingering. "In what way?"

"You make me dizzy, for one."

Megan dipped her head and met Allison's eyes. "In a good way?"

She straightened and nodded, refusing to break eye contact. "We're so different, but that's part of what draws me to you, I think."

"And women for you—"

"Are new. Admitted. But I've asked myself candidly, and I can honestly say that I'm not chasing a novelty. This feels...real. And I wish I could explain it better, but I don't have anything to compare it to. But ever since I've discovered these feelings, the world is suddenly alive in a way it never has been before."

"I believe you. Come here," Megan said quietly and held out her hand. Allison took the two steps between them and pulled in a little extra air to adjust to being in Megan's space, so very close to her.

"Hi," she said in a near whisper, taking in Megan's scent. Being this close to Megan had her skin tingling and her stomach flip-flopping and her legs a little shaky. At the same time, her breasts longed to be touched, and a small throbbing took up residence between her thighs. It was almost too much to handle, all of it at once, but at the same time, an experience she never wanted to end. She had no idea her body could react this way to another person without any prompting from her brain. Had she always had this capability and just didn't know it? Megan slowly slid a strand of hair behind Allison's ear. Her lips parted. It was one thing when she'd leaped in and kissed Megan without thinking, but this slow unravel was another experience entirely.

Megan's gaze dropped to her mouth, then lifted to Ally's in question. She was asking for permission, and in that moment, there was nothing Ally wanted more than to be good and kissed. She offered the smallest of nods and watched as Megan leaned in slowly, giving her every opportunity to back away. When her lips brushed Allison's, the Earth shifted. She heard herself murmur—or was that a whimper?—against Megan's mouth, absorbing the shockwaves of new sensations that hit her everywhere. Megan's lips were as soft as she remembered. Her mouth was warm, and everything about Megan drew her in. She angled her head and melted against the feeling of their lips moving in slow tandem. She was drunk on it. Gone. Then, ambitious. Hunger took over, and she noticed herself moving closer and increasing the speed of the kiss, which Megan had no trouble accommodating. Her own skin went hot, and that throbbing between her legs had tripled as she melded her body against Megan's, wrapping her arms around her neck. She longed for Megan to touch her, knowing innately it would be nothing like she'd ever experienced. As if reading her thoughts, Megan's hands slipped under her shirt to the small of her back. She gasped at the contact, at the fingertips on her bare skin, and pressed in closer, acutely aware of Megan's breasts pressed against hers.

"Should we stop?" Megan asked, after pulling her mouth away. Her cheeks were flushed and her breathing shallow. Allison took a moment to blink and watch, amazed that she had elicited that kind of response.

"Maybe a little more," she answered, only to have Megan reach for her at the same exact time she reached for Megan. They were off. Kissing and walking, Megan steering her backward until her back hit the wall with a thud. *Yes.* Allison closed her eyes as Megan kissed her jaw and then her neck. She gripped the fabric of Megan's shirt and held on for the most delicious ride of her life. But then she had to participate. She had to touch, explore, and maybe even lead. Crazy. She pulled Megan's mouth back to hers and took over, moving them to the couch. Megan took the cue and lay back, pulling Ally down with her. She saw stars when she settled on top of Megan, living out a number of recent fantasies.

"Oh, wow," she said as she stared down at Megan, who reached up and touched her cheek tenderly.

"You're so beautiful." The earnest quality with which Megan looked at her was everything. She meant it.

Ally caught her mouth and settled in. Before she knew it, their legs were intertwined, and with Megan's thigh between hers, they were going to be done before they got started. The pressure that steadily built was almost too much to bear or control. She pushed against Megan's leg and felt herself too close to the edge. Her body was overwhelmed, and she couldn't keep up. She tore her mouth from Megan's and focused on the smooth leather of the couch to regain some semblance of control.

Megan covered her eyes briefly. "God. Okay. Maybe we should press pause."

"Yes," she said reluctantly. Her body raged against the decision, begging her to change her mind. But the one thing she didn't want to do was rush full speed ahead before looking both ways. A difficult task, given the fire raging between them. They shared a small smile, her seated and Megan on her back, propped up on her elbows. "This is all new to me, so tell me this. Was it just me, or was that really, really…?"

"Definitely not just you."

She exhaled in relief, and Megan laughed. "I think I should go, but know that it's the responsible part of my brain speaking, and not the really insistent other part."

"You don't have to offer an explanation, but I happen to very much like the one you just gave." She stood and offered her hand. "Let me walk you."

They lingered at the door, neither wanting to say good night. Instead, they let their lips do it, clinging to each other a little longer in a slow, wonderful, toe-curling kiss. "I'll see you soon," Megan said.

"Good night."

Allison could have sworn she floated down that hallway, unable to comprehend how this was an aspect of life she'd gone this long without. Before hopping on the elevator, she took a moment, closed her eyes, and allowed herself to memorize every moment of tonight. She was pretty sure there was nothing better. Well...maybe one thing. She smiled and headed home on a strange new high.

CHAPTER NINE

A llison Eileen Hale."

The biting tone in Betsy's voice said everything. Allison closed her eyes and adjusted the phone, preparing for the onslaught. She was going to have to explain herself to her sister, whether she wanted to or not. "Hey. What's new Betsy?" she said in her most upbeat voice.

"You know damn well what's new. The question is what the hell are you thinking, and even more importantly, why wasn't I told that there was even an issue between you and Brent?"

She winced. She'd known this conversation was coming. She had just hoped to put if off a bit longer and have the news come from her. But she'd apparently waited too long, the cat was out of the bag, and here she was. "Oh. Well, Brent and I have taken a break, if that's what you're referencing."

"A break? Or a breakup?" Betsy practically shrieked. "They're different."

"I think that's what we're figuring out."

"This makes no sense at all. You had your whole life laid out like a perfectly wrapped Christmas present and he was so excited. Why would he end it? What did you do?"

She sighed. "This is more about me. I had doubts, and he was understanding."

"This is just unacceptable. I'm coming over."

"No, no, no. You really don't have to—" The phone went dead, and thirteen minutes later Betsy was on her doorstep with angry eyes. Allison, accepting her fate, held the door open for her sister, who breezed in and planted herself on the couch with a pointed look on her face. She wore exercise clothes and picture-perfect makeup, of course. Nary a crisis could get in the way of her outward perfection.

"Well?"

Allison stood in front of her with her hands placed on her hips. "It's been an interesting time. I can admit that."

"You're engaged to the most eligible bachelor in Texas and throw it all away because of an *interesting time*. Sweet Allison, I don't know whether to hug you or shake you, but I'm here now, and maybe it's not too late to turn this ship around and fix things. Put the wedding back on track."

"No. That's not the best idea."

"It's the only idea, and thank God in sneakers I'm here to talk some sense into you. Why didn't you call me the moment you had a doubt? I'm your *sister*, dammit."

Frustration bubbled. "Because of this. You don't listen to me. You've been here two minutes, and you've already decided what course I should be on in life and are prepared to thrust me onto it, even if it's not what's best."

"That's because *I love you*, and as your big sister, sometimes I can see things that you can't."

"But I'm not twelve years old anymore, Bets. This is not you telling me to watch out for Mr. Bonner's algebra class. For God's sake, this is the rest of my life we're talking about." She'd gotten loud, shouted even, which was not normal behavior.

Betsy matched her. "Which makes it more crucial than ever. There are angles you haven't even considered."

"I doubt that."

"And what brought this on in the first place? Did you fight?"

Allison closed her eyes. "No, we rarely fight. I met someone very unexpected."

The sentence landed with a thud. Betsy just stared at her. Finally, her jaw dropped.

"What? You're not going to say anything?" Allison took a seat and a breath, slowing them the hell down. "Look, I didn't plan on any of this. It's upended my whole life, but sometimes you have to take a moment."

"What's his name? And where in the world did you meet him? You don't go anywhere, and when you do, it's with Brent." She seemed to be searching desperately through her brain. "Oh my God. That cocktail party of Megan Kinkaid's. You met someone there."

Allison felt the blood drain from her face at the mention of Megan's name. She wasn't ashamed that Megan was a woman, but it was a big deal to announce that particular detail when she wasn't sure she had all the facts yet herself. She'd thought there'd be more time. "Nothing happened at the cocktail party."

"But he was there. You can admit it."

She closed her eyes at the misuse of the pronoun and ignored it. For another time. "Yes."

"Who is he? What does he do?"

Allison dropped her head. "None of that matters."

"Of course it does," Betsy snapped. "Is he successful?"

Of course that was where Betsy would focus. She hesitated, knowing she needed to explain further. "Yes."

"Well, at the very least, there's that." She sighed. "Poor Brent. I just can't imagine what he must be feeling."

While Allison felt bad for Brent, too, she couldn't help but note that her sister wasn't interested in Allison's well-being, or how *she* was handling all of this. In fact, she hadn't asked once. Her main goal was to chastise, cast doubt, and redirect Allison back where she wanted her. While it wasn't anything new, it made her sad.

She turned to Betsy. "I don't like hurting Brent, but honestly, he seemed okay. Confident, in fact, that everything will work out."

Her sister threw her a pointed look. "Allison, listen to me. You need to make sure it does. For the sake of everyone."

Allison recoiled, blinking as she turned over the implication in her brain. "What does that mean?"

"That there are a lot of people involved. A lot is riding on this pairing."

"You sound like this is the 1600s in Europe. Marriages aren't about strengthening the relationship between two families."

"And yet sometimes that's how they wind up."

"I can't think that way."

Betsy stood. "No. But time will surely tell what the fallout will be. Don't let it tick away for too long, little sister."

She headed for the door and let herself out, leaving Allison bruised and shaken. She hadn't expected overwhelming support, but she'd thought she'd see *some*. A hug. A word of reassurance. Something.

When her phone buzzed from the arm of the couch a few minutes later, she was afraid to touch it. Mustering her courage, she checked the readout.

You okay? For some reason, you're on my mind. Megan. She smiled, already transported out of this room, beyond the difficulties of life, to sitting in front of kind eyes and feeling supported, understood, and even a little bit special.

I will be, she sent back.

But she wasn't entirely sure she believed it.

❖

"Mom. Hey, Mom?" Megan said a little louder. "Mom, you're not on the screen anymore. All I see are the refrigerator magnets." Namely, one in the cutout shape of a photo of her from the ninth grade with braces. She'd begged her parents to take it down, to no avail. She was forever commemorated as an awkward fourteen-year-old to anyone who visited the house.

"What the what?" her mother said, sliding back into view but holding the phone too close, so Megan got a hearty glimpse of half her face. "This good now?"

Megan smiled at her mother's warm voice. She was trying. "That's perfect."

Half her mother's face smiled back. "We're going to the grocery store today and then to a movie but not a late one. I like being home early, these days. Ever since we hit our sixties, we're in early. Is that some kinda rule?"

"Nah, you just like your house at night."

"Your dad wants to see the flying space machines again. I feel like we see flying space machines way too often."

"None this year!" her father yelled from somewhere in the room.

Megan was pretty sure they were talking about the most recent Skywalker saga, but if she pushed, they'd be on the topic for far too long. She decided to get right down to it. "I was hoping to come and visit you guys, if you're up for it. I carved out a weekend for myself and scheduled the staff to handle the weddings without me. What do you think?"

The camera dropped, and the next thing she knew it was both their faces in the frame, beaming at her. "We love the idea," her mom said.

"Can you come this weekend?" her dad asked eagerly. "You can watch the game with me. I'll even make my famous popcorn with Parmesan."

"Sadly, no. I'm booked solid, but what about next weekend? That's when I have time."

"You just sold me," he said. "Just like that. I was gonna golf with Don, but I've just canceled it. I'll make a banana bread, too." She loved her dad's baking. He was gifted.

"And I'll eat it," her mom chimed in. "You're welcome here any day, anytime. You know that. I'll tell the dog. He'll be thrilled enough to get off the couch. Well, we can hope, at least."

"Don't bother Lefty," her dad fussed. "He's only just started his fourth nap and needs his beauty sleep."

"That's true. I won't be telling Lefty just yet, Megan. It will have to wait until he's lucid because your father feels so strongly about his sleep quality."

"Fair enough. I wouldn't want to overexcite a schnauzer with a couch addiction." Megan laughed because the image on her screen was now the ceiling. She let it go. "So, I'll firm up my plans and get back to you. Looking forward to some seaside air."

"We got plenty," her dad said. "Love you."

"Not as much as me," her mom countered sweetly. "I'm the winner."

Her father's left eye appeared on screen. "She always wins."

"Love you both, too."

She clicked off the call and slid out of her car, which sat in the driveway of a modest and sweet looking home. Allison's. Tan bricks, dark brown roof, and a matching door. Homey, but not flashy. Very much like Allison herself. As she made her way up the walk, with flowers in hand, she felt the familiar flutters that hit anytime she saw or thought about the woman who had stormed into her life and tossed everything in the air. They'd talked on the phone throughout the week, but Megan's work schedule had made get-togethers at a reasonable hour hard, what with Ally's early bird schedule for school and the twenty-five-minute drive between their homes. But they'd made a plan for a drink at Allison's house so Megan could see her place and glimpse a bit more of her life. She'd been looking forward to their meetup all day like a second grader about to go on a field trip to the zoo.

Ally swung the door open before she had a chance to knock. She wore soft-looking jeans, a yellow knit top, and brown booties. The best part was the smile. It lifted Megan and energized her in a manner she couldn't quite believe. "Welcome to my humble abode," Ally said with one outstretched hand. "Don't let the drywall and outdated carpeting impress you too much. The eighteen-year-old cabinetry might make you swoon. That tends to happen."

"And what a welcome that is. Hi."

"Hi," Allison said. "Are those for me? Gifts were certainly not required but always celebrated."

"On the first day I meet your house? Like I would show up without an offering. Big day."

"Well, now the pressure is on. Except it's not. These are gorgeous." She smelled the bouquet. "My house is just a house, but it's mine. Get in here and see it. I've missed you."

"I've missed you, too," Megan said. She heard the wistful quality in her voice, one she didn't fully recognize. She was such a softie lately, and that had her a little nervous. This was new territory and had her out of her comfort zone.

"That's why you should get in here. So I can gape at you without giving the neighbors a show."

Megan laughed, and as Allison opened the door wider, she slipped inside. It smelled like baking apples, her favorite. The lit candle on the entryway table identified itself as the sweet source. As they moved down the hall into the living space, Megan spotted two more. "I'm a big candle lighter," Allison explained. "They feel like friends."

Megan nodded. "I've never thought of them that way." But Allison made her see the world differently, and now she'd see candles as infinitely friendlier, too, which sounded nice. "Have they met the fuzzy gloves?"

"Most definitely. They have long chats."

The living room was small, but cozy. Matching blue sofas formed the shape of an L and a folded white blanket sat on the back of each one.

A few pieces of well-chosen art hung on the wall, reminding Megan of Ally's good eye for artists. "You have a Richter of your own."

"I don't at all. I have a Richter *print* mass-produced for chain stores that sell bath mats. Some of us aren't as fancy."

"Prints count."

Allison beamed. "Good. No one told me."

The kitchen was adjacent but in its own separate room, and Megan couldn't help but imagine the space would feel much bigger if the architect had opened up the floorplan, but the house had to be nearly forty years old and seemed perfect for Allison. The kitchen was just as homey as the rest of the place. All kinds of cooking utensils clung to spindles, and a giant mixer sat on the corner of the counter. "Chocolate cake is my forte," Ally said. "I'll make you some if you're good."

"Don't go making promises you don't intend to keep. You've already turned me on to Froman's, so the bar is set high."

"Have I let you down before?" Ally asked in challenge.

"God, no." It was the damn truth. "And I keep waiting for you to."

They went quiet for a minute. Megan's sincere confession had broken the playful patter, but Allison didn't seem to mind in the slightest.

"You have the best eyes. Brown and amazing. I think you get prettier every time I see you," Allison said with a tilt of her head. "How do you do that?"

"I have a theory." She moved to stand in front of Ally, who had her back to the kitchen counter. She placed her hands on either side of her waist, and that earned a smile. "The more you get to know someone, and the more you click with that person"—she pressed her lips to Allison's, stealing the kiss she'd been longing for since arriving on the doorstep—"the better-looking they become."

Allison blinked in the happy haze of being kissed. "Nope. That's not it."

Megan's mouth fell open. "You're rejecting me outright? It's a good theory."

With one finger, Allison traced the skin along the collar of Megan's maroon sweater even as it dipped dangerously low. Goose bumps broke out on her arms, and it was harder to get a deep breath. "It's not a bad theory, but it's not the case. You're simply gorgeous all on your own, and I'd think so even if you were the Ursula the Sea Witch of wedding planners, and we didn't click at all."

Megan wanted to laugh at the quip, but the way Ally's finger was dangerously close to the curve of her breast had her swallowing back a burst of lust instead. She liked this version of Allison, the one who took sinful liberties. It added a whole new layer of steam.

Ally met her gaze. "The truth is, when you walked into our first consultation, I was blown away by how pretty you were. The photos online did not prepare me. And that was before I knew I wanted to… do things to you." She traced the line of cleavage visible above her neckline and Megan closed her eyes. "With you."

Seduced in a recently engaged schoolteacher's kitchen. She did not have this on her bingo card. Megan took a step closer, settling firmly into Ally's space, her mind wandering to sexy places. Because, oh, she'd wanted to do just as many things to Allison, too. She fantasized about them daily. Yet she wanted Allison to have the reins and direct their pace. "When did that part begin for you?"

Allison looked away and shook her head. "After that damn dream I had. It was like my mind unlocked a part of me I had no idea was there. After that"—as she listened, Megan slid a strand of soft blond hair behind Ally's ear and waited—"I realized I'd never been more attracted to another human being in my life." Ally exhaled. "And I'm not saying that lightly. Being this close to you right now makes me feel like I might burst into flames at any moment. At the same time, it's the most wonderful and relaxing feeling in the whole world. I breathe better when you're around. Your turn."

Megan nodded and sent her a soft smile. "I never saw you coming. All warm and teacher-like and unassuming." She sighed. "But beautiful as hell. And when you look at me, really look at me? The whole room goes still. How do you do that?"

When she spoke, Allison's words were soft, delicate. "I think it has more to do with my subject and what I see when I look."

Megan couldn't resist this woman another moment, not with those luminous blue eyes searching hers. She inclined her head and caught Allison's mouth in a heated kiss. Allison received her and gave back just as much while Megan marveled at how well their mouths fit together, and how easily they moved in tandem as if they were always meant to find each other one day and had, their perfect fit. When Ally opened her mouth, Megan's tongue found entrance, and she lost herself in a haze of longing and arousal and Allison. From kissing alone, her desire fired. Her skin went hot, and her center ached. She wanted to pick Allison up and carry her to the bedroom she'd yet to discover, drop her right in the center of the bed, and learn every inch of her body until Ally cried out with pleasure.

As their make-out session escalated from slow and steady, to hot and heavy, to desperate, Megan checked in. "Are you okay?"

Allison swallowed and nodded, clearly attempting to regain her composure with a slow exhale. "That was more than okay. It's just…a lot."

"Let's go slow. One step at a time, right?"

Allison pressed her forehead to Megan's. "What if I'm not good at it?"

"At what?" Megan asked, her mind still foggy and straggling behind.

"Sex," she said quietly. "I've never. With a woman."

"You need to trust me on this when I say that won't be possible. Will it be new? Sure. But never bad. Not if it's us."

"I want to have that glass of wine with you," Allison said, raising her gaze. "But can I touch you first?" Allison asked, slipping her hands under the front of Megan's shirt and sliding them slowly upward. Allison met her eyes, waiting for a response before moving farther.

If only Megan could remember the meaning of words that had once felt so natural to her. Instead, as a shot of heat hit hard and fast between her legs, she nodded. Allison's fingertips traced the skin of her stomach up to her rib cage until they met the satin of Megan's bra. She trembled. She heard Allison take a steadying breath before palming Megan's breasts lightly through her bra, lifting them into her hands and softly moving them in a circle against Megan's body. She bit the inside of her lip as heat flooded. Her own breath hitched, and she grasped the fabric of Allison's shirttail, anchoring her desire. She'd been touched a good number of times in her life, but none had felt as sensual or erotic as this. Her panties were wet, and her responses were in overdrive. Every sensation magnified as she watched Allison's eyes darken with desire.

With her hands still under Megan's shirt, Allison gently pulled the cups of her bra down, freeing her breasts of the fabric. Megan's eyes slammed shut as Allison's thumbs found her nipples and circled them slowly, gently, and then less gently. Allison let Megan's breasts fall and then picked them up again, massaging, exploring, and damn near causing Megan to lose control. She heard the sound of her own ragged breaths. Despite her best efforts, the pressure inside began to build steadily with each knead and intimate touch. She was subtly aware of her hips moving, pressing against Allison's thigh, which had somehow made its way firmly between her own. The dampness between her legs had tripled. Desperation took hold, and the lip-biting no longer helped, erasing from her brain any intention of going slow. It was simply no longer her choice to make. Allison matched her rhythm, and Megan realized she had sensitive breasts that seemed to be so much more connected to the rest of her body than she'd ever known.

Allison rolled her nipples between her thumbs and forefingers and pressed her thigh against Megan's throbbing center. Megan's eyes fluttered as she attempted to control the rising intensity within her, the momentum of the speeding train heading her way. She could do this. Mind over matter. In a move she didn't predict, Allison removed one hand from beneath her shirt and slipped it firmly between her legs, pressing the seam of her jeans against her most sensitive spot. She heard herself whimper and cry out, and it was only a matter of seconds until Megan saw colors spring to life behind her eyes as pleasure erupted, ripping through her center to every part of her body. She rode Ally's hand in part shock and part bliss as sharp, wonderful bursts of pleasure flooded to every nerve ending, accosting her and overtaking her reality. She let the orgasm have its way with her, and as the shockwaves receded, she blinked in utter amazement. Not a stitch of clothing had been removed, nor had they strayed from their spot in Allison's kitchen. What in hell? She wasn't someone this happened to. She didn't even know she could achieve such a thing.

"I came over for wine," she said simply. That's when her wits floated back to her, and she found Ally's face and what could only be described as a look of awe.

"No, I think you came *before* the wine," Ally said as her expression shifted to pride and wonder. She rested her forehead against Megan and whispered, "Maybe I'm not bad at it?"

Megan laughed quietly, her breasts still dislodged from her bra and her legs still shaky. She pulled Ally in. "I think we've answered that question and then some." She placed a soft and slow kiss on Allison's lips, leaned back, and exhaled slowly, beginning the process of putting herself back together. "Maybe that drink?" That earned a joint laugh.

Allison, who couldn't stop smiling, turned to the cabinet behind her. "Coming right up." As she poured two glasses of red, Megan waited, surely flushed and happily owning it. Shortly after, she joined Ally on one of the blue couches, took a big sip of the dry wine, which was exactly what she needed in this moment, and stared at Allison.

"Hi," she said with another laugh. She wasn't sure how else to dive in after such an unexpected encounter.

Allison smiled. "Hi." She hooked a thumb in the direction of the kitchen to their left. "I'm not usually someone who takes bold, sexual liberties with my houseguests in the kitchen, minutes after their arrival. Just for the historical record."

Megan nodded, forcing herself to appear thoughtful. "No? Because this was my first visit here, and I have nothing to compare it to."

"I promise. Not a regular practice." Allison leaned in and kissed her. "But I regret nothing."

That sent an enjoyable shiver. Megan placed her palm against Allison's and threaded their fingers together. "It was really hard to stop."

Ally's eyes went dark again, which made total sense. There'd been no release for her, something Megan regretted, but at the same time, she didn't want to push. This was new territory for Allison. Not to mention, her life probably felt like a big question mark about now, and the last thing Megan wanted was to make her even more uncomfortable.

"I can tell that you're letting me set our pace, and while that's respectable of you, I'd rather these kinds of decisions be a two-way street."

Megan raised a playful eyebrow. "So back to the kitchen?"

Ally laughed, and Megan absorbed the sound that now climbed the charts to her number-one favorite. "Maybe not just yet."

"Fair enough." She gave their still joined hands a shake. "Tell me what's new. I feel out of touch with your week."

"Well," Allison said, scooting a little closer, which was wonderful. "I told Betsy about the broken engagement and my status with Brent, which was hard."

Megan made the shape of an O with her mouth. "And how did she take it?"

"Not well. She'd heard it from Brent, which is not the way I wanted it to happen, but that's my own fault for dragging my feet. I knew my family would be upset, and that's always been a hang-up for me my whole life. Disappointing them."

Megan sat up straighter, needing to make this point. "Of course I understand that desire to keep the people you love happy, but I worry you're prioritizing it. This is your future we're talking about. That's too big a sacrifice to make for others. Marriage is a big deal."

"And I think tonight I demonstrated that maybe there's more to me than even I planned on." Allison looked at the wall as an amazed smile brushed her lips. "I've felt so free lately and so happy when I think about you. It's a hobby, really."

"Are you saying that hasn't happened before when you've dated?"

Allison nodded. "Exactly what I'm saying. When I was with someone I liked, I'd always look forward to seeing him, and I'd have a great time when we're together, but I focused on me and my trajectory when we weren't. I didn't dwell, or pine, or fantasize. And now I'm thinking I should have noticed that."

"Maybe you hadn't yet met the right person."

"I'm starting to think you're right."

Megan understood that Ally was placing her in a different category. It was easy to let her heart take off with that piece of information. But their scenario was a precarious one, and Megan was someone capable of assessing risk, whether in business or her own life. When there was uncertainty, she didn't take the risk. Simple as that. The practice had never failed her, so she would continue to assess things with Ally as they went. But she wouldn't let herself get too comfortable. At least not yet. But she could identify with Ally's journey. "I remember the first time I had a crush on a woman. My freshman year of college. Her name was Francesca, and she sat near me in my Introduction to Spanish class." Megan shook her head at the formative memory. "She would pass me these looks that made everything in me come to life. I'd never had that with boys before. Even my longtime high school crush—who, I might add, I lost my virginity to on prom night in a bedroom at his friend's house."

Allison's mouth fell open. "Oh no."

"Oh yes. I'm a high school cliché. Most disappointing three and a half minutes of my life."

"I'm so sorry," Allison said, but she was laughing.

"I'm not. It was entirely enlightening." She shook her head with a smile and took another sip.

"What happened with Francesca?"

"She invited me over to *study*." She put the last word in air quotes. "She was two years older than me, so of course I found her to be the most worldly creature I'd ever met. Brown hair about to here"—she indicated halfway down her back—"and these eyes that seemed to see right through my nineteen-year-old bullshit. We cracked our books but were making out before we could say 'biblioteca.'"

Ally's eyes went wide. "That was probably a big deal for you."

"Please." Megan waved off the understatement. "It exploded my world. I didn't know those kinds of feelings, both physical and emotional, before her. As scary as it was, it was the best thing that ever happened to me. Changed my life."

The grin that took up residence on Allison's face was everything. "I love the way you put that. The more we learn about ourselves, the better life is, right? At least in the end. It's the fallout that happens in the meantime that's hard." She watched the smile on Allison's face dim, because for her, there was a lot at stake.

"I think the answer is yes to both." Megan finished the last of her wine. "And now the drink I came for is gone. I should go."

"You don't have to."

"I want to leave you wanting me to stay, rather than the alternative." She stood, and Allison joined her.

"That's the thing. I can't seem to imagine that alternative happening."

"Come here," Megan said automatically, giving Allison's hand a tug. She did. And as they stood together, sharing each other's space, Megan placed a hand on Allison's cheek, cradling her face. "I had the best time tonight, and that keeps happening."

"Sometimes I feel like I'm floating when we're together. Even just sitting and talking on the couch."

She smiled and met Allison's gaze. "Let's do it again soon. I need a little more floating of my own."

"You're on."

"Walk me out?"

"I'm nothing if not hospitable."

Megan laughed as flashes of their kitchen antics hit. "Um, you can say that again. I'm definitely leaving satisfied. What was it you said at my place? Five stars. Definitely recommend a visit."

That earned a bark of laughter. They walked hand in hand to the front door and stepped out onto the quaint covered front porch.

"A rocking chair would look really nice right there."

Allison followed her gaze to the empty spot in front of the window. "You know, I've thought that before, too."

"Reading books. Sipping your coffee. Growing old peacefully."

Allison looked pensive. "Might need two."

"Good point." The night was young, and she was reluctant to leave but knew baby steps was the smart way to go. "'Night, Ally."

"I like it when you call me that."

"Does no one else?"

"They do. It's just different when you say it." She slid her arms around Megan's neck, a position that just seemed to work for them. "Thank you for tonight."

Megan leaned in and stopped just shy of those gorgeous lips. She felt the electricity right away. "I had the best time." Allison closed the distance, catching her mouth in a kiss that made her forget her whereabouts entirely. "'Night," she murmured against Ally's mouth. She turned to the three steps that led from the porch to the sidewalk and paused, staring straight into the eyes of Allison's older sister, Betsy.

"Oh, hello," Betsy said blandly.

"Hi, Betsy," Megan said. She looked back at Allison, who hadn't moved. In fact, she'd gone entirely still and looked downright haunted. Megan's heart clenched. This surely wasn't how she wanted to talk to Betsy about all she was learning about herself, and yet here they were. Exposed. She wasn't sure what the best move was. Leave the sisters on their own to speak, or stay by Allison's side in case she needed support. She was certainly willing to do that, but she needed a sign.

"I think I understand things a lot better now," Betsy said, folding her arms. It wasn't the most supportive of physical gestures. She looked from Allison to Megan and back to Allison again. "You're having an affair with your wedding planner." Apparently, Megan was going to be here for this.

"First of all, she has a name. Second of all, I'm not having an affair at all. I'm not engaged, Betsy."

"In this moment. You know very well it's temporary, and what you're doing now is going to destroy everything. You think the Carmichael family is going to stand around while stories of Brent's fiancée running off with another woman trickle down the society columns? You need a wake-up call because that's not how these things go."

"In Allison's defense, I don't think either of us could have predicted what's happened. But sexuality aside, I think—"

"And for the record, this has nothing to do with whether you're a man or a woman, Ms. Kinkaid. I donate and attend all the marches."

"Admirable," Megan said evenly.

Betsy turned back to Allison. "This is about the way people talk and the details that will only titillate the masses, as they laugh at poor Brent." She whirled on Allison. "Is that what you want for him? If not, don't do this. Put what you want aside, and think about him."

Allison, to her credit, held strong. "Brent knows Megan is a woman. He told me to take this time to explore my feelings. That's what I'm doing."

That seemed to shut Betsy up for a moment.

She straightened, the expression on her face dialed to righteous. Oh, Megan didn't like this woman. How were she and Allison raised by the same parents? "I'm sure that was him giving from his heart, thinking of you. Maybe you could do the same for him, and in the meantime wake the hell up and seize what's right in front of you." She gave Megan a once-over. "Don't throw your life away for a dalliance. We all have…proclivities. It's how you handle them that counts." She shook her head, in what seemed to be disbelief. Her focus was clear, however. Saving face, and that meant protecting Brent Carmichael. "But I'll leave you two to it." She turned to go and then remembered something, holding up the canvas bag in her hand. "Dad made his famous chicken noodle soup. I said I'd drop some." She placed the bag on the sidewalk, apparently not willing to get any closer to Allison or the porch. "He's always so thoughtful of others. Maybe you could take a page."

They watched as Betsy returned to her car, parked along the curb. Once she was safely inside, Megan marched right back up the steps.

"I'm so sorry that happened. I should have been more thoughtful about our—"

"We didn't do anything wrong," Allison said blandly, as if all emotion had been drained from her body. She looked like a shell of herself, and Megan detested that she'd contributed. Hell, she'd been the abject cause.

"That part's true. But I know this isn't how you imagined telling your family."

"No, it's not. But maybe it's better this way. Rip off the Band-Aid. You heard Betsy. She doesn't care about whatever this implies about me, or what kind of journey I'm on." Allison had a point. Betsy was focused on pretty much every factor but Allison and her feelings. "This is about landing a Carmichael and protecting the investment." She said it with a sigh. "Which was never a goal of mine."

Megan nodded. "What can I do?"

Allison turned and their eyes met. In that moment, Ally visibly came back to herself. "Nothing. You've been caring and supportive, and that's all I can ask for. If anyone should be apologizing, it's me to you for what you just witnessed." She gave Megan's hand an affectionate squeeze.

"That was nothing," Megan said with a grin. "Have you ever seen a bride when her flowers are late to the ceremony?"

That pulled a laugh from Ally, comforting to hear. "Thank you for minimizing the situation. But if I really want to do the right thing, I should probably head to my parents' house and get ahead of the story. They should hear everything from me."

Megan nodded. "Do you want me to go with you? I can sit in the car while you talk. Offer moral support on the drive. Google knock-knock jokes and deliver them with gusto on cue."

Allison seemed genuinely touched. "No. I think this is something I have to do on my own. But maybe we can try the knock-knock jokes out next time." She leaned in and placed a soft kiss on Megan's lips, which said she wasn't ready to pack it in just yet. A lot of people would have run for the hills with so many complications involved. It spoke to Ally's character, which Megan grew to admire more and more.

"Promise me that you will call and update me."

"I promise."

She gave Ally's chin an affectionate shake and headed home,

awash with conflicting emotions. The evening had been wonderful until the moment it wasn't. And as much as Megan wanted to give herself over to all the incredible feelings she was experiencing, she couldn't lose sight of her precarious position in all this. People in her shoes always lost out, didn't they? And the more she let herself fall for Allison Hale and get used to the idea of an *us*, the greater that loss would hit. She was up against Brent Carmichael, for God's sake. She could skip across clouds all day, or she could stay measured, realistic, and with one foot on the ground. She nodded in understanding of what simply had to be her path.

CHAPTER TEN

The porch light glowed with warmth as Allison made her way up the winding sidewalk to the house that had been her childhood home. She used to play hopscotch on the driveway and dive onto the Slip 'N Slide in that very front yard with the neighbor kids, Tina and Terry, across the street. But there was something daunting about the house as she approached it now, as if once she crossed the threshold, nothing would ever be the same again. She took a fortifying breath. That was okay, because things were only going to get better, a concept she told herself to hang on to.

She let herself in after a loud two knocks, her standard practice. Her father was doing dishes in the kitchen, and her mother sat at the kitchen table with her laptop open, likely updating the books, a once-a-week practice. She took off her work glasses when Allison walked in. "Well, to what do we owe this surprise?" Her bottle-red hair was a little crazy, which meant she'd been shoving her glasses all over her head.

"Hi, guys," she said, planting a kiss on her mother's cheek and stealing a chair at the kitchen table. "I decided to swing by and see what you were up to." Her heart was beating way too fast.

Her dad held up a cereal bowl and shook his head. "It's too exciting to put into words."

Her mother turned her screen around to show off her spreadsheet. "Truly riveting." She studied Allison. "It's later than you usually visit us. I'm suspicious."

Allison laughed. "Well, I have updates if you have a minute or two."

Her father, wearing his comfy, oversized Dallas Cowboys around-the-house-pants and white T-shirt, turned off the water, appearing interested. "Fire away." He stood at the edge of the counter in anticipation.

Her mother was also now watching her carefully, her brow furrowed. "Is everything okay?"

"First of all, yes. Everyone is healthy and safe." A pause. "But I need to let you know that I gave the ring back to Brent."

Her mother blinked and looked to her father and back again. For a moment, neither said anything. "I don't understand. What in the world? Why?"

Her father's only response was to drop his brow in concern and shift his weight. He liked to collect all the information before reacting.

"I know that to you this seems out of left field. But the truth is, I was questioning things between us, and we agreed that it was better to wait until I was sure. Brent felt strongly that we should spend some time apart, and I agree. There's no use planning a wedding when we're not clear on if there will be one."

She could see the wheels in her mother's head, as if she was trying to keep up. "Allison. This isn't like you. I'm scared now. What's going on? Are the two of you fighting? You must be so rattled. Are you okay?" Her mother took her hand in both of hers, and the soft touch and sympathetic gesture hit Ally square in the chest. Her mother cared about *her*, more than the engagement, and it meant so very much.

Tears crept into her eyes and her voice felt scratchy. "I hope so. I think I am."

"So this means I don't have to wear a tux?" her father said, coming to sit at the table with them. He offered a soft smile.

That broke the tension, and the three of them shared a laugh, which allowed Allison to catch her breath and regain momentum. "Let's wait and see," she said, but part of her knew that ship had sailed.

Her mother looked her in the eye the way only a mother can. "You still haven't told us what prompted all this."

Here it goes. She gathered her little ball of courage and went for it. "I started to develop feelings for someone else. At first, I shrugged it off as a silly crush. The kind that passes with time."

"But it was more than that?" her mother asked, kindness in her voice.

Allison nodded. "I tried to shove it aside and live my life as best I could. Didn't work. I told Brent all about it, and he suggested we step back."

Her father nodded, his gaze locked on the table. "It's a shame if it doesn't work out between the two of you. You're a great couple of kids, but you know we have your back whatever you decide. You're our little girl."

Ally nodded, and relief flooded. "You have no idea what those words mean to me." She touched her heart, her hands shaking. "But there's one other thing. The person I developed feelings for is a woman. Megan Kinkaid, who was planning the wedding."

"Oh," her mother said, clearly surprised.

"It's no more of a shock to you than it was to me. I promise. But I wanted you to know about that part of my journey."

No one said anything, and behind them a teakettle began to whistle. "I'm sorry about that," her mother said and rushed to take the offending kettle off the stove. "You know I take nightly tea."

Allison nodded and turned to her father, searching his face. Sensing the attention, he searched for words. "The way I figure it, it's what makes a person happy that matters the most. It's how you treat people in this life, and how they treat you that's important."

She wasn't sure what she expected, but those simple yet meaningful words resonated.

Her mother returned to the table with a cup of tea for herself and one for Ally. "It's new for me, to think of you in a relationship with a woman, but if that's what happens, then that's what happens." She looked at her husband. "He's right, though. We always hoped that you'd grow to be kind and thoughtful, and you're both of those things. That's everything." And then her mother did something amazing. She smiled.

Allison attempted to smile back, but the emotion that swelled and swarmed made it so very difficult. "Thank you," she managed, her heart filling up full as she sat there. "I wasn't sure how you'd feel. If you'd be disappointed or—"

"We love you," her mother said immediately. "That's always going to be our first response to anything."

"She's right. She's always right," her father said with a sly shrug.

"I love you, too." She took a sip of hot tea, noticing that her hands still shook. "But I also know you think the world of Brent."

Her mother inclined her head from side to side. "I will admit to being very excited that he was going to be your husband. He's always treated you nicely."

"Brent's a stand-up guy." Her father left it there.

"And who knows? Maybe you two will still find a way."

Allison nodded solemnly, even though with each passing day she felt less and less confident about that happening. She finished her tea as they moved on to lighter topics: foot traffic at the store, her father's pesky car breaking down again two blocks from home, and her mother's new favorite commercial with the talking cat. It wasn't until she was washing out her cup and preparing to leave that she broached another angle of the breakup.

"Have you heard any more about the Dash Bar deal from BeLeaf?"

Her father was quick to shake his head. "Waiting to receive our first order. I'm sure it will be any day."

"Me, too," she said. "Regardless of my relationship with Brent, the Carmichaels were really impressed with the bar and want it on the shelves."

"I hope so, but that's not something you need to worry about," her father said and placed a kiss on top of her head as he passed.

"Well, I do," she admitted.

"We're just fine," her mother said, opening her laptop again, the very one that would likely tell her the opposite when she finished the books.

Ally hesitated, not sure there was much else she could say. "Well, I'll get out of your hair."

"Come by for dinner this week," her mother said. "Spaghetti and meatballs."

"I'll try." She smiled, realizing that the world still stood and her parents still loved her. This was a good night. She drove home listening to quiet music and taking in the evening's sequence of very surprising events. She was shocked by her behavior with Megan in her kitchen but also a little proud, sad about her run-in with Betsy shortly after, and warmed by her visit to her parents' house. How quickly the world moved these days. If nothing else, it encouraged her to just keep pressing forward. Learn, grow, and be kind. Those were the only things she could control in life. That and remembering the beauty around her. She smiled up at the stars that gleamed bright and clear in the night's sky, saying hello and thank you for the blessings in her life. Each and every one of them.

❖

Megan walked the hallways of the Soiree offices in search of the agenda for the Baker-Smythe wedding. "Who do we have on Baker-Smythe?" she asked Demi, who only gave it a moment's thought.

"Lourdes's client. She's in her office."

"Perfect. Thank you." She turned and headed back down the hall, enjoying the click-click-click of her own heels on the floor.

"Freeze." Kelsey stood outside her own office door and moved one finger in an up-and-down motion in Megan's direction. "What's with the sass? You're walking with a new swagger."

"No, I'm not." But Megan was grinning. She could feel it.

"Yes, you are. I saw your hips swinging and that little purse in your lips that said you have the mojo."

"I don't have the mojo."

"Do," Kelsey countered.

Cade popped out from his own office. "I saw mojo, too. Wasn't going to blatantly call it out, but since Kelsey has. You're guilty."

"I third," Lourdes said, folding her arms in her respective doorway. "Looking for me?"

She swept her gaze over the three of them. "My hips are innocent. I am simply enjoying a nice day. Can't a woman do that in her own office?"

Kelsey raised an eyebrow in challenge. "She can if she's willing to spill each and every detail that motivated said enjoyment."

She looked at Kelsey and dropped her tone. "Later."

"And then even later you'll tell us? I'll confirm your vendors for this weekend," Cade said to Kelsey.

"Not a chance." She then offered him a subtle nod.

"Hey!" Megan said. "I saw that. Trading insider information for grunt work is against Soiree rules."

"No," Cade shot back. "Check the bylaws."

Megan narrowed her gaze. "We don't have bylaws."

"Exactly," he said.

Didn't matter. She was enjoying the afternoon, the weather, her coffee, and even this showdown in the hallway had her amused. She shook them off and focused on Lourdes. "I heard Ms. Baker has called in distress."

Lourdes, who had her dark hair pulled back in a tight knot at her neck, covered her forehead with her palm. "We've had three lengthy calls today. She's convinced the bridesmaids' dresses are a hint bluer than the material she picked out. She's even dropped the word *lawsuit*."

"Well, are they?"

"No. She's also convinced the three-tiered cake she ordered is likely to fall, but that anything smaller will make her look like she's not taking the event seriously. She's also worried that the pinks in the bouquets will overshadow every other color, and what had she been thinking, and why didn't we stop her? That we're incompetent automatons."

"Automatons? That's a new one. Okay, let's get her on the phone. Have you gone with understanding and sympathetic?"

"Yes. Didn't work."

"Problem-solving?"

"She's convinced there are no answers."

"Perfect. Then tough love it is."

"This is why I look up to you."

"Watch and learn," Megan said, taking a seat in the chair across from Lourdes's desk. They had Maryanne Louise Baker on the phone in no time.

"Maryanne? It's Megan Kinkaid. Hi there. I'm here with Lourdes in her office. I heard you're having a rough day."

Maryanne seemed to perk up at the mention of Megan's name. "Oh, thank God it's you. Yes, all the details are wrong, and I don't know what I'm going to do about it. Lourdes has been a great planner, and I need to apologize for any names I've called her, especially the overly positive mynah bird, but I feel like eloping at this point."

Megan took a moment to laugh in order to lighten the mood. "You wouldn't be the first bride who felt like escaping. But listen to me. We're not doing that, okay? I've gone over your portfolio of choices for your big day, and I have to say I'm impressed."

"I don't see how. It's all wrong. I can see the truth of that now, but the wedding's in days, and there's nothing I can do about it. Nothing!"

she wailed. This had taken quite a turn, and Megan could hear her gulping for air. Fantastic.

She made eye contact with Lourdes as if to say, *And here it comes*. "Maryanne. I need you to stop that immediately. We're not doing this." Tough love in session. She put her game face on and leaned close to the phone on speaker. "But I'll tell you what you *are* going to do because it's in the best interest of your wedding. You're going to stop second-guessing yourself and enjoy the days leading up to what is going to be a gorgeous event. No more crying. No more overthinking. And definitely no melting down or name-calling. You're stronger than that."

A pause. "Okay," she said in a much meeker voice.

"I'm a professional, and everything I see here is absolutely gorgeous. Do you think I'm bad at my job?"

"No. Not at all." She sounded a little more put together now, rushing to reassure Megan.

"Good. Because I worked really hard for my reputation, and I wouldn't put Soiree's name on a wedding I thought was anything close to problematic. I'd fix it first, and I don't see anything here to fix. That says a lot about your good taste."

"Oh. Thank you," Maryanne said. "I'm already starting to feel better just hearing that."

Lourdes sat back at her desk with a smile. Held up both hands as if to say, *How do you do it?*

Megan silently raised a shoulder and returned her attention to the call. "And if you start to feel yourself going downhill again, you just remember what I said. You know what you're doing. I know what I'm doing. And Lourdes definitely knows what she's doing. I would trust her with my own wedding in a heartbeat. No question."

"Okay, thank you. I will do that." It sounded like the tears had perhaps been dabbed away, and new strength had settled. "I appreciate you taking the time to talk me down." She added a laugh.

"Maryanne. Anytime. I mean that. My door is always open to you. That's what I'm here for."

They concluded the call, and Megan stood. "Let me know if you have any more trouble. I think the event is going to go smoothly. Great venue, great list of vendors, and she really does have a good eye. She's just lost her mind. Too common."

"But it's you who has the charmed touch with these brides. I don't know what it is. When you speak, they just latch on."

"Wedding magic." She offered a wink and sashayed her way back down the office halls to a series of playful catcalls from her friends and loved every second of it.

After work that night, she met Kelsey at Shakers, where they stole two seats at a table near the bar. Kelsey was there first and had a couple of martinis ready to go. Dirty for Kelsey. Mango for Megan.

"You don't waste time," Megan said.

"Not when there's dish." She slid a martini closer to Megan. "Drink. Discuss. I'm antsy."

She took a sip and let the citrusy drink envelop her. "The highlight reel is this. I ran into Allison Hale at the Cramer wedding. The one I worked with Cade."

"Gasp. Drama."

Megan held up a finger. "The Carmichael wedding, the one we lost, is off."

"Shut up. Why isn't this news everywhere?" Kelsey looked around like there should be banners posted in the bar.

"I think the Carmichael side believes it's going to be short-lived and is therefore keeping the news to themselves. Riding out the hiccup."

"And what do you think?"

"I think there's been indication on my end that that may not be the case."

"Hold on. I'm gonna need this." Kelsey lifted her glass and took a long, sustained drink. At the same time, she made a *give me more* gesture.

"She came over to my place. I've been to her place. I came *at* her place, and that's where we are." She smiled at the joke she'd borrowed from Ally.

Kelsey set down her drink, choking on the liquid she'd consumed and reaching for a napkin. Megan handed her one calmly. Once Kelsey recovered, she turned her focus to Megan. "You cannot just blurt something like that out, but God, I love that you did."

Megan smiled. "And now you're updated."

"Sounds exciting and complicated."

"It's both. She's taken over my thoughts lately, and everything is so different with her. We're so different. It's jarring in a really good way."

"Preoccupation when it comes to women is not something I'm accustomed to witnessing in you. But I now suspect you're a smitten little minx of a kitten." A pause. "But how are you handling it all? Not about to run for the hills, are you? Don't get spooked. This is new ground, letting someone in."

"I understand. I do, but I'm actually holding steady. I'm happy, Kels. It feels really good to let my guard down. But there are some moments when...I freak the hell out. What if I let myself go there with her, and then it's over?"

"We don't know that's gonna happen."

"But there's a chance. I don't want to end up one of those brokenhearted people calling into radio stations." Megan stared at the wall as she shook her head. "And who would have ever predicted that I'd fall for a *bride*? Never in a million years would I have imagined this could happen. I'm not proud of that part."

Kelsey's dark eyes met hers knowingly. "As someone who has fallen for the most unavailable people on the planet, I can identify with how you feel."

"See? And look how that's worked out for you." Kelsey's string of relationships, even the ones that she put her heart and soul into, had all crashed and burned in monumental ways. "Reminds me of that woman who said you'd changed her whole world."

"And then went back to her ex-girlfriend two weeks later? Yeah. That one was rough."

"It sounds eerily familiar. That could happen to me."

"No, no, no. Do not backslide or allow my bad luck to interfere with the happy little thing you have going. Allison strikes me as a sincere and forthright person." She sat back. "I don't get the vibe that she'd yank you around. Don't let her scare you."

"I can't help it. It's like I have one foot on the sidelines." She covered her heart. "She's been honest from the start, but if I'm also being honest, I think she's lost and maybe confused, too."

"Well, the highest profile engagement in Dallas just came crumbling down at her feet." Kelsey sipped her drink. "Not sure I blame her. My advice? Give her time, and take some for yourself. What's the rush?"

"What's the rush?" Megan repeated, nonchalant. "I like that."

"If I've learned fucking anything, it's that time reveals all things."

She touched her now empty glass to Kelsey's in cheers. "I'm going to hell for two on a weeknight, but let's order another."

"I like you better now already." Kelsey flashed a smile and signaled the bartender.

CHAPTER ELEVEN

Allison moved about her empty classroom early that Friday morning, preparing for the math-a-thon her students had been studying for all week—essentially, a series of math games, in which the class would divide into two teams for friendly competition. The rules stated that as long as everyone tried hard and behaved with good sportsmanship, both teams would share in the lunchtime pizza party that would follow. The winners, however, got bragging rights.

"You look happy," Lacey said, popping her head around the door to Ally's classroom. "That's a positive sign."

She smiled. "It's math-a-thon day and hours from the weekend. How could I not be?"

Lacey came farther into the room and politely pulled the door closed behind her. "I was just texting with my kid sister, Luna. She works at this cute little bookshop, and her boss just got engaged to this famous romance novelist who came in for a signing. Talk about fate."

"How crazy. And romantic. I love that."

"Right?" A pause. "Forgive me for dropping in on you, but—"

"I drop in on you all the time. Demand things. I even text you at home, badgering you for advice. So what can I do for you?"

"Just wanted to see if you had any file folders? I'm completely out."

"File folders?" Allison raised an eyebrow. "Sure, you can steal a box, but they have tons in the supply room." She thought for a moment. "Which is actually closer to your classroom than walking all the way to fourth grade. You're caught in a lie and now must confess all." Ally folded her arms.

"Fine." Lacey blinked. "I was just taking the long way, actually, and, thinking about the bookshop romance, was wondering how things were going with Megan."

"Lacey Turner of the fifth grade!"

She squinted, hands in pockets. "You don't have to use my full name."

"You care. You care more than you've let on." Allison grinned. "It means we're friends now. You can't escape it."

Lacey held up a hand as she moved about the perimeter of the room, taking a handful of rulers and helping Allison place one on each desk. "Well, I can't just send my advice out into the world and hope it all works out." She shrugged. "So, fine. I was hoping for a little update."

Allison tried to smother the grin, but it wasn't going anywhere. "I've felt...lighter lately. I always feel like I have something to look forward to, no matter what I'm doing. It's really nice."

"You're gaga."

"Yes. And so very alive." She paused, mid ruler distribution. "I've never felt more energetic in my life."

"So, you've had *sex*." Lacey dropped her voice on the last word, given they were within the walls of an elementary school.

"Not exactly. Kind of." She frowned. Made sure the door was closed. And decided to just say it. Lacey was her friend and now consultant. She could level with her. "We've fooled around. Second base. Third, maybe? I don't know the bases very well to say."

"We can skip the baseball analogy."

"Okay. The point is that..." She dropped her voice to a whisper. "I want to do more, and I feel like that's on the very near horizon, but..." She couldn't say the words.

"Oh, and we have a man down." Lacey studied her. "Just say it. Turn off your brain and just blurt out the words like an assembly line."

"I don't know how." Allison closed her eyes and braced herself.

"To say it out loud?"

She opened her eyes again. "To have full-on, no clothes sex. With a woman." She'd said that way too loud and winced, dropping her volume again and scurrying closer to Lacey. "It seems so much more involved than with a man, and I have no experience with this sort of thing. I need to rent some lesbian movies. Are there classes? Study sessions? I'm a dedicated scholar."

Lacey blinked. "I think we should go back to baseball."

Allison nodded, prepared to listen to her friend and write down whatever information might be most important. She'd always been a studious note taker, and this was maybe one of the most important tests she faced.

"You've landed on some bases. Vague that may be, but we're going with it. You clearly have some experience to draw from, and honestly, so much is instinct. You have to trust yours."

"Trust me. When we're together, there are so many very powerful instincts. My hands have a mind of their own, my mouth does things before I tell it to, and I take liberties that I'm shocked I take. In kitchens."

"Very impressive. You sound like you have all the necessary tools." Lacey met her eyes. "I think you just need to get out of your own damn way. You're in your head."

"Weren't you? I mean, your first time?"

"Hell, yes. It was awful. Awkward and sometimes uncomfortable. Dark in the room, which made everything confusing." Allison's face fell hearing that. Lacey leaned in. "But still the most amazing thing I'd ever experienced. And it only got better from there."

She exhaled slowly. "Well, that's something."

"It's everything."

Two days later, from the comfortable chair across from Megan's desk at Soiree, Allison asked her a question. "Is it weird to not know what it's like to be excited about life until one day you are?" At Megan's invitation she'd swung by for a little extra time together. They hadn't seen each other in three days, and that began to feel like way too long. In fact, the more time they spent together, the more she craved it.

Megan smiled, and Ally melted. She was so beautiful it damn near hurt to look at her. She wore jeans and a brown tweed blazer on top of a white dress shirt. "Is this your way of confessing to me that you've been happy lately?" She came around the desk and leaned against it in front of Allison, arms folded. So sexy.

"Yes." Ally looked up at her. "You know that it's been hard to navigate my path lately, but underneath it all is this undeniable giddiness about everything that's ahead. I try to just focus on that, and it sees me through. You. Me. You, again." She sighed and gave Megan's hand a slight shake. "I think about you way too often. You're zapping my brain time."

"You're not alone. I imagine you in your classroom throughout the day. Check the clock to see if you're on lunch soon, because I know I'll get a sweet text from you."

"Always," Allison said. Even in this sincere exchange, every part of her was longing to be physically closer to Megan, to touch her cheek, kiss her lips, hold her. Would that need ever fade away? She simply couldn't imagine that.

"Not to be a mood killer. But how are things with your sister? Have the two of you talked?"

Allison shook her head solemnly. "My parents have continued to be incredibly sweet and supportive, but Bets?" She sighed. "May take more time. The interesting part? It's not a comment on sexuality, at least not directly. I think this has more to do with me and Brent, and everything that relationship brought to the table. She *liked* the idea of being an in-law to the Carmichael family. It came with such status, and that's what drives her." She shrugged. "We just value different things."

"Well, that name carries a lot of weight in this town. I can't help but wonder a little bit, too."

Allison tilted her head. "What do you wonder?"

"How long it will take for the newness of all this to wear off before you start remembering all the perks that come on Brent's arm."

Allison deflated, surprised to hear Megan's words. Her fear. She stood and leaned against the desk alongside Megan. "I want you to listen to me, okay?"

"I always listen to you."

"I like where we're at. I'm not thinking about Brent, or the engagement. It's my hope that my future is with you." Okay, maybe she was sounding a little too serious, and nerves crept in. She rushed to reassure Megan that she hadn't already decided on paint colors for their future home. She didn't want to scare her away. "Not that I expect us to be there just yet. It's just a little daydream I have, which I probably should keep to myself."

Megan, to her credit, didn't seem too spooked. In fact, she wasted no time in leaning down and kissing Allison, which prompted an outbreak of goose bumps on all her limbs and stoked a physical longing Ally was growing used to.

"I have a new gay friend." That was the sentence she uttered the moment the magical kiss ended. She wished she could explain why, but here they were.

Megan blinked, amused. "I'm sorry, what?"

"A friend from work is gay, and she's been a great sounding board about all this. Lacey. I might send her a five-layer dip to say thank you. It's a specialty."

"I'll need to try it. Lacey's a lesbian colleague?"

Allison's cheeks went hot, hearing how this all must sound. "Yes, and she's been so helpful in the listening department. She's fifth grade. They're wise."

"She's been your Kelsey."

"Oh." Allison enjoyed this insight. "Kelsey is your person?"

"Mm-hmm. I tell her everything, and she helps me see the world clearly and not run screaming from my own emotions." She frowned. "Mostly. Sometimes she encourages me to chuck my common sense out the window and run into traffic, but together we make our way through. Mostly."

Ally stood in front of Megan and placed a soft kiss along her jaw. "I'm happy you have her. I hope she likes me."

"She says you're okay."

Allison's eyes went wide. "I can send her a five-layer dip."

"I'm kidding."

"Oh, good."

"You're cute."

"You're sexy. Really. A lot."

Megan laughed and turned her head, catching Ally's mouth in a hungry kiss that finally brought them together. "What am I going to do with you?"

"That's the part I have very little clue about, but I was hoping it might be sooner rather than later that there's doing." There her mouth went again, running away with its damn self.

"Yeah? I think we can arrange that. Just waiting to hear these words first."

"Well, I've said them now. Can we do this some more first?" Ally asked, leaning back in and hovering just shy of Megan's mouth before sinking into the kiss, which went from zero to sixty in no time, wedging her body between Megan's legs, which she was finding was one of her favorite places to be. Tongues, lips, and unmatched chemistry. *Oh, my.*

"I love the way you kiss me," Megan managed between kisses. "Your lips. God in heaven."

With that kind of encouragement, she slid her hands into Megan's jacket and around her waist, savoring the warmth coming through her shirt. She felt so connected to this woman, so enraptured.

"Do you want to come over tonight?" Megan asked, her voice low and husky. Allison loved the way it sounded when she was turned on. Given their exchange, she'd be coming over for a lot more than a friendly glass of wine. God, she wanted that. Longed for it. Yet at the same time, alarm bells sounded, and her brain switched to panic mode, searching for a bailout button.

"What about tomorrow?" Better. Less daunting, because tomorrow was a long time from now. The pivot would buy her a full twenty-four hours to calm the hell down. Or twenty-four hours to overthink everything. So that might be bad. She should just jump and embrace all the signals her body was giving her, because it had a lot of opinions when Megan was in the room in a blazer like this one.

"Tomorrow is great. You say when and where, and I'm there." Megan placed a slow kiss at the base of Allison's neck that made her knees forget their purpose.

"More," Ally whispered, closing her eyes.

She felt Megan smile against her neck before kissing her there once again, slowly, softly. She placed another kiss on the underside of Allison's jaw. She realized distantly that while Megan's mouth was on her neck, her hands were on her ass, cupping it. How did she miss that moment, and more importantly, how did she continue to stand up with everything so warm and strange and wonderful?

"I can come to your place tomorrow night, if it's available?" Allison said. The heat passing between them begged it to be available. What a crime it would be, unavailability. She needed more time to stare at Megan, talk to her, and—God—touch her. She was like a damn drug that made every aspect of life better.

Megan laughed, pushed off the desk, and ran her fingertips through Allison's hair, smoothing it, returning it to its original state. Always orderly. "I'll make sure it is. I have no memory of renting it out."

Allison's body decided to hold on to her arousal, which was not at all helpful as she drove home, alone with her racy daydreams that both excited her and sent her into a fear-laced spiral. She gripped the steering wheel and focused on the road, terrified, excited, and terrified again. This date they'd just made had her feeling like she was about to leap off a cliff, a beautiful cliff, but a cliff all the same. Every part of her screamed for more with Megan, which had to be a very telling signpost. She should shut down the overthinking, punch the self-doubt in the face, and remember how special Megan made her feel. Her vibrating phone pulled her from her thoughts as it danced in her cupholder. Stopped at a red light, she checked the readout: *Brent*.

She went still.

In so many ways, it felt like her old life was calling her up on the phone, reminding her who she was and to get the hell back to regularly scheduled programming. A return to stasis would calm the waves, sure, and that offered relief, but at what expense? She knew the answer, her own. She cared a lot about Brent Carmichael, but the door to that world was closing, and the path in front of her seemed bright, and infinitely more suited to her. The traffic light turned green, and the phone's vibration ceased. Ally drove on, exhaled, and nodded.

She was headed in the right direction.

❖

It was getting close to lunch the next day when Megan exited her office in search of a cup of coffee to get her through. She'd lost herself in a sea of client calls, checking in with her nearly there brides to be sure they were up-to-date on their to-do lists, and to let them know that their decisions would soon be final, giving them the opportunity to rethink a detail or two before there was no turning back. Mornings like this one, when she needed to be *on* for hours at a time, seemed to fly by in a haze of too much smiling and lots of reassuring. This coffee would help save her. When she came face-to-face with Brent Carmichael speaking to Demi in the lobby, she snapped right out of mission mode, pulled up short.

"Brent," she said, forcing the happy-to-see-you energy. Anything to mask the shock and concern at his appearance at her workplace. "It's lovely to see you."

"Is it?"

She felt her smile dim, but she refused to let it disappear. "Of course."

"I don't have an appointment. I thought maybe you could spare a couple of minutes."

"Sure. Why don't you come into my office? It's a bit more private." She and Kelsey, who'd emerged from her office, exchanged a look. She didn't expect any kind of trouble from Brent, but the curt nod Kelsey gave her let her know that she had Megan's back and would keep an eye on the situation. They had two or three brides in the office meeting their respective coordinators, and Megan had no desire for a scene. Not that Brent seemed the type. Though you never knew how a normally grounded person would react when they felt scorned.

Brent nodded and followed her, work-ready in his very expensive blue suit. Once behind closed doors, she turned to him. "I wasn't expecting you."

"I realize." He unbuttoned his jacket and took a seat in the chair she indicated.

"What can we do for you? New event coming up?" She sat behind her desk with a smile, knowing full well this wasn't a business call.

"I thought we should probably have a friendly chat given recent events. We're old friends, right? Can we do that? Level with each other like two adults."

"Of course we can." She paused and folded her arms on her desk. "This is about Allison."

He nodded, the smile faded from his lips, and she could see that this was a man in turmoil. That part didn't feel good. Could he be an arrogant oblivious knucklehead? Sure. Was he a bad guy? No. "I'm worried about her."

"I can understand that. But if she's taught me anything, it's that she's an astute girl. I think the world doesn't give her enough credit."

His gaze narrowed as if he didn't appreciate the education. "I would never underestimate Allison. She's amazing and capable of taking on pretty much anything. It's what first caught my attention about her. One of the things I love, still."

"But?"

"But this is different." His jaw tightened, and he glanced to the side. "She's got cold feet, and I think it's confused her. She's mistaken her nerves, her jitters"—he threw a hand in the air—"for something else."

"And that something else would be her feelings for me."

"Yes." He gripped the armrests of the chair. "I don't know what kind of spell you've cast on her, but it would be nice if you could take a look at the bigger picture and help her understand what's actually happening and uncast it."

"You want me to help her see that she's just nervous." Megan exhaled, because it was apparent that Brent didn't have a good read on the situation. Allison had never struck her as someone nervous about marriage. If anything, her attraction to Megan seemed to ruin the plans she was on board with. "The problem is that I'm not sure I agree with you. I think Allison is learning things about herself on legitimate terms, independent of your engagement. The timing, I can admit, was not ideal."

"Yeah, well, I thought this learning about herself phase would have been over by now, and we'd be back on course. So you can see my growing concern."

Megan wasn't sure what to say to that. "I can imagine that you're upset. But I think you have to take her seriously."

"I'm asking you to back off. Plain and simple. That's something I'm serious about."

"I hear you, but what if I can't do that?"

"Then I'd say you're dishonorable because you'd be ruining her life. I mean that sincerely and with no malice. Help her find her way back to herself."

Megan hesitated, staring at her desk before raising her gaze back to his. "Look, I think we're both insane if we think this is our decision and not hers. I know that you're hurting, and I get that this is hard."

"You forgot fucking embarrassing." He looked up at the ceiling, uncomfortable. "She left me, and people are starting to realize it."

Ah, yes. The Carmichael reputation. "I think this is probably a conversation for you to have with Ally, not me."

"Oh, so it's *Ally* now? We're there?" he scoffed.

"Brent."

"Don't." He stood. "I've never had anything against you. You've always been a stand-up person, respected in business, and fun around a punch bowl. But this is different." He was getting a little loud. "This is my life. So you think long and hard."

Was that a threat? This wasn't like him. But he was desperate and grasping at straws. "Or what?"

"Or you'll leave lasting damage." His shoulders sagged. He held up a hand and let it drop. Defeated. "You can have nearly any woman you want. Why this one? You'll go on with your life when it ends, and hers will be in shambles. Do something before that happens, Megan."

"I have no intention of hurting Allison. We've been very clear with each other."

"Are you sure you haven't already?" The question hung in the air, unanswered. He buttoned his jacket. "I'll see myself out." Moments after he excused himself from her office, Kelsey appeared, wide-eyed.

"Hey, you okay?"

"I'm okay." She was rattled, though. That was for sure. She exhaled slowly and gripped the edge of her desk. "It could have gone a lot worse."

"He didn't go all Gaston on you?"

Megan laughed because the Disney comparison to Brent wasn't inaccurate. "I didn't say that. But he held his temper for the most part, and we had a civil, if strained, conversation. I think the guy's starting to realize that she might be serious."

"Is she? And where's your head?"

"God, K." She frowned and took a seat. "I need to tread carefully here. While part of me wants to grab Allison's hand and run off into the sunset, it's entirely premature. We're still getting to know each other. If anything, this has reminded me that there are factors beyond my control at play. And they could come back to bite me if I'm not careful."

"Don't you dare run scared. That's not who you are."

She smiled. "It's not typically, no. But it feels like there's a lot on the line."

"Good things are worth the price tag they come with. You don't pick up a Chanel bag for ten dollars for a reason."

She softened and reflected. "I do like Chanel."

"We all do. So work for it."

A pause. "She's coming over tonight. Big night."

"The plot thickens." Kelsey raised an eyebrow, tapped the doorframe, and pointed at Megan. "Stay the course. Find your Chanel happiness like you damn well deserve. Shut out the rest of the noise."

But alone in her office, Megan heard Brent's words over and over again in her head: *You'll leave lasting damage.*

The question was, damage to who? She had a sneaking suspicion she might be standing in front of a speeding train. She closed her eyes and leaned back in her chair as a sinking feeling came over her because the reality of her situation was getting harder and harder to ignore.

CHAPTER TWELVE

After ten tries, Allison finally decided to go with the white knit top because she'd been told in the past that it really flattered her figure. She'd added a necklace because it softened the look. Gray booties that Betsy insisted were in topped off Allison's faded, slim-cut jeans that cost more than she had any right spending on a teacher's salary but fit her better than any pair she'd ever owned. Yet as she stood in front of Megan's door, she wasn't sure she had the courage to actually knock. As always, soft tunes floated from inside. She imagined Megan opening a bottle of wine, waiting on Allison to arrive before partaking herself. Once she saw Megan and those gorgeous brown eyes, she would be fine, right? Because every part of her trembled with anticipation, and if they weren't good in bed together, what did that say? Would it even matter? No, she decided, because this felt like more than sex. Sex was a bonus. Saucy. Exciting. But it wasn't the be-all end-all to happiness.

At the same time, there was no way in hell they wouldn't be good together.

Just knock.

She shifted her weight, fully aware of the overnight bag on her shoulder, which felt so deliberate she was almost blushing. *Here I am for a sex date.* That was her.

Just knock.

Should she add a touch more lip gloss? She might have rubbed it off with all the nervous pursing of her lips on the way over. Before she could come to a decision, the door opened, and Megan looked back at her expectantly.

"Are you having words with yourself in your head while you stand in my hallway? An internal debate?"

She had been, yes. "How did you know?"

"Well, you've been standing out here for a couple of minutes now, and I know that you tend to overthink. And talk to yourself. I figured both were likely afoot."

"Afoot, indeed." Allison exhaled, already feeling better because she was understood. "You're a spy."

"Well, the building helps. When a visitor is on their way up, the door folks buzz me."

She nodded, but really her attention was on Megan, once again in bare feet, which just made her so human and damn attractive. Maroon nail polish, and her hair. God. "Your hair is down. It's so pretty."

Megan absently touched the back of it. "You get the chill version of me tonight."

"That's my favorite. When you're relaxed."

A pause.

Megan eyed her. "Would you like to stay in the hallway? Totally up to you. I don't boss my guests around."

Allison laughed, realizing the ridiculous nature of her behavior. "I'm most definitely coming inside." She didn't wait for further invitation and breezed past Megan, finding her confidence. It was close to eight, and they'd agreed to meet up after dinner since Megan had had a late meeting, the only time that week the entire staff was free.

The apartment was quiet except for the soft music playing from the sound system. She was beginning to feel more at home in the space, the more she visited. In fact, it was becoming a great getaway spot for her. A soft place to fall and relax after the whirlwind of her life.

Megan gestured to the open sliding glass door. "I was out on the balcony before you arrived. It's a beautiful night. Wanna join me?"

Oh, she very much did. "I'm in." She accepted the glass of wine Megan offered and dropped her presumptive bag sheepishly near the door. Luckily, Megan hadn't paid it any attention.

She'd taken a peek out onto the balcony before but had never spent any time there. Megan had two comfortable chairs and a small table outside overlooking the gorgeous, twinkling lights of downtown Dallas.

"Wow. This is something." There was a slight chill in the air, but nothing she couldn't handle. When Megan put her arms around her from behind, she warmed instantly, and the world settled. In fact, she wasn't sure she'd ever felt more satisfied, so she pushed back against her, wanting more. "Hi," she said quietly.

Megan kissed her cheek. "I've missed you. More than I should admit."

"Oh, please admit. Because I've missed you back. Since I saw you yesterday, I've been thinking about tonight a lot."

"Letting you go home last night was hard. I was…keyed up." Her darkened eyes told the larger story. Megan had been turned on thinking about her, and that had Allison grappling for strength. Her eyes moved over Megan's body. She wanted nothing more than to step into Megan's space and take what she desperately wanted. Toss that shirt to the side and unbutton those low-rise jeans that Megan looked so damn hot in.

"Hard for me, too," she said instead. They had time, right?

She took in the dark sky, the few stars that shone through the cloud cover, and the brightly colored office buildings, one of which changed color every ten seconds or so. "It must be nice to sit out here and watch that guy shift colors." She gestured with her head to the building.

Megan came to stand next to her at the railing, their shoulders touching, which made the whole left side of her body warm. "Ah, that's an office building. A Bank of America on its most prominent floors. They added those LED lights a few years back, and now it's a nightly show. Relaxing to watch one color fade into the next with a glass of red after work."

Ally turned to face Megan. "You know everything."

Megan's eyes went wide, dancing. "That's probably my most favorite compliment I've ever received. I'm going to have you write it down later. Stick it to my fridge."

She burst out laughing. "It would be. You're so type A. Is your apartment ever a mess?"

"Um, yes. But I couldn't stand for you to see it that way."

"But I have to. It's my new goal." She touched Megan's cheek. "You're going to have to let that guard down eventually, you know. Just me. You. Your secret messy apartment."

Megan exhaled. "I will try. But know that I don't let a lot of people in that way." She kissed the inside of Ally's hand.

"Well, I want to be one of them."

"And I want you to be."

The sentence sent Allison's heart soaring and her lips seeking Megan's. She meant the kiss to be celebratory, but it quickly escalated from slow and steady to hot and illicit. She very much liked illicit kissing. "We're making out in full view of all of Dallas," Allison murmured. The idea had her even more turned-on.

"It's about time they know."

Allison smiled but noticed it was hard to keep her hands to herself. "Tell me about your meeting." A hand at Megan's lower back, just under her shirt.

"It was enthralling. We constructed a new timeline form." Megan's eyes dipped to the opening in Allison's top. It showed off a little bit of cleavage, by design. She was a sex panther now, apparently, and owning it. "We discussed how to get what we want out of vendors the day of, and how, more often than not, honey goes a lot farther than vinegar, which one should reserve for after the event." She swept a strand of hair from Allison's forehead and then ran a hand up and down her arm. Such a simple action inspired goose bumps...everywhere. Even the air felt charged, tension-filled like a taut bow ready to release its arrow.

"I've always been a fan of honey, myself." Her hand, which had developed an agenda of its own, slipped lower, grazing Megan's ass because, c'mon, she was human, and the ass was amazing.

"Honey, you say? Now that you mention it, you might have some right there," Megan said, eying Ally's lips and leaning in with a grin.

"Oh, you're really good."

"I'm even patting myself on the back." Megan captured her mouth in a hungry kiss. "Hmmm. No, I was wrong. No honey. That's just you, which is better."

"So smooth."

"Thank you," Megan said, taking their nearly empty wineglasses and setting them on the table before taking Ally by the hand and leading her inside. "Little more privacy, you know?"

"I do. I approve."

As if by design, the music on the sound system was slow and a little bluesy, like the universe was in on the plan to bring them together. As if they needed it.

Allison was nervous, but not. She was excited, but steady.

There was no part of her that wanted to run, and that said so much. Sex had always been something she could take or leave. Tonight, she craved Megan's body, her touch, and any combination of the two beyond all measure.

"I want you," Megan said, meeting her gaze. Ally felt those words down to her toes. Her lips parted. She didn't have the words so instead nodded as Megan reached out and cradled her cheek. "Yeah?"

"Yeah," Allison said, holding eye contact, ready to combust as she stared at the sexiest woman she'd ever seen.

"This way," Megan said, killing the lights in the living room with one switch on the wall. Allison followed her wordlessly to her bedroom that smelled wonderfully of Megan and vanilla and cinnamon. She never wanted to leave this place, an idea that doubled when Megan pressed her against the wall nearest the bed and melded her curves to Allison's. Her body went hot and still as she absorbed the pangs, shouts, and aches of need that overcame her. They were kissing. Expertly. Allison granted entrance, and Megan's tongue moved into her mouth, causing the world to slow down and speed up in unpredictable intervals. It was the best kind of drunk. The room was dim. Megan must have had one of the fancy lighting systems that allowed a person to pick a setting. This was a good one, but it still allowed her to see, and that was important.

Somewhere in the middle of that, though, Megan slipped her hand between Allison's legs, on top of her pants. "You're wet," Megan whispered. "God. I can tell."

Allison's eyes fluttered closed, and she bit her lip, moving with Megan. "Since the balcony. You looked at the dip in my top."

"Damn right I did."

The reminder must have snagged her attention because she easily lifted the shirt over Allison's head, leaving her there in her red bra. Megan's eyes dropped and she took in the sight, swearing quietly. "May I?"

Allison nodded and watched as her bra was easily unclasped and tossed to the floor. Her breasts weren't big, though they definitely weren't small. But the way Megan stared at them made her feel more confident than she was used to, and how liberating was that? Megan dropped her head and pulled a nipple into her mouth, sucking long and hard. Allison saw stars and gripped the wall behind her for support. Megan's hand dipped down the front of her pants, and a finger traced the border of her panties. Torture. Plain and simple. She adjusted, trying to engage, force contact, find release. Megan took her time. The other breast. She had an agenda. She bathed it with attention, circling her tongue around Ally's nipple while softly tracing a line across the crotch of her underwear with one finger. This woman was multitalented, but then this was Megan Kinkaid. She was not used to her body responding in such an intense manner, and the throbbing of her center was more than she could handle. She didn't want to rush them, but she wasn't sure the choice would be hers for much longer. "Megan," she said quietly. That one word, that plea, was enough. Megan nodded, kissed her one time, and moved them to the bed. First, she laid Allison down gently and took the rest of her clothing off, one piece at a time, watching intently as each new part of Allison was intimately revealed. She was completely exposed to Megan's heated gaze. "Allison. You're gorgeous," she said, running her fingertips from Allison's shoulders, to the curves of her breasts, down her ribs, to her thighs.

She then repaid the favor, standing and taking her top off slowly, allowing Allison to watch, and God, she did. Her mouth went dry. She'd never seen anything so hot in her life. She stared in sheer captivation as Megan stripped down to her matching yellow bra and underwear and lowered herself on top of Allison.

Bliss.

That's what the weight of Megan on top of her amounted to. She placed her hips between Allison's legs and rocked slowly, pushing against her insistently, which quickly built the pressure between Allison's legs and had her breathing shallow and quick. She was simply overcome with sensation she didn't recognize. How in the world did this woman know how to drive her absolutely crazy? Megan's hips continued the wonderful torture. She was so close. And then the rocking stopped. Allison nearly wept. That was until her legs were parted gently, and she felt the warmth of Megan's mouth kissing her center, then licking her softly in small circles. The noises she heard in the room were hers, but she wasn't aware of the effort it took to make them. She was quite simply undone and traveling at a fast rate of speed toward something important. Megan reached up and found her hands, intertwining their fingers tightly as she pulled Allison into her mouth fully. "Oh my God," Allison said, digging her nails into Megan's skin until she came in a glorious wash of unhinged pleasure. Her hips were off the bed, but Megan had her, reclaiming her hand and pushing her fingers inside, which doubled the payout. Allison rode her hand, not holding back, feeling sexy and satisfied with each wonderful wave.

"How?" was all she managed when she came back to herself again. She tried for air, but it was scarce.

"You make it really easy," Megan said, lying alongside her.

"I mean, did you feel that, though?" She shook her head, still not quite sure she believed how amazing that orgasm had been.

"I felt every second of it. Trust me."

"We're not done," Allison said automatically.

"We don't have to immediately—"

"Oh yes, we do," Allison said, unable to wait another second to have her way with Megan, something she'd daydreamed about a million times. She shoved her nerves to the side and followed her instincts. She climbed on top, kissed the tops of Megan's breasts, unclasped her bra after only two and half tries, and let her breasts tumble out. Stunning. She blinked at the image of Megan on her back, topless and ready. She slid the yellow underwear down her legs and exhaled, calming herself. Her touches were timid at first, but as Megan responded, offering encouraging sounds, she used them as a guidepost. She allowed her fingers to play between Megan's legs, learning what she felt like, what kinds of touches she liked. She smiled when Megan closed her eyes and gasped, feeling the kind of heady power she could get used to. She crawled up Megan's body, kissed her neck slow and lazy as she pumped her hips nestled between Megan's, luxuriating in the connection she felt to Megan when they came together. "I'm so close," Megan said weakly, almost in awe. Allison didn't stop. In fact, she picked up her speed, pressing more firmly against Megan's center, taking her nipples into her mouth one at a time. On instinct, she bit down.

"Yes," Megan hissed, tossing an arm over her eyes, her hips moving wildly.

Allison reached between them into wetness and found her most sensitive spot, pressing firmly in rhythm until Megan whimpered and went rigid, her back arched in the most beautiful display. Allison memorized the image, allowing it to burn itself into her brain.

When Megan floated back to them, she found Allison's face and pulled her down to her. "Are you okay?"

Allison didn't hesitate, on a high. "I'm struck. I'm in…awe. That was so much more than I had planned on."

Megan pushed herself up on her elbows. "In a good way?"

Allison laughed. "In the best way." She lay back on the pillow and grinned at the ceiling, like a kid who'd just been presented with a new bike on Christmas. "You know, I'm usually a one and done kinda person. But I could do this a lot more. Tonight, even."

Megan laughed, and looked up at Ally. "I'm happy to have inspired your appetite."

"You inspired a lot more than just that." She captured Megan's mouth for a kiss she never wanted to end, doing everything in her power to savor the feeling of Megan's naked body pressed beneath hers, the manner in which their curves melded together perfectly, and how poignant it was to experience Megan's heartbeat against her chest. She would remember this night for the rest of her life and knew with unshakable certainty that she'd never look at the world the same way again. How could she when she'd been forever changed?

❖

Megan awoke to sunshine streaming in from the picture window across from her bed. Of course it would be a sunny morning. It had to be. The cheerful beams that nudged her awake were the only possible greeting on a day like this one. When her eyes had fluttered open a few minutes before, she found herself snuggled up to Allison's warm body from behind, inhaling the now very familiar scent of her shampoo, smiling, and closing her eyes again to absorb the wonderful moment. Bask in it.

The night before had been everything, exceeding her expectations. The newness, the chemistry, the off-the-charts lust, and that didn't even touch on the depth of feeling that swirled within her. She shook her head in awe of the heat they'd managed, which was usually something two people worked up to, once they knew each other's bodies well enough to act blindly. They shockingly hadn't needed the practice and fit together by perfect design. Her heart ached pleasantly at the memory of the tenderness. She brushed the thick blond hair off Allison's neck and placed a soft kiss there, already aroused from her glimpses of her naked body beneath Megan's sheets. At the same time, she didn't want to wake her, because she looked so much like an angel dropped to Earth. The decision was a war for the ages. Luckily, she didn't have to leave for that Saturday's wedding until lunchtime, given that it was just a few blocks away at the Adolphus. Low-stress travel for her.

She traced one finger along the skin from Allison's shoulder to her forearm. So incredibly smooth. Gorgeous skin. The sheet left Allison's right breast partially visible to just below the nipple. Megan inhaled at the perfection of its shape and continued to trace, this time the curve of Allison's breast. At the soft touch, Ally adjusted, pushing closer against Megan's touch. She kept her fingertips featherlight, circling the breast widely and then in smaller circles until she got closer and closer to the nipple. When Ally's breathing went noticeably shallow, Megan smiled. She was awake. She placed a slow kiss just below Ally's earlobe and pulled a soft murmur of appreciation as Ally's backside was pressed into Megan more firmly. "Good morning," Megan whispered only to see the corner of Ally's mouth turn up in a smile.

"Hi, you," Allison said quietly. "What amazing things are you doing to me at this hour?"

"Just hoping to wake you up a little. Slowly, of course. No rush."

Because she couldn't seem to stop touching Allison, Megan slid her arm beneath Ally's for better access. She cupped the breast from behind and did the same on the other side. This allowed her to pull Ally against her, which shot up her own want several notches. As she massaged Ally's breasts, pushing her back against her body, Ally's hips began to rock subtly. Megan knew the cue. She pinched her nipples, and Allison gasped, squeezing Megan's wrist and then encouraging the circular motion, silently asking for more. She slid the sheet down Ally's body, exposing more of her beauty. Holding their position, she trailed one hand lower, gliding her fingers along the skin of Allison's rib cage, the small swell of her stomach, to the spot between her legs, where she slid her fingers between damp folds. Ally whimpered, rocking against her hand, slowly and then quicker. Megan held her around the waist with one arm and went to work between Allison's legs, exploring, touching, teasing, listening to the amazing soft sounds of pleasure Allison offered. Finally, with two fingers, she slid into warmth and found a steady rhythm that Allison matched. She kept her eyes on Ally, watching what she could see of her face. Her eyes were closed. Her lips parted. Her breathing ragged. When she cried out and went taut, Megan held her tighter, slowing her movement, bringing her down from the heights of pleasure slowly until Ally finally went limp in her arms.

"Mornings at your place deliver," Allison finally blurted.

Megan laughed and turned Ally to face her. "This one is unique."

"Ooh, good answer."

They shared a kiss, and Allison stared into her eyes. She seemed so relaxed, happy. "People are getting married today."

"They are. Romance is in the air. Henry and Frederick. They have good taste and the wedding should be fantastic as long as the venue remembers our food-allergic guests. There are six of all varying types."

"Wow."

"My job is to keep them alive and away from tonight's shellfish."

"I have faith in you." A pause. "When will I see you again? I hate sending you away to work. We should just stay right here."

Megan smiled and enjoyed being wanted because she wanted right back. "As soon as humanly possible. You can stay here if you'd like. In this very bed. Or the living room. Kitchen. My place is yours. Or you can leave and come back tonight. You can also summon me to your place like royalty. Send an owl with a telegram and a smile. Smoke signals work. I'm at attention."

"How about I check in with you later and see how you feel?"

"I can already tell you. After a wedding, I'm always exhausted and starving. I inhale junk food, and it's not pretty in the slightest. A messy plate of nachos is my favorite. There will be cheese all over my face, which I think is what you were requesting to see last night. The dark side. Have I mentioned that I love to share nachos?"

Ally laughed. "You did not."

"Well, that's how I'll feel. Starving. Messy. Generous."

"A great combo because I'm someone who accepts nacho handouts freely and without guilt."

"A kindred nacho spirit? How does this keep getting better? Speaking of food, want some breakfast? I feed people here, too. In fact, I have a waffle maker that will knock your socks off."

"I have no socks." She glanced beneath the sheets. "No clothing at all, it seems. You share nachos, cook food, and steal clothes."

"And I'm not ashamed."

Megan sat up and slipped out of bed. She watched as Allison's gaze roamed her body, her arm tucked behind her head to aid her viewing. It sent a lovely flutter as she found her robe.

"Your body," Allison said with a shake of her head. She covered her eyes briefly. "God. Just look at you."

"That sounds like a positive endorsement. Meet me in the kitchen in fifteen?"

Ally appeared in five wearing pink and white striped shorts and a top. Satin. "Aww. You brought pajamas to this sleepover. Cute ones."

"Feels silly now given what I know, but yes."

"Well, you're always welcome to my clothes, you know."

"You said always."

"Mm-hmm." She poured the batter into the waffle maker.

Allison eased herself onto a barstool across from her and rested her chin in her hand with a grin. "That means the future. You're projecting more sleepovers."

"Yes." Megan paused, set the empty bowl on the counter. "I heard it, too. The future. There. I said it, again. It's what I want."

"Good."

They shared a smile and enjoyed the happy silence as she made them both breakfast. Midway through, she caught Allison staring intently at her robe, which, as she worked, had fallen partially open. She didn't bother adjusting it, enjoying the attention. They ate together at the kitchen table as Megan peppered her with all the details of what her job at a standard wedding entailed, all the while aware of the pleasant feeling that she'd had sex the night before. Still tingly and little bit sore, in the best sense.

"And then there's whatever band or DJ we're working with the day of. While they're announcing the first dance and hopefully playing the agreed upon song, the event staff should be slicing the formally cut cake, so we can distribute it immediately following the toast. At least that's my preferred order. Other planners surely work differently."

"I have no idea how you keep everything straight," Allison said, cutting into her second waffle. "All those dangling tasks would drive me mad. Like a game of Whac-A-Mole."

Megan laughed. "I think you just summed up my job. I play event

Whac-A-Mole for a living." She distantly wondered if talking about weddings tugged at Allison, given that she'd just been in the midst of planning one for herself. She tried not to think about it, but that was hard. Surely, it was just as hard for Ally.

"Hey, you. Where did you just go?" Allison asked, placing her hand on top of Megan's and giving it an affectionate shake. "A million miles away all of a sudden."

"Oh. Sorry. I'm right here," Megan said, brightening again. "Just lost in memories of last night." Not a total lie. She was that, too.

Allison set down her fork, her cheeks coloring pink. There was a noticeable pause before she dived in. "I'm not wrong, am I? In thinking that it was...good? Between us."

Megan popped a bite of waffle into her mouth and smiled at Ally around it. "Mm-hmm. It was."

"I can't tell if you're being real with me right now, which you totally can be because I'm so ridiculously new at all this that I'm confident there's room for improvement in terms of, ahem, skill level, but I'm highly motivated."

"New at what exactly?" Megan squinted, feigning confusion.

Allison took a minute. "Sex." Her eyes went wide with accusation. "You know exactly what, too."

"I just like seeing you blush. Say it again, so I can watch you go all red."

"Sex." This time came with confidence.

"Now that's nice." She pointed with her fork. "So was last night. And this morning. And this moment. In fact, *nice* is a dumb as hell word for it because it's so much better than that. Fantastic is more like it. Highly memorable. Another waffle?"

Ally laughed. "No, no. I'm already so full. But I'll take to heart the word *fantastic*. I might put it on my fridge in colorful magnets."

"Well, you'd be entirely deserving. You earned those colors."

As Megan washed their dishes while Ally cleared the table, she knew the transparent thing to do would be to mention Brent's visit the day before. She didn't want to upset Allison in the midst of their date, but this morning felt like an opportune time.

"Hey, I do need to tell you something." She turned off the water and met Allison's eyes. "Brent stopped by my office yesterday."

"Oh. He did?" Allison took a moment, her face clouded with concern and then defeat, like a child at the zoo when someone let the air out of her balloon. "What did he say? I'm sorry he did that."

"It's okay. I think he's feeling worried that maybe your time away from him is turning into more. He thought you'd have come back to him by now."

Silence. "Oh." No mention of whether or not she planned to. That hurt. After last night, Megan didn't really see Allison moving in that direction, but she couldn't seem to shake the fear from the recesses of her mind. Anything could happen here, and she needed to be ready for it. Emotionally.

To cover the lack of reassurance, Megan pressed on. "He asked me to back off."

"You're kidding."

"No."

Allison came around the counter until she stood facing Megan. "I don't want you to back off, just so we're clear." Her blue eyes searched Megan's in earnest, and she believed her. Part of her relaxed. *Part.*

"Okay. It helps to hear that from you." She wanted to push. She wanted to say that she needed more reassurance if she was going to let herself go where her feelings were so desperately tugging her. She was falling for Allison faster than she'd ever fallen before, and that was a very dangerous prospect. This was not the kind of scenario Megan would have planned or wanted for herself, but she focused on the fact that Ally was worth it. Every day they spent with each other showed her that. She needed to stay strong and hang in there because waking up next to Allison had been everything she'd ever wanted.

"I can imagine his visit probably rattled you. But I hope it didn't scare you away. Because I'm not scared."

Okay, that helped. "No?"

Allison went up on tiptoe and placed a soft kiss on Megan's lips. "No."

But she *was* scared, more than she was willing to admit. It wasn't a feeling she was comfortable or familiar with, leaving her grappling with her own thoughts, too unnerved to divulge her fears to Allison. Too embarrassed to admit to being *that girl*. "Do you hear from him much?"

"Um, some. He's texted a couple of times, checked in casually, but hasn't broached the subject of the breakup. Honestly, because of that I thought he was doing well."

"I'm not sure that's the case."

"Huh." Allison seemed struck, upset even. It made perfect sense that she'd care about his feelings. Megan couldn't begrudge her that. "He's always so confident. It's strange to think of him struggling with anything."

Megan smiled. "Yeah, well, you're not just anything. You're Allison, and you matter a lot. To both of us apparently."

"I wonder if I should reach out."

Megan winced. "I'm afraid that might fuel the fire."

"Yeah, me, too." She seemed dejected, as if sitting in front of an advanced puzzle she had no ability to solve.

"But listen to me, time will help heal, and all of this is going to work out. You can't control Brent or his emotions. All you can do is manage what's going on here." She touched Allison's heart with her palm, and Allison covered it with her hand.

"That's what I'm trying desperately to do, and right about now, I'm feeling damn successful."

"I like hearing that," Megan said, grinning. She inclined her head in the direction of her bathroom. "I better hop in the shower and start making strides toward being a professional today. Interested?"

Allison's cheeks dusted pink again before her eyes darkened. She nodded and gave the tie in the front of Megan's robe a pull, prompting it to fall open. Megan passed her a look and a raised eyebrow.

"What? I'm helpful."

With a laugh, Megan turned and led the way to the best damn shower she'd ever taken.

CHAPTER THIRTEEN

Sometimes it was the quieter moments that spoke volumes, Megan had come to realize. The mundane times with Allison, where they simply existed in everyday domesticity, had become her favorites. Working side by side on the couch at night. Reading books together. Did the back and forth between their houses, the schlepping of overnight bags, after-dinner meetups, and late nights in bed steal from her time and sleep? Yes. In a big way. Did she care? Not in the least.

As she sat on Allison's couch going over her day planner as Allison constructed lesson plans for the upcoming six weeks of school, she took a moment to just absorb the perfection of the evening. Soft instrumental music played from the Bluetooth speaker in the corner. The windows were cracked, letting the cooler winter air sneak in.

"Are you busy this weekend?" she asked impulsively.

Allison looked up, taking a moment to pull herself out of the fourth grade and into the present. "Uh, let me think. I have a shift at the Nutcase, but nothing other than that. Are you asking me out?"

Megan laughed. "I am most definitely doing that." She chewed the inside of her lip, realizing she was about to take a rather large leap. "Hear me out. I'm going to see my parents in Corpus Christi and thought, I don't know, that maybe…you'd like to come." She hurried with the next part, already selling it. "They live near the beach. It's really pretty. I think you'd love it, actually. You could see where I grew up. Meet the important people who made it happen."

"You're dangling the beach as bait?"

She stared into blue eyes that danced. "I do what I have to do."

"For the record, more time with you is all you need to dangle, but the beach is certainly a bonus, as is meeting your parents." She seemed to work a brief equation in her head. "I bet I could persuade one of the other employees to cover for me at the store."

Megan crawled down the couch, eliminating the space between them. "Does that mean we're taking our first road trip together? I like to sing really loud in the car and sometimes even direct my singing to the drivers of *other* cars. They love my work. A passenger offers a whole new audience."

"You can sing your heart out." Allison laughed and leaned in to Megan, who was still on all fours. She hovered just shy of her mouth. "You pick the music. I'll pick the snacks. Kissing is optional, but I vote for at least some."

"The hell it's optional," Megan said, capturing Ally's mouth. "Listen to me. You're so cute when you work. I keep staring at you instead of my planner."

Allison blinked, almost as if she was surprised to hear it. "I had no idea that I had you…preoccupied."

Megan stole another lingering kiss. "You have me wet," she whispered in her ear, "and you haven't even moved from your spot on the couch." She pulled her face from next to Allison's ear and met her gaze, which went decidedly dark. Ally opened her mouth and closed it. Yep, that seemed to have gotten her attention. Allison calmly set her laptop on the end table and slid down onto the couch, pulling Megan's body on top of hers. Wordlessly, Ally grabbed her face and pulled it down, meeting Megan's lips in a hungry kiss and murmuring her appreciation as Megan settled her weight on top. She was fairly accustomed to Allison's sounds, and that was a good one. "Wow, that was all I had to say?" Megan nipped at the spot just under Allison's jaw just as Ally tugged Megan's shirt up and over her head. Megan sat up, giving Allison access to what she knew she wanted.

"Yep. That did it. Those words." Her palms found Megan's breasts immediately. "Oh, hello."

"Filing that sentence away."

Allison laughed, her eyes never leaving Megan's breasts. "You have to mix it up. That's the fun part."

Megan closed her eyes and swallowed at the wash of need that hit as Ally pulled the cups of her bra down and caught a nipple in her mouth. "Challenge accepted."

As they lay in Ally's bed an hour later, exhausted in the happiest sense, Megan began making plans for their weekend, imagining Allison meeting her parents, seeing the place she grew up. She dared to allow herself to imagine Christmases there, or visits in the summer. Maybe they'd rent a little place on the beach for a couple of weeks when Ally was out of school. Megan could work remotely. She trusted her staff, and maybe it was time she gave them a little bit more autonomy.

"You're smiling," Allison said, tracing her cheek. "The moonlight gave you away."

Megan turned to the window and the great big moon that hung over everything as if offering its blessing. For tonight, she allowed herself to turn off her concern, silence her worry, and concentrate on what she could control—the here and now. She had to say, the present was pretty damn awesome, and why not let herself bask in that for a while? "I'm just really happy right now."

Allison, her blond hair splayed across the pillow, her face glowing in the dim blue light, beamed back at her. "Me, too. Really happy. I mean not alone with you on a beach happy, but pretty damn close."

Megan laughed. "Soon." She placed a soft kiss on Allison's nose and pulled her close. "You're gonna love it."

❖

The sun against that clear blue sky was gorgeous. Ooh la la. She could get used to the sound of those waves, too. Allison had been to Corpus Christi a couple of times as a kid. It was half a day in the car and an easy vacation for parents who couldn't exactly afford Disney World. But knowing it was where Megan grew up had her seeing it with fresh eyes. They'd paused on their way into town for a short walk on the beach to say hello. As they walked barefoot through wet sand, the tide tickling their feet, Megan, who had her hair up with little wisps flying in the breeze, smiled at her.

"I always relax the second my toes touch the sand. They know I'm home."

Allison looked out at wave after wave that seemed to be rolling in for miles. "It's so peaceful out here." In the few minutes they'd walked hand-in-hand, they'd only passed a couple of other people. The day wasn't exactly warm, and the chill had them both in zip-up hoodies, but the sunlight had certainly shown up to welcome them to town.

"I used to come to the beach to sort my thoughts out," Megan said. "I'd pick out a spot in the sand, take a seat, and just gaze out into the ocean until it all seemed to settle down in my head and get quiet. That's when I could see the world, my problems, for what they were and make a clear-headed decision."

Allison smiled. "I imagine you were sixteen going on thirty-five."

"My mom used to say something similar."

"Good. I can't wait to meet her. Harriet, right?"

"Harriet and Richard. But everyone calls him Rich. The dog is Lefty, named for the direction he chose to chase his tail. Mom cooks the most, but Dad is better at it. We don't point this out, but it's generally understood. They'll have a room set up for you out of courtesy but will turn a blind eye to us shacking up after they've gone to bed."

Allison's eyes went wide. "We're going to sneak around?"

"We are."

"And you're sure that's okay."

"I am."

"That might be kinda…hot."

Megan stared at her in all seriousness. "Everything with us is. I've stopped being surprised."

Allison smiled. As on fire as she was around Megan, she truly enjoyed that it went both ways. She'd never felt more powerful than when she could affect Megan with just a subtle look, a touch, or when she wasn't even trying. She'd watch as Megan's eyes changed, and she got that look on her face that said she was turned-on. It had made all the difference in Allison's recent history. She carried herself differently, picked out different clothes, even. The newfound confidence was liberating in a way she never could have known. She now wore heels on occasion, for God's sake, feeling sexy and worthy of the look. Her! Allison Hale, little sister to the beautiful and talented Betsy, was a sassy minx with a really hot sex life and a wonderful woman to hold her hand on the beach. How? She still couldn't fathom it all.

She'd been looking forward to today ever since Megan had extended the invitation. She'd searched far and wide and found the perfect bouquet to present to Megan's parents, hoping they liked her. When Harriet Kinkaid opened the door with a warm smile and outstretched arms, she knew her wish was likely to come true.

"Well, hello, visitors from the north!" she said, embracing first Megan and then Allison. "And who is this?" Mrs. Kinkaid asked her daughter, accepting the floral bouquet with a grateful gasp. "Someone thoughtful. That's for sure."

"Mama, meet Allison." Her mother didn't hesitate and went in for a second hug.

"You're just adorable is what you are. Come in and meet the hubby. He's playing golf on his fake green and pretending it's the Masters."

"So just another weekend around here," Megan told her with a wink.

Mrs. Kinkaid hadn't been lying. They found Megan's dad in the living room, putting on a miniature stretch of fake grass, wearing an entire golf getup, complete with a lime argyle sweater and a cap with a little orange ball on top. He held his arms to the side and grinned. "I got all dressed up for you."

"Dad, you did this to embarrass me, and you know it," Megan said with a laugh and placed a kiss on his cheek.

"Never," her father said and extended his hand. "Rich Kinkaid, famous golfer in the living room."

"Allison Hale, mere schoolteacher." She fought the urge to curtsy, already liking these people very much. The two-story home screamed of warmth but also fun. A glass owl full of lollipops sat on the counter that separated the living room from the kitchen and also created a feeling of a window connecting the two spaces. The family room was medium sized with a couch and two comfortable looking forest-green armchairs, where she could imagine Megan's parents watching the news at night, side-by-side. Family photos lined the entryway, and Ally couldn't wait to steal a moment to check out little Megan, who probably carried an attaché to elementary school. This was going to be fun.

"Let me show you to the guest room, Allison, and then we girls can have margaritas and a chat outside. That old guy can join us if he wants."

"Shall I bring my mariachi music?" they heard him call as they made their way down the hall.

"Not if you want to stay," Harriet hollered back.

Harriet showed her to a quaint guest room decorated with a blue and white quilt and a gray chair in the corner. As she placed her bag on the floor, Harriet motioned for her to follow them. "You gotta see our girl's room. I haven't changed it much since she left home at eighteen for Baylor." She'd said the words with a great deal of pride, and when they entered the room two doors down the hall, Ally understood why. The bookshelf across from the bed with the pink comforter was jam-packed with trophies and medals of all shapes and sizes. There was hardly enough room to hold all of them.

"Oh, man. Look at all the accolades," Allison remarked and whirled around to catch Megan's highly embarrassed face.

"I liked to participate."

"She was a hard worker," Harriet said. "Stayed up much later than her dad and me, studying, practicing, whatever she had to do. She didn't just participate—she *won*."

"I'm not at all surprised," Allison said, having every suspicion about Megan's drive confirmed on this one shelf. "Oh, and a yearbook?" She picked up the checkered book positioned in the middle of the desk.

"Don't you dare," Megan said. "I was still figuring out hair products, and you can't unsee what's in there."

"I love your hair. Soft and silky."

"You can thank my hot iron and conditioner." She pointed at the yearbook. "That girl had neither."

"That sounds like all the more reason to meet her." They spent the next half hour poring over Megan's school photos and memorabilia, Harriet acting as the perfect tour guide. Megan's abject embarrassment grew by the moment, delicious icing on the cake. Later, they enjoyed cocktails on the patio before a dinner of taco salad and fresh cantaloupe from the local farmers' market.

"You guys know how to host a gathering," Ally said, as she helped Harriet with the dishes. Megan and her dad were in the backyard catching up, and it gave her and Harriet some time to talk.

"So, Megan tells me you two have really hit it off."

"We have." Allison smiled. "I feel that way, too."

"She also says this is new for you?"

She took a moment, understanding Harriet's meaning. "She's the first woman I've ever dated, if that's what you mean."

She nodded. "It is. Just know that I applaud you and your journey. Admire you even."

Allison accepted a plate to dry. "Thank you. That means a lot."

"And your family is supportive?"

"For the most part, yes. My sister is working on it, but my parents have been great."

"That's important. I know what it's like to catch your family off guard. When I brought Megan's father to our family picnic, there were a few eyebrows. Some disapproving mumbling. Who's this white guy?" She waved it off. "They got over it quick. Love us both now."

"I hadn't thought about that. I guess when your family has an idea of what your life is going to be like, it takes some adjusting when it doesn't go that way."

"Give that sister some time."

"I will."

"One more thing." Harriet hesitated, and it was clear there was something on her mind. She kept her eyes on the margarita glass she washed, her tone delicate. "I don't know if you've noticed, but my daughter doesn't take a lot of big risks without guarantees. She'll jump in with both feet if she's confident in her chances of success, but when she's not..." Harriet met her gaze.

"She holds back."

She passed Allison a warm smile that let her know her words were meant to help, not hurt. "She gets timid, which is not a place she's comfortable, and then she backs away altogether."

Allison nodded, internalizing Harriet's meaning. She'd wondered more than once about the depth of Megan's feelings for her and what she wanted from all of this down the line. While it was a conversation she thought would come naturally, maybe she would need to be the one to take the lead. To let Megan know that she was in this and happily so, in spite of the tumultuous backdrop. "Thank you for the insight. I can definitely use it." She peered out the window to see Megan and her father laughing. Megan's bright eyes lit up with mirth, and everything in Ally tightened pleasantly. The world felt so different now that she knew Megan was in it, and getting to see her childhood home, meet her parents, and experience where she came from only added texture and layers to an already impressive woman.

After a lively night of conversation and a game of Spades played at the four person kitchen table, during which Megan's parents soundly trounced them not once but four times, it was time for bed. Allison slipped into a pair of gray sleep shorts and a light yellow T-shirt, having thoroughly enjoyed her day. With only two doors separating them, it was torturous not to be able to wrap her arms around Megan, kiss her neck, her lips, her breasts. She sighed dreamily at just the thought.

Meet me at my place immediately, a text message on her phone beckoned. *Megan*. She smiled, held the phone to her chest, nervous about breaking the rules and dying to do just that. Were they even rules? Megan didn't think so. And while she wasn't sure herself, she'd been given the guest room, and grown woman or not, she respected Megan's parents. Her body had its own argument, though. Surely, they'd understand if she sneaked out for a little alone time with Megan. The room was likely just for show, to make everyone comfortable.

Come HERE, a second text message read. The emphasis sent a chill, and Allison was not strong enough to fight against all caps. She cracked her door and peeked out, gazing down the dark, still hallway. No voices. No movement. Just the quiet hum of the heater and a slash of lamplight beneath Megan's bedroom door. Then as if there wasn't a moment to spare, she scampered—yes, scampered—from the guest room to Megan's, bursting through the door with wide eyes.

Megan chuckled. "Hello, Speed Racer. Someone chasing you?"

"I never sneaked out as a teenager. I didn't have anywhere to sneak out to, but I still never did it."

"I did," Megan said.

She stood in the doorway as Megan approached from where she sat on the bed in a white and blue striped nightshirt with four large buttons. It brushed the tops of her thighs as she walked, and Ally felt it between her own. The small lamp by the bed was the only illumination, but she caught the look in Megan's eyes just before she captured Allison's mouth in a toe curling lip-lock. Her hands were immediately beneath Megan's nightshirt from behind, and to her amazement, she had nothing on underneath. "You're naked under here," she managed. "I'm cupping your naked ass."

"Mm-hmm," Megan murmured against her mouth, pressing against her deliciously.

Allison's hands dipped lower, touching Megan intimately from behind, pulling a sharp intake of air from Megan. God. She was wet and ready, and what was Ally supposed to with that just a short walk from Megan's parents? She was going to hell, but damn if she wasn't going to have a good time on the way. She pressed Megan against the wall gently, careful not to make noise, lifted the nightshirt to her waist, and stroked her softly between her legs as they kissed, Megan's hips rocking in rhythm. As Megan got close, Allison broke the kiss and looked down, marveling at the sight, her hand moving in and out, taking this other person to heights of pleasure. She was drunk on lust, power, and satisfaction. To her surprise, it didn't take long, and Megan strained and gripped Allison's shoulders tightly as she came.

Then finally, "You're really good at up against a wall," Megan whispered.

Allison laughed quietly. "My first time."

Megan smiled. "Never would have known it. It rivals against the kitchen counter." She leaned in close to Ally's ear. "Get in bed with me."

"Yeah?" Her legs felt a little shaky, and the tickle of Megan's breath caused her to ache pleasantly between her thighs.

She allowed herself to be tugged toward the double bed with the pink comforter and slipped beneath the cool sheets next to Megan, who didn't hesitate to lift, shift, or displace her clothing to gain access to her body. Allison turned herself over to Megan, letting her explore, take her time, and quite simply drive her mad. She bit the inside of her cheek rather than allow a single cry to escape her lips when the pleasure washed over her, bold and bright.

Allison threw an arm over her eyes. "We just did that in your childhood bedroom."

"Nothing childlike about it now."

She peeked out from behind her arm to find Megan looking rather accomplished. "Another trophy for the shelf?"

Megan lit up at the idea. "It would be my favorite of the bunch."

❖

Megan was on an extended high. The trip home was turning out to be better than she'd even dared hope. Things had felt different between her and Allison from the moment they drove out of Dallas, almost as if they'd left every last complication in the rearview mirror and could just…be. Exist. Enjoy each other. They'd stolen looks across her parents' dinner table, laughed happily unencumbered, and Megan found herself focusing on the present, no longer preoccupied with what might lie ahead. To say it was relaxing would be an understatement.

They decided to drive down to the beach the following afternoon, and her mother had insisted on packing them a picnic lunch. It wasn't exactly warm out, but they'd donned hooded sweatshirts and jeans and headed out.

Megan spread out a blue blanket for them as Allison hugged herself and looked out over the water. "I can't believe all of this was in your backyard growing up."

She let her gaze settle on the peaceful horizon. "I took it for granted. Not anymore. It calms me whenever I come back to the water. Tropical vacations are my favorite."

Allison joined her on the blanket and sat close, looping her arm through Megan's and snuggling against her. "Do you think we'll take one together someday?"

"One? If I have my way, we'll take many. See the world. We'll go on cruises. Luxury jaunts to Jamaica. Greece. The South of France."

"We're so fancy in this fantasy. I'll need a new wardrobe."

Megan looked at her, meeting those fathomless blue eyes. "I mean it. Those are the kinds of things I want us to do. Someday."

The smile on Allison's face faded, almost as if this had all become very real. "Then we have to do it. Jamaica first." The smile reappeared. "I'd die if I got to go to Jamaica. I'd sip rum from a coconut. Do they let you do that there, or am I falling for the cliché on TV commercials?"

Megan slid her right leg behind Allison and pulled her in, her chest to Allison's back. Ally rested against her as she sun shone brightly on them, creating a small patch of warmth. "We'd find a way. Coconut drinks or bust. Plus, you can meet my extended family. They're incredibly friendly, but bossy about food. My great-uncle won't let anyone near his outdoor grill. He'll toil over his meats all day, and let me tell you, they deliver."

"I like him already. Maybe after, we'd find a nice little club and slow dance."

"And dinner on a beautiful balcony, overlooking the beach at sunset."

"Oh, I like that one. A cabana by the pool."

"Champagne room service. With strawberries."

"I'm having second thoughts. I don't want to move from this spot."

Megan tightened her arms and could identify with the sentiment. It was nice here. With this woman in her arms, and the sea air gracing her lungs, she was more than content to never move again. They had the stretch of beach mostly to themselves. Occasionally, a jogger or dog walker made their way past, but the real action was closer to town. She watched the next series of waves roll in, the white frothy foam encroaching and retreating. In an hour, it would be on top of them if they weren't careful. "So, what do you think of my parents? Don't hold back. Let me have it."

"I think they're adorable, especially the way they bicker and then pause and laugh about it. That's how a marriage should be. At least I think so. You have to *like* the other person, not just love them. Wanting to rip their clothes off is the best kind of reward, though." She sighed dreamily.

"I can't argue there." A pause. "Will I get to meet your parents?"

A breeze hit and lifted Ally's hair. "Yeah, of course."

It was early. Megan could admit that, and she hated how needy a question it was. "Good. No rush or anything. I was just curious."

"Fair warning, though. They're huge fans of Brent's. He could do no wrong in their eyes, so even if they've been incredibly supportive of my relationship with you, I'm sure they hold out hope—"

"For it to be Brent in the end."

Allison winced. "Yeah."

"Everyone loves Brent. I feel like that should be a TV show."

Allison glanced back and kissed her cheek softly. "They just don't know you is all. Everyone who does adores you, including me."

"But I'm not a Carmichael."

"Neither am I. I'm pretty sure that's not a requirement in life."

"Still." She stared out at the ocean, hating that she'd let their issues follow them to the beach, of all places, and banishing the insecurities from her brain. "You know what? I don't want to talk about him any more today. I want to enjoy this time with you, and remember it always."

Allison pulled out her phone and focused the camera on them. "Then that's exactly what we are going to do." Megan snuggled her chin over Allison's shoulder and smiled softly into the lens. "Captured.

Forever. There," Ally said, reviewing the photo, which had come out as a wonderful representation of their afternoon.

They looked happy, carefree, and like a really striking couple, if she did say so herself. Megan marveled. "You know what? We look like we go together," she said, running her finger over the image, incredibly pleased. "I love it."

Allison turned back to her, the sunlight illuminating her hair. "Because we do."

Megan leaned in for a kiss, and when her lips met Allison's, she closed her eyes and savored every second. Today was a very good day. "Let's eat."

CHAPTER FOURTEEN

When Allison pulled into her parents' driveway that next week for her brother-in-law Dell's birthday dinner, she paused at the atrocious new addition to the yard. Placing her car in park, she gaped. What in the world? She approached the *for sale* sign that stood in front of the one-story home with the winding sidewalk slowly, not believing it was real. She made an accusatory circle around it as she let the realization settle. Her parents were selling her childhood home? No, no, no. That was the porch where she'd sipped hot chocolate when it rained. She'd Rollerbladed through that garage, making lap after lap while listening to the Spice Girls. She'd not heard a word about selling from anyone and was desperate to find out why and, more importantly, if she could change their minds. Not seeing her sister's car in the driveway yet meant she'd have a moment alone with her parents to sort out what was going on. She stalked up the sidewalk, let herself inside, and found her mother fluffing the couch cushions in the living room Allison now wanted to weep over.

"Hey there, sweetheart," her mother said. "Hand me that one?"

Allison picked up a wayward cushion and tossed it to her mother. "So are you going to tell me what's going on? I'm freaking out over here."

Her mother straightened and held out her hands to the room. "We're celebrating! That's what's going on." A happy birthday banner hung across the mantel above the rock fireplace, and several balloons hung in various locations around the living room. In the kitchen, she could see a cake for Dell. None of which was the point.

"I'm talking about the sign in your yard. Mom, what in the world? Talk to me. Please."

Her mother quirked her lips to the side, as if still in party setup mode. It was a cop-out, a way for her mother to act like nothing big was going on, and the most important thing in the world was which ice-cream scooper to pull out. "Oh, that. Well, we decided it would be best if we downsized. You kids are grown up and out on your own. What do we need with this much space?"

But the home was modest, not at all luxurious, and they'd put the extra rooms to good use. An office for her parents and a guest room for when the aunts and uncles came to visit. "I just feel like this is coming out of left field. You've never once mentioned wanting to move or downsize."

"Just because I haven't mentioned it to you doesn't mean it's not something we've talked about on our own."

Panic struck. They were serious about this. "What aren't you telling me?"

Her mother opened her mouth to respond, but a voice from the kitchen beat her to it. "We can't afford this place anymore. After a second and third mortgage, we don't have any more recourse. It's time to find something cheaper."

Ally stared. Numb. Sad. "I knew things were tight, but I had no idea they were this bad." She turned to her father, because he was the one telling it to her straight. "What about the Dash Bar licensing? If you can just hang on a little bit longer then—"

"The Carmichaels aren't taking or returning our calls any longer, and I get the feeling that's not likely to change. Deal is dead. Just how it goes in business sometimes."

She swallowed, and a sinking feeling came over her. Her limbs went heavy almost as if she was being pulled underwater. Was this because of her?

"This is not your fault." As if reading her thoughts, her mother rushed in. "I don't want you thinking that for a moment, okay? Sometimes things just don't work out even when you really want them to. Part of life." But she looked sad, and that made Allison feel worse. She swallowed, her jaw tight.

Because of course this was Dalton Carmichael's vindictive response to her walking away from a marriage to his son. He was a powerful man, and when you were in his good graces, he showed you the best side of himself. When you weren't, he reminded you of what he could do. She'd heard him tell stories over dinner of going to war with the people that crossed him, as his family nodded their approval, chuckling about his ability to turn on a dime. She'd sat there slightly horrified by his bragging but knew enough to sip her champagne politely and discuss it with Brent later.

"You know that's not the way I do business, right?" Brent had said, loosening his tie once they'd arrived back at his place one night after a particularly eye-opening gathering at his parents' house, during which Dalton had regaled them all with a story about one of their vice presidents and how he'd not only been fired for missing an important deadline for the company, but they'd arranged to have him evicted from his apartment building that same day by gently pulling a few strings.

"I know you're not, but wow."

"I know." He sat on the couch with a thud. "It's always been this way. He's my dad, and I love him, but he can be an asshole when he wants to be. He's got a vindictive streak. We got the same treatment as kids."

"I'm really sorry to hear that." She sat next to him and took his hand.

"When my baseball team lost the state championships my senior year of high school, he didn't talk to me for two weeks because one of my errors led to the loss."

Her heart had broken for him then, and it broke for her parents now, who'd worked so hard and thought they'd finally arrived at a little success. And then she'd gone and ruined it. Had it been selfish of her? She wasn't unhappy with Brent. She just wasn't sure that was the path for her, and with each day that passed, it seemed she'd been right. It didn't make her guilt any easier. She didn't have a chance to say much more because the door opened and Betsy and Dell arrived with shouted hellos, and everything shifted to the celebration.

"Glad you could make it," Betsy said, eyeing Allison. She'd only exchanged brief messages with Betsy since their run-in outside Allison's home, but to her credit, she flashed Ally a friendly smile.

Allison sent one back, hoping they could reconcile. "I wouldn't miss it for anything."

Betsy looked around. "Feels a little strange without Brent here. Like we're down one."

And there they were again. "I know. Strange for me, too." Brent would have immediately shaken Dell's hand, and the two would have been off, talking loudly about business and sports and who knows what else. They'd always gotten along, happy to be future brothers-in-law. Though she stood strong on her choice, it felt a little empty there without him. She could admit that. She imagined that was normal when things were still new. While her parents made a big deal over Dell on his big day, she turned quietly to Betsy. "Did you know about the house?"

She nodded, her face solemn. "They searched for another way. Talked to the bank a hundred times, but they're just too far behind to recover without selling."

Allison nodded grimly. "I had no idea things were already to this point."

Betsy raised a shoulder and said in her sweetest, most passive-aggressive voice, "All you have to do is ask. I do it all the time."

More guilt.

She'd been a little caught up in her own life lately, and though she still pitched in at the store on weekends, she should have inquired more about how things were going. She felt awful. Midway through the gathering, when her mother slipped into the kitchen to take the potato casserole out of the oven, she followed her and pulled her into a tight hug in the moment they had alone.

"Well, what is this for?" her mother asked, returning the squeeze.

"I'm just so sorry things have been difficult lately. I should have done more to help. Been around. I don't know." She released her mom and met her eyes.

"No. That's nonsense. You've got your own life. We're going to be just fine. Like a couple of cats. We always land on our feet, your dad and I." But there was a hollowness in the way she said it that let Allison know this time was different. Her mom was worried underneath the bravado, and now so was she. This was new ground.

She told Megan about it the next night while they snuggled on her couch. "I wish there was some way I could help. I can't believe Dalton is doing this to them, all to get back at me. I mean, I *can*, but still."

Megan sighed. "I hate it, too." But there was something else in her voice. She was distracted or closed off. Something. Allison turned in her arms. "Are you okay?" She touched her cheek. "You seem off."

Megan pushed herself up into a sitting position, and Allison followed her. "I don't want to add to your stress, but I'm afraid the plot thickens."

Allison frowned. "What do you mean?"

"Soiree received notice that our services would no longer be needed for the BeLeaf fundraiser scheduled for late spring, or any future events, for that matter. They're paying out the portion of the spring contract they're obligated for, but our relationship is over beyond that."

"You're kidding." Allison's mouth fell open. "I'm so sorry. Is this a large loss?"

"They were our biggest corporate client, and with the number of events we handle for them annually, yeah, it's going to hurt some." She shook her head. "Doesn't matter. We'll just try to cover with more weddings. Smaller events. We have the demand."

Allison stood, needing room, because her thoughts were blazing, leaving her unsure which of the many trajectories to follow. She dropped her head back as she paced. "What else?"

Megan watched Allison cautiously. "I was going to use a *wait, there's more* voice, but you beat me to it."

"Fantastic." Allison nodded as she stared up at her ceiling. "Lay it on me."

Megan hesitated, clearly not wanting to add to her distress.

She made the *give it to me* gesture and nodded. "This is the time."

"I sit on the board for the Women in Business Association."

"I remember you mentioning that."

"Right. We do a variety of things, but the one most important to me is the assistance we provide to women who are struggling to find employment. We set them up with clothes for their interviews, coach them on what to expect, and prepare them for success at work when they're hired."

"Right. Incredibly valuable."

"Well, they asked me to step down this morning, without much of an explanation. The only thing I can come up with is—"

"Let me guess. The Carmichaels are big donors."

Megan smiled. "You spoiled the big reveal!"

Ally laughed, because what else could she do? Megan was

working hard to keep her delivery light when the situation was anything but. "That asshole. I'm so sorry. You're free to walk the hell away from me at any time. You really, really should, in fact. That's my expert advice because I'm apparently a wrecking ball. An assault on your professional life wasn't supposed to be part of the deal." She shook her head and squeezed her fists. "I'm so angry. At them. At myself for not knowing better."

Megan stood and came to her. "Don't be angry, especially not at yourself. You followed the proper channels. You were open and honest. No one should be forced into marriage." She kissed Allison's hand. "Look at me, okay?"

Allison did begrudgingly, guilt still flowing like water through a freshly broken dam.

Megan's eyes were friendly and focused when she met them, calming Allison's turbulence quickly. "Do you see me running because I lost a seat on a board? No. If a bridezilla can't rattle me, then the power-hungry Carmichael family can't. Do you know what I am going to do?"

Ally felt herself relent, smiling. "No clue. What? Don't TP their house."

"I'm going to raid your fridge and find us some rough-times ice cream. I know you bought some. I saw it the other day."

"I only have the regular kind." She stuck out her bottom lip like a kid.

Megan, who'd already raced into the kitchen and probably had the freezer door open, called back, "You're wrong. This is it! This is the perfect rough-times ice-cream, and there's also hot fudge in here, which means you understand life's principles. Congratulations!"

"Well, everyone should have hot fudge." She frowned, thinking about the sad people who didn't. "Are you staying tonight? Say yes."

After some beeps from the microwave, Megan came around the corner, carrying two bowls of ice cream topped with warm hot fudge, a comfort-laced salve. "I'll stay if you still want me to. I was planning on it before our depressing discussion." Megan punctuated the sentence with a smile for contrast, still trying to cheer Allison up. She wore calf-length leggings and a Baylor University sweatshirt that exposed part of her left shoulder, the one with the small mole. Ally was growing to love her collection of Megan details and was eager to add more.

"I want you to."

"Good. Then you have an overnight guest." She placed a soft kiss on Ally's lips and turned to her bowl, which was honest-to-God the best possible way to drown a difficult day and drain all the life out of its suckage.

They flipped on the TV to a mindless reality show that would allow them to decompress and not think too hard. Megan slid back on the couch and patted the spot in front of her. "Get over here, and let me take some of that tension off."

"You don't have to beckon me twice."

She nestled between Megan's legs and sighed in surrender when warm hands slipped onto her shoulder blades beneath her shirt and squeezed gently, releasing the pent-up tension. "How's the pressure? Okay?" Megan asked quietly.

"You'll have to ask someone else. I'm in a pleasure trance and refusing to come out."

She heard Megan chuckle quietly, and as they watched rich women vacation together and argue on a vapid TV show that was also the best show ever invented, Allison systematically began to discard her troubles, one muscle group at a time. The one thing she couldn't seem to escape, and thank God, was the effect Megan's touch had on her. Not only was she feeling looser, but warm and full of very recognizable sensations. Her body loved being touched by Megan and was responding. She had a feeling her cheeks were flushed, which seemed to match her now shallow breathing pattern and an inability to concentrate on the show. Megan's hands were at the small of her back, gently moving in circles with medium pressure. She closed her eyes and tried to enjoy the attention to her muscle groups, but the rest of her was jealous and wouldn't shut up.

Megan had gone quiet, lost in the show, or perhaps her thoughts. Her hands moved from Ally's back to her stomach, no longer applying pressure, just moving in lazy circles. Allison rolled her lips inward as those hands inched up her rib cage toward breasts that longed to be touched, fondled, held. Okay, maybe Megan hadn't gotten lost in the show. A shot of need hit low. She was wet. She wore no bra, something she was now thankful for. As Megan's hands found the undersides of her breasts, Ally sucked in air. She pressed her back against Megan, encouraging her with quiet murmurs. Instead of the overt attention she craved, Megan touched the center of her breasts with her fingertips, featherlight. Intoxicating, torturous, wonderful. She circled her nipples slowly, refusing to give more. Ally didn't hide what this was doing to her. Her fingernails dug into Megan's legs, bracing. She could hear the sound of her uneven breathing, and surely Megan could, too. Her hair was swept to one side, and warm lips slowly began to kiss the exposed skin. Languid. Megan was clearly all about taking her time. Megan's lips caught Ally's earlobe, pulling it into her mouth as she increased pressure on Allison's breasts, holding them firmly, lifting and releasing in rhythm with her mouth.

"Good God," Ally whispered. Her arousal was intense and spreading like a fire long out of control. She could scarcely form a thought in the midst of the pulsing ache between her legs that seemed to grow exponentially, moment by moment. Her thoughts were too hazy to piece together. "What are you doing to me?"

"I missed your body. That's all," Megan said, pulling her hands from beneath Allison's shirt and running her fingertips from Ally's knees up to her inner thighs. Allison was seconds from combustion. "Lie down." Megan's voice was husky, and the words were firm, a command. She eased back on the couch and watched as Megan slid the leggings she wore down to her ankles and off. Her panties were on the floor two seconds later. Megan was between her legs, holding them expertly in place. Warm lips kissed her intimately, and Ally thought she might levitate off the damn couch. She couldn't stop herself from pushing against Megan's mouth, asking for release already. Megan's tongue traced gentle circles, and Allison's hips rocked of their own accord. She was merely along for the ride, which she could tell would not be a long one. She covered Megan's hands with hers, and when Megan zeroed in on Allison's most sensitive spot, sucking softly, the pleasure ripped through her like a shooting star through the night sky. She heard her own voice cry out, not at all like her, but the powerful sensations that jolted her body from every nerve ending had taken her over and catapulted her into a new understanding of the word *orgasm*.

With that relief, Allison felt the stress and concern evaporate. In that moment, she was exactly where she was supposed to be, beneath the touch of this astonishing woman, who'd come to mean so much to her in such a short period of time. As each new ripple took its turn with her, she saw her life in sharp clarity and knew in her heart she'd followed her heart. Nothing had ever felt so right. With Megan, she fit. And she wasn't sure she'd ever fit before.

She threaded their fingers together on both hands as she floated back to Earth. "Is there a tip jar for the massage therapist?" She grinned. Megan laughed and slid alongside her on the couch, kissing her cheek.

"Not an official one, no."

She tipped Megan's face toward her and sought her mouth, sinking into it and reveling. "Then I'll have to get creative."

She watched as Megan's brown eyes darkened, sending goose bumps to Ally's already alert skin.

"Let's adjourn to the bedroom." Ally stood.

"I don't have to be asked twice," Megan said, allowing her arm to be tugged. That night, with a new shut-out-the-world attitude, Allison let go. She took liberties with each caress, boldly taking what she wanted and enjoying every inch of Megan's body. She wasn't shy. She followed every instinct she had, surprising even herself when she flipped Megan over and took her from behind. It turned into the most freeing experience of life.

"How do you feel?" Megan asked her later, as they lay facing each other, their limbs all tangled.

"I feel like me," Allison said honestly. There were quite a few consequences for claiming a new life for herself, ones that she'd never seen coming. But in the end, those things couldn't dictate who she was. Her heart knew. It had recognized Megan the moment she met her, even if it took her brain a little longer to catch on. And their connection continued to grow even right up to this moment. Her feelings bubbled and swirled, taking center stage.

"I could get lost in you," Megan said. "What if I already am?" She wasn't smiling when she said the words, which left Ally concerned. This was becoming a theme.

"I'll find you," she said softly, trailing her fingertips down Megan's back as she looked into moonlit eyes. She knew innately that, together, they could accomplish anything. They just needed their shot. With each passing day, her heart swelled and clung, until she knew beyond anything else that life was better with Megan at her side. The problem? She was beginning to wonder if Megan felt the same way.

❖

One month made a huge difference in business. Megan found that out the hard way. In that short amount of time, most of the business on Soiree's corporate side had dried up to crumbs. Clients were pulling out of contracts. Others were going with their competitors for annual events that had always belonged to Soiree.

Megan had known there could be further fallout from the Carmichaels after losing her seat on the board, but she'd clearly underestimated their reach. With the extra time, she'd devoted hours to expanding the bridal side of their business, and luckily, there seemed to be no shortage of women with big weddings to plan. Still. Her pride was hurt. She valued her position in the Dallas event planning space, and it seemed like the big guys no longer wanted her in the game. She'd always imagined that if anything got in her way, it would be the racial bias present in the elbow-rubbing circles of high society, not a war with the damn Carmichaels, of all people. But she'd been forced out, and that hurt. A lot.

She kept herself busy as much as possible and focused on the bright spots in her life. Her friendships, her existing clients, and Allison, who'd become not only her girlfriend, but her honest-to-goodness best friend as well. Though they'd spent Christmas apart with their respective families, their reunion was nothing short of historical. She'd never missed anyone more.

Nowadays, they rarely spent nights apart even if it meant Ally had to sneak away early to prepare for school or Megan got home late after personally working an event. She saw Brent Carmichael in passing at luncheons or events within the professional organizations they both belonged to. He was cordial—she'd give him that. In all honesty, she didn't credit him with the blackballing. It had Dalton Carmichael written all over it, and he had certainly kept his distance from Megan with the exception of a wedding she'd worked and he'd attended. When their gazes met during dinner, he'd simply raised a glass of champagne in her direction and smiled victoriously, sending a chill up her spine. He was making sure she understood his role in her recent struggles, happily claiming responsibility. She glanced away with a pit in her stomach and focused on her job.

The scope of the fallout had taken its toll, however, and it was hard to stay light on her feet. While Allison was everything she'd ever wanted in a partner, the ground beneath her felt precarious, and she had trouble giving herself over entirely, waiting for the other shoe to drop. She wondered if Allison had noticed. One night after a dinner of Chinese food out of cartons, one of their favorite traditions, Ally asked the question.

"How do you feel about me?"

Megan paused, chopsticks in the air. "What in the world kind of question is that? I adore everything about you. You know that." Back to eating.

"Well, I'm falling in love with you," Ally said, almost by way of a blurt. Her face heated red. "In fact, I'm starting to believe that I'm already head over heels." She rushed to explain, "I realized recently that we don't talk about our feelings too often. We don't take stock, and I get that's because you're very practical, but I'm less so, and it's important to me that we communicate. You know, discuss these kinds of things." She watched as Allison clenched and unclenched her fists at her sides, something she did when she was nervous. Megan liked that they were close enough now that she knew her tells. But honestly, she also had no idea where to go with this. Allison might have been nervous, but Megan was terrified and unwilling to admit it. This whole conversation made her feel uncomfortable, like she'd been backed into a corner without warning. This emotional stuff was not her thing, and no matter how strongly she felt, it was hard to let herself admit it.

She took a deep breath to process what Allison had just confessed and to formulate a response she was okay with. Hell, this was what she did on a daily basis for brides, right? Kept them calm. Happy. Pacified. Her voice remained measured and even. "I can tell you that I'm really happy with where we're at." She added a big smile to prove it. None of it was false.

"Okay," Allison said, drawing the word out, nodding, likely waiting for more. Megan didn't offer it and was left feeling like she'd somehow failed. She searched for any remaining reassurances to smooth things over, but she just couldn't say the three words Allison needed her to. Not because she didn't feel them—she did. But their situation felt riddled with complications and fallout, and saying the words would send her right out onto that scary ledge ready to fall at any given second. Could she give herself over to such uncertainty? No. She took a step back to safety instead. "I think we're on the same page, don't you?"

Ally hesitated, and who could blame her? "I'd like to think so, but I wonder what goes on in your head. I used to know. Lately, though, you've seemed withdrawn. Sad."

Megan used the power of touch to bury her shortcomings in the conversation. She took Allison's hand and pulled her close, holding her at the waist and gazing into her eyes. "I'm not sad about you. We're great in so many ways. We have the best talks, and amazing chemistry, fabulous ice cream sessions." She looked skyward. "The sex cannot be spoken of without exclamation points."

Allison smiled. "I agree with all those things." She seemed to relax in Megan's arms. "I miss you a lot when we're not together. I think about your day. If you're smiling or too busy to smile." A pause when Megan didn't respond. "Do you ever do that?"

Ah. Okay. Allison was attempting to pull Megan out of her emotional shell, which these days was easier said than done. She couldn't tell Allison that the very fact that she was on this Earth had Megan energized in the morning like never before. That she dreamed of the feel of her skin and the soft scent of her shampoo when they were apart. She couldn't articulate that she counted the moments until they saw each other, until she could bury her face in Allison's hair, or kiss the lips she'd grown obsessed with and daydreamed about during her workday, as her coworkers teased her for the dreamy smile on her face. She most definitely couldn't announce that her feelings had accelerated leaps and bounds over anything she'd ever felt for anyone because speaking those words out loud would make them all too real, and the more real they became, the more terrifying the stakes seemed.

What if she was just a break from Allison's regularly scheduled programming and eventually she was going to run back to the life she knew? It was self-protection. She couldn't fully enter the race unless she knew she'd come away successful. The more Megan felt for Allison, the more she held it in. The mere thought of losing Ally hurt too much to dwell on, so she shook herself out of it, understanding that getting too close was likely dangerous. She focused on the very specific question Allison had asked instead.

"Of course I think about you. How could I not?" It wasn't the complete answer, but it was all she could allow herself to offer. She gently cleared a strand of hair affectionately from Allison's forehead. She was smiling back at Megan, but it was a carefully constructed smile that gave very little away. It wasn't a beam or one of her relaxed bubbly grins. She was guarded, and that was not at all like Allison. Her chest tightened. This conversation wasn't going well, and neither of them was acknowledging it.

That night as they fell asleep, she pulled Ally close, needing to feel her heartbeat against her own and shroud herself in the love that was already bursting from her chest no matter what she did to quell it. Dammit. With Ally's face tucked below her cheek as she slept, Megan lay awake, staring at the ceiling and the shadows that danced a haunting routine above her, lost in her thoughts, and worried that the carefully guarded castle was about to come crumbling down.

Chapter Fifteen

S omething's going on," Allison said and took a bite of her sandwich. It was a begrudging bite. Her stomach had been off all week, and her appetite had drifted from her like an untethered boat in a current. Who knew when it would return? But if she didn't eat, she would get lightheaded during math instruction, which required her to be on her feet more than any other time of the day, especially when they were working on difficult multistep word problems like today. She needed sustenance. She frowned and met Lacey's questioning stare. "And I don't like it."

"What kind of something? Do your neighbors have secret meetings they don't invite you to? I've wondered that about mine before."

Allison went still. "I had no idea you dealt with such neighborly suspicion."

"I brush it off."

The more she got to know Lacey, the more her endearing quirks seemed to emerge. She supposed that meant they were truly on their way to friendship.

"For the best."

"Sneaky bastards. So what's your thing?"

"Megan. I'm doing the whole taking-stock thing and coming up a little short."

"Trouble in Sapphic paradise. I know it well. Proceed."

Ally nodded, needing to talk this out. "So, here it goes. We were doing great, everything moving in the right direction. We have a blast together—we just click. Plus, the sex. I can't even. My vocabulary doesn't stretch adequately."

"You saucy vixen. You've come so far on your foray into ladyland. But?"

"I can feel her pulling away a little at a time, and I don't have a clue what to do. The more I feel for her, the more she recedes. I'm helpless to stop it, and it's beginning to affect...everything."

Lacey frowned and popped the last bite of her oatmeal cookie into her mouth. They'd gotten in the habit of eating lunch together in Lacey's classroom, a practice Allison had come to look forward to. "Is it possible she's just overrun at work? Didn't you say she takes on a lot?"

"She does. But this feels different somehow." She shook her head, trying to pin down the appropriate words. "She still devotes the same amount of time to us. She's available, but she's also less...present, like she's distracted." She sighed, facing a more likely, though awful suspicion. "Or maybe she's getting bored. The shine might be gone on her end. I tried to have a talk with her the other night, tell her how I feel about her, but she didn't give much back and then changed the subject. Things feel...unsteady, and I hate it."

Lacey frowned. "Well, has she had many relationships in the past?"

Allison hesitated. They'd talked about it. "She's had girlfriends, sure. I don't think anything extra-long-term."

"Might be a red flag. When things get serious, she's out. We might've just stumbled on her pattern."

"Right. God. That sadly fits." Allison nodded, forcing herself to face the very upsetting possibility. Megan had touched on the fact that before Allison, she spent time at Shakers with Kelsey and met women here or there. She'd confessed that these meetings had rarely turned into much because she was a busy person and not one to get sucked in easily. Back then, Ally had taken that as a compliment because Megan *was* interested in *her*.

This was an awful pill to swallow. Did that mean that they would just dead-end at some point? She just couldn't imagine it, and yet, she had to prepare herself.

She pictured those kind, dark eyes that felt like they belonged to her now, and every part of Allison hurt, physically hurt, at the idea that Megan might be drifting away for good. She thought of her parents. The *for sale* sign in their yard and the deal with the Carmichaels, which was over because of her. Lastly, she thought of Brent, who'd never done anything but support her with a smile on his face, who'd never wavered in what he wanted, and she'd given it all up for Megan. She didn't regret it, but she was becoming increasingly aware that her head might be just as valuable as her heart when navigating this situation. She had to keep her wits about her.

When Brent called later that night, something he did once or twice a week these days just to check in, she deviated from her usual plan to let the call roll over to voice mail and, on impulse, decided to pick up.

"Hey there," he said, sounding surprised to hear her voice.

"Hi, Brent." She closed her eyes. His voice was so familiar that she relaxed into a comfortable zone she'd missed recently. "How are you?"

"Oh, ya know. I've been better. Calling to see how you are, though."

She smiled. "I'm doing all right. Grades are due in two days, so I'm—"

"Slaving over your laptop at the kitchen table until they're in. Likely with a glass of white, but just one because it's a weeknight."

She laughed because she was sitting in the very spot he'd just described, wineglass half empty. "Yes, that."

A pause on the line. "You will likely say no, but can we grab a cup of coffee? Take a walk in the park. I'd love to catch up. No pressure. Just want to hear all you've been up to. It's been a couple months."

She took a long moment with that request, conflicted in so many ways. But it seemed harmless enough, and she was feeling so much at sea these days. Seeing Brent and reinforcing their new friendship dynamic might actually be helpful. "I can swing that."

"Fantastic. When?" His voice was now energized, eager even.

"Um, what about tomorrow?" Megan had already begged off the dinner that they usually had together. Her office was hosting a monthly cocktail hour for their stable of brides.

"Done. I'll meet you at the teddy bear statues in Lakeside Park at, say, six o'clock? How's that?"

"Yeah, I love those statues."

"I know you do."

They said their good-byes, and she clicked off the call, guilt nestled tight in her chest. Doubt crept in like an uninvited guest. What the hell was she doing exactly? Fresh tears arrived hot and thick, falling down her cheeks. She wrapped her arms around herself to feel anchored, whole. It was a losing battle.

The next day, with the sun shining and the light of day to calm and soothe her soul, she sat on the park steps that led down to the teddy bear statues just yards away. A young bear playing with an older one, adorable and unexpected in the middle of the path. She'd always imagined the bears were mama and baby, and it made her heart swell, just as it did today.

"There she is," a deep, familiar voice said from behind.

She stood and turned as Brent descended the steps in a dress shirt and jeans. "What? No tie today? Who are you?"

"I knocked off work early and ditched the fucker. It chokes me."

"It chokes you," she said simultaneously. She shook her head, and they laughed. How strange to be laughing with Brent again. Yet familiar, comforting at the same time.

With his hands in his pockets, he surveyed the statues. "I'm glad we chose this spot. These guys missed us," he said, gesturing to the large and small bear.

"Me, too. Haven't been out here in a while." Back in their early days of dating, they used to meet up at the statues on Saturday morning. He'd pick up coffee to-go for both of them, and they'd walk the trails, getting to know each other. She remembered testing out his sense of humor and realizing that he was virtually unflappable and could match her wit. It seemed like such a faraway time now, and that made her heart tug. She studied his face. He seemed thinner, but still Brent, striking no matter what he did.

"Shall we walk?" he asked.

"I'll follow you." At first, neither of them said anything as they made their way down the cozy path. It was chilly, but not cold, and that made for a pleasant early evening as she took in the trees, ready to rebound from the winter into the fresh green of spring.

He spoke first. "One of the reasons I invited you was that I wanted to apologize."

She nodded, absorbing the offered olive branch. "Can you be more specific?"

"My family, as you know, is protective of me. And when they

learned about the engagement, they made some moves I wasn't aware of and don't support. But I want you to know that that stops now."

"You're talking about blackballing Megan."

"Yes. And I spoke with my father about it as soon as I heard."

"I appreciate that. It didn't really seem your style. I'll admit, it was upsetting."

"It's not who I am. I hope you know that. I've asked him to stand down. If I'm being honest, I don't think she'll earn back BeLeaf's business, but maybe he can get out of her way when it comes to the larger community."

"And is that going to work? You simply asking."

"I'm hopeful." He hesitated, looking grim. "But you know Dalton."

She sighed. "My parents put their house on the market. They were counting on the BeLeaf orders for the Dash Bar."

He closed his eyes. "Christ. I'm sorry, Al. Not sure I can get him to budge on that one. When he's embarrassed, he's a whole different version of himself, which quite frankly sucks. Especially since the bar should be on the shelves based solely on its own merit. This wasn't supposed to be a favor."

"I realize." She paused. "I hope you know that I would never want to embarrass anyone. Especially you."

He seemed to chew on that for a moment. "I know that you're a good person just trying to figure it all out, but yeah, it fucking hurts to be jilted in front of everyone." He stared straight ahead. "But the harder part is missing you. You were my right hand, you know. My sounding board."

"Your girl Friday," she said, pulling up a reference he used to make. Life with Brent was always so easy. She knew exactly what she was in for and rarely stressed.

His laugh came with a nip of nostalgia, too. "Yeah, exactly. How's your family? We already know mine is a little out of joint."

"Surprisingly in good spirits, given all the setbacks. Betsy isn't taking the changes in my life so great."

"Because no one saw it coming."

"Not even me. Isn't that strange?"

He paused their walk. "Do you think you're a lesbian?"

She shrugged, keeping her eyes on the trees that lined the trail. "I think I'm just a person trying to figure it all out. The label doesn't really fit. I'm not sure what label does."

"Because when we were together, it didn't feel like—"

"I know." She'd never found their sex life wanting, exactly, but then she'd never met Megan before either. There was before Megan and after. "Maybe it's more about the person, for me. But I can definitely tell you that my attraction to women is not a fluke or a phase. It's real. But so was what we had. None of this erases our life."

"And Megan Kinkaid is the one?"

"Maybe." She hesitated. "I don't have all the answers."

"No." He seemed to concede. "I can't imagine you do. Just hard, you know. I'm not ready to give you up."

"Well, you haven't. Here we are, taking a walk. Shooting the breeze."

He grinned. It wasn't what he was asking for, but wasn't it something? She didn't want him to vanish from her life altogether. Maybe there was some wiggle room for a real friendship. "You have a point."

They walked on and talked about work, the changing seasons, and whether Brent should bite the bullet and get that dog he'd been talking about getting for years. But just one. Shocking how natural their exchange was, given everything that had happened.

She went home that night feeling a little lighter for having reconnected with Brent and that part of her old life. She dived into bed and grabbed her phone, ready to tell Megan all about it.

Just got home. I missed you today, Megan's text read.

She grinned like a kid and typed back. *Me, too. Gonna kiss you into next week tomorrow. Get ready.*

Now that's all I'm thinking about.

Join the club. Ally bit her lip and typed back, wishing Megan was there with her. *Sleep tight. Until tomorrow.* She set her phone on the nightstand and turned off the lamp, snuggling in for bed, fully aware that she'd not told Megan about her walk with Brent. She wanted to keep their good night light.

They'd get to it.

Eventually.

❖

They had two days before what Megan called Wedding Weekend would hit, where they'd booked themselves to slightly over capacity. Five high-end weddings happening simultaneously throughout the city, with her team divided into subgroups, her top vendors splitting their time, and Megan acting as quarterback with an eye on all the moving parts. It would be quite the weekend, and she'd scheduled a Soiree meeting to make sure all the ducks were in a row.

"What about Take the Cake? Are they on top of it this time?"

"Seem to be. Delivery for the Sherman wedding at two p.m., well in advance," Kelsey said. "The country club will get them set up. I'll be with the bride at the church for pre-photography."

Cade looked up from his laptop. "The Fairmans are also using them. Delivery is cutting it a little close for my liking, but we'll manage. They only have the one driver, so I'll have Demi at the Hilton to meet him, and I'll stay back for formal photos at the church postceremony."

"Good, good. But stay on top of them. They always understaff on busy days, and I don't want a late cake."

Both Cade and Kelsey nodded and typed.

As a group, they came up with a schedule for their part-time junior planners to move from one event as it closed to another, midway through. They were all going to be exhausted, but she had faith that her team was up for the challenge.

As they gathered their things, Cade lagged behind, practically toeing the ground. She watched him, waiting for whatever he had to say.

Finally, "I saw Allison in Lakeside Park yesterday. She looked great."

Megan perked up at the mention. "Oh yeah. I didn't know she went."

She watched as a series of emotions crossed his face. "She was on a walk with Brent. Carmichael."

"Oh yeah?" Megan played it cool, but the information surprised her. Why in the world wouldn't Allison have mentioned that? It seemed like it would have been a headline, given all the Carmichael fallout she'd been through, and they had talked the night before. Allison hadn't said a word.

"Seemed very casual," he added, "no big deal." She imagined he'd weighed whether to say anything or not. Everyone knew the story by this point and saw Allison as Megan's plus-one.

"Oh yeah, I'm sure it was."

Later, though, as she packed up and headed home, the information clung to her like a monkey on her back. Of course she wouldn't want Allison to stay away from Brent if she chose to spend time with him, but the secrecy of it cued alarm bells sounding quietly in the distance. Nothing horribly concerning, but at the same time, she took note.

Allison was already inside Megan's apartment, slicing up cheese for a mid-evening snack for the two of them, when she arrived. "Welcome home. I have snacks. I hope you like the state of Wisconsin."

The sight of her so at home in Megan's kitchen seemed to erase everything. Allison lit up the room, and Megan counted the blessing. "Hey there, gorgeous. You're a sight for sore eyes."

"And look, honey, I cooked!" Ally said, showing off her sliced cheese like a Food Network hottie.

Megan laughed. She was beyond cute. She'd give her that. She snagged a slice of sharp cheddar and nodded her approval. "You did great."

Allison dropped the show, came around the counter, placed her arms around Megan's neck, and kissed her just as soundly as she promised she would, igniting every one of Megan's senses as she held Ally close, taking her in, absorbing as much of *this* as she could. The best kind of salve. "How was work? I know it's your everyone-in-the-world-is-getting-married busy week."

She held out a hand ready to tick off her tasks. "Ran around at twice my usual speed, argued with a florist, talked a bride off a ledge, and booked three new weddings, trying to fill the corporate gap." She relaxed. "But we ended with a team meeting that made me feel so much more prepared for the events. We have our ducks in a row and will conquer wedding weekend."

Allison looked thoughtful. "You in a Wonder Woman–type outfit from her early days in Themyscira makes me a little weak in the knees. We probably shouldn't even talk about it, or I'm going to be preoccupied."

Megan raised an intrigued eyebrow. "This is new and valuable information."

"Always here to help and announce my weaknesses at any given moment." Allison returned to her station and poured them each a glass of wine from the decanter, in the long-stemmed glasses Megan loved. "I will miss you this weekend but will happily await your victorious return." She handed Megan a glass. "What else is new?"

She sipped casually. "Cade said he saw you in the park. A get-together with Brent?" She made sure to keep it light, pretending to survey her options on the cheese board as she spoke. This was not an inquisition, just an honest curiosity.

Allison paused, her glass midway to her mouth. "Yeah. He called. I answered. It was actually a nice get-together. We took a walk and sorted through a few things."

Ah, so maybe it was just closing a few loops. Megan could kill the images in her head of Allison and Brent rekindling their romance beneath the tall oak trees, staring longingly into each other's eyes, an image that gutted her. She was overreacting and needed to dial it back. "Why didn't you mention it?" The one dangling detail she needed to tackle.

"I should have. I planned to."

Megan nodded. "Good. I don't want you to think that I have any problem with you seeing or speaking to Brent. I mean, you guys were engaged. It's only normal."

"I don't think that."

"Good."

Silence. Why were they being weird now? "And I want you to feel free to tell me."

Allison nodded. "I think I needed to talk some things out, and he's good for that."

Ouch. That landed a little differently. "Anything I should know about?" Her heartbeat thudded faster than normal. She placed a casual hand over it because it was a foreign feeling. She wasn't someone to get rattled by a detail, but if Ally was reaching out to Brent for comfort and not telling her about it, then maybe things weren't as they seemed. She hated herself even more for jumping to silly conclusions.

"Nothing like that. We talked about the fallout from the breakup. His father. You should know that he doesn't condone Dalton's behavior."

"Good. I think we're all just trying to sort through our lives without hurting anyone in the process."

"Yes, and Brent is in agreement. Beyond that, we just caught up with each other." She hesitated, and Megan waited, almost afraid to move. "I'd love it if he and I could find a way to be friends. I would hate to say good-bye to him altogether." She frowned. "What do you think about that?"

"Being friends?" Megan relaxed, because it was a perfectly natural request. "I think that you are a mature, smart, and capable woman who would make a great friend to anyone."

She watched Allison visibly relax. "And you are the one person who has consistently made me feel like I'm all those things."

"Then I deserve more cheese." She reached across the counter and scored a triangle of smoked Gouda and sighed. "I'm really glad to be home."

CHAPTER SIXTEEN

A llison pumped her arms, realizing it was the only way to keep
up with her power-walking sister as they hustled through
her neighborhood in a race against no one. She and Betsy had seen
considerably less of each other lately, mostly due to their rift over the
Carmichaels. But she'd arrived ready to defend her choices and to cut
Betsy a break for taking longer to absorb the reality of the situation than
everyone else. What she hadn't accounted for was how off-balance she
felt about her choices. Megan had been aloof and noncommittal, and
lately, she wasn't sure where they were headed.

"I wish that you could focus on the bigger picture is all," Betsy
said, walking fast but never seeming at all taxed. How?

"You're going to have to explain that one to me." She managed
the words around her own huffing and puffing. She really should work
out more if she didn't want to resemble the Big Bad Wolf.

"All you had to do was coast to easy street. Your life isn't just
about sex and who you lust after most. If that was the case, I'd be
married to my personal trainer, who barely speaks and drives a beat-up
Honda." She'd managed to say all those words without a single gulp
of air. Madness. "This is marriage. It's not meant to be a fairy tale. It's
a journey, a shared life with many different components and driving
forces." Her arms pumped like a maniac, and Allison tried to match, a
perfect metaphor for her entire existence alongside her sister. She never
could keep up.

"That's the most unromantic thing I've ever heard in my life."
They'd reached the end of their route, thank God, and had looped back

to where they stood in front of Betsy and Dell's gorgeous two-story with the perfect garden and side fence.

Betsy closed her eyes. "And that's exactly where you've gone wrong. You've watched too many movies, Allison. Shake out your romantic notions." She paused, one hand on her hip, the other taking her pulse with two fingers on her neck. "Think about what it would mean to Mom and Dad. To walk you down the aisle and place your hand in Brent's. It would rekindle the partnership with the Carmichael family. Put everything back into place. They could keep the house and finally have a good night's sleep. Don't they deserve as much?"

Her heart sank because she *could* do that for them. But at what cost to herself?

"Just think of how many burdens it would ease. Brent's hurting. He looks like a shadow of himself."

"I know," Allison said, conceding. "Breakups are awful, but we're working on a friendship, and maybe over time, that will be enough for you guys, as well." In fact, she'd made plans to see Brent later that week.

Betsy nodded several times, taking in her words. "I guess I'm just disappointed in you is all. I don't want to watch you throw your life away."

The words were so incredibly harsh that a lump grew painfully in her throat. "Well, no, I don't want that for myself either, which is why I'm following my heart and trying to do what's right for everyone."

"That's the last thing you should follow when figuring out your life," Betsy said, hustling up her sidewalk to the house. She turned back, but her smile looked forced. "Want to come in for a Gatorade and towel off?"

Betsy had barely broken a sweat, but Allison was a different story. "Thanks. I think I'll just run home and grab a shower."

"Ah. A hot date with the wedding planner. Got it." Her voice was flat.

"Megan. You used to know her name. Hell, you used to fawn over her."

"That's before she ruined my family."

"Harsh."

"Real."

Allison sighed. "Well, I'm not sure this has been productive, but it was at least good to see you. Been a while."

She watched as Betsy's posture relaxed and her expression softened. "I know I'm kicking your ass over this, but it's because I adore the hell out of you. Plus, I'm Betsy the bitch. It's what I do." She walked back down the sidewalk, grabbed Allison, and pulled her into a tight hug, sweat and all. "You're gonna be okay. No matter what happens in the end."

It was the first time she'd heard Betsy offer any kind of support, and it sent tears to well in Allison's eyes. "Thank you for saying so. I needed to hear it."

Betsy released her and held her tightly by the shoulders, meeting her gaze fiercely. "Just promise me you won't let your emotions make all the decisions. The world is a difficult place to maneuver, and that's why God gave us brains to help."

"Got it." As narrow as Betsy's focus was, that little nugget of advice was actually helpful. She did need to keep an eye on the big picture and try to resist blindly following the hearts in her eyes. Megan, as much as she wanted her to, wasn't offering Ally much reassurance and left a giant question mark about her feelings. If she was falling desperately in love with someone who was growing bored with her, she'd like to know about it. In fact, she needed to find out now, before she got in much deeper.

"Hey, you," Megan said, picking up on the second ring. Allison hadn't even made it out of Betsy's driveway before needing to hear Megan's voice.

"Hi." She exhaled slowly, relief trickling in. She placed her hand on the steering wheel. "I don't have a reason for calling. I just needed t—"

"You don't ever need a reason to call me."

"No? Well, that makes me happy. Will I see you soon?"

"God, I hope so. I'm working late tonight. Tomorrow?"

"I'll see you then." A long pause. She wanted to say *I love you* but knew it would put Megan on the spot. Instead, she held the words in, close to her heart, just for herself. "Good night, Megan."

"Night night, Ally."

She clicked off the call and stared up at the darkening sky as the stars made their debut. "What are you trying to tell me?" she asked the universe, quiet and unhelpful in its reply. "Head or heart? Just give me a sign. An arrow. A pat on the head. Okay?" She locked her gaze on the brightest star in the sky. "I promise I'll listen."

❖

Wedding Weekend lived up to its hype and more. Over the course of the weekend, Megan raced between events, picking up the slack for vendor mistakes, running cover, and making sure all of their eight couples were not only happy, but ecstatic with how their big days went. When she arrived at the Coleman reception with the two additional kegs of beer the liquor supplier had neglected to deliver, she knew she could finally exhale. This was her last stop.

Kelsey was lead on the event, which was perfect. The reception should ease into self-sustaining mode soon, with most of the formal events out of the way, leaving the guests to party the night away. Bring on the dancing and mingling, which meant she could finally catch her breath and even relax a little with her best friend, who'd seriously killed it this weekend.

"You're alive!" Kelsey said, beaming as Megan appeared at her elbow. She wore their company's customary navy with her hair in a chic knot at her neck, as always looking like she came off a runway. Clients loved that about Kelsey. So did the women she enchanted.

"Barely. Extra kegs are here. Seems you have this one running smoothly."

Kelsey waved off the comment. "These guys are not hard. So in love with each other that it's all they're focused on. They barely batted an eye about the missing kegs."

Megan touched her heart. "These are the weddings that made me want to go into business in the first place, the ones that celebrate the purity of love."

"Said only the way someone in love could articulate." Megan let that one go as they watched the dance floor. The groomsmen strutted around in sunglasses to "Macho Man." Very few straight weddings ended without this very scene taking place.

"What if I am in love?" Megan blurted. God, why had she done that? Putting it into the ether was the last thing she needed, yet she was so stressed, barely sleeping the last two nights, it was as if the words had taken over and burst forth from all the pressure.

Kelsey swiveled. "You are. I was just waiting for you to catch up." She beamed, clearly proud of herself.

Megan shook her head. "Ever feel like you're walking into oncoming traffic?"

"Who, me? Daily. It's what I live for. You, on the other hand, prefer to play it safe on the curb."

She faced Kelsey. "She's hanging out with Brent again. Isn't that step one before getting back together?"

"She is?" Kelsey frowned, examining the details. "I don't think it has to mean anything. Maybe they're working on staying friends."

"That's what she says."

"There you go. So stop it. I've seen the way she looks at you when you walk in the room. That's not a fluke. It's not a fling. It's real." She sliced through the air with her hand. "I've spoken."

"She's seeing that new *friend* again this weekend. The same friend who's rich and powerful and can give her family everything they need to keep their lives afloat. Did I mention he desperately wants her back?"

"Did I mention that it's you *she* wants? I think her feelings count for a little more in this scenario, don't you think?"

"She said she's falling in love with me."

"Then take her at her word. She's a grown-up, and from what I've seen, a smart one." Just then, the hotel's coordinator signaled Kelsey, and she was off. "And stop thinking about it. Know your worth and stand tall."

As Kelsey departed, Megan found herself literally doing just that. She was Megan Kinkaid, she reminded herself, and Carmichael or not, she had a lot to offer. And on that note, maybe it was time she started offering more, being honest with herself and Allison about her feelings. Just the thought had her heart thudding at an uncomfortable pace. Why was she so bad at this? But she needed to face that fear if she wanted to hold on to the kind of happiness that she'd never imagined. Oncoming traffic, indeed.

❖

Allison rested her chin in her hand as she listened. Brent was talking a mile a minute about the first-quarter sales report that saw his stores spiking. "It's just a relief to know that plans I put into place are actually flourishing. My region is on top."

She popped a fry. "Why is that? The surprise and relief. You've grown up around these stores and know them better than anyone. Of course you're capable of elevating them."

"Thank you." He grinned at the compliment. "The loyalty program alone has paid off in spades. Not even Dalton can argue that point, and he was against the idea."

She popped a fry. They'd met up at Harley's diner again, which felt neutral and fitting. This time for lunch. Maybe it would be their new postbreakup location, which she was fine with because they had excellent BLTs. "Well, I'm thrilled for you, especially since it's in Dalton's face."

"Well, you may not remember this, but it was you who encouraged me to think bigger, outside the box, when it came to initiatives at work."

She grinned. "Did I? Go me."

"Mm-hmm. You were always a great cheerleader and a source of great advice. I miss it."

She felt the corners of her mouth relax out of the smile. She didn't know what to say to that. This was a delicate situation, and she wasn't fully equipped. Sure, she missed him back, but not in the same way. She missed the familiarity of their life, the ease of how they were around each other, but she could now clearly see the difference in *happy* versus *fine*. "Well, toss me a nickel. I'm full of busybody opinions about any and all jobs."

He laughed. "Fair enough. Holding you to it." He set down his huge burger. "So, how's Megan these days? Look how mature I'm being."

This was a step forward for him, acknowledging her relationship. Maybe there really was hope. "Color me impressed. She's great. Busy. This weekend is killer for her. They're actually overbooked, so all hands on deck."

"She hate me?"

Ally grinned around a fry, taking her time to answer. He didn't deserve the easy way out. "No, but would you blame her?"

"I have mixed emotions and am probably not the most impartial person to ask."

She gestured with a fry. "Fair."

"I'm guessing it's serious, between you two?"

Allison nodded, all the while shouldering that nagging feeling that she was maybe more serious than Megan was. "I think so."

He nodded and watched his food. "I don't love hearing that but at the same time can be happy you're happy." He seemed to rethink. "Well, some of the time I can. I'd like you to keep an open mind."

"Brent."

He grinned ruefully. "I know. I hear myself. But I have to say it. We were good together, Ally. Our lives click and we just…work."

"I know. But there's more to consider, you know?"

He tossed his napkin onto the table. "Yeah, I do. And I'll take you any way I can get you, and if this is the new us, then I will work on being grateful."

"You can do it."

"Of course I can." He signaled for the check. "Gotta get back to the office, and then I'm heading to the store on Lovers Lane. We have a whole reorganization in place to better suit traffic flow."

"It's the weekend. You're gonna shake up the Shake 'n Bake?"

"You know it. Let's do this again soon. You can regale me with the details of your love life, and I'll bite my cheek. If we do it enough, maybe I'll lose the cheek biting."

"In spite of the biting, I'm glad we're doing this. I would hate seeing you disappear from my life."

"Yeah, that didn't feel like a great option."

"Are you thinking of dating at all?" It was strange to even say it, but it was time.

He offered a half smile. "Maybe. There's been interest."

She wasn't shocked. The second he was whispered to be single, she was confident that the sharks began to circle. The women in his world had batted their eyelashes and giggled at him even when he'd been spoken for. She could only imagine the attention he received now.

She held up a hand. "Just don't go crazy, okay? Keep your wits about you."

"That's what I have you for. To keep me grounded." He signed the credit card slip their server presented, and they were off to their respective days.

She called Megan on the drive home and left her a voice mail, wishing her an easy end to wedding weekend. She got a short and sweet text message back later that night. No call. Guess they would connect later.

She headed to school on Monday morning feeling weirdly off-balance, as if something in the universe wasn't right. She couldn't quite put her finger on it, but as the day pressed on, the feeling evaporated in favor of spelling words and interpersonal conflicts at recess. At the end of what felt like a very long workday, Allison tried to unwind on her drive home by zoning out to the radio.

When the local station returned from commercial, the DJ offered a brief local news update: *"Quick update on the incident just south of town. Brent Carmichael, son of BeLeaf Foods mogul Dalton Carmichael, was transported by EMS following a serious four-wheeler accident. Tune in to our sister station WFAA for more at five..."*

Ally could tell the male voice had moved on to weather, but his words stopped carrying true meaning. She stared at the radio in disbelief. Her heart stopped and started in a weird do-si-do. She covered it with her hand to try to regain some control and get her thoughts together. This was bad. She knew how dangerous those ATVs could be and had told Brent on more than one occasion that she worried for him. How could this have happened while she'd been teaching compound sentences?

She pulled over at a gas station along the highway to figure out what to do. Her fingers started to move across the screen of her phone but stopped because she wasn't sure what to type, or who to call, or what to do. As she stared helplessly, her phone rang. Megan. Thank God. "Hi," she said, after sliding on to the call. Megan would know what to do. She was the cool-headed type in any situation.

"I'm not sure if you've heard but—"

She closed her eyes, willing it away. "Brent was in some kind of accident."

"Yes, that's why I'm calling. The news is making its way through social media. I tried to find out what I could."

"Megan. I told him to take it easy on that thing. What did you hear?"

"It happened just outside of town. Apparently, Brent took the day off to go four-wheeling with a few of his buddies." It wasn't anything new. One of his favorite ways to blow off steam. The guys would shoot their mouths off, drink some beer, and drive around the Carmichaels' rural property until the sun set. "They didn't get too far into their day when Brent flipped his vehicle while taking a corner at a high rate of speed. They transported him to Presbyterian, and I don't want to upset you, but it sounds serious, Ally. I know he wasn't conscious when he was transported."

She blinked. Processing. "Why wasn't he at work? He was rolling out a new floor plan for one of the stores, and now he's hurt. How does that just happen?"

"I don't know," Megan said, her voice sympathetic. "I'm so sorry this happened. Let me finish a client meeting, and I'll come by, so you're not alone."

"No." She tried desperately to make her brain work faster. "I think I'm going to head to my parents' house, let them know. Can I call you later?"

"Oh." A pause. "Yes, definitely. And if I hear more, I'll let you know immediately."

The sky was inexplicably clear, and the sun shone brightly, like any other day. How odd. How did the sun not know that a good person was fighting for their life? The sunbeams that lit up her half of the car felt warped and out of place.

She pulled her car into the driveway of her childhood home and in desperation, needing to know more, placed a call to Jeff, Brent's younger brother. It was possible he hated her, but they'd always had such a great relationship in the past that she hoped he could overlook all that had happened, given the circumstances.

"Please don't hang up on me," Ally said when he answered. "I need to know what's going on."

"I wouldn't do that." She exhaled. Thank God.

Tears sprang into her eyes. "How is he?"

She heard him exhale. "They're taking him upstairs in a few minutes," Jeff said. She could hear him walking, probably putting distance between himself and the family. "He was driving so reckless, Ally. I told him to knock it off, but he wouldn't listen. He just had this look about him. Wild, you know? I tried."

She pushed back against her seat as if it would absorb some of her concern. Guilt flared. He was having a hard time lately because of *her*. "Hey, this isn't your fault," she told Jeff. "It was an accident. Is he going to be okay?" That last sentence she was only able to choke out, emotion having robbed her vocal cords of their ability. God, what if they lost him?

"We don't know. Broken ribs, a broken wrist. His nose." She rolled her lips in, hating those details. "His face was cut up a little when I saw him."

"What now?"

"We're waiting on a CT of his head, to see if there was any trauma. I don't see how there couldn't be. That thing was on top of him."

That last part rattled her. "Let's just wait." And she did. Megan checked in with her, which was nice, and propped her up in the midst of the sickness that swirled and thrashed in her stomach. Not much news was coming her way. Allison went home and didn't move. She sat on her couch, staring at the wall as the excruciating minutes ticked by.

Eventually, her phone rang. Jeff. "Like we thought. Multiple broken bones, and his brain is swollen. They'll be watching him overnight and doing what they can to bring the pressure down. That's their first priority."

"Okay, but did they seem hopeful?" Her voice sounded scratchy, even to her. It was after one a.m., and every part of her body ached from the tension it carried.

"They said they'll sit more comfortably once the head injury has been stabilized."

"Good. Okay. Then we wait for that. It's going to stabilize. I can feel it." After hanging up, she sat back and let her gaze, once again, settle on the wall across the room and allowed her mind to drift to happier memories. When her parents opened the shop. On the beach with Megan's arms around her. Brent's birthday when she'd bought him that sweater three sizes too big, and they'd laughed until they had tears streaming. She bit the inside of her lip to tamp down the emotion, realizing how very blessed she'd been with the people in her life. She nodded, reminding herself that there would be more memories to come with Brent. He would find a way through this, not the type to give up. His body would fight now.

She had to believe that, will it to happen.

CHAPTER SEVENTEEN

The Soiree office suite felt unusually quiet in the early morning hours. Megan was used to the commotion of her staff as they moved around the space, teasing each other, working together on details, or taking client calls that drifted down the hall, mingling in a jumble of energetic voices. With Allison out of pocket and looking in on Brent this entire week, she'd had trouble sleeping. When that happened, her best remedy was to busy herself. Arriving at the office at six a.m. had actually turned into a four-day streak she'd grown fond of. The alone time gave her a chance to tackle things like email, organization, and big picture project managing without so many small interruptions.

"Oh, my Jimmy Choos, you're here early again." Kelsey.

"Well, you're early, too," Megan said, squinting at the clock. It wasn't yet eight. Kelsey was more of an eight forty-five kinda girl.

"I know. It's horrible, too. I have a bride who can only meet before work, so here I am like a dutiful little wedding bitch."

"That's how I think of you, too."

"You sleeping any better? You don't look it."

"Thanks." Megan shook her head. "I wish. But everything is just so weird right now."

"What's the update? How's Brent?"

"He goes home tomorrow. Most likely. I guess he still has to pass a few physical therapy tests. Show he's able to move around without danger, something like that."

Kelsey nodded. "Good for him. Do you get Allison back soon?"

She winced. "I don't want to push. He asked for her the second he woke up, and she's been there, helping out ever since. She's where she needs to be, I guess. And I'm just…doing me. Supporting her through calls and texts. Occasionally I glimpse her."

"You're a mess. I can tell."

Megan closed her eyes. "I can't argue. I don't even recognize myself. I used to be confident and calm, not the insecure lunatic staring back at me in the mirror. But he needs her. It's just that the more time they spend together—"

"The more convinced you are that she remembers her true place in life, by his side."

"Isn't that the story?"

"No, that's the *cliché* everyone always claims is the story when it has no basis in reality."

Megan sighed, knowing Kelsey's statement to be true. "It's not that he's a man. It's not her sexuality I'm afraid of. It's an ex-fiancé thing. I'm starting to feel like maybe I was the rebound girl for someone who was panicking about a very permanent commitment. What if I'm legit the rebound girl?"

"Is that what it feels like when you're together?"

"No. At least I don't think so."

"Then shut up, and listen. You're in your own way. *You.* You're doing this, so stop it. Unless Allison gives you signs that she's no longer interested, then you have to stop making decisions for her and then punishing her for them."

"Fine," Megan practically yelled back in frustration. She lobbed a Sharpie good-naturedly at Kelsey for being reasonable.

She dodged it easily. "I was inches from a workers' comp case just now." She pointed at Megan. "You're dangerous. I'm off to my meeting. And lastly? Stop it."

"Will do."

"No, you won't."

"Probably not."

Once alone, she thought back to the night before. She'd invited Ally over to decompress. She'd declined because Brent's doctor was scheduled to come around soon, and he preferred she be there rather than his mother, who tended to not listen and asked too many questions. Two days before that, Ally had canceled their dinner date because Brent had texted her that he was feeling low, and his left hand, in which he had two broken bones, was giving him trouble. She'd headed to the hospital instead, forgetting to text good night later because she'd been too tired. More and more, Megan felt like an outsider or a burden that Allison had to tend to before breaking free. She'd noticed herself texting less and less, avoiding the disappointment of a delayed reply and hating the feeling that she was intruding.

But she missed Ally. Her smile. Their talks. Their nights. And God, those lips.

She sat back in her chair, wondering if they'd ever get back to the way things had been and cursing herself for taking that time for granted. She'd never been happier, and yet rather than enjoying the moments they'd had together, she'd questioned it, held back, and now? Well, now maybe it was too late.

❖

"What do you think?" Allison asked Brent once she had him settled on his leather sofa. "Good to be home, right?" She smiled widely, trying to sell the momentous occasion to a somewhat grumpy patient.

He nodded, his eyes appearing sleepy from the large doses of drugs they had him on to keep the pain away. "Yep. This is what I need."

She knew he'd been done with the hospital for days now and had been clawing at the walls. "Now you can relax and get better, and things can start to feel normal again."

Though nothing about the past few weeks had been normal. While he'd healed slowly in his hospital bed with Allison bringing him daily jokes, magazines, and her company, outside, spring had inched in, warming them all and zapping the world with vibrant greens and pinks and yellows. She'd hardly had a chance to notice.

Her kids kept her busy during the day, and she'd check in on Brent, seeing what he might need after school let out. That left her very little time for anything else. She'd given up her weekend shifts at the Nutcase, and her personal life had taken a woeful hit. But this new existence had become a routine at this point, and though she cared very much about Brent's recovery and getting him back to good health, she was beginning to wonder how long this process might take. When could she slowly hand over the reins to Jeff or one of the other Carmichaels? They'd been so eager to see him open his eyes that first week in the hospital but had come around less and less once it was clear he was out of the dangerous section of the woods. Maybe this important step, arriving home, would transition him to a new phase of recovery. Maybe she could start to become a person again, too. *Maybe.*

"I'll get you settled in, start some dinner, and then Marlene should be by."

"She's not you," Brent said in a playful voice. They'd met the at-home nurse who would be helping Brent around the house at the hospital. Older, efficient, and with a warm grandmotherly quality.

"What? She seems your type," she told him with a wink.

He winced as he lifted his left foot, currently in a half cast, and placed it on the coffee table. Two broken bones in that foot.

"But be nice. I'm serious. We want to keep her."

He frowned. "Do we, though? Let's think this through."

"Yes," she said emphatically. "I have a job, and it's not tending to reckless four-wheel drivers who need to be smacked upside the head."

"What about if the reckless comes with dimples?" He flashed his and she relented. Now that the swelling had gone down around his face, it was nice to see his normal facial expressions start to make appearances again.

"Not enough of a perk."

They teased each other more these days, partially to keep the mood light after such a terrifying experience, partially because it was a new way for them to communicate in their new dynamic.

"Big plans tonight? Is that why you're leaving?"

"Yes." She gave his kitchen counter a good scrub down.

"Is that all you're going to say?"

She came around the island and faced him. "I'm meeting Megan for a drink."

He went silent for moment.

He might have forgotten their circumstances, but she hadn't. When she wasn't with Megan, she was thinking about Megan, and she didn't like the fact that the in-person aspect of their relationship had taken a back seat to her new sense of responsibility. She'd pretty much put everything on hold when Brent went into the hospital, understanding that part of that tug to step in came from the guilt she carried from leaving him. Broken up or not, she couldn't just turn off caring about his well-being. Still, she wondered about the fallout. Megan had been incredibly supportive, but at the same time, things between them had been less than steady before the accident, and now they felt more distant than ever. She hated that and vowed to work toward fixing it. Step one? Get Brent back on his feet and slowly hand over the reins to his nurse and his friends and family. It was time for her to start stepping back and reclaiming her own life.

"Tell her I said hello," Brent said evenly, a pleasant but unconvincing smile on his face. He turned on a soccer match while she organized his medication along a counter in the kitchen.

An hour and half later, she scanned the room at Shakers, looking for Megan, her heart already squeezing pleasantly with the knowledge she was about to finally spend time with the person she missed more than anything. Spotting her, Megan held up a hand from a table in the middle of the semi-busy bar, and the world seemed to burst with life again. *At last.* Her hair was down and fell in more natural waves. She wore dark jeans and a white blazer with a black cami underneath. The matching black heels made her legs look long and sexy. God, she was the most gorgeous woman in any room, and Allison's stomach went tight with attraction and pride. That was her girlfriend. *Hers.* And she couldn't have been more proud, happy, and excited about picking up where they'd left off.

She hurried over and closed her eyes when Megan pulled her into her arms and held her for a long moment. She inhaled her scent and nearly teared up at how wonderful it was to be back with her after so many long days away. "Hi, hi, hi," she whispered. "God, it's good to see you." When she pulled back and gazed into Megan's eyes, it was clear that she wasn't alone in her sentimentality. The corners of Megan's dark eyes creased with happiness as she grinned back at Ally.

"You are a sight for sore eyes. Are you okay?" Megan asked.

"Now I am."

"You must be exhausted." They sat, and Megan indicated the waiting glass of wine in front of Allison's chair. "I ordered you a glass. I hope that's what you wanted."

"It's perfect." They sipped. They smiled. They sipped. They were still feeling each other out, searching for their groove, but happily so.

"You look great," Megan said. "Really pretty, especially in that blue." Ally glanced down at the blue top with cap sleeves and three buttons, the top of which she just might have left undone on purpose.

Oh, that compliment felt nice. Warmth hit her cheeks. "Thank you. How's work? How's Kelsey? Tell me everything. What did you have for dinner? I feel so uninformed, and I hate it. Did I mention how much I've missed you?"

Megan laughed. "It feels good to hear it. Let's see, we had two new bookings at work. Cade had a meltdown because he found out they'd discontinued the everything bagel at the cart on the corner. Kelsey broke a heel and was noticeably shorter all day, which we all loved. I had a chef's salad for dinner. And I…have been busy trying to keep busy. Missing you. Now you go."

"My parents are in good spirits, but sometimes I think they just say that to make me stop asking. Betsy is looking to redo her kitchen, and it's a whole thing with the color gray and its many different shades. My fourth graders are preparing for track-and-field day, and I've taught them my secret tug-of-war trick."

"And what's that?"

"No. Uh-uh. You're not in the fourth grade." Megan's foot pressed against the side of Ally's leg beneath the table, causing her to roll her lips in. "Seriously? Puppy dog eyes and under-the-table flirting?" God, she couldn't resist either.

"Yes."

Allison laughed. "Okay, I'll give you anything you want." She leaned in, divulging state secrets. "The trick is you all get really low at the same time and pull like hell, and the other team will fold almost immediately. But you don't start that way. You wait for the captain's cue to drop. It's all very coordinated, but do not tell the other fourth-grade classes. Do you hear me?"

"Good Lord, you're adorable. I forget how much until you're right in front of me caring so desperately about the best things."

Allison picked up Megan's hand and kissed the back of it. "Adorable?" She got hit with a good dose of lust and dropped her voice. "Do you still find me adorable when I'm on top?" Yessiree. She did just go there in the middle of a public bar. Highly unlike her, but it'd been quite a while, and she fantasized about Megan more than was probably normal.

She watched as Megan grappled with the swift change. Her mouth opened and closed, and she blinked. Finally, she fanned herself. "You have to warn a girl."

"More fun this way." They held eye contact, the delicious kind that made Ally tingle in all the right places. It felt amazing to be in Megan's presence again, and she couldn't wait to leave this bar so she could show her. Slowly.

Megan grinned. "How's the patient?" she finally asked, breaking eye contact.

"Home and seemingly pleased to be there in his own space. Now he just has to learn how to navigate it with the bad foot and hand, and busted ribs. His wrist is braced, too, and giving him a lot of trouble."

"I'm glad to hear he's out of the hospital, at least. Do you think you'll get a little breathing room now? You've been going so hard." She sipped her mango martini. "I worry about you."

"I think it will ease up. I'll stop by after school and see what he needs, and his nurse will check in on him."

"Every day after school, though?" A pause as Megan seemed to consider her next set of words. "Do you think that maybe this is the time, during this transition, to maybe step back from every single day?"

Strangely, Allison felt a little on her heels, the spell from earlier broken. "I just don't want to drop him when he's still so far from recovery. I feel like he still needs me."

"Right. No. I get that," Megan said and then seemed to survey the room. It felt like they'd just taken a giant step away from each other, and Allison wanted to undo it. Explain. Get rid of the cold gust of air that had just ruined everything.

"If I can get him through the hard part and over this initial hump, then he'll be more than ready to take over soon."

Megan set down her drink delicately. "Yes, but he's Brent Carmichael, right? Doesn't he have a million friends and a very tight-knit family circle for that kind of thing, not to mention more money than Midas? Does it have to be *you*?" She offered a smile, probably to soften the inquiry.

Allison swallowed. Whether she wanted them to or not, her defenses flared. She tried to keep her tone super casual. "Yeah. I think it does. Not only is he still my friend, but I've been the one there for the physical therapy appointments. I have the information about what's going on, what exercises he needs to do. I know the medications and am the one who keeps them straight, on schedule." She nodded a few times to punctuate.

"I'm sure that's all knowledge that can be passed on."

She rolled her lips in and shook her head. Silence reigned. "Why are you making this so hard for me?" Honestly, weren't things difficult enough? She didn't need outside pressure from Megan, too. Not when she'd been spread so thin and trying so hard.

Megan held up a hand. "You know what? You're right. I'll stay out of it. Your life, not mine." She offered a tight smile, but the pretense of a casual conversation was already gone.

"How can you say that?" Allison stared at her drink blankly. "It's not just my life."

Megan sighed. "But it is, Ally. Hasn't it always been?"

That one hurt. "It sometimes feels like you project that on to me because maybe it's what you want. Your own space where I come and go. No real focus on anything concrete or permanent."

Megan's dark eyes flared. She seemed offended. "I've done nothing to give you that indication."

"You avoid any and all talks about how you feel. You're available less and less but prefer to blame the distance on me, when really that's not fair."

"That's the thing. None of this is fair." Megan let her hand fall onto the table in defeat. Like she was giving up. How could that be?

Allison took a breath to let them both settle. This was not how tonight was supposed to go, but she could see the frustration written all over Megan's drawn features and felt it tighten in her own chest. "Maybe we can hit the reset button? I really want to enjoy tonight." She tried to smile. "I've been looking forward to it for days."

Megan nodded. "Yes. Let's do that." A soft smile. "Resetting in progress. I apologize."

"So do I."

Megan gave her hand a squeeze. "How's the wine?"

She laughed. "In the excitement of seeing you, I forgot to pay attention." She sipped and paused, pondering. "It's a pinot, isn't it? Mellow. A little jammy."

Megan leaned in. "I love it when you say words like *jammy*."

"Yeah? Well, I wear them, too. My pajammies."

Megan closed her eyes. "Only you, Ally. Only you would say something like that."

"What?" She laughed. "Why are you making that face?"

"It's why I can't get enough of you. You say something ridiculous, and it's still sexy as hell. Who else can pull that off?"

"Oh, that's a good endorsement." They were pinging again. Back on track and she could breathe.

"So, did you bring any with you tonight?" An easy rise of the eyebrow came next. Oh, there were the flutters. Good ones, too. She felt the familiar stirrings lower that only Megan could elicit in her. Some sort of magic she'd never understand.

"Well. I didn't want to assume anything." They were just being playful now. Of course she'd be staying over, and they both knew it.

"My bed misses you as much as I do."

"So what do we do about that?" Her phone buzzed in her purse. She glanced down, deciding to ignore it.

"Should I get the check?" Megan asked, following her cue.

The phone buzzed again. If it was possible, it seemed louder this time, more insistent. She closed her eyes. "I better check. Just in case."

Megan made a go-ahead gesture. "Yeah. Please."

Brent. She slid on to the call, planning to make it quick. Maybe just a question about his meds. "Hey, everything okay?"

"Ah, I think so. Honestly, I'm not sure. I fell in the hallway, and now I have this shooting pain up my arm."

"You were wearing your brace, though, right?"

"I took it off just to let my arm breathe a little. But I realize how stupid a mistake that was now, and I'm thinking I should ice it, but I just finally got settled upstairs, and I'm afraid of falling again if I go back down."

"Don't do it alone. Get your nurse to help."

"She already left. I told her I was good and going to sleep. Another mistake."

"Yeah. It was." She sighed. Trapped. Megan watched her carefully. Brent waited quietly on the line. "I'll swing by. Give me fifteen."

She could hear the relief in his voice when he said, "You're a lifesaver and a saint."

"Yeah, yeah." She clicked off the call. "Brent."

"Yeah. I ascertained."

"I'm really sorry." She gestured to the phone. "But he's had an incident and hurt himself and needs a little assistance."

Megan went still. Finally, she nodded. "Of course. No. I understand."

They stared at each other, Ally's mind racing with how to make this work. "Why don't I see if I can get him settled and then head back over later tonight? We could pick up again. Please? I will make this up to you."

Megan stared at the table before raising her gaze. "You know what? Let's not. I think we've both had long days and could use some sleep."

A pause. This was not the ending to the evening she'd wanted. "Megan. Please. I'm sorry."

But Megan was already standing, dropping several twenties on the table. "You have nothing to apologize for. I think we both know you're where you're supposed to be." She kissed Allison's cheek and turned to the bar. "You know what? You go on ahead. I think I'll have one more at the bar. My night has suddenly opened up."

Allison nodded, helpless, but doing what she felt was best, even if it meant sacrificing herself and what it was she wanted. They'd get through this, she reminded herself as she drove the near twenty minutes to Brent's place. And then at last, they could finally live their lives. Take those vacations they'd daydreamed about. Maybe they'd even move in together at some point. The thought brought a much needed smile to Allison's face as she imagined domesticity alongside Megan. Doing dishes. Laundry. Arguing over TV shows before falling into bed together and doing it all over the next day. Nothing in the world would make her happier.

She just had to be patient. That's all.

CHAPTER EIGHTEEN

The gossip surrounding the Carmichaels' oldest son had run rampant. But Megan held her tongue.

"Did you hear about Brent?"

"The word on the street is that he might not walk again."

"I heard it's worse, that he also is experiencing neurological deficits. It's very sad for everyone. The Carmichaels are devastated. He's taking a leave of absence from the company. May never be back."

"I heard he might be disfigured."

Megan moved through the throngs of guests at the Throckmorton home, picking up snatches of conversation as she went. There was certainly a most talked about topic, and it was Brent. This one was a smaller event than they usually handled, but the Throckmortons were not only former clients, but they'd become friends of Megan's from the social scene. As such, she was off the clock. Midge Throckmorton, the family matriarch, had hired Soiree to handle the details of the party but insisted Megan attend as a guest. That meant she had Lourdes as the point person, and Demi there to assist.

Brent was indeed the topic of everyone's conversation these days. Rich people loved to gossip about one another, and the Carmichaels had given them quite a lot to chew on this year.

"Things are a little crazy here tonight."

Megan turned to find Jeff Carmichael at her elbow, smiling warmly. She'd always had a soft spot for Jeff. As the younger son, he wasn't the poster child for the family the way Brent was. In fact, he was often overlooked. The also-ran. "I wasn't aware you were speaking to me."

He winced. "I'm not someone who holds grudges. Plus, Brent can fight his own battles."

She touched her champagne flute to his. "I'd rather not fight anyone at all. Life's too short for that, don't you think?"

"Even better. You on your own tonight?" He scanned the room from his spot alongside her.

"If you're asking about Allison, no, she's not here."

"A shame. She would have loved these fancy appetizers."

Megan smiled. She couldn't disagree, but it had been a week since they'd met at Shakers, and other than a few surface level conversations, there hadn't been much contact. Mostly her fault. She could accept responsibility for being unavailable, tied up at work, or just not willing to engage in much deeper interaction. She had her armor up and wasn't quite sure how to get it down again. Old habits died hard, especially when the stakes felt so unbelievably high. She was adrift and damn well knew it. "She's probably at Brent's. She seems to think he has no one else."

"I feel bad about that. I've offered to step in, but he turns me down every step of the way."

"Of course he does. He's no fool." Her champagne glass was empty, and that was a shame. Luckily, a server passed by with a fresh tray at that exact moment. She helped herself, knowing the alcohol would take the edge off. "Who knows? Maybe they're meant to be. Maybe this whole accident was the universe's way of bringing them back together, so they can live happily ever after in a big house."

"I don't know about that. I can't even begin to weigh in when—"

"Jeff." She turned to him with a smile. "You don't have to. He's your family. I would never expect you to speak ill of someone you love."

"You're a good human. I just hope it works out well. For everyone."

She smiled ruefully. "Tricky."

"Yeah. I know." He raised his glass in farewell and turned to go.

She just couldn't resist. "Jeff?" He looked back. "Do you think she still loves him? Honest opinion."

He hesitated, clearly off-guard. These were not waters he was comfortable wading into, but she was floundering and looking for guidance, insight.

"Please?" she asked.

He looked away and then met her gaze. "From what I saw daily at the hospital, I think it's a possibility."

"That's all I'm asking." Megan nodded and sent him a grateful smile. "Thank you."

He nodded back and disappeared into the sea of guests. Her body felt cold, heavy, and sick. She set down her nearly full glass of champagne, no longer able to consume it because she was pretty sure that Jeff Carmichael had just confirmed her worst fear. She wanted to run from the party, take shelter in some way, hide, escape it all and, at the same time, recognized the lunacy of it all. She couldn't escape the loss that was heading her way. All she could do was minimize it and figure out a way to move forward.

❖

Something was going on. If Megan had been unavailable before, she was exponentially MIA ever since their almost date at Shakers. She bore part of the responsibility, still riding the guilt train for having left her at the bar. Yes, Brent needed her, but when she examined how the whole scenario must have made Megan feel, she understood how it might have hurt her feelings. Megan saw her racing to her ex-fiancé's side rather than spending the evening with her, the first real shot they'd had at alone time in a while. Not only that, but she'd been at Brent's place nearly every day after school since, and Megan knew it.

Their conversations these days were polite but short. Megan generally ended them, explaining that she had an appointment or an engagement and that she knew Allison needed to get back to Brent. Those comments hadn't escaped her. The nagging feeling that Megan was simply using this scenario as a reason to step back from Allison also tugged at her. Maybe Megan missed the freedom of dating other people. Maybe the luster of the new relationship had dimmed.

"When am I going to see you again?" Ally asked that night, the phone pressed to her ear as she lounged on her couch. It was late. She should be in bed getting what sleep she could before her early workday, but after her time at Brent's, followed by an intense session of grading backlogged papers, all she could think about was how desperately she missed her happiness, Megan.

"I know, right? It's been too long." Well, at least they agreed on that much.

"Tomorrow night. You, me. A couch. We can catch up. Maybe take a bubble bath. What do you say?"

"That sounds amazing. Let me see how my day goes."

"That feels like a blow-off. If you'd rather not see me, just say so."

"I definitely want to see you, it's just…this all feels very complicated, and I'm just trying to stay focused on what's in front of me."

"I want to be in front of you. In fact, I'm on my way over." Allison stood and searched for her shoes as the adrenaline surged. This had gone on long enough, and it was time to find a way forward.

"No, don't do that. You have work tomorrow. It's not the best time."

"Well, then you can tell me that when I knock on your door, and I'll go."

"Ally," Megan said quietly.

"I'll see you soon." She clicked off the call and drove to Megan's apartment, feeling discouraged, but for once she was taking the bull by the horns and fixing things once and for all. She was nervous as hell with clammy palms and heart beating, waiting outside Megan's door.

"Hey," Megan said with a smile when she opened her door for Allison to come inside. That was something.

"Thank you for letting me in."

"I would never turn you away, and you know it. I don't think I'm capable." She was friendly enough, but there was a weariness to her demeanor, as if she'd not slept well or had very little emotional energy. She wasn't sure, but it was possible Megan had been crying. Her eyes were red-rimmed in a manner Allison had never seen.

"Good." She tugged on Megan's hand, pulling her to the couch and savoring the feeling of Megan's skin touching hers. "I'm here because we need to talk. You've been distant. I've been MIA, and I just want it all to end."

"Right. Yes. All of that." Megan's delivery was less than convincing, but she was at last right there in front of Ally and listening. That was something.

She sat on the leather couch, which was cool beneath her fingertips. The lights in the living room were off, but the bleed-over from the kitchen left them enough light to clearly see each other. She felt comfort within these walls, already filled with so many of her happiest memories. She wanted more, but she couldn't be the only one. Allison was one hundred and fifty percent in this thing, but she needed to know Megan wanted her back. She met Megan's eyes and searched for the words, coming up short because this moment felt so very important. "I feel like I've let you down." It was a start. "And I hate that. I keep trying to come up with all sorts of ways to make it up to you, and I will."

"Do you think that maybe that might just be a little bit of guilt popping up?"

"Of course I feel guilty. After the accident, I've not had the same amount of time, and we've only seen each other here and there, and to top it all off, this is someone who was very important to me we're talking about."

"I guess I was referencing guilt that you embarked upon this journey with me, opened this whole can of worms when you got cold feet over your wedding, and now you feel this sense of obligation to, I don't know, see it through. But to what end? This is your life we're talking about."

That pulled Allison up short. "If I've ever given you the impression that you're some kind of obligation, let me correct that right now. You're my priority."

Instead of answering, or lighting up, or taking Ally's hand, Megan studied the ceiling. That didn't bode well. Every muscle in Allison's body went tense, painfully so.

"I think your life is really complicated, and the best thing for everyone might be to simplify."

"You want me to drop Brent. The thing is that he's not in the best place—"

Megan pinched the bridge of her nose as if dealing with a difficult problem. "Look, I don't think either of us thought this would last forever."

A gut punch. This wasn't happening. "No?"

Megan met her gaze and inclined her head. They stared at each other, Ally in mystification. Megan in resignation. "Ally," she said finally. The tone of her voice was sympathetic, which was awful. It made Allison feel like a victim, a fool, for not getting the game at hand. She could be naive, but she was sincere, always. Had Megan not been?

"No. Don't just say my name like that. Explain what's going on."

Megan swallowed. Calm. Dammit. No. "I feel like we had a really good time together, and we both learned a lot. But I think your old life is calling. And so is mine."

"That's awful. How can you say something like that so easily?"

Megan passed her a reassuring smile. She had on her professional face now. The one Allison had seen her assume when she calmed down a hysterical bride or tried to reason with a vendor to get what she wanted at a certain price. "I don't mean for any of this to sound awful, but I'm someone who tries to look at the big picture."

"And we're not in it," Allison said flatly.

"This was a journey of self-exploration for you, and I think it's telling that it's all led you back to where you first started."

"Don't push this off on me." She exhaled, calming herself. She needed her wits about her.

"He loves you."

"And you don't."

Silence. Megan didn't comment, likely because to do so would be cruel. *I'm not in love with you* were harsh words to utter, especially when she could let the unspoken do it for her.

Megan seemed to choose her words carefully when she finally responded. "I'm just trying to look ahead and do the right thing for all of us. Why drag this out and make it even harder?" Her fingers smoothed her jeans, and Allison became overly aware of every little sound and action. Yet she couldn't get her brain to work, to process what was happening. Someone had pulled the chair from beneath her, and she was backtracking, attempting to understand how, why.

"It's the Band-Aid method, huh? That's what you've chosen for me?" Allison nodded, as her stomach roiled. When she'd made the decision to drive to Megan's place, she'd been nervous but energized, excited to get them back on track. She'd imagined them talking things over, kissing, maybe falling into bed where she could savor their renewed connection, inhale the scent of Megan's hair, and never let her go. She'd slowly step away from Brent to give him time to adjust to new people taking care of him until he was better. What she'd never imagined was any of this. They were going to reconnect and get back on course and live happily ever after. Now that she'd experienced what they were like together, how would she live without it? Didn't matter. As crushing as this was, she had to hold on to her dignity, her sense of self-worth, if that was at all possible.

"Please don't think this is easy for me," Megan said. "I promise you. It's not. But I don't think that we're meant for each other."

If words could crush a soul, these did. "I guess not. I hadn't gotten that memo until now." She looked around the room for help, not exactly sure what to say or do. Would this be her last time here? How awful that sounded. "Are you sure?" she asked meekly.

Megan nodded. Her brow was creased, highlighting the discomfort she felt. Was she just waiting for Allison to leave so she could get back to her real life?

Impossible.

She was sitting across from a stranger. Allison flashed on all they'd shared. The coffee dates, the romantic nights, the trip to her parents' house where they'd stolen looks and relished the private moments, that wonderful picnic on the beach, and the imagined moments ahead. So many of them, in fact.

"Okay, well, you'll have to forgive me for grappling. I had a different idea of what was happening here."

"Did you really, though?" Megan asked. "Be honest with yourself because I'm not sure you're seeing what the rest of us are."

"Honesty has never been something I struggled with, Megan. But thank you." She stood. "I guess that's that." One last look around as her heart clenched and the pain nearly choked her. "I'll see myself out of your apartment and your life."

As she passed, she saw Megan close her eyes. What was she feeling? The mixed signals made it hard to know. She heard footsteps behind her. Megan was following her to the door, which she so did not need. She didn't turn back. She couldn't.

❖

"Ally, wait." She felt guilty for using the familiar form of her name, but that's who she was to Megan, her Ally, and in this, the most awful moment of all, even she couldn't deny that. Stripped raw, and clawing her way through this, Megan was depriving herself of everything that was important to her. She was setting Allison free, but she was also destroying her own life in the process. How easy it would have been to take Ally into her arms tonight. To lose herself in the security of her kiss, and to shut the rest of the world away and just *be*. The two of them against the world.

But she couldn't shake the evidence right in front of her. There was a magnet pulling Allison back to Brent. First in friendship, then in his time of need. She also couldn't shake Jeff's words. He thought Allison still loved Brent. Someone stronger would have stayed and fought, and that was something she was going to have to learn to live with. She wasn't strong enough to do that. Weak people got out early, and when it came to her heart, Megan had discovered the one area of her life where she was not at all in control.

She followed Allison into the hallway outside her apartment and said it again. "Wait, please." Allison paused but didn't turn, her back still to Megan. Now what? "I just need you to know that this, us, all of it, has meant a lot to me."

"Was it real?" Allison asked, but her voice was gone. She sounded hoarse and strangled, the emotion having gotten the best of her. Everything in Megan screamed for her to undo it, to apologize, to tell her to come back in the apartment and that they'd find a way to talk it out, fix things.

Because she didn't have the right words, she turned Allison around and placed a kiss on her lips that she hoped communicated everything her heart couldn't dare say. She took a step back and nodded. "It was."

Allison stared at her, searching. "I don't know if that makes this better or worse." The tears pooling in those blue eyes would be Megan's undoing if she didn't get herself out of there and quick. She felt the onslaught of emotion—grief, regret, defeat, and sadness—all closing in on her like a tidal wave that would break over her in a matter of seconds.

"Take care of yourself, okay?"

"Yeah," Allison said numbly.

She didn't watch her go. She couldn't. Instead, she excused herself back into her apartment and closed the door behind her with a click that came with such finality, she nearly couldn't take it. She'd just dismissed the brightest light she'd ever known, her own true happiness. But it had never really been hers to begin with, right? She'd been on borrowed time and waiting for the time's-up alarm no longer seemed like a possibility.

The silent sob hit first. Her throat constricted, and her face contorted. She covered her mouth as she walked straight forward, desperate, needing assistance, but searching for…what exactly? There was nothing in her perfectly appointed apartment that could help her. She was alone and, about now, felt certain that she always would be. She wasn't cut out for love and the vulnerability that came with it. Seeing the woman she loved walk away, likely into the arms of someone she preferred, had been enough to convince her of that.

She called in sick to work the next day, something she'd never once done since opening the doors to Soiree all those years back. There was no way she could get it together enough to face people, feign a smile she didn't feel, or concentrate on everyday tasks when she was quite simply broken and bleeding. She stayed in bed and declined phone calls, even from her parents, who left a message that the lantana was blooming, and spring was going to be so beautiful in Corpus this year. As the hours marched on, she turned inward to self-reflection. She needed to figure out what it would take to move her past this, past Allison, and back to her old self. She came up empty each time because she didn't want to go back. She'd had a girlfriend who she was crazy about, who had made her world sparkle, gave her a glimpse at a possible future, before it all came crashing down.

"But here's my question," Kelsey asked two days later over lunch in the little bakery on the first floor of their office building. The place was always bustling, and with only four tables, it was hard to snag one. Kelsey had insisted that Megan eat with her and leave the office behind for an hour. The homemade chicken salad on a croissant that she usually pined for sat untouched on her plate.

"All right. I'm ready."

"Did she *know* you were crazy about her?"

Megan squinted. Her eyes still felt scratchy from the crying sessions that seemed to hit out of nowhere and did not at all go with the Megan Kinkaid brand. She'd resorted to wearing sunglasses any chance she could safely get away with it, opting for fashionably chic rather than emotionally crumpled. "Yeah, she knew."

Kelsey nodded, moving her chef's salad around with her fork. "Because you told her?"

"Because I *showed* her. She saw the effect she had on me. She had to. I lit up every time she walked in a room."

"Words are different. You're clearly in love. I know that because I have the past-you to compare to. Allison is new at decoding Megan."

Megan sagged in her chair. She'd avoided the word for as long as she could because the concept meant she had so very much to lose. But hell. She'd lost everything now—what did pretense matter? "I am in love with her. And no, I didn't say it. There was never the right moment to go there."

"You were scared out of your mind."

"Fine. I was scared."

"My only point here is that maybe Allison would have done well with that information when she was navigating what had to be a slippery slope, balancing her newfound sexuality, her intense feelings for you, and her ex desperately needing her and probably laying it on pretty thick."

The way Kelsey put it did make Allison's plight sound especially dicey. "Which is why I chose not to complicate things further with declarations of love."

"It's interesting you used the word *complicate*." She delicately took a bite, somehow managing to hold on to her perfect lip gloss. "I would have gone with *simplify*."

Megan balked. "In what world would me declaring myself make it easier for Allison?"

Kelsey laughed. "It's like you've never watched a romantic movie in your life. Love topples all. If you'd armed Allison with the knowledge that you loved her, maybe it would have seen her through this mess, helped her along. You sent her into a crisis with your relationship on less than sturdy legs."

"No," Megan said automatically. "Ally is where she wants to be, even if she can't see that."

"I know I always love it when people make decisions for me. So do you. We all adore it, really."

Megan frowned because she damn near hated it, and Kelsey knew that. "Okay, that's a semi-valid point, but it doesn't change the circumstances."

Kelsey set her salad to the side and picked up her sparkling water. "But you could have. Still can. If you can somehow find your swagger again."

"No. That ship has sailed." Megan stared out the window at the large number of people in business attire coming and going like the world was a normal place. Surreal, yet a reminder that her own pain was just that, hers to get over. She wondered about Allison's day. It was weird not speaking to her for days. How was she? Did she understand why they hadn't worked out? Was she back in Brent's arms? Had she rebounded? Questions she'd likely never have answers to. She faced Kelsey. "And I will find my swagger."

If only she actually believed that.

CHAPTER NINETEEN

"Could you hand me the Pledge?" her mother asked, pointing to the yellow bottle of cleaning solution. "I want to give the living room another once-over before the showing."

"Only because you seem to really want this," Ally said, passing her the bottle and the rag sitting next to it. "I, for one, would still like to find a way for you to keep the house."

Her mother smiled. "I've made peace with it. Still lots of life for us to live out there, and a smaller place will probably do us good. A new adventure."

Allison didn't buy it for a second, and her heart sagged, heavy.

As her mother dusted with Allison pitching in on a nearby end table, she passed her a sympathetic look. "You feeling any better about the whole Megan situation? I hate seeing you so dejected."

She wasn't, but it had been nearly two months since Megan had handed her walking papers, and even though she still felt like a shell of herself, it was time she stopped dragging the rest of the world down with her. "No, I'm good. Feeling much more like myself these days. Just took a little time." A lie. But the good kind. Her mother had too much on her plate to overcrowd it with worrying about her. Ally'd much rather that she focus on her father and their home and business. Ally would take care of herself.

Her mom straightened. "Well, that's the best news I've had all week. Should we sneak some wine?"

Allison looked around the empty living room. "Is there someone who will have an issue with it?"

"No, but lately I've taken a great deal of comfort in pretending I'm getting away with something."

"Well, by all means. Let's ninja our way to the kitchen and break into the wine cabinet before they see us."

"Now you're talking."

Allison led the way, making sure to look both directions in case imaginary eyes were on them. She located an unopened bottle of dolcetto from a vineyard she'd not heard of before and did the honor of popping the cork. She'd always enjoyed one-on-one time with her mom, and with her father closing at the store that night, she had her all to herself.

"I hear Brent is much more himself these days."

Allison nodded. "He's back at work and on the mend. No more physical therapy, but he has to take it easy or he gets sore." As shocking as it was, he had been a huge source of support for her when it felt like the world had dropped out beneath her feet. He'd been her friend in a dark time, and given the way she'd hurt him, it had been a surprising turn of events.

"Do you think he's still hoping for something more?" Her mother said it so casually as she turned her wineglass in her hand. But her eyes danced with hope.

Ally sighed and reflected back on the past week.

"You're here. My day can begin," he'd said the last time she'd swung by. They'd watched a reality singing competition and rooted for different contestants over delivery pizza, ham and pineapple on her side, every topping on the planet on his. Earlier in the week, he'd also been a little flirtatious, complimenting her jeans and how her smile always took over a room. He'd held her gaze when he said it, unwavering. She couldn't deny that spending time with Brent was comfortable, easy, and nonthreatening. Three things she needed about now. It would be easy just to slip back into that rhythm. Hide out in the familiar.

"He might be."

"And what are your thoughts? I imagine you're still not ready for anything romantic."

She wasn't. She couldn't imagine it. And yet, she seemed to seek out his company, the shelter it provided. Was it fair to him to just go along with it? Because she could only imagine that the more time they spent together, especially in the midst of her new single status, the more he would hope, wonder, expect. She'd shelved the notion because she simply wasn't equipped. She took another sip of wine, already feeling it working, unwinding her thoughts.

"I think I don't have a clue what I want."

"Then just float along for now, okay?"

She loved that advice.

❖

"Dad's talking about throwing in the towel on the shop. He said so yesterday," Betsy told her over milkshakes, an outing Allison had suggested to reconnect with her sister. She'd forgotten Betsy didn't indulge and had waited for her to pore over calorie counts on any and all flavors, finally opting for the bland sugar-free stuff at the end of the display case. Allison, having no shame, had gone for the double chocolate spun shake with extra whipped cream.

"I was worried it would come to that."

"I keep hoping now that you and Brent are on better terms that there might be hope for the BeLeaf deal to come through. If it did, I have a feeling it would open so many other doors for them. They'd have a proven success story to take to other buyers and distributors. They'd have a real shot."

Allison sighed, hating being the one stuck in the middle. "I think it's time for me to say something to Brent."

Betsy's entire face transformed. "I know it's not a likely scenario anymore, given the changes in your relationship status, but it couldn't hurt, right?"

"No."

"And you've been there for him, Ally, every step of the way."

"I've tried to be."

Her sister went quiet. "I know that I wasn't the most supportive of your relationship with Megan Kinkaid." Hearing her name spoken out loud still hurt in a manner she was never quite prepared for. She'd never felt pain that manifested itself both mentally and physically, but she felt it all over, and it showed no signs of dulling. She missed Megan with everything she had in her, but the ending of that relationship had done more than hurt her. It had taken a little part of her away, the part that leaped at life, that moved through the world without fear. She was different now and didn't like that about herself. At the same time, it felt safer. "But I can tell that the breakup really did a number on you, and no big sister likes to see that."

"Thanks, Bets." She shrugged, trying to avoid delving too deeply into the topic. Self-preservation and all. Her face felt heavy, and the corners of her mouth pulled down, which meant she needed to do something to snap herself out of this. "But I've been doing okay. Going for walks."

"My friend Angela saw you and Brent at dinner. Anything there?" She held out a hand. "Not that I'm applying any pressure. Lesson learned."

"I don't mind you asking." She shrugged. "We're just living life. Being us, but no, nothing romantic has happened. I honestly don't know where his head is on the topic, but mine is far from anything like that." The idea of moving on after Megan was a no-go. How would anything else compare?

"But you're not ruling it out?"

"Betsy. I'm tired. I'm banged up." She shook her head. "And I'm just looking for a break from any and all trauma."

"Hear me out, and then I'll shut up." She made a zipper gesture across her lips. "I know you're confused and hurt and searching. But keep in mind that Brent Carmichael can offer that and a lot more. Just don't forget." She waved a hand. "That's all I'm saying. I know him, and he would never abandon you. Who knows? Maybe this whole journey was just meant to reassure you that you were where you were supposed to be all along. What is it they say? There's no place like home?" She pretended to lock her lips and throw away the key, dusting off her hands to complete the sentiment.

She nodded, half of her rejecting everything Betsy had said, and the other half finding the idea of safety a comfort. Brent would take care of her. No, her happiness level wouldn't be anywhere close to when she and Megan had been together, but the resulting hurt was maybe a good argument to avoid those kind of extremes. Safe and in the middle lane wasn't sounding so bad. How in the world did she wind up in partial agreement with Betsy of all people? Her life was becoming less and less recognizable.

❖

It had been three months. Three damn months of awful. There were some nights when a person just needed to go numb. Let it all fall off of them—the hang-ups, the hurt, the preoccupation with the past, and the damn second-guessing. That's what Megan needed, and she wouldn't find it sitting home alone, blinking at the wall. She had abandoned Shakers, opting for a more discreet bar a few blocks away. She'd also skipped her typical martini tonight and went out on a limb with a rum and Coke, her second so far. Time to stretch the norm and live a little differently.

"You're Megan Kinkaid."

She blinked, turned, observed. A blonde. Pretty. Smiling. A short dress. Yeah, that rum was hitting. "Yes."

"I tried desperately to get you to plan my wedding. You were hopelessly booked."

She forced a smile, wanting to be anything but work-Megan right now. "I'm sorry about that. Truly. I hope it was a great event." She turned back to her drink, absorbing the bluesy music piped in through the inexpensive sound system.

"It wasn't. We canceled it last year, and she's been on a serial dating streak ever since. Bullet dodged."

"I guess that's another form of congratulations."

"Let me buy you a drink."

"You don't have to do that."

"I want to." She signaled the bartender. "It's happening."

"Fair enough." She was really quite beautiful, this woman. At any other time in her life, she would have been instantly attracted to her. Was she truly that broken?

The woman sat down and smiled. "Mara."

"Megan."

"Oh, I know."

She smiled back at her. "Right, right."

They chatted casually, and halfway through Megan's third cocktail, she felt herself start to relax, and instead of sending not-interested signals, she turned on her barstool and faced her new friend, intermingling their knees, returning a bit of the flirting, and even allowing Mara to lean in to her space as she moved her cocktail straw in a circle around her drink. Mara was most definitely hitting on her, and though Megan never would have predicted it, maybe this was exactly what she needed to jump-start herself out of this damn heartbroken rut.

"Should we get out of here?" Megan asked, feeling bold and willing to run with the sexual tension that had been building between them all night.

"I live across the street," Mara offered.

"Ah. Another downtown dweller."

"Convenient, no? Interested?"

She had pretty great lips. Megan would give her that. "Yes." She said the word instantly, leading with her gut and not her heart. It felt amazing.

Mara grabbed the bill and settled, took Megan by the hand, and led her out of the bar. Carefree, that's how she felt, and she was embracing the bliss of it as they walked the streetlamp-lit street to just a block away. She didn't get to see much of Mara's studio apartment. Megan was through the door and pressed against the back of it before she had much chance to survey the space. Mara's lips were warm and insistent, and her body responded, which meant she wasn't dead. She allowed her hands to roam beneath the hem of Mara's shirt and up her back. She closed her eyes to better engage, Mara's lips now on her neck. This was good. She was her old self again. She was living and surviving, maybe even enjoying herself. There could be life after Ally.

Pause. No.

At just the thought of her name, Megan flashed on a pair of big blue eyes smiling across the table at her over a romantic dinner. The tickle of Allison's hair on her shoulder. The way she kissed Megan, the feel of her fingertips across her skin, which felt markedly different than this woman's touching her now. She shrugged away the thoughts, ordering herself to focus on the here and now. She murmured her approval at the soft kisses being placed on her neck as Mara moved her way down to her neckline, anything to pull herself back in. But it was like Allison was now all that existed in her brain, and her body refused to engage. She heard Ally's laugh in her ears, remembered what it was like to anticipate her arrival, to inhale the soft smell of her vanilla-scented perfume once she did. Mara's lips were once again on hers in a steamy lip-lock, and her fingers worked on the buttons of Megan's shirt.

She couldn't. Megan pulled her mouth away, seizing air, her eyes darting to the ceiling.

"You okay?" Mara asked. Megan's shirt was now unbuttoned all the way, and this was awkward. She caught Mara softly by the wrists and paused their intimate progress.

"I'm just having a night, I think. Dizzy. A little tired. Possibly drunk." She left out completely in love with someone else and missing her more with each damn day. She was sunk.

"Maybe we just slow down," Mara said, caressing her cheek. But now, even that felt wrong, like she was betraying her own heart, which was ridiculous and not. She was the one who sent Allison away, and whether or not her intentions were altruistic, who the hell cared now? She was flapping around in the world alone and full of regret, and the only thing that seemed to offer any kind of relief was the idea of calling Allison. Yes, she'd finally just admitted to herself that maybe she'd made the wrong decision.

"I think I need to go instead," she said, wincing. "I'm really sorry. This is all on me, and you were wonderful."

Mara took a step back, placed her hands on her hips, and nodded. "It's totally okay. Maybe we can exchange numbers. Try this another time?" Her kind eyes overflowed with hope. She was a nice person, and Megan felt awful for suggesting they go somewhere together, following her home, and then bailing.

She sighed. "I'm going to be honest and tell you that this is not the best time for me. Things are complicated."

"Ah. Well. I get that, too."

"But thank you for the conversation, the company." She inclined her head, sheepish. "And more."

Mara opened the door for her. "Anytime, and I can honestly say I mean that."

She was grateful for the understanding. Megan let herself out, feeling like maybe it was time to face facts. She was miserable and couldn't take much more. She walked the handful of blocks back to her place with a lot on her mind. Because the late spring air was warm, she took an extra block, gaining momentum in her conviction with each step. She could call Ally. Would that be so horrible—to admit that she missed her, and loved her, and had made a horrible mistake? Maybe Allison would tell her to go fuck herself and hang up the phone. She shook her head. That wasn't her style. And the only way to find out how she'd react was to pick up the phone and call her.

Maybe.

She stood in front of her building and stared up at it.

"Nice night," Chip said. "Good for working things out." He tapped his temple.

She stared at him. "How did you know that's what I was doing?"

"It's my job to know my people. Heading in?" He opened the door.

"You're too good at your job." She accepted the offer and passed through the door, feeling the swift blast of cool air from the newly turned on air conditioning.

"You know what I always tell myself when something weighs me down? Sleep on it, and if you feel the same in the morning, you really mean it."

She paused and turned back. "That's actually really good advice. You know what? You're getting extra cookies for the holidays this year. Maybe even booze."

"Let's hope you still feel that way in the morning."

She laughed, already feeling lighter, like she had a sense of direction after so long. Maybe this was the time in her life when she needed to be brave, take a stand, and declare herself no matter how daunting it might seem. She stared at herself in the mirror before bed and really looked herself square in the eyes. She was only on this Earth once, and there wouldn't be any second chances. She had to take control of her life and wrestle it away from the fear of failure that had haunted her since she was a kid. So what if she failed? At least she'd know she'd tried, and wasn't Allison worth it? "God, yes," she told the mirror with tears pooling in her eyes. "Definitely."

When she awoke the next morning, everything felt lighter. The sun shone brightly as she exited her building and ushered her into the world, hot coffee in hand. She popped on her sunglasses and smiled, prepared for whatever was ahead. She felt stronger and well equipped, ready to take her life back into her own hands.

When she arrived at the office, Demi handed her the paper and a handful of messages, which she would tackle after email.

"You look great," Lourdes said, offering a nod of approval as Megan made her way down the hall in her heels and gray suit. "Million bucks."

"Thank you," she said and grinned back. When she arrived at her office, she found Cade waiting outside.

"Good morning, sir."

"Good morning." Though his face said anything but.

"Everything okay?"

"Yeah." A pause. "Yes. But I wanted to check in with you about something that you may already know all about. If so, please just ignore me."

She eyed him as he shifted his weight and thrust his hands into his pockets. He was nervous. Very unlike Cade. "Come on it. What's going on?"

He did so and closed her office door behind him, which told her this was a sensitive subject matter. She wondered if he'd lost a client. It was unfortunate, but it happened, especially if the couple's aesthetic wasn't gelling with their own style and approach. Having been there, she was ready to talk him down once she heard him out.

Cade took a seat. "I had dinner with my friend Jason Sontera last night."

"Oh, from Vows and Veils?" The competing agency was slightly smaller and took a more boutique approach to event planning but was well respected in the community. She often sent referrals there herself when Soiree was booked up.

He nodded. "He told me they'd taken on a new and exciting client—they would be handling the Carmichael wedding."

She paused midsmile, dissecting the words for their meaning, but feeling like her brain was woefully stuck. "Jeff?"

He took a moment. "Brent and his bride, Allison. They're apparently wanting a rush job, sparing no expense. He's lead on the project and entirely stressed out about it."

"Oh," she finally managed and nodded. "So they're going ahead with the wedding after all." Her brain was racing a hundred miles a minute. Adrenaline shot through her system, and panic struck smack in the middle of her chest.

"You hadn't heard."

She forced a burst of energy, anything to save face in the midst of a devastating, humiliating moment. "No, but good for them. Right? I'm glad they managed to patch things up. And so soon. Wow." She grinned and moved the mouse around aimlessly on her computer screen, which was exactly how she felt. Directionless.

"Are you sure you're okay with this? You would have every right to be surprised, upset."

She and Cade were fantastic colleagues who'd even socialized on occasion, but he was not someone she planned to come undone in front of. "Honestly, I'm fine. That ship had sailed for me. We had a good run, but Ally is where she should be."

He hesitated. "Okay, but I'm here if you want to talk. About anything."

"Noted. Thank you for telling me. It's big news."

"Yeah," he said, nodding uncomfortably. He turned, opened the door, and nearly smacked headfirst into Kelsey, who was beelining straight for her office. Did that mean she knew, too?

"Pardon me," Kelsey said, dancing around Cade to get herself into Megan's office and Cade out. She shut the door behind her, leaving the two of them alone. Kelsey stared at her with those soft brown eyes, and that told her all she needed to know. Kelsey had always been her soft place to fall, and that look in her eyes was all it took. Megan couldn't speak. The lump in her throat was too overwhelming, and the tears were milliseconds behind.

"Come here," Kelsey said, opening her arms and moving to Megan, who didn't hesitate to stand and move straight into them. She couldn't hide what she was feeling from Kelsey even if she wanted to. Not something as crushing as this. "I got you," Kelsey said, smoothing her hair from behind, as she heard the first sounds from the back of her throat. Thank God these walls weren't thin. But this was not the best location for her life's very first breakdown. "It's okay."

"It's not," Megan managed, but her voice sounded like a strangled whisper, and she was noticeably shaking.

"It will be."

She looked around her office, feeling wildly trapped. "I don't think I can do this. Be here. Not today. Not around weddings." Fresh tears. Oh no.

"Say no more. We'll cover your day. That's why you have a team."

The tears streamed down her face as she nodded. Helpless, like someone had punched her in the stomach and knocked the air straight from her body. It felt like there would never be air again, and so much of this was her fault for not fighting, declaring her love, offering Allison everything she had. Then anger took its turn. "I never should have let myself fall in love with her. I should have seen this coming a million miles away."

"I disagree. You can't police who you fall for."

"It wouldn't have worked anyway," Megan said helplessly, returning to her chair like a dejected child. "All arrows pointed to her, and they were neon."

Kelsey scooted the chair across from her desk a little closer and took a seat. "I think there's something to that, don't you?"

"That it was meant to be for me to have my heart stomped on, run over, and pulverized."

Kelsey winced. "I see your sadness hasn't stripped you of imagery."

"A meat grinder comes to mind. A jackhammer." She shook her head, feeling nauseous. "How in the world did I get here?"

"By doing the very human thing of falling in love." Kelsey folded her arms and sat back. "I, for one, don't think you leave it here."

Megan squinted. "What's that supposed to mean?"

"She's not married yet."

"No." Megan held up one finger. "I'm not begging her to abandon the life she chose and come back to me."

"Don't you mean the life you chose for her?"

"Semantics," Megan said. She stared at the open notebook on her desk with mundane notes about other people's happily ever after. Her face crumpled all over again, and she closed it right along with the hope she'd been carrying since deciding to reach out to Allison. All gone now. She was so stupid for thinking she could right the course.

"If the Megan I know is still in there," Kelsey said, standing, "she won't let this wedding happen without having herself heard first. The words *I'm sorry* and *I screwed up* go a long way, you know."

"It's too late," Megan said, resolute. "I'll send a gift."

"Stop that."

"What do you want from me? I'm trying to survive here."

"I want you to take today, lick your wounds, and then explain to Allison what you're feeling. Let her decide. For all she knows, you're living it up, enjoying the single life, happy to be rid of her."

"That's the most ridiculous thing I've ever heard."

"Not everyone's in your head, Megan. You have to express yourself to be understood."

"I don't know that I have that in me."

"Well, I beg to differ, and I hate seeing you like this. You've been a shell of yourself for a long time now. Ever since you ended it."

"You know, I made the decision last night that I was going to ask Ally for another chance. I woke up this morning even more sure of myself. Only to hear she's on the fast track to marriage. How's that for my timing?" She let her head drop back onto her chair. "If that isn't a clear signal from the universe, I don't know what it is."

Kelsey tossed her hands in the air. "I don't know what to do with you. I love you. I'm here for you, but sometimes you frustrate the hell out of me."

"I can see that," she said dully. "The little lines on your face are all furious."

Kelsey touched her face in outrage. "See? You're aging me prematurely. Also, I'm calling your mama."

Megan sat up. "Don't you dare."

"Oh, I'm doing it. You need to listen to reason, and she's the only other hope we have. Mama Kinkaid is getting a call soon."

She didn't have the energy to fight. She could barely string a thought together after emotionally downshifting with the news. "Fine. You win. Call her. Honestly, nothing really matters at this point. I'm going to take today and come back tomorrow, resigned and ready for... whatever." It was lackluster at best, but it was all she had. She felt depleted, as if someone had turned down the volume on her soul. The vibrancy she walked into work with was long gone, along with Allison, the only person on Earth she wanted to speak to.

Yet Ally was long gone.

CHAPTER TWENTY

I have no idea why we have to accomplish all of this in two weeks," Betsy said in a huff, trying on her fifth dress of the day. She stood atop a small stool surrounded by three mirrors in the bridal salon. Allison had already selected her own dress, opting for simple and, hopefully, classic. A white A-line dress, slightly off the shoulder with a short train, accented with a small amount of lace. She didn't feel the need to go all-out the way she always imagined she would. This whole thing had been kind of a whirlwind, and honestly, that was how she preferred it. Why drag it out? Brent had asked her sincerely to reconsider his proposal late one night on his couch after they killed two movies and a bowl of buttery popcorn.

"We're great together, and I miss you," he said sincerely. "I miss the us that used to be, and I can't help but hope that now that the clouds have cleared, your path seems a little more clear. Is there a chance of that? Marry me, Allison. Let's do this."

And rather than agonizing over her feelings for one more uncomfortable second, she'd said yes.

"Do you mean it?" he asked, standing from his spot on the couch. He didn't get on bended knee this time, and there was no fancy setup. No, this discussion was just the two of them in a living room. No fanfare. No photographers. No audience.

She nodded. "Okay. Let's get married." The words felt heavy as they left her lips, but freeing at the same time. They'd been spending so much time together, but he hadn't so much as kissed her yet. That came next. Once he heard her answer, his lips were on hers, and she closed her eyes, bracing for whatever feelings would burst forth.

Fondness. Familiarity. Comfort.

Okay. Those things counted for a lot, and to compare would be wrong.

No, she didn't sink beneath his lips like she did Megan's. She didn't yearn for more the very second they touched, but in so many ways, that was exactly what she needed now. A steady, nonterrifying ship to calm her waters. Plus, she really liked Brent, and they would have a good life together. And maybe once they were married and settled, she could finally shelve the thoughts, memories, and longings of the person who still visited her dreams and left again each morning like a cruel trick.

She shook herself free of the memory and turned to Betsy, as she examined her profile in the mirrors. "Two weeks is completely doable, and wouldn't you say we've drawn this thing out long enough?"

"Well, I can't argue with that. But there's so much to do, to accomplish. I'm going out of my mind on your behalf. I mean, do you even have time to enjoy it? What do you think of this one?" She turned, showing off an emerald-green sleeveless dress that looked dynamite on her.

"A, actually, the faster planning is fun. B, you look gorgeous. Let's go with this one. Yeah?"

Betsy placed a hand on her hip, kicked the hip to the side, and struck a sexy pose in the mirror, the same one she'd employed since they were teenagers to test out her sex appeal. Highly obnoxious but it also made Allison smile. That was Betsy for you. "I vote yes. I could work the aisle in this."

They made an appointment for alternations, Allison handed over Brent's credit card, and they were off to meet their wedding planner, Jason, to sample a round of cake flavors. Unsurprisingly, these appointments reminded her so much of Megan and their consultations in the early days. Jason was no Megan. He was detail oriented, efficient, and friendly, but he didn't come with that magical flair that made her feel as if everything was going to be perfect. That was Megan's gift alone.

"What are you feeling about this one?" Jason asked, pursing his lips in anticipation. His incredibly round glasses perched on his nose, beckoning her to answer, and making her think she wasn't hip enough to meet his expectations. He nailed the sexy nerd vibe. "The strawberry custard filling is very popular."

"It's great," she said. "This will work."

"We don't want it to work, Allison." He placed his hand on her forearm in earnest. "We want it to astound you. Are you astounded beyond measure? Really think."

She paused and met his gaze, trying to impress upon him how thoughtful she was. "Yes," she said, finally. "I find this strawberry filling to be astounding beyond measure." Just easier that way. Megan would have laughed her ass off at this guy.

"I love every second of this," he said, as if she'd just made the most crucial decision of her life.

"Me, too," she said, matching his overly reverent tone.

"Shall we head to floral selections? I have us scheduled for a two o'clock and a three at my two favorite shops. There are some gems I think you're going to clutch your pearls over."

"Let's do it. I left my pearls at home, though."

"Sweetheart, I have a spare set."

She went through the motions, checking items off her Jason-created to-do list over the next few days, having snagged some time off work to make it all happen in the shortened timeline. Before she knew it, she was one week from getting married and a little shocked about that.

"How are you feeling?" she asked her father after dinner at her parents' house after a long day working with Jason. Her mom's spaghetti, meatballs, and garlic bread comfort meal was just what she'd needed. She'd be thrilled to get back to school tomorrow and let him see to all the follow-through. She'd made the decisions, and now he would handle the rest.

"Oh, I'm good. Got a little more wind in my sails. Been going to bed earlier." He smiled. "I'm happy if you're happy."

"I am. Mom says that that you have a meeting with BeLeaf about the Dash Bar. That's pretty great." Of course the talks were back on again now that the happy couple was on the way down the aisle. Typical, but she was not about to lose this opportunity for her family, even if the timing did irk her. She'd love to tell Dalton Carmichael where he could shove his negotiations. Unfortunately, her parents needed his stores.

"It's a relief to have something encouraging in the pipeline."

"Maybe you won't have to sell the house after all."

He smiled at her warily. "You know that all those things are just second place to you, right? I don't care if we have to move, or abandon the bar and find a smaller store. I don't care about any of that as long as you girls are happy." He stared at her as if he was able to see right through her, to the essence of who she was, to her soul. It was unnerving that he seemed to see her so clearly, but then her dad had always been extra intuitive, a sensitive guy.

She blinked against the tears that gathered in her eyes. "It's been a roller coaster of a year. I can admit that. But I'm really doing okay and feel that things will only get better after next week." It was more her hope than her belief. But it was all she had.

"There's no harm in waiting a little longer, you know. Making sure that your heart is where it's supposed to be."

She placed her hand on top of his. "This is the path for me. I just needed some time to see that."

"Then why are you all misty?" he asked.

Well, that did it. She blinked back the tears, but a couple spilled out, traitorous suckers. "I don't know. Just under a lot of wedding stress. My app says it's normal."

"Just know that you can change your mind at any point, okay?"

"Well, I won't be doing that. Ever since I said yes to Brent, I feel like I can breathe." That part was true. He threw her a lifeline when she was drowning, and thank God for that. She now had a sense of direction, purpose, and she would maybe find a way back to the light once again.

"If you say so." He didn't seem convinced. "But I'll be ready with the Nissan in gear, ready to drive you out of there if you give me so much as a nod. Pedal to the metal."

"That's because you're the best dad."

"Be sure to tell Betsy. She raided the fridge and fussed at me for drinking whole milk."

"We'll gang up on her next time."

"Deal." He looked behind him at the dinner dishes. "Guess I better do my part. She cooks. I clean."

"I'll help."

Side by side, they systematically washed and dried, and turned the spaghetti-splattered kitchen back into its original self. The busywork coupled with the familiarity of her family's kitchen settled Allison's emotions, and when she returned home that night she was more determined than ever to walk down the aisle, having gathered her ambition once again. She closed her eyes with a sigh, hoping against hope that a pair of brown eyes didn't overtake her dreams the way they so often did. It was time to move the hell on. She would be so much better for it.

❖

No one discussed the Carmichael wedding at Soiree, which was interesting because it was shaping up to be quite the social event if you listened to gossip, and weddings were practically all they talked about. Yet Megan's coworkers were kind enough to spare her the chatter and even seemed to shield her from errant calls from vendors who were confused about who was now handling the affair, after their initial partnership with the bride and groom.

The wedding was in four days.

Megan knew because she was counting every last one of them, with dread coursing through her veins as they slowly approached Saturday at six p.m. when Allison Hale would walk down the aisle to become Mrs. Brent Carmichael. Shortly after, Megan would no doubt see a splash of photos on social media from mutual friends and read about the nuptials in the society column with a heart full of regret and despair. While she ached for Allison, she had no intention of undoing what Ally so clearly wanted. She was just sad to see she had been right about that all along.

"I talked to Kelsey, and I don't understand." Her mother was already fussing at her through the phone, and they'd barely said hello.

"I told her not to call you."

"She better call me the second she's worried about you. Why didn't you tell me you broke up with Allison?"

She pinched the bridge of her nose. "It just didn't come up."

"Well, that's not quite true. I know when my child is lying to me. Don't try it."

Megan sighed, acquiescing. "It wasn't going to end well. She was still tied up with her ex-fiancé, and now they're back on."

"Because you sent her back."

"No." A pause. "Maybe. Honestly, I don't know, Mama. I'm not in her head."

"Well, I didn't have to be in yours to know that you were in love, and it was so nice to finally see."

A long pause. "You saw that?"

"Clear as day. Your father and I were simply struck by it. Never seen you so happy, so enamored in our lives, and now you ran away."

"I don't know that I would call it that. Self-protection maybe?"

"Chickening out maybe. This is like that time you trained for months for the dance team tryouts in high school and then didn't even show up the day of because you were certain you wouldn't make it."

"I probably wouldn't have."

"Well, now we'll never know. Is that how you want this thing with Allison to play out? You never knowing if things could have gone differently if you had shown up for tryouts?"

She chuckled sardonically. "Oh, if only it was that simple."

"It is that simple." Her mother's voice came through the phone louder and with frustration. "You say what's in your heart, and then you wait for them to talk back. How hard is that?" Her mom was not speaking into the phone when she added, "I swear, this child of yours…"

"Don't bring Dad into this."

"Well, I'm here, too," she heard him call. "You're on speakerphone. Aunt Brenda is also here. She's visiting for beach time."

"I brought extra sunscreen this time," she heard Brenda call from somewhere in the background.

"That's great, Aunt Brenda." She winced. "You're all there talking about my love life. Wonderful."

"Well, someone has to talk about it," her mother fussed. "You're pretty tight-lipped. Did I mention that I didn't raise you to run away?"

"You probably did."

"I can say it again louder."

"No need." She had been blessed with a mother with lots of feelings and opinions, but sometimes they made for true obstacles to getting the support she needed. "It's just been a really confusing and difficult time."

"Then let me help. You go to her and you say your piece."

A long pause as she considered this. "And if she tells me to get the hell away from her?"

"Then at least you know, for heaven's sake, sweetheart. This is not the moment to lose your nerve."

The words hit like a thud. She *had* lost her nerve. Hell, she hardly recognized herself. Her mother wasn't wrong. She'd always been a scrapper, but fear of failure was certainly her Achilles'. "Maybe," she said, making an excuse that she had an urgent bride call on the other line. When she hung up, she pulled up Ally on her phone and let her thumb hover over the call button. All she had to do was press down, and she'd be connected to the one person's voice she longed to hear more than all others.

"Hey, you ever had any trouble with the priest at St. Holy Trinity?" Miranda asked, popping her head into Megan's office. "He's banning the videographer at the Kelly wedding and limiting the photographer to one location at the back only. When I gently pressed, he started yelling at me."

"Father Frank? He's usually easygoing. Are you sure you were gentle?" It was something they were working on with Miranda. Her people skills.

"I mean, I didn't tell him that he was an obstinate blowhard, but there was an insinuation."

Megan closed her eyes and set down her cell phone. For the best. "Let's talk to him together and see if we can change his mind. Take notes, and learn how to behave."

"You got it, boss."

As she put out the fire, her heart tugged at another missed opportunity. She'd almost had the nerve to place that call.

Almost.

CHAPTER TWENTY-ONE

Allison awoke on her wedding day much earlier than was usual. It was like her body knew that this was a special day and wanted her awake for every· moment of it. She'd not stayed at home the night before, and not at Brent's. They were getting married at the Rosewood Mansion, a five-star hotel the Carmichael family frequented for events and the housing of out-of-town guests, and Brent had rented them each a lavish suite. Hers was overly large with towering ceilings, a lush king-size bed, french doors that opened onto a Juliet balcony, and a sitting room that looked like it came out of a decorating magazine, all decked out in mauves and tans with towering bookshelves and large imposing artwork on each wall.

She walked around the space, still wearing the T-shirt she'd slept in. In just a matter of hours her suite would be buzzing with hair and makeup people, her photographers, her family, her attendants, and more. This was the last little bit of solace she'd have, and she took a moment to savor it. Things had worked out so differently than she ever would have planned on just months ago. Her phone rang, jarring her from the quiet. Brent.

"Yes?"

"It's our wedding day. Are you stoked?"

She grinned at his Brent-speak. "So stoked. That's what I said when I woke up. Wow, I'm feeling *stoked*."

"Right? I'm off for a round of golf to loosen up, but I'll see you at six and then again every day." He'd made a great deal of progress with his recovery but was still moving slow. Though he didn't have his old stamina back yet, his friends would watch out for him on the course, and he could use the golf cart to get from hole to hole.

She smiled at his words, and her heart ached in her chest. He sounded so happy, and she was attempting to match him with everything she had in her. It was hard to admit that she was coming up short, but she knew that it would take time, and that much they had going for them. "I'll be there. The one in white, probably stumbling over her vows."

"Even better for when I nail mine." She bit the inside of her lip because he was partially serious.

When Jason arrived, the day took off. He was by her side constantly, which, of course, just reminded her of Megan. She noticed herself getting quieter as lunchtime moved into the afternoon. The suite was full, and Betsy held court, chattering away with the visitors as if it was her own special day. For once, Ally was grateful for Betsy's over-the-top presence that allowed her to fade a bit. Her stomach felt off, and her hands were clammy.

"It's just normal wedding-day jitters," her mother told her when they were alone in the bathroom.

"Right?" She shrugged it off. "Everybody gets nervous on their wedding day. It's the exact day to do it. I'm totally normal and should shut up and enjoy it."

Her mother adjusted a strand of her hair in the mirror. "If it helps, I nearly fainted while we stood at the front of the church on my day. Your father had to steady me. He does that with his eyes."

Ally smiled at the idea. And then she frowned, because her mother had been standing at the altar with her person, and what if Allison wasn't going to be? She gripped the countertop as her vision swirled.

"You all right, sweetie?" her mother said, placing both hands on her shoulders. "You just went incredibly pale."

She squeezed the sides of the bathroom counter with everything she had in her, hoping to ground herself and calm the hell down, find some air, and get the swirly room to stop. "Am I doing the right thing?" She turned to her mother in desperation. Not a conversation she ever thought she'd be having on her wedding day.

"Yes," her mother said without hesitation. "It's scary, one of life's biggest steps, but I know that Brent's the one for you. Everything has pointed in that direction."

"Everything feels like it's happening very fast."

Her mother nodded. "Now that part I can agree with, but that doesn't change the outcome, does it? This is what you said you wanted."

"You're right. You're completely right," she said as she stared at her reflection in the mirror. Her makeup was done, her hair was up. All that was missing was the dress.

An hour later, when she stepped into it as Jason held it open for her, she just knew it would all fall into place. That magic validation she was searching for was surely waiting for her to see her reflection as a bride. As the room full of friends, future in-laws, family, and vendors gasped as she was buttoned in, she turned to her reflection. The woman she saw staring back at her was elegant, beautiful, and so startlingly put together that she didn't know what to do with the culmination of emotion. Was that really her? She looked like a princess. "Wow," she said simply. This was a surreal moment, and time seemed to go extra slow. How many times had she imagined herself as a bride growing up? Here she stood.

"More than wow, little sister. You're going to dazzle," Betsy said, squeezing her shoulders from behind.

She turned to Betsy, who had misted up. "Thank you, Bets."

"I mean it." A pause. "You okay?"

She nodded. "I am."

The next forty-five minutes seemed to fly in a series of shutter clicks from the photographers' cameras in various parts of the hotel, until they were moments away from the ceremony and the biggest moment of her life. She'd seen a serene little garden on the grounds earlier and had a thought.

"Jason?" she asked.

"What can I get for you?" he asked. "I have about five minutes before I head to the ceremony to get prepped."

"Perfectly fine. I'm going to catch my breath in the little garden near the front. Is that all right?"

His brow creased. "The guests might see you."

"I won't be long. I really need a private minute to clear my head." She needed a pep talk, is what she needed. The gravity of the situation weighed heavily on her. More so with each passing second.

Jason nodded, and while the photographers worked with her cousins on her father's side, she slipped away, mindful of the time. A short elevator ride and a couple of hallways with impressive ceilings led her to the outdoor sitting area she'd seen earlier. Lots of greenery, bright flowers in pinks and yellows flanking the space. Once she was alone with the fresh air on her skin, she closed her eyes and let the sunshine fall on her face. There it was just like always, ready to comfort her and guide her on this journey. The warmth on her skin grounded her, and she could, at long last, breathe. She savored the relief of air to her lungs.

"You look beautiful."

She didn't open her eyes. She knew the voice and had to be imagining it. Megan had shown up in her dreams most every night since they'd said good-bye. Of course she'd find a way into Ally's thoughts now. Of course. But when she opened her eyes, the startling reality was that she hadn't imagined the words at all. Incomprehensibly, there she stood. Right there in front of Allison. Not a mirage, not a dream. She wore jeans and a soft purple T-shirt.

For a long moment, neither of them moved. Allison's heart jackhammered, and her thoughts were all but suspended. Her world, the serenity from moments before, had just been tossed in the air.

Finally, Megan held out a hand. "I'm not here to upset you. I don't want to do that, especially not today."

"Then why are you here?" she managed to say. "I'm getting *married.*"

Megan took a deep breath. "I know. And I shouldn't have waited so long." She closed her eyes. "I tried. I did. I just couldn't…" She opened her eyes again, and Allison's resolve shook at the sight of them. Big, brown, and expressive. She used to get lost in their depths and loved it.

"You tried to…what?" Allison asked, searching her face for some kind of clue or explanation as to exactly what was happening, because there was no sound reason for Megan's presence here.

"I was a coward," Megan said simply. "I was so scared of what I was feeling, what it meant, and how much I had to lose that I ran from the one person I never should have run away from."

"No. You don't get to come here and say that."

Megan held up her hand. "I was so caught up believing that you were moments away from running back to Brent at any given second that I held myself back from you, and there was a lot you didn't get to hear, to know."

Allison pinched the bridge of her nose. This wasn't happening.

"But the truth of the matter is that the last thing I wanted was to lose you. I woke up terrified every day until I finally convinced myself that stepping back was the right thing to do."

"Yet here you stand." It was an accusation. "I'm not doing this, Megan. I can't. I'm moving on. This isn't fair of you, to show up like this."

Megan's gaze fell to the ground in defeat. "I know. Trust me, I'm well aware, but I couldn't let you walk down the aisle and pledge your life to someone else until you knew the truth. I fell in love with you, Allison. I knew it back then, and I know it even more now. I miss your smile, our talks, your touch. In fact, I've been just sick without you."

Allison stared at her, attempting to process the words she'd longed to hear for so long. Megan loved her. But they felt all wrong now. They were here too late, and so was Megan. "You should go."

Megan nodded, tears filling her eyes. "Yeah, I guess so." She turned down the stone pathway that led out of the garden to the front of the hotel. Allison watched her go, making peace with her decision, because dammit, it was the right one. Love was one thing, but stability was something else entirely.

She nodded to herself, set on her path and ready to begin the rest of her life.

She picked up her train, and with one last moment alone with the sun, she took a deep breath and headed off to find Jason and get this show on the road. It was almost time.

❖

It had been a killer Saturday. Megan had attempted to stop one wedding before wrapping up another for work. She normally headed home for the comfort of her couch and junk food to unwind, but tonight she didn't quite think she could handle the silence. Her heart hurt, and though she understood quite clearly that she carried the responsibility for that, she still sought relief, and the bottom of a glass seemed like the best place to find it.

Kelsey beat her to Shakers and had a picture-perfect martini waiting for her on the table when she arrived.

"You think ahead."

"I learned from the best."

Megan, having changed from her navy wedding clothes into jeans, flat shoes, and a simple black top, sighed in awe of the drink.

"Before you drink, let me propose a toast."

"Is that really necessary?" Megan asked, squinting. The day had sucked, everything hurt, nothing more than her heart, and she just wanted to get on with it. "Let me toss this back like a fish, and please be prepared to walk me home. I feel like I might need three of these things."

"It's rare you get sloshed, so I can accept my best friend responsibility and deliver you safely to your door."

Megan stared at the exposed brick on the back wall. "You should have seen the way the Jacksons looked into each other's eyes during their first dance tonight." She shook her head, remembering the love and adoration that made her want to gouge her eyes out. "Love is highly overrated."

"You have every right to say that for a little while. A free pass, but it does have an expiration date."

"You're no fun."

"I'm actually the fun one in this duo. See that woman over there? We actually had a lot of fun last night. Maybe you should try something similar."

"Tried it. I'm broken. Love's fault. Toast already, so I can swan dive into the drunk end of the pool."

Kelsey lifted her glass, a lemon drop martini for her. "To taking chances."

"No." Megan set her glass right the hell down. "I don't want to toast to that. Risk sucks."

"You did something brave today, Meg."

"Debatable. Pathetic comes to mind. But"—she nodded reluctantly—"I stand by it. I'm glad I put myself out there even if I crashed and burned in the most horrifying sense."

"Except I'm not so sure you did."

"If this is a speech about following my heart, you can skip it. More about the erasing-my-memory portion of the evening. Let's get to that."

"Not yet."

"I'm really starting to resent you."

"She didn't marry him." Kelsey raised her eyes from her glass to Megan and waited. Megan studied her friend's face, noting the small smile that played on her lips. She wouldn't screw around with Megan's feelings right now. Did that mean that her words were true?

She made the come-here gesture. "What are you saying? I need more of the words."

"I'm saying that Cade and Jason are at a bar about ten blocks from here, and Jason is regaling Cade with the dramatic events of his day working the Carmichael wedding. Or should I say the wedding that wasn't."

She blinked. She stared. She tried to understand.

Sensing her confusion, Kelsey set down her drink. "Apparently, moments before walking down the aisle, Allison asked to speak with Brent privately. Jason balked because tradition and all, but she insisted. No one knows what was said in that room, but the wedding was called off. Brent made a brief announcement to the already seated guests, Allison took off with her dad in his Nissan like a bank robber after a job, and the decor was quietly taken down. No one got married there today."

Megan didn't know what to do with this information. All of a sudden, she had energy coursing through her limbs, and her mind was now overly alert, not like she'd just worked a wedding and had her heart stomped on. As she sat there, she felt hope creep in. She'd not heard from Allison, though. Not a word, and she certainly hadn't been happy or relieved to see her at the hotel this afternoon. That was worth paying attention to.

"We don't know why?"

"Well, I think we *do*. She's in love with you and can't ignore it."

Megan frowned, searching the bar as if it would have her answer. "Then why haven't I heard from her? Why hasn't she told me she called it off?"

"I didn't say she was happy with you. I wouldn't be."

She sat back in her chair. "Huh." A pause. "Be right back."

Kelsey stared at her in confusion as she excused herself to the sidewalk in front of the bar and placed a call. Her father answered on the second ring.

"You okay?" he asked immediately. "It's after ten."

"I'm completely fine. But I'm in a spot." She was pacing because she had all this scattered energy. "I went and saw Allison before the wedding. I told her how I felt."

"Do you want Mom for this?"

"She yelled at me last time. How about you fill in?"

"How about I hold the phone but keep her in the loop?" he asked. "Sold."

Her father's voice drifted away. "She talked to Allison, you know, the girl she loves, before her wedding. She stormed the wedding!"

"Course I know who Allison is. Give me that. What did she say?" her mother asked, breathless, probably grabbing the phone.

"I'm still here!" her father yelled.

"Don't delay. What did she say?" Her mother had the phone now. "You stormed the wedding?"

"I don't know about stormed, but I went there and talked with her, and she told me it was too late. Sent me away."

A pause. "Oh," her mother said. "Why'd you sound so happy, then?" she asked her dad, followed by the sound of a smack to the arm she was quite familiar with.

"Didn't know that part yet."

Megan continued, "But here's the thing. She called it off after I left."

Her mother didn't hesitate. "*Ahhhh!* She loves you back! Ding-dong it all, I knew it. I saw it when you were here. I just *knew*."

"Ding-dong, indeed," Megan said. "Now what? Your tough love instructions apparently worked, as scary as it was."

"I didn't even raise my voice. You just don't like being questioned, but I'll tell you what now, because I happen to know. Moms do. You go very slow and approach her with caution."

"Slow."

"Patience," her father yelled. "Like you're approaching an unhappy animal in the wild. How I won your mother over. Had to systematically convince her I was a good one."

"He's *pretty* good," her mom said, by way of mild concession. "Still leaves his clothes on the floor."

"Allison can throw her clothes anywhere she wants to if we can just be together."

"Aww," her parents said in unison.

"That's a sweet thing you just said," her mother said. "Bring her back to Corpus for some more fun."

"I'm gonna do my best." A pause. "Patience, huh?"

"The only way."

She sighed. She could be patient when it came to work or seeing a movie she was excited about, but when it came to her life, to Allison who she missed more than was possible, how was she supposed to sit on her hands? How?

"You called her, didn't you?" Kelsey asked, eyeing her as Megan returned to her chair.

"I did no such thing. What? You think I have no patience? Just checking in on my parents. Standard stuff."

"I'm impressed at your willpower."

She exhaled slowly. "I think if I want another shot with Ally, then I'm going to have to play the long game."

"Ooh la la." Kelsey sat back, her eyes dancing. "I cannot wait to watch take-charge Megan Kinkaid sit on her damn hands when we both know who she wants them all over. Start the movie already."

"Yeah, yeah," Megan said. But for the first time in a long while, she was smiling genuinely. There was actual hope, and she planned to hold on to that. No way in hell she was going to blow it this time. Been there. Done that. Now it was time to get serious.

Let the waiting begin.

CHAPTER TWENTY-TWO

The fourth grade had been extra rowdy today. DJ had slugged Taylor for using his ruler without permission, and Evelyn and Claire had ended their best friendship over a disagreement about BTS. The whole class was inattentive, and Ally hadn't remembered to breathe deeply when her workday smacked her in the face.

"You look awful." She glanced up from her overcleaning of the dry erase board to find Lacey staring at her from the doorway. "If the fourth graders suck so much, please do not send them to fifth grade. No room at the inn."

"Better start brushing up on your BTS backstory now, or you have no hope of settling the arguments. These girls mean business."

"Good thing I'm an aficionado already." A pause. "Remember when you played runaway bride?"

It had been nine days since she'd fled the scene of her wedding. She squinted. "Only vaguely."

"How's that going?"

She dropped her towel to her side. "It was the right move. I stand by it now, but I don't feel better about it." She slipped on top of the nearest student desk. "Brent and I have talked briefly. Giving each other some space. He understands. Even takes responsibility for rushing things."

"Is there hope there?"

"For a romance?" She shook her head. "No. Too hard after…"

"Yeah." Lacey slid her hands into the back pockets of her black pants and surveyed the room as if super interested in the decor. "About that. Her. You talked to her?"

"Nope." That was Allison's cue to go back to angry scrubbing of the whiteboard. "She kicked me to the curb and then successfully ruined my wedding day, moments before I was set to walk down the aisle."

"I know, right? Damn her." Another long pause. Lacey took a stroll around the perimeter of desks, trailing one finger along their surfaces as she walked. "You did skip the wedding, though."

"Yes."

"So maybe she had a point? Maybe there's some unfinished... something...I don't know...there?"

"Are you on her side now?" Ally asked, straightening midscrub, hand on her hip.

"Not if you're going to shoot me looks like that." She held up her hands palms out and backed slowly toward the door. "Just checking in is all."

Allison nodded, not taking her eyes off Lacey as she retreated. "Well, to answer what seems to be your question, no, I don't plan on reaching out to Megan."

"I know, right? Blech. Wedding ruiner. Who wants that?" She offered a wave. "See ya later, Hale." And just like that her friend took off like a scared kitten. She didn't often have that effect on people, but she was admittedly extra feisty these days. Angry, confused, and adrift. But no. She wasn't cutting Megan a pass on this. Let her stay downtown and plan her weddings and stop popping into Allison's head uninvited, looking sexy and beautiful and kind.

"A mirage," she murmured through her persistent cleaning. "Not going there."

Once she had everything in its proper place for the opening of the once-a-semester school store, she headed home with a weary sigh. She felt clobbered and needed a pick-me-up. Knowing just the place, she made a right turn, changed course, and arrived at Froman's, land of amazing caffeinated dream drinks. She happily took her place in line, ignoring the menu because she would be having a Toffee Crunch Dream. Iced this time because Dallas was incredibly warm these days. She was up next and gave the shop full of people a perusal. Meetings, friends catching up, some working on their laptops. Pause. Rewind. Ally froze because there by the window, laptop open, a neat stack of folders to its right, sat Megan, who stared back at her with a conservative smile. Allison nodded and for the life of her didn't know what to do. She forgot her order, how to place it, what money was.

She was up and the cheerful barista smiled. "Your usual?" Oh, thank God. Ally smiled and nodded, handing over the credit card she now clamped way too hard. Once she'd received her drink, she had a call to make. Walk by Megan's table like a normal person and say hello, or stroll the hell on out of there. She exhaled, knowing herself and how she was raised. She found her smile and approached the table, her chest tight and her stomach full of butterflies.

"Small world," Allison said.

"Isn't it?" Brown eyes found hers, and the familiarity of their connection was startling. How was it still this strong after everything? Surely time would have dimmed its luster. No such luck.

"I guess it is my fault for introducing you to this place."

"It's pretty hard to forget about." Megan studied the room. "It's a good escape to work or read."

"You've been coming here to read."

Megan nodded. "Only just recently." She shrugged. "Better chance of running into you if I'm here more."

Ally dropped her gaze to her drink and the pillowy hills of whipped cream on top. "You might have heard. I didn't get married."

"I did hear. I'm sorry."

She shook her head. "No, you're not."

"No." At least she had the courage to admit it. "That wasn't your life you were heading toward."

"Interesting," she said, which was impressive of her because what she really wanted to ask was why Megan had to ruin every good thing Allison had going for herself. The anger tightened around her heart like a vise. "Well, enjoy the rest of your workday. That's a nice spot you've got for yourself." She didn't wait for a good-bye.

When she swung by Froman's the following Monday after a leisurely weekend of doing absolutely nothing that took place off her couch, she was surprised to see Megan reading a book in one of the comfy chairs in the corner. It was Monday afternoon. Didn't she have clients to meet with? Why was she all of sudden taking up residence at Ally's favorite coffee shop?

"You're stalking me," she said to Megan, who seemed to finish the sentence she was on before looking up from her book. She smiled, and Allison felt it all the way to her fingertips. She planned to ignore that.

"I'm reading a book in a public place. Are you gonna stick around?"

She'd actually been planning to. "Yeah, just to unwind. I'll sit over there," she said and pointed to an open table currently being cleaned off by an employee. It offered enough space.

"Suit yourself, but there's a perfectly good chair right here." Megan pointed to the armchair next to hers, a small table at its armrest.

"This table is fine," Allison said and headed to it. "Enjoy."

Only, a couple of teenagers beat her to the spot, and she was left looking around for a place to sit like an idiot. This place really picked up in the late afternoon. She felt Megan's gaze on her, tracking her plight. When she turned back, Megan silently gestured with one hand to the chair.

"Fine," Allison said. "Desperate times and all."

"You're sitting here under protest, and it's been noted for the record."

"Yes," she said, setting her things down, sipping from her straw, and feigning intense interest in her phone. Megan went back to her book, and dammit, she'd missed the title. As she mindlessly scrolled and people-watched in rotation, she became wildly aware of Megan's favorite lotion. She wore it daily, and it took Ally right back to the days and nights they'd been inseparable. *Happy*, her heart added. When they'd been carefree, blissful, and eager for each new day together.

"What is it you're reading, anyway?" she finally asked, hearing the annoyance in her voice.

Megan raised her head, and glanced at the front. "Just a little self-improvement." She flashed the cover, a drawing of a woman with lots of little faces coming out of her head. "It's called *Flight Risk*. It's about how our emotions influence the risks we're willing to take in life."

"Huh," Allison said. "Interesting."

"I figured I could always use a few tips. Sometimes I run away from things because I get scared."

"Right," she said, eyeing Megan suspiciously. Was this for real?

"Hey, how's that little guy Levi doing?"

"He's asking his friends about whether he should become a movie star or not. Most have said no, but his parents have convinced him that there's no other route for such a dashing young man. We're working on how to stay humble."

"Oh, he's going to be a handful."

"He is, until some girl gets ahold of him and sets him straight."

"Or some boy."

"Good point. He's just a runaway train of charisma." She caught herself smiling in the midst of her dishing. She'd forgotten to be angry, hurt, and unforgiving. She'd have to work harder. But it felt ridiculously good to just talk to Megan again about something as casual as work.

"I have every confidence in your ability to help guide him."

"Yeah…" Ally said, letting her voice trail. She glanced at the door. "I better get out of here and to work on grading today's creative writing assignment."

"Oh, that sounds fun," Megan said. "I bet you get such a variety. Do you have any superstars?"

"I do. Take care." She hightailed it out like the place was close to bursting into flames, when in fact, maybe she was the one about to. All because of the effect Megan Kinkaid had on her. She muttered to herself the whole damn way home, but she did something ridiculous and came back the next afternoon, scanned the place as she approached the counter, and absorbed the disappointment that surfaced when she realized Megan was nowhere to be found. "That's not why you came here," she whispered to herself because she was apparently that person now, who whispered to herself in public while others looked on curiously. She was here for the coffee that made her world sparkle and no other reason. She was stronger than that!

Megan wasn't there the next day either, and that was perfectly fine, preferable even. But four days later, when Augustus threw up all over the stack of math homework, Allison decided she deserved an after-work treat. Megan was in line when she got there. She took her spot behind her.

"We have to stop meeting like this," she said when Ally arrived.

"I'm simply going to my standard coffee spot. I think if anyone is crashing, it's you."

"Oh." A beat. She looked struck and a little sad. "Well, I don't want to take this place away from you if I make you uncomfortable."

"No, no. I'm just...being difficult. This place is as much yours as mine." Another pause. "What'll you have?"

"I've actually been traveling the menu, giving everything a shot. Today I'm going with almond cappuccino."

"I'm impressed. That's a real drink."

"So is a Toffee Crunch Dream."

Allison sighed. "Let's be honest. It's not. It's a perfect dessert but not a serious coffee beverage. Your latte will laugh at my dream."

"I won't let it. Want to grab a table together?" She said it so casually. How?

Allison could lie to herself all she wanted, pretend that was the stupidest idea ever and make an excuse to hit the road, but the reality was that the suggestion sounded really nice. Like a warm bath after an especially tense day. A glass of water to someone incredibly thirsty. "I guess so. We're both here."

"I noticed that, too," Megan said with a wink. She got her drink first and snagged a table, and when her Dream was ready, Allison joined her. What in the world were they supposed to talk about? She was now hyperaware of everything. The way she lifted her own drink to her lips. Megan's perfectly applied makeup, which made her look gorgeous, even though she didn't need any of it. The soft rock playing on the speakers. Why couldn't she just relax? *Because she broke your heart and upended your whole world.* Could that be it?

But then Megan launched into a story about a bride she'd met with that afternoon that wanted a circus-themed wedding, including tightrope walkers and flame eaters, and they were off.

"Do you need some sort of insurance on that kind of event?"

"I've already placed a few calls to find out. This is the creepy part. She wants to walk down the aisle as a clown."

"Stop it. No one will attend." She was already laughing at the lunacy, which certainly helped the tension dissolve.

"And she wants that silly instrumental circus music for the processional. Apparently, this is her lifelong dream."

"And her partner is going along with it?"

"Oh, he was there, too. He's going to dress as a lion tamer."

Ally closed her eyes and placed a hand on her chest. "Bless his heart."

"Bless his sweet little heart. He loves her."

"Enough to don a whip?"

"Definitely planning the whip."

Allison laughed again. "You have to get photos."

"My portfolio is gonna be poppin'."

"Wedding planning, especially in a short period of time, is not for the timid. I don't know how you do it. I have new appreciation for the industry."

"Is it weird for you, talking about the almost wedding?"

She considered the question, a little surprised by how not weird it was. "No. It's a part of my life, and I'm coming to terms with it."

"Have you come to terms with my role in it?"

She stared into her drink. "No. Not quite."

"Yeah, I kind of got that impression. I don't know if it matters now, or maybe if not now then someday, but I'm truly sorry. For all of it."

She raised her gaze and found Megan's eyes. Her expression was heartfelt, sincere. "Thank you for saying that." She left it there. While Megan still had a clear effect on her, some kind of magnetic pull she couldn't shake, her heart was now guarded and closed.

"You don't have to say anything. Just listen." Megan placed her hand on the table right along Allison's. Megan didn't touch her, probably on purpose, but the proximity forced her to swallow and remember to breathe. "I haven't given up on us. I know you likely have, and that's okay. But I'm here as your friend…or whatever else. If you tell me to stay away, I will. I don't plan to make any big moves or make you feel uncomfortable. But if you ever feel like taking a step in my direction, I'll be here and would very much welcome that opportunity to show you how unafraid I am now. Of you, of me. Of us."

Oh, those were some rattling words. It took Allison a moment to digest them, turn them over, and decide how she felt. A part of her couldn't resist celebrating their meaning. That was the part that still held on to her amazing memories with Megan. The other part of her screamed *hell no*, still bristling from abandonment and betrayal. Megan didn't just get to waltz in and out of her life on a whim. Allison was a person with real feelings and vulnerabilities, and she wasn't about to hand Megan the power to undo her all over again, whenever she felt like it.

"I hear you. I do. And I honestly don't have the perfect reply."

"Then let's leave it there and talk about something else. The weather, your parents. How are they?"

"Surprisingly good. Brent was kind enough to put his foot down with his father, and for once he was heard. The board got involved and decided the product stood on its own, and they're moving forward with the licensing. The Dash Bar is going into fifty stores across Texas, and if it does well, they'll expand."

"Wow, so what does this mean for them?"

"They can breathe a little easier. Take their house off the market, for starters."

She smiled. "Well, I'm shocked to be saying this, but I'm proud of the Carmichaels for setting the personal aside."

"Me, too. And it takes away some of the guilt."

"You don't have to feel guilty about following your heart. You get to make your own choices."

She took a moment to sort her thoughts because there were so many. "I feel like I'm on a journey right now. I'm learning who I am, but I'm also learning who I want to be. I like the strength I've discovered and plan to continue building on it."

Megan seemed impressed. "I envy you."

"Why? You're one of the strongest people I've ever met."

"Um, you might want to rethink that, given recent behavior."

"You know something? You're right. You're a chicken."

Megan's mouth fell open. "I suppose I deserve that. Not a term I'm used to owning, but I can do it, as long as we can move it to the past tense." Her face took on a determined quality, her eye contact unwavering. "Because that's not where I'm at now."

"Yes, you've indicated as much." That was about all she was willing to agree to, and in the midst of their conversation, she'd slugged down about three-quarters of her Toffee Crunch Dream. Not much left holding her here.

Megan must have picked up on her shift. "You're about to leave, aren't you?"

Allison nodded.

"Okay, well, maybe we'll see each other again sometime."

"Yeah." She stood, paused, and forced herself to relinquish a little bit of her resentment. "Thanks for the talk. I mean that." She offered a soft smile to punctuate, and she meant it, too.

She drove home feeling better than she had in a long while. Unclear on exactly what she was feeling and what was happening, but she was trying not to overanalyze. *Just float*, she told herself. That's all that was required.

❖

Megan tried not to think too much as she navigated the spring into summer transition. Soiree was about to enter its busiest season, and it was important she stayed focused on the things in front of her that she could control: her work, her ability to be a good and kind person, and not overthinking. That last part was key, and it would be to her detriment if she let her overworking brain convince her that her efforts to rebuild her relationship with Allison brick by brick were for nothing. They weren't. Simply talking to Ally again was a salve. Allowing a little bit of her light to spill over into Megan's life was an actual gift, and that's what she chose to concentrate on.

If they were meant to be, it would happen.

The idea that they weren't was too much to consider at this point.

They'd made it a couple of times a week habit to meet up at Froman's and catch up. Their short talks had gradually grown longer until sometimes they sat there for two hours or more. Nothing romantic had happened between them, but the connection was impossible to ignore. She reminded herself that Ally could have stopped coming to their impromptu coffee dates, or dodged her when she arrived.

"How many more weeks until your summer break?" she'd asked Allison earlier that week. She'd adjusted her drink order to an iced latte to compensate for the approaching summer scorchers.

"Seventeen school days, but who's counting?" Allison wore gray pants and a white dress shirt, having come straight from work. She really rocked the outfit, and if they were together, Megan would have been trotting after her like a puppy.

"Not you. Big plans?"

Allison sighed and slid a strand of hair behind her ear. It was longer these days, sexy. "Maybe I'll go somewhere with sand."

"I seem to remember it looking good on you." She'd paused to watch the blush hit Allison's cheeks, and it warmed her, too. She didn't take the reminder of their picnic on the beach any further, but she had a feeling Allison remembered the day as clearly as she did. It had been a fantastic afternoon, one she hoped they'd get to repeat sometime. Maybe.

"Good point. Maybe I'll look more seriously at a vacation. I could use one. Or I'll take a cruise to the Caribbean and leave it all behind."

"You should. You do so much for your kids all year. You deserve to be pampered."

Allison looked over at her, and she could see the conflict play out on her face. There was more Ally wanted to say, but she was holding back, which of course, Megan understood.

"I do enjoy a good cruise, provided it's the quiet luxurious kind."

"You speak from experience?"

"I do. I could show you the ropes. The twenty-four-hour pizza kitchen is not something you want to discover on the last day."

They stared at each other for a long moment, lost in the fantasy of the two of them at sea. Well, at least Megan was.

"Another life, right?" Allison said uncomfortably.

"Really? Because we have so much left in this one."

Ally blinked, processing. "It's not that easy. I can't seem to trust you. We were on a tightrope together, and you let go." Her voice was quiet, vulnerable, and Megan more than appreciated her honesty.

She swallowed. Her hands trembled. "I won't ever let go, Ally. I can guarantee you that."

"Yeah," Allison said, glancing away. The moment was charged, and Megan found it hard to breathe. "It's not that I don't want to… or that I don't feel…" It was almost as if she didn't have the energy to complete a sentence. "I just can't."

"I understand." Her heart thudded dully, and her gaze landed on the table in defeat. And there it was. In spite of the time they'd spent together, their connection, and her patience, it seemed they'd reached an impasse. "I don't want to let you go," she said, lost, to the wood grain of the table. Her heart hurt, her head swam, and her fortitude was all but dashed.

"I know," Allison whispered. "But I think we have to."

It was a conclusion. It offered no hope, and that meant it was time for Megan to take Allison at her word. "I guess I've crashed your favorite coffee shop a few times too many. Time I return it to your care." She stood and slid her hands into the back pockets of her black jeans.

"I'd be lying if I said I haven't enjoyed our talks. It makes things a little easier, you know?"

Megan nodded. "I think that's called closure. I'm glad I was able to give that to you." It hadn't been her intention at all, but she had to glimpse a silver lining in a moment of such utter sadness. "You take care of yourself, okay?" She heard the strangled sound of her voice, indicative of the emotion she couldn't seem to tamp down.

Moments later, Allison's arms were around her neck, and she held on to Megan tightly. "I'll never forget us," she whispered, which just made it that much harder. How could it possibly be over? The two of them apart quite simply felt like it went against the universe. She closed her eyes, held on, memorizing every detail, and braced for the inevitable moment. When Allison let go. The loss was like a blast of cold, uncomfortable air that left her sad, alone, and hating herself for what she'd done to them. After a final look back, Allison walked out of the coffee shop. Megan sat, grappling, trying to make her brain process the finality of that moment. The room felt dull. Muted, as if the color and life had been drained from her surroundings.

She sat there for what felt like a few minutes or a few hours until she was able to gather herself and her belongings and head to her car. She paused as she approached because there was a woman leaning against it. No, not just any woman.

Allison.

When she heard Megan approach, she turned, and those bright blue eyes, brimming with emotion, told her everything she needed to know. "I couldn't leave," Ally said. "I don't want to leave you." She reached for Megan, who moved to her instantly, overcome. She took Megan's face in her hands and kissed her right there in the damned parking lot of Froman's Coffee, and the world stopped on its axis. All that was left was this magnificent feeling that she was right in the spot she was supposed to be, and those lips—dear God, she had missed them.

"What are you doing to me?" Megan asked, coming up for air.

"I think I'm changing my mind. Am I allowed to change my mind? Say yes."

"Yes," she answered automatically. Laughter followed, the really good kind that allowed her to release some of that pent-up tension. This was actually happening. She leaned in and kissed Ally again, lingering, reveling in the familiar taste of her lip gloss. She was ready to burst with joy. "Are you sure?"

Allison nodded. "I am, and I've known it for a while. I've just fought against it with everything in me, and for what? To live in my own unhappiness because I can't forgive you. That's stupid. When I walked out of that coffee shop, I was trying to be someone I'm not. I'm yours."

"You're scared. I get that. You're allowed to be. But if you're willing, let me take that on. You can just coast. Eat breakfast in bed and plan the trips we're gonna take on breaks from school. I love you and nothing is going to change that."

Something unexpected happened. Allison started to cry.

"Oh no. Was that the wrong thing to say?"

Allison shook her head, wiping away the tears from her scrunched-up, adorable face. "It was the perfect thing to say. I love you, too, even when I'm so mad at you I can't see straight."

"Maybe that means we're meant to be." Megan pulled Allison to her and held on. They attracted an occasional stare from a passing car, but nothing that fazed her in the slightest. "What now?" she whispered. The options seemed endless. Her heart soared as she celebrated this gift of a second chance. "Can I see you later?"

Allison pulled back, looked up, and held her gaze. "Your place or mine?"

CHAPTER TWENTY-THREE

Kissing Megan in the middle of the parking lot had been just the thing to break the spell. In that moment, so many of her worries floated away, and she remembered with startling clarity who they were, and how well they fit together. Who knew a kiss that was sexy and goddamn satisfying could also ground a person so effectively?

The release that hit after finally giving in to her feelings staggered Ally. She'd driven to Megan's apartment that night on a high, almost as if her car didn't touch the road. She'd floated her way there. When Megan had opened the door in crop jeans, bare feet, and an off the shoulder yellow T-shirt, Allison nearly melted. This had been the right decision.

They stood in that doorway grinning at each other, high on their reclaimed dynamic, almost like they couldn't quite take their eyes away. "Come here," Megan said, taking her by the hand, pulling her right the hell in so that their bodies pressed against each other.

"Hi," Ally said. Megan's greeting was a little more intimate. Her lips were on Allison's in a searing hello. "Oh, my. Your greeting was better," she said, her voice now a little lower.

Megan laughed. "I'm feeling a little greedy. Come in."

"What should we do?" Allison asked, trailing a finger along the countertop she'd long missed. She nearly inhaled the place, taking in every familiar detail. The soft summer breeze tickling the window. Soothing jazz music playing from the speakers. The blanket on the back of the couch she'd curled up with more than a few times. The soft ticking of the silver clock on the wall. There was something about these details that were so uniquely tied to her understanding of who she was that it felt like she'd arrived somewhere near and dear to her heart, which, in fact, she had.

"Are you hungry?"

Allison shook her head.

"Wine?"

"I'm good for now."

Megan's grin grew along with her understanding. "Backgammon."

"Not a chance."

She looked skyward, a smile tugging. "Well, as your hostess, it's up to me to make sure you're happy."

"Happy? Well, that part is already taken care of." She exhaled. "Did you see that? I feel like I can breathe again, and that's worth celebrating."

Megan nodded. "I want you to know something. I recognize that this is a big step, and believe me, I'm not taking a single moment for granted. And we can go incredibly slow if that helps." Those beautiful brown eyes were soft when she said the words. Ally already found herself lost in them, and how wonderful that she could now allow herself to just *be*. No more fighting what was right in front of her, warring with her thoughts. This was where she belonged. It felt right.

"Why don't we take it one moment at a time?" she said, depositing her bag on the barstool closest to her. She made her way to Megan, who grinned as she watched her approach. "The thing is, I like slow. But fast is fun, too." Megan's eyes darkened, and her smile dimmed.

"Oh," she said. "And how are we feeling today?"

"I thought we could improvise."

"Sold."

They were kissing in two seconds flat, Allison up on tiptoe for maximum access. Slow and sensual was up first, leaving her a little drunk. Megan's hands were on the small of her back but moving upward. Her tongue was in Ally's mouth, causing murmurs of pleasure she only distantly registered came from her own mouth. Before Allison knew it, she'd been slid onto the counter, giving her a newfound height advantage. Once deposited there, Megan took a moment to just look at her and take her in. She slid a strand of hair lovingly behind Ally's ear as her eyes dropped lower. Wordlessly, she pulled Allison's top over her head and feasted her gaze on the pink bra with more than a little cleavage revealed. "Seriously?" she whispered to no one. Allison leaned back on her hands and grinned, loving the foreplay, having missed this part desperately. She trembled in the best sense when Megan pulled the straps of her bra down to her elbows, kissed her neck tenderly, and made her way to the tops of her breasts, licking the space between them, following the path with her tongue. Ally's head dropped back as she reveled in the combination of pleasure and desire that coursed through every inch of her. Her eyes were closed and her bra was off. That much she became aware of as Megan, with her hands on Ally's waist, began to tease her mercilessly with her mouth. God. But she needed give and take. She straightened, pulled Megan's mouth to hers, and kissed her with the passion she'd had building for weeks. She turned her around and kissed her neck from the side as she palmed her breasts through her shirt. Megan didn't hesitate and took the damn thing off, tossing it to the floor as the music kicked into extra soulful, punctuating the moment. Perfect. She pressed Megan's breasts back against her body as she caught her earlobe in her mouth. "I think we may need to move this party somewhere a little more comfortable."

"Counters can be fun," Megan said, turning to her.

"Later."

"Your ambition is my favorite."

They kissed their way to Megan's bedroom, stopping for a time on the arm of the couch, then up against a wall in the hallway, before finally finding a bed. As hot as they were together, as always, everything about this time also felt different. There was a reverence to it, an expression of the love they'd recaptured and faced head-on. Each touch was softer, each moment of eye contact that much more intense. When Megan took her to heights of pleasure and brought her down again, there were tears on her cheeks.

Megan tenderly wiped them away and laid her face along Ally's. "Hey there. Are you okay? Talk to me."

"I'm more than okay. I'm…home."

She kissed her. "You are. And you're never leaving again. Ever. You hear me?"

"And if you get scared, or nervous, or feel the least bit insecure, then—"

"I will scream it from the rooftops, so not only you, but every neighbor we have knows how I'm feeling."

"We have the same neighbors?"

"Well, yeah. Eventually." In the dim light of the room, she could see that Megan was nervous. "I'm ready for that now, but listen, we can hold off. Summer is a good time to move, though. You're off work."

"Wait a minute." She placed her hand on Megan's cheek and turned her face so their gazes connected. "Megan Kinkaid, wedding planner known to many, are you asking me to move in with you? Officially asking?"

"Yes, fourth-grade teacher. Please do. Anytime you want. Today, tomorrow, next year. The offer is there. Or I'll move in with you. Either way, I want it to happen."

Allison grinned. "You'd miss this place, and honestly, so would I."

"As long as I'm with you, I can breathe. Tested the theory. Never want to again."

This was such a big decision, but she honestly didn't have to think very long. "Yes. When school's out. Let's do it."

"And a Caribbean vacation. And maybe Italy at Christmastime. Chianti and carols pair perfectly."

"Your mind is my favorite when you're naked." She slid on top and settled her hips between Megan's legs, watching as her eyes fluttered and darkened.

"I love you," Megan said. "Do you hear me?"

Allison kissed her in answer.

"I'm gonna say it all the time. You need to be prepared. I plan to tell other people, too."

"Good."

Megan smiled. "I love you."

"What was that?" Allison looked skyward.

"I love you. A lot."

"I love you, too. Oh, and there's a lasagna dinner at my parents' house tomorrow night. You're coming with me. I already talked to them, and they're thrilled to meet you."

"The parents? This is getting serious."

"You have no idea."

Those were the last words spoken before she lost herself in Megan, in total expression of her own love and passion. As they lay together after a more than memorable evening, drifting off to sleep beneath a wash of moonlight, happy and sated, Allison reflected on her journey over the past year, hardly believing any of it was possible. The path had certainly not been an easy one, full of twists, turns, and giant rocks in her way. Hell, toss in an evil gnome or two. A troll under a bridge. But if it led her right back to where she was in this perfect moment, she would go through every damn second of the journey again. It was now part of her and her newfound identity. It was fantastic finding Megan, but even more of an accomplishment to have found herself. And now that she'd opened up to love, as scary as it was, the path ahead looked pretty damn exciting. She wasn't sure how, but everything in her knew with unshakable certainty that she and Megan were about to live a long and wonderful life together. In fact, the knowledge brought tears to her eyes.

Megan, who she thought had drifted off to sleep, actually hadn't. "Are you crying?" she asked, gently swiping a tear with her thumb. "Why are you crying?"

"Because we've made it to the beginning."

She quirked her head. "The *beginning*?"

"Of the rest of our life. It starts today."

She watched the smile begin small on Megan's face and grow beneath the moonlight to a thing of beauty. "I love you, and I love our beginning."

Allison answered with a kiss, long and meaningful. A first kiss all over again for the woman she loved, who Ally planned to spend every moment of her life showing how much.

❖

Megan couldn't believe she was about to set foot inside a BeLeaf Foods after all her history with the Carmichael family over the past year. Part of her wondered if she might burst into flames as she moved through the automatic double doors into a blast of air conditioning.

"Stop worrying."

"I'm not. I'm just nervous."

"There's nothing to be nervous about," Allison said and squeezed her hand. School had let out for the summer three weeks ago, and summer-Ally came with a relaxed, slightly tan glow that Megan couldn't get enough of. Her blond hair sported sun streaks from time spent at Megan's pool, and her eyes were happy, bright, and bluer than ever. She slept in each morning, and Megan loved getting to cover her in kisses before she left for work each morning. "I already told Brent you'd be here, and he's bringing the woman he's seeing, too. So there. With this partnership off the ground, I think it's a new leaf for us. No pun intended. Well, maybe a little because it's too good to pass up."

It hadn't shocked her how fast Brent had rebounded from the left-at-the-altar fiasco. She was sure there had been throngs of women knocking at his door ready to console him, and he'd certainly done some wound licking. It had been a few months since she and Allison had reconciled, however, and it was good to hear that he was moving forward and had forgiven Allison for the decision she'd made.

With a bouquet of flowers to celebrate the big day, they traversed the grocery aisles of the store to the center station where they spotted Mr. and Mrs. Hale handing out generous hot samples of the Dash Bar, huge grins on their faces as they spoke with interested customers. The bar had been selling well, and this was their shot to introduce it to those shoppers who might not take a chance on a new product without giving it a taste test.

"This is the blueberry. My personal favorite," Mr. Hale said, handing a customer half of a warm oatmeal bar. "Oatmeal on the go. No spoon or bowl needed."

The woman studied the bar after taking a bite. "Oh, okay. I can see how this can be convenient when I'm dashing to work."

"You just said it all right there," Mrs. Hale said, grinning like a celebrity. Her red hair was up in a beautiful twist. "When you're dashing."

Allison was simply bursting with pride and raised her shoulders to her ears. "They're so happy," she whispered to Megan. "Look at them." Her parents had yet to acknowledge their arrival because they were so overrun with customers.

"They're holding their own on the shelves, too," a male voice said. She looked behind them to see Brent standing there in khakis and a green BeLeaf polo. He looked good. Robust and healthy. You'd never know he was seriously injured less than a year ago. "Good signs for a reorder."

"Do you think that will happen?" Allison asked, hopeful. "Oh, and hi."

"Hi." He leaned down and kissed her cheek. "I'd say so. The

display is eye-catching, and they already have community support from their shop." He then turned to Megan. "Didn't mean to ignore you. Been a while," he said with a tentative smile and offered his hand, which she accepted good-naturedly. They'd seen each other a handful of times recently and were on good terms. Truly.

"Good to see you, Brent."

"Yeah, you, too. Oh, and guys, this is Mandy," he said, stepping aside and allowing them both to shake hands with a perky blonde.

She grinned and nodded, likely a little nervous. "It's nice to meet you both. I've heard a lot."

"Good things," Brent tossed in with a nervous laugh. "I promise. I didn't tell her about the jilted groom thing at all."

"You should have," Ally said solemnly. "Think of the sympathy points."

"I'll work it in."

Megan had to give them credit for being able to joke about it.

"Well, maybe one day we can all get together," Allison said, gesturing to Mandy and Brent. "Dinner or something. Toss the awkward right out the window."

"Yeah, I'd like that," Brent said sincerely. He was truly making an effort.

"Megan, you're here! Come try the strawberry. This is the one I was telling you about the other day," Mr. Hale said. She grinned and headed his way. The family had been incredibly warm, and even Betsy seemed to have come around, inviting Megan to her baby shower, noting that she just might be the little one's aunt someday.

"What do you think?" Mrs. Hale asked, grinning as she sampled the bar with the warm strawberry filling. "Any good?"

"Amazing," Megan said.

"I'm gonna make you a fresh batch to take home, next time you're over. You guys should come to dinner on Thursday, in fact."

She glanced behind her. "I'm free if Ally is."

"I'm free," Allison said, beaming and looping her arm through Megan's. "What am I free for? What's happening Thursday?"

"Dinner with us. I'm thinking taco salad. Extra avocado."

"I can make fresh bread," Mr. Hale added.

"We'd love it," Megan said, and Allison squeezed her hand.

Everyone was finally finding their rhythm, Megan included. She'd loved her life before Allison, but she had no idea how much she'd been missing out on. Allison was everything, and at the end of a long day, there was no other face she wanted to see across the dinner table, next to her on the couch, or alongside her in bed that night. Her life had texture and purpose, and that made her excited for each new day. With each wedding she attended, she celebrated the love on display, happy in the knowledge that she knew exactly that kind of everlasting love herself. She might even have shed a tear at a few of them, to Kelsey's raised and amused eyebrow.

"What time is our reservation tonight?" Allison asked, as they made their way through the parking lot, back to their car. It was Friday night, and they'd made a habit of setting it aside for date night, exploring new restaurants and movies together.

"Seven. Why?" She grinned. "Wanna stay in tonight instead?"

"I wouldn't mind a little lounge time. Maybe we can sit on the balcony and watch the city?"

Megan kissed the back of her hand. "It's like you read my mind."

"Takeout and ice cream with hot fudge?"

"Even better. Guess what?"

The setting sun brought out the radiant color of Allison's eyes. "Tell me."

"I'm wildly in love with you."

Allison beamed. "Then take me home and show me."

"Easiest request ever."

EPILOGUE

One year later

The idea that Megan Kinkaid wasn't in control of her own wedding made Allison grin as she stared at herself in the mirror in her simple A-line white dress that she simply adored. Was it wrong to want to wear your wedding dress every day? It was going to be hard not to. She could tackle fractions in this glamorous baby. She turned to the side, once again admiring the seamstresses' work on the designer's subtle applique.

"Tell me more about how she's keyed up," Allison said to Kelsey, who had taken on the task of floating between the two brides before assuming her role as maid of honor on Megan's side.

Kelsey laughed and adjusted the simple drop diamond necklace on Allison's neck. "Well, she can't sit down and keeps staring at the clock, willing the minutes to move faster. She over and over again picks up her sparkling water, only to realize she's not really thirsty, and then repeats the whole process. It's amazing."

Allison grinned. "It's hard for her not to be in complete control of a big day like this. In fact, it's downright cute."

"Yes! Which is all the more wonderful for our team. Speaking of which, Cade's already in place and on headset with Miranda. The guests have settled. We're going in five." She gathered Allison's hands and faced her. "The museum hall looks gorgeous. Are you ready to do this?"

"I've never been so ready for anything in my entire life." She spoke slowly and deliberately. "Get me to that woman."

"Funny. She answered almost in the exact same way." Kelsey kissed her cheek. "I'm thrilled for both of you. I'm going to go join our girl. See you all out there."

Ally turned and waved to the grouping of couches where Betsy and Lacey, who would serve as her attendants, sat in anticipation along with her parents, who would jointly walk her down the aisle as Megan's parents did the same. She took a moment to hug and thank each of them as excited energy danced through her body. If there was a photo of happiness, it had to be her in this moment.

The next half hour of her life floated by like a daydream of the most wonderful kind. The Dallas Museum of Art was jaw-dropping in its beauty. They stood with a minister beneath three white arches surrounded by fabulous statues and works of art. The place was overflowing with fresh flowers, and elegant black folding chairs housed their guests in neat little rows. The place stole her breath, and Allison couldn't believe this was her wedding. Leave it to her future wife to pull off the most beautiful event she'd ever seen.

That wasn't even the best part.

Megan wore a long ivory dress with the most intricate beading. Her hair was swept up in elegance. Her smile radiated with love as she took Allison's hands in hers and vowed to cherish her forever. After a few of the more traditional vows they'd agreed upon, they added words of their own.

Megan's voice was filled with confidence when she looked Allison square in the eyes, causing her to melt. "Believe me when I say that I had no idea there was a you, or anyone even close, who could make me feel the things that you do. The second I did, my life was never the same, and I never want it to be. When you're nearby, everything is better, right down to the taste of ice cream on a lazy Sunday night. You're a bright spark in everyone's world, Allison, and I'm so honored to get to call you my wife. I love you more than I ever thought it was possible to love another human. You're my light. My everything."

Well, that did it. How was she supposed to speak after absorbing so many wonderful words? Even though it was her turn, Allison had to take a moment because the emotion had bubbled to the surface and robbed her of her voice. She held up one finger to their nearly two hundred guests to signal for a minute, which prompted laughter. That helped.

Finally, she gathered herself. "Megan, you make me weak in the knees and transform me into my most calm self, all at the same time. I'm still trying to figure out what kind of superpower that is. Your charisma is only matched by your kindness, and when I'm not in your presence, I count the minutes until we're together again. That sounds like a cliché, but I actually do it. I like that you let me wear your clothes and never make fun of me for enjoying the art projects at school just as much as my fourth graders." She smiled, knowing her kiddos were sitting happily in the fifth row. "The idea that I'm about to embark upon spending every last day with you is nothing short of a miracle. I'm the luckiest human on Earth, and I thank God that I found you. I believe in fate now, and that we were meant to be each other's person. Please know that I am ecstatic to marry you, and I will cherish you and our love with every fiber of my being until my last day."

Megan smiled, tears in her eyes threatening to spill over. *I love you*, she mouthed to Allison, who mouthed it right back. When they were announced as Mrs. and Mrs. Megan and Allison Kinkaid, a name selection Allison had insisted upon, the room erupted, and every part of Ally blossomed with happiness and excitement for everything wonderful to come. Christmases, vacations, cookouts, parties, birthdays, vacations, and maybe even a little addition or two to their family. The idea of a little Megan running around about did her in.

When she danced with her wife for the first time in the spotlight beneath a panel of three-story-high windows, it was a slice of heaven she would never forget. "You're so beautiful," Megan whispered in her ear as she held her close, their family and friends looking on.

All Ally could do was marvel. How did she get here? Pressed against her as they swayed to the music was everything Allison had ever wanted. "Is this real?" Allison asked, reaching up and touching Megan's cheek.

Megan considered the question. "If it's not, it's the best dream I've ever had."

After a life of feeling ordinary and adequate, Allison had finally achieved her very own fairy tale. "I think it's real."

Megan nodded. "I'm yours and you're mine."

"That's us." Allison grinned. "Forever."

They sealed the words with a kiss as the photographer's flash went off, capturing the blissful moment for all eternity. As it was meant to be.

About the Author

Melissa Brayden (www.melissabrayden.com) is a multi-award-winning romance author, embracing the full-time writer's life in San Antonio, Texas, and enjoying every minute of it.

Melissa is married and working really hard at remembering to do the dishes. For personal enjoyment, she spends time with her Jack Russell terriers and checks out the NYC theater scene as often as possible. She considers herself a reluctant patron of spin class, but would much rather be sipping merlot and staring off into space. Bring her coffee, wine, or doughnuts and you'll have a friend for life.

Books Available From Bold Strokes Books

A Convenient Arrangement by Aurora Rey and Jaime Clevenger. Cuffing season has come for lesbians, and for Jess Archer and Cody Dawson, their convenient arrangement becomes anything but. (978-1-63555-818-0)

An Alaskan Wedding by Nance Sparks. The last thing either Andrea or Riley expects is to bump into the one who broke her heart fifteen years ago, but when they meet at the welcome party, their feelings come rushing back. (978-1-63679-053-4)

Beulah Lodge by Cathy Dunnell. It's 1874, and newly betrothed Ruth Mallowes is set on marriage and life as a missionary…until she falls in love with the housemaid at Beulah Lodge. (978-1-63679-007-7)

Gia's Gems by Toni Logan. When Lindsey Speyer discovers that popular travel columnist Gia Williams is a complete fake and threatens to expose her, blackmail has never been so sexy. (978-1-63555-917-0)

Holiday Wishes & Mistletoe Kisses by M. Ullrich. Four holidays, four couples, four chances to make their wishes come true. (978-1-63555-760-2)

Love By Proxy by Dena Blake. Tess has a secret crush on her best friend, Sophie, so the last thing she wants is to help Sophie fall in love with someone else, but how can she stand in the way of her happiness? (978-1-63555-973-6)

Marry Me by Melissa Brayden. Allison Hale attempts to plan the wedding of the century to a man who could save her family's business, if only she wasn't falling for her wedding planner, Megan Kinkaid. (978-1-63555-932-3)

Sweet Surprise by Jenny Frame. Flora and Mac never thought they'd ever see each other again, but when Mac opens up her barber shop right next to Flora's sweet shop, their connection comes roaring back. (978-1-63679-001-5)

Protecting the Lady by Amanda Radley. If Eve Webb had known she'd be protecting royalty, she'd never have taken the job as bodyguard, but as the threat to Lady Katherine's life draws closer, she'll do whatever it takes to save her, and may just lose her heart in the process. (978-1-63679-003-9)

The Edge of Yesterday by CJ Birch. Easton Gray is sent from the future to save humanity from technological disaster. When she's forced to target the woman she's falling in love with, can Easton do what's needed to save humanity? (978-1-63679-025-1)

The Scout and the Scoundrel by Barbara Ann Wright. With unexpected danger surrounding them, Zara and Roni are stuck between duty and survival, with little room for exploring their feelings, especially love. (978-1-63555-978-1)

Can't Leave Love by Kimberly Cooper Griffin. Sophia and Pru have no intention of falling in love, but sometimes love happens when and where you least expect it. (978-1-636790041-1)

Free Fall at Angel Creek by Julie Tizard. Detective Dee Rawlings and aircraft accident investigator Dr. River Dawson use conflicting methods to find answers when a plane goes missing, while overcoming surprising threats and discovering an unlikely chance at love. (978-1-63555-884-5)

Love's Compromise by Cass Sellars. For Piper Holthaus and Brook Myers, will professional dreams and past baggage stop two hearts from realizing they are meant for each other? (978-1-63555-942-2)

Not All a Dream by Sophia Kell Hagin. Hester has lost the woman she loved, and the world has descended into relentless dark and cold. But giving up will have to wait when she stumbles upon people who help her survive. (978-1-63679-067-1)

Protecting the Lady by Amanda Radley. If Eve Webb had known she'd be protecting royalty, she'd never have taken the job as bodyguard, but as the threat to Lady Katherine's life draws closer, she'll do whatever it takes to save her, and may just lose her heart in the process. (978-1-63679-003-9)

The Secrets of Willowra by Kadyan. A family saga of three women, their homestead called Willowra in the Australian outback, and the secrets that link them all. (978-1-63679-064-0)